Someone To Wed

Book 3 of the Lost Girls Trilogy

CHERYL HOLT

Praise for *New York Times* Bestselling Author
CHERYL HOLT

"Best storyteller of the year . . ."
Romantic Times Magazine

"Cheryl Holt is magnificent . . ."
Reader to Reader Reviews

"Cheryl Holt is on my 'favorite authors' list. I can't wait to see what she'll write next."
The Reading Café

"A master writer . . ."
Fresh Fiction

Here's what readers are saying . . .

"OMG! I just started reading this series yesterday. It was hard for me to close my Kindle and go to bed. So, so good!"
Artemis

"Cheryl Holt has packed in so much action that the reader is constantly spellbound. So many characters, so vividly portrayed! Rogues, unfaithfulness, loyalty, and delightful dialogue. You will love this book!"
Gladys

"It was fabulous! I laughed, I cried, I got angry, and I smiled. I read the whole book without stopping."
Robin

"Action, drama, and intrigue. I read it in one afternoon. I couldn't put it down!"
Gina

"You just can't wait to turn the page to see what happens next. Outstanding!"
Margaret

"This book is such an emotional roller-coaster. I cried and laughed and cheered. It was so good!"
Colleen

BOOKS BY CHERYL HOLT

Someone To Wed

Prologue

"YOU LITTLE MOPPET," CAPTAIN Ralston said. "What will become of you? I can't imagine."

As he asked the question, Joanna stared at him, her eyes wide. She'd like to tell him not to fret, that good things would happen on her life's road. Her mother had promised her before she'd died.

Her mother had had a special gift. All of the women in Joanna's family did, and as her mother's infection had spread, she'd shared many stories with Joanna so she wouldn't be scared once she was left alone. The end result was that she was worried about her present circumstance, but she wasn't frightened.

Since her mother had perished, she'd frequently appeared in Joanna's dreams, and Joanna viewed each one of them as a gift to guide her on her way.

She wasn't yet possessed of her mother's secret talents. They would slowly develop when she was bigger, and when they blossomed, she would have to be very cautious.

There would always be people who wouldn't understand her peculiar skills, and they'd be afraid of her. It was why her mother and Joanna had had to flee England. Her mother hadn't been safe there.

Captain Ralston was a kind man, and he was concerned about her, but she thought he should be more concerned about Libby and Caro. *They* would endure plenty of sorrow in the future, but Joanna would be fine.

She didn't tell him that either. He wouldn't have believed her, and she was only four. She'd learned to be very quiet, to observe and to speak just when it was necessary.

"Do you suppose you'll ever talk again?" Captain Ralston asked. "Or has this ordeal rendered you mute?"

Joanna frowned. Of course she'd talk someday. Recently, she'd been silent simply because she was wary and vigilant, and she liked to keep track of details.

It was better now. *He* had made it better by rescuing them. When he'd arrived, they'd been marooned for so long that none of them could clarify the length with any accuracy. He'd fixed what was wrong.

She was cradled in his arms, propped on his hip, and loafing at the bow of his ship as it cut through the water. He'd been explaining the roll of the waves and the flight of the birds, about the current and the wind conveying them forward.

She felt cherished and happy, as if she was his daughter, and she liked to rest her ear on his chest, to hear his heart beating under his ribs.

They'd be in Jamaica in a few hours. It was the spot where she'd been headed with her mother when the storm had struck in the night, and their own ship had sunk in the tempest.

Afterward, they'd washed up on a deserted island. Originally, there had been six adults with them—six out of an entire vessel of passengers and sailors. The adults had gradually passed away until the only ones remaining were her, Caro, and Libby.

They weren't her sisters. She didn't have any siblings, but they'd grown to be her sisters. She was younger and smaller than they were, and they took care of her. She would miss them after they were parted, but her mother had warned her to be prepared for it to occur.

It didn't seem possible that she wouldn't see them again, and it was why she was being so quiet. She was marking their every act and comment, committing them to memory. She'd lost her mother, but how would she survive without them too? She'd suffered too many losses, and she was ready for them to stop.

"Gad, but you're precious, aren't you?" Captain Ralston said. "I predict those green eyes of yours will land you in trouble with the fellows when you're older."

Joanna knew that wasn't true. She was descended from an ancient line of women who didn't attach themselves to men. They didn't marry. They didn't carry on normally in society. They stayed separate in a manner that others deemed threatening. Men weren't important in their world.

She nestled closer and whispered a request to him, but it had been ages since she'd spoken aloud, and he blanched with surprise.

"So you can talk after all. I'm delighted to discover it, but what was that, peanut? Your pretty voice was so soft that I couldn't make it out."

"Will you watch over us?" she asked.

"Haven't I from the very first minute?"

His reply indicated she hadn't been clear in what she meant. She hadn't been referring to that very moment. She wanted him to *always* watch over them. She wanted him to *always* protect them.

"I want you to watch over us forever," she said. She laid her tiny palms on his cheeks and added "Forever!" as if it was a new word he didn't comprehend.

"Forever, hm?" He chuckled. "Well, yes, Miss Joanna, I can promise you that. I will watch over the three of you forever. Don't you fret about it. I will be your guardian angel. How does that sound?"

He put her on her feet, which left her very sad. He was tall and strong, and she liked to snuggle in his arms, to pretend he was her father. She'd never met her own father, so Captain Ralston was the perfect substitute.

"You run along and find Libby and Caroline," he said. "The cook is baking a cake—to celebrate our arrival in port. Tell him my orders are that the three of you can have a slice before anyone else."

She smiled up at him, and he smiled back, and she dawdled, cataloguing his features, aware that she wouldn't be with him many more times in her life and being desperate to never forget a single detail.

Chapter

1

Twenty years later . . .

JOANNA JAMES WALKED OVER to the window and peered out. The sun had set, and the sky was a soothing lavender color that would swiftly fade to indigo. She was inside the manor, the ostentatious Ralston Place, and she hadn't planned to tarry. It would be dark when she reached her cottage.

She never liked the dark. It was a lingering fear from her childhood when she'd survived the shipwreck. The dark scared her. Storms scared her. Bodies of water scared her, and she'd definitely never board a ship again. She'd learned the hard way that they could sink, and she'd used up all her luck in that one terrible incident.

She could see her dog, Mutt, faithfully sitting under a tree. He was a big, clumsy animal, his coat multiple shades of brown and black, his paws huge and his ears floppy. He looked harmless, but his calm demeanor was deceptive. He could be a fierce warrior when provoked.

She'd freed his leg from a hunter's trap and had nursed him back to health, so he was devoted and loyal. He'd guide her safely through the woods to her home.

With the shadows lengthening, the colors were vibrant, the greens so green, the blues so blue. It had been a beautiful summer day, and the night would be even lovelier. She wouldn't need a shawl to ward off the chill.

She was a grateful and fortunate person, and she laid a palm on the window glass and sent a prayer winging out to numerous people, some alive, some not. To her shipmates Libby and Caro. To little Clara, the orphaned girl she viewed as her niece. To her mother—dead for two decades. To her wastrel, despicable father she'd still never met and didn't intend to ever meet. To her mother's sister, Aunt Pru, who was deceased too.

When Joanna had been brought to England from the Caribbean, she'd been claimed by her Aunt Pru. Pru had adopted Clara as well—shortly after she was born. Clara had been raised by Pru when her relatives might have abandoned her in the forest to die. She'd been that unwanted, but Pru had wanted her. Joanna wanted her, and they were a family.

Aunt Pru had been gone for the prior four years, having passed over when Joanna was twenty. It was just her and Clara now, getting by as best they could, and they had plenty.

She picked up her basket and exited by a rear door. Mutt rushed over, his tail wagging. She patted him on the head and said, "You're sweet to wait for me."

I know . . . he seemed to respond.

The cook in the kitchen had given her a meat pie for her supper. She searched in her basket, broke off a corner, and held it out for him to gobble down. She stood for a minute, letting him lick the crumbs off her fingers, then she started off with him trotting by her side.

Aunt Pru had warned her that they didn't dare keep a pet. History proved an animal could be dangerous to women with their backgrounds and habits. While Pru had still been with them, Joanna had obeyed the edict, and she probably would never have ignored the solid advice, but she hadn't sought out Mutt. *He* had found her.

After his leg had mended, he wouldn't leave. She'd struggled to convince him to return to his former master, but he'd refused to heed her. Clara doted on him, so they had a dog, and she had to remember that England was a modern country. A woman could have a pet without it being a sign of nefarious tendencies.

They strolled across the park, and at the edge, she paused to study the manor. It was a grand mansion, three stories high with hundreds of windows reflecting the last of the waning light. There were turrets on one end, with the older section having been a castle in the ancient past.

The moon was rising, so the grey brick shimmered with an eerie silver hue. There were candles burning in several of the rooms, so it looked like an enchanted place where a princess might reside.

She faced the moon, its power flowing over her, as she whispered another prayer, that she be imbued with the strength she needed to heal others. That was her goal in life: to do good deeds, to be helpful, to be a blessing to others.

She'd lived on the Ralston estate for a decade, with Aunt Pru having a friend who'd offered the spot to them when they'd been in a hurry to move from their previous town. They'd settled in without too much difficulty, but there were changes on the horizon, and they'd be dramatic and overwhelming.

She sensed it in her bones, and she wondered if she shouldn't read her cards to receive a hint of what was approaching, but it was usually pointless to inquire about herself. She was nearly always blocked from divining her own fate, but occasionally, she felt greedy and attempted it anyway.

One truth was front and center: Whatever was meant to be, it was meant to be. She couldn't fix or deflect it, so it was ridiculous to try to discover more than the universe chose to reveal.

She spun away from the house and walked to the path in the trees that would lead her to her cottage. It was a long distance, but with the moon up, she would easily find her way.

She hadn't taken a dozen steps when Mutt woofed to notify her of someone's presence. The same moment, she smelled smoke from a cheroot and saw the glowing tip of a cigar. A more skittish maiden might have been alarmed. After all, it was growing dark, and she was alone. The servants at the manor were finished with their chores for the day, so if she shouted for help, there was no one to assist her.

But Mutt was a great judge of humans, and his bored bark apprised her that the man was friend not foe, and he posed no threat. If he ultimately turned out to be a fiend, Mutt would subdue him quickly enough. Generally, he was sweet-natured, but he could be vicious when riled.

"I didn't scare you, did I?" the man said, and his voice was a rich, deep baritone that tickled her innards. "If so, I apologize."

"No. My dog told me you're harmless."

"Harmless! Since I view myself as being very tough and masculine, I like to think there are better terms to describe me than that."

Mutt went over, eager for some vigorous attention. The man obliged him, which made her like him immediately. She was partial to people who liked dogs.

"What's your name?" he asked Mutt rather than her, the two of them bonding in a thoroughly male fashion.

"It's Mutt," she answered.

He snickered. "You're not very clever at naming your pets."

"It just seemed appropriate, and he doesn't mind."

Mutt lay down at his feet as if he'd decided they would tarry and chat.

"He likes you," she said.

"He should like me. I'm a likeable fellow."

"Modest too."

He chuckled over her assessment, then he pitched his cheroot into the dirt, grinding out the flame with his boot.

"I've been spying on you since you left the manor," he said.

"I can't believe you'd openly admit it."

"You were gazing at the house as if you might devour it."

"I like to see the candles shining in the windows. It's like a fairy castle in a storybook."

"I've never stared at it from this angle."

"You should try it more often. It's very soothing, especially when the colors are so intense and the evening so pretty."

"I don't remember us ever being introduced," he said. "Who are you?"

"Miss Joanna James. And you?"

"Captain Ralston."

She blanched. Captain Miles Ralston was the sailor who'd marched onto her tiny island when she was a little girl and had whisked her away to safety. She still dreamed about him, and she'd never stopped pretending he was her father.

But the dear man was long dead, and she smiled at her silly error.

"Captain *Jacob* Ralston, I presume?" she said.

"At your service, Miss James."

He pushed away from the tree where he was leaned, clicked his heels, and bowed, but it was in a teasing way.

"We were informed that you were coming," she said, "but I wasn't aware that you'd arrived. You've been away for an eternity. Why are you lurking in the woods? Have you even gone inside to announce your presence?"

"I've been inside, but I swiftly found myself craving some fresh air. The manor always seems very stifling to me, so it's difficult to settle down and feel comfortable."

It was a brash confession, and they were strangers, so she was surprised he'd uttered it. She supposed the black night and the quiet forest made it easy to offer comments that normally wouldn't have been voiced.

In the ten years she'd lived at the estate, she'd never previously met him. Due to his being in the navy, he was rarely home, and when he was in England, he wasn't too keen on visiting the property.

He'd inherited it from his father, but he hadn't been fond of his shrewish mother, Esther Ralston. She'd been a spiteful harpy, renowned for her out-of-control raging and foul moods, so his childhood had been incredibly dreary. Mrs. Ralston was deceased now, and with her exhausting specter having vanished, perhaps he'd visit more frequently. She would wish for that to be his ending.

She hated to see families quarrel or not support each other or have members assuming they'd rather be alone. She had only Clara to call her own, so she could categorically confirm that being alone was no fun at all.

"Are you settled and comfortable?" she asked.

"Not yet."

"How long does it usually take you?"

"Too long. Typically, I leave before any contentment appears."

"Maybe it's not possible for you to be content in any one spot. It sounds as if you're filled with wanderlust, and you need to keep moving."

"You could be right."

He stepped nearer, and he studied her in a manner that was thrilling. She was very petite, so he towered over her. After her ordeal in the Caribbean, she'd never gained the height and weight another woman might have. She was just five feet in her slippers, and she was thin to the point where people thought she didn't have enough to eat and were always giving her gifts of food.

She ate plenty, but it never added weight or stature. She was destined to be small.

"What color is your hair?" he inquired.

"What an odd question. Why would you wonder about that?"

"It's too dark for me to be sure, and when I want to know something, I ask. I don't blunder around and guess."

It was likely a habit developed because he was a ship's captain. He barked orders and had them obeyed.

At his query about her hair, her arrogance flared. They resided in a land where almost every female had blond hair and blue eyes, so she—with her auburn hair and green eyes—was very different. Pride was a great sin, but she couldn't stop being vain about her looks.

She constantly tried to tamp down her conceit over her exotic features, but she never succeeded. Her Aunt Pru had claimed she'd inherited her conceit from her father who'd been an earl's wastrel son. It definitely hadn't come from her mother who'd been kind, modest, and even a tad shy.

"Well, if I'm being charitable with myself," she said, "I'll declare my hair to be auburn, but if I'm being brutally honest, I'll have to admit it's red."

"Ooh . . . a red-haired woman! How absolutely fascinating. Do you have the temper to match?"

She chuckled. "No. I'm the most placid female in the kingdom."

"There's no such thing as a *placid* redhead."

"Then let's call it auburn."

She never wore it in a proper chignon, so it was hanging down and tied with a ribbon. He stunned her by reaching out and grabbing a dangling strand. He wrapped it around his finger, using it as leverage to draw her closer. Her pulse thundered with a peculiar excitement, and she was frozen like a statue, puzzled over his intent.

He pulled her even nearer, and she could smell alcohol on his breath. Obviously, he'd been drinking, which was a sign that his homecoming had been difficult—as he'd mentioned—but that it was even more wearisome than his comment had indicated.

As he assessed her, she assessed him. She suspected his hair was black and his eyes blue. He was very tall, six feet at least, his shoulders broad, his waist narrow, his legs very, very long. Masculine vigor practically oozed out of him.

She couldn't wait to bump into him in the light of day, and she was curious if he'd turn out to be as handsome as his father had been. In her very vivid memories of Captain Miles Ralston, he'd been dashing and marvelous. She was certain his son would be very much the same.

He realized he was being very forward, and he dropped the strand of hair, but didn't step away. He remained where he was, enjoying their proximity. She was enjoying it too.

A burst of energy had ignited between them, as if their physical positioning was generating sparks, and the sensation was exhilarating. Their bodies were potently attuned, their anatomies recognizing each other on a subconscious level that was strange and electrifying.

"Are you one of my tenants?" he asked.

"Not really."

"What are you then? Are you wandering across my park for no reason?"

"I live in a cottage in your woods, but I'm not a tenant."

"Are you a vagabond? Are you a squatter? Should I gather some men and have them run you off?"

She tsked with exasperation. "No, it's nothing like that."

"What cottage is it? I hope it's not far. I like to assume the estate is very safe, but I'm not anxious to have you walking much of a distance by yourself."

"Mutt will be with me, and it's not far," she said.

It was a small fib. Her house was located at the end of the forest, at the end of his property. She figured he wasn't even aware it existed. He'd never exactly been a dedicated landlord.

"You insist you're not a squatter or a tenant," he said, "so how have you earned yourself lodging?"

"I care for your people."

He cocked his head as if it was the most bizarre reply ever. "How do you care for them?"

"I nurse them when they're sick. I deliver their babies. I stitch their wounds and ease their suffering."

"You manage all of that? How can you? You can't be much more than a dozen years old."

"These dark woods are shielding my age."

"Which is . . . ?"

"Twenty-four. Almost twenty-five."

He scowled as if he didn't believe her, and it was a common mistake. She looked very young, and her adult torso had never filled out as it should have.

"How long have you been at Ralston?" he asked.

"It's been a whole decade."

"Why haven't I ever heard of you?"

"I can't imagine. Perhaps you weren't paying attention as you ought."

"You must have moved in when you were fourteen. Were you healing my tenants and servants back then?"

"I was helping my Aunt Pru. She tended them before me, and she taught me her skills. Did you ever meet her?"

"No, but then, I've never spent much time here. My career has kept me away."

That was a false excuse. It was his mother who'd kept him away, but Joanna swallowed down the remark.

"What's in your basket?" he asked.

"A few concoctions for your sister."

His scowl deepened. "Margaret is ailing?"

"Her melancholia has flared again."

"She's not melancholy," he said. "We're Ralstons. We don't ever despair. We're much too sturdy for a bit of anguish to weaken us."

He talked about his sister as if he knew more about her than Joanna. Since he'd just arrived after a very lengthy period away, it was quite a vanity for him to suppose he had much information about any topic.

"Her fever is bothering her too," Joanna told him.

"What fever?"

It was bewildering that he hadn't been apprised of the problem. He was thirty and his sister, Margaret Howell, was twenty-eight. She'd been in Egypt for ten years with her husband, but he'd died, and she'd come home. She didn't have much to show for her adventure in the foreign land except a tropical fever that occasionally plagued her.

Her malady could be fierce, but more often than not, it was simply a nuisance that drained her energy. It was her lingering sadness that was more of an issue, and Joanna had had no success in making it go away. She hated for anyone to grieve and be unhappy.

"If you'd like to learn what troubles her," Joanna said, "you should inquire of her rather than me. She can provide the details she feels like sharing."

"I will pester her, but can't you give me a hint? Why would you claim she's sad? Is she mourning her husband? She didn't like him enough to be upset that he's passed away."

"Captain Ralston!" she scolded. "What a horrid comment, and you shouldn't suggest such a notion to me."

"Why not? Will you rush out and tell the world?"

"No. Your secrets are safe with me, but you shouldn't risk it. Not when I'm a stranger. Who can predict how I might behave? Not you certainly."

"I'm a good judge of character, and I deem you to be eminently reliable."

"What if you're wrong?"

"I'm not," he pompously stated, "and I won't apologize for being blunt about Margaret's marriage. If you've been in the area for a decade, then I'm sure the facts are not a mystery to you. Her husband, Mr. Howell, was a somber, depressing cretin, but my mother insisted she wed him.

She thought Margaret was too vibrant and silly and that she required the stern hand of an older, awful husband. Mostly, my mother didn't want her to enjoy her life too much. Mother was exhausting that way."

He'd just repeated much of the gossip that swirled, and from Margaret's miserable condition, Joanna wondered what sort of dire experiences she'd endured in her marriage. She'd been back for a few months, but she wasn't anymore content than when she'd first returned, and Joanna couldn't figure out how to improve her mood.

The herbs and teas she prescribed weren't having any effect, but then, some people were simply destined to be morose, and there was no fixing it. Margaret needed an interval to lament what had happened to her, and Ralston Place was the perfect spot to heal.

"You're determined to air your dirty laundry," she said.

"It's late, I'm bored, and you're too polite to stomp off in a huff. It's easy to unburden myself."

"I might stomp off—if you grow too verbose. There are many things about you I don't care to know."

"I wish it wasn't so dark. I'd like to check your eyes for veracity, for I'm positive that's not true. My family's foibles are like a bad theatrical play, and every person in a hundred-mile radius is cognizant of the rumors. You must be too. There's likely not a single story you haven't heard a thousand times."

"Maybe I haven't listened to any of them."

"I doubt that very much. Who could resist the juicy tales that are told about us?"

"I like to imagine I'm above lurid babbling."

"I shall remain skeptical about your high motives until we are better acquainted and I can assess more accurately whether you're that noble or not."

"My face is an open book. It's impossible for me to lie and get away with it."

"You and I should gamble then. I'll be able to fleece you blind."

"I don't have much to lose, so it would be a quick walk to penury."

"Everyone has something to lose."

"Not me."

That wasn't necessarily correct. She had her cottage and her work. She had Clara and Mutt. She had the neighbors who sent for her when they were feeling poorly. If she had to relinquish any of it, but most particularly her small house, she would be devastated.

She was relishing their conversation more than she should, and she said, "I should be going."

"We've only just begun to chat."

"My niece is waiting for me. She'll be fretting."

"I suppose I must offer to escort you. I can't let you traipse off on your own. If you suffered a mishap, I'd blame myself forever."

"What mishap could I suffer?"

"You could trip over a tree root and sprain your ankle. You could be eaten by wolves. You could be attacked by brigands."

She chuckled. "Other than the prospect of tripping, I can guarantee those other fates will not befall me."

"You're awfully certain."

"I'm always certain."

There was mischief approaching on the horizon, but it wouldn't occur yet, and she wasn't entirely convinced it would happen to *her.* She couldn't ever totally predict an outcome with complete confidence, but she could definitely stagger home without worrying. She didn't explain why she was so certain though. He'd never understand.

He leaned in so close that the tips of his boots slipped under the hem of her skirt. Those pesky sparks ignited again, and she perceived every little detail about him. She was drawn to him on an elemental level, as if every pore in her body was on fire.

She could smell the soap with which he'd bathed, could sense the heat emanating from his skin. There were other odors too, manly ones of tobacco, fresh air, and horses. An even slighter aroma was detectable, and it was extremely tantalizing. She couldn't describe what it was, but it made her want to rub herself against him like a contented cat.

It was a heady, exhilarating moment, and she felt special and exotic. She was being bowled over as she shouldn't let herself be.

The women in her family never had suitors; they never married. They never considered it. They were busy and powerful, and men interfered in ways that couldn't be tolerated. She'd never loafed with a beau, had never stood with a handsome man and reveled in his potent scrutiny.

"Don't leave." His voice was low and intimate, as if they were sharing secrets.

"I think I'd better."

"I'll see you to your door."

"I *don't* think you'd better."

"You are a hard nut to crack, Miss James."

"I've heard that my whole life."

"If I get sick while I'm home, will you tend me?"

"To the best of my ability."

"Then I shall hope to become ill, so I can have the pleasure of your company again very soon."

"Are you a flirt, Captain Ralston?"

"Not usually, but you're the sort of female who brings out the worst in a fellow. I won't be able to resist misbehaving around you."

"I will force you to mind your manners."

"What fun would that be?"

The moon had been hidden behind a cloud, and suddenly, it burst free, its silver light shining down. He was staring at her so intently, and it was very strange, but Time seemed to stop, as if the universe was marking the encounter.

She would mark it too. Over the coming days and weeks, she'd revisit every single word they'd uttered.

"Goodnight, Captain."

"I'm walking you, Miss James. Don't let's argue about it."

"You're drunk."

"I am not," he huffed.

"Well, you've been drinking then. Go inside and take to your bed. Or check on your sister. It would make her happy."

"I'm barely acquainted with my sister. Why would I be the person who could make her happy?"

"If that's even remotely true, then I must advise you to work on your relationship with her." She stepped away so the sparks could settle. "And I'd appreciate it if you'd cease telling me things I shouldn't discover. You'll regret it in the morning."

"No, I won't," he said. "I've never regretted any conduct I've ever perpetrated."

She smirked. "Why does that not surprise me?"

She skirted by him, wishing he'd reach for her, but being relieved when he didn't. She hurried away, but she could feel him watching her, his gaze like daggers in her back. She'd suspected he'd follow her, despite her demand that he not, and when he stayed put, she couldn't decide if she was glad or not.

Eventually, just when she would have flitted out of his sight, he called, "Miss James?"

She halted and glanced over at him. "Yes, Captain?"

"Will I see you tomorrow? I'm afraid I have to insist on it."

"You should know a very important fact about me."

"What is it?"

"I never do what I'm told, especially not when a man insists."

He laughed at that. "Apparently, you're sassy, but a bit of brazen attitude is exactly what I'd expect from you. After all, your hair is red."

They exchanged a charged look, then she yanked away and continued on. But she grinned the whole way home.

Chapter

2

"I'm bored already."

"You're always bored when you're not on a ship."

Jacob Ralston grinned at his friend, Kit Boswell. Kit's father and Jacob's father, Miles, had served together in the navy, and when Kit's father had died, Miles had been named his guardian. Kit had come to live with them when he was a boy and he'd never left.

He and Jacob were the same age of thirty, and they'd been raised together, so they were like brothers, but not like brothers too. While Jacob's mother had paid for Kit's schooling, she'd refused to purchase a navy commission for him. Once Jacob had sailed off at sixteen, Kit had stayed behind, but then, he'd never wanted to be a sailor.

He was content to pass the slow days at Ralston Place, and his slothful habits were catching up with him. His eyes were still brown and alert, his hair also brown and showing no signs of grey, but he was developing quite a belly paunch, his face puffy and lined from dissipation. While Jacob was fit and vigorous, Kit was indolent and idle.

He ran the estate for Jacob, so he had important, steady employment, and he'd tolerated and dealt with Jacob's mother, Esther, in a
manner Jacob had never managed. Jacob was grateful to have him on
the property, for his presence meant Jacob didn't have to loaf at home
and tend things himself.

During his current visit, his goal was to ascertain if he could bear
to muster out of the navy and return for good. He was about to engage
himself to his cousin, Roxanne. After he was a husband, shouldn't he
retire? Could he stand it?

His mother had been such a miserable shrew that he'd avoided the
place as much as possible, but she was deceased, so she wasn't around to
nag and upset him. Her ghost seemed to linger in every corner though,
and he wished he knew a magic spell that would chase her away.

A house was just a house. A farm was just a farm, but her awful aura
pervaded every inch of space, and it rocked him with bitter memories.

He and Kit were in the estate office at the rear of the manor and
enjoying an afternoon brandy. It was nice to be away from the rest
of the household, to have a few minutes to chat. Jacob was sitting at
the desk, and Kit was slouched in the chair across. Jacob figured Kit
yearned to grouse that the office was Kit's, that the desk was Kit's, that
they had their seats backward.

Kit wouldn't dare complain about it though. The desk, the chairs,
the mansion, the acreage, and every blade of grass on it, belonged to
Jacob, and while Kit was viewed as family, he was still an employee.
It was a terribly snobbish attitude for Jacob to have, but he was an
Englishman through and through. Status and position counted in
every facet of their existence.

"I met the most intriguing woman last night," he said.

"An *intriguing* woman? At Ralston Place? I can't fathom it."

"It was a Miss James?"

"Yes, Joanna James."

"She claimed she's nursing Margaret."

"Your sister has been under the weather, and I argued with her to send for the doctor, but the housekeeper told me she's suffering from *female* troubles, so Miss James is a better choice."

"What sort of female troubles?"

Kit shrugged. "Who can guess? It's the sort Miss James is supposedly adept at fixing."

Jacob snorted at that. He'd been home for twenty-four hours, and he'd barely seen Margaret. She was hiding in her room and not particularly excited that he was back, but what had he expected? Their mother's grim attitudes and stern habits had ensured he and Margaret weren't close.

They had another sister, Pamela, who was two years older than Jacob. She'd eloped with a man their mother would never have allowed her to wed. The disgraced pair had fled to America, so he never corresponded with them and had no idea if she was happy. He hoped she was. He'd like for one of the Ralston siblings to have a good ending.

His cousin and fiancée, Roxanne, was in residence too, but he'd hardly seen her either. It had him feeling like a stranger, which he mostly was. He deliberately stayed away, and if Roxanne and Margaret weren't exactly glad he'd staggered in, he had no one to blame but himself.

"Apparently, Miss James has a cottage?" he said.

"It's the small one out by the London road."

"Do I have a cottage out by the London road?"

"It was empty for years because it's so isolated, so I gave it to her aunt." Kit rolled his eyes. "Honestly, Jacob, now that you're here for an extended period, why don't you ride around your property. Learn about what you own."

"I might try that. Maybe it would cure my boredom."

He finished his drink, stood, and started out. Kit didn't rise with him, but asked, "Weren't you planning to examine the account ledgers?"

"I changed my mind. It's too pleasant an afternoon to spend it talking about expenses and debts."

"I agree."

Kit toasted him with his glass, then Jacob escaped.

He realized that he ought to show more of an interest in the place. It had been his since his father had died when he was ten. A relative had managed it for him when he was still a boy, then Kit had taken over after they'd become adults.

He never questioned Kit over any issue, but why would he? Kit was paid to be in charge, and Jacob wouldn't sneak around behind him, nitpicking and second-guessing. He probably shouldn't be so trusting, but so far, he'd never had reason to rein in Kit or revoke any of his authority.

He couldn't force himself to care much about the day-to-day workings of the estate. He wasn't a farmer and never had been. He was a sailor, descended from a lengthy line of sailors, and he knew about wind, water, and currents. He didn't know about crops or forage or herds or orchard health, and he didn't really want to know. That type of discussion put him to sleep.

The prior night, when he'd met Miss James in the woods, he'd told her he always needed to settle in when he arrived, and he'd been serious. About the time he was more comfortable, it was time to leave again.

He thought about proceeding to the front parlor, searching for Margaret or perhaps socializing with Roxanne. He ought to get acquainted with her, but in his present mood, he was too edgy. Roxanne would wax on about the engagement party they were hosting in September, after which the betrothal would be official, and he couldn't contemplate it yet.

His mother had arranged the match shortly before her death. Roxanne was a distant cousin who might have grown up to be his bride, but she and her mother had moved to Italy when she was fifteen, so it hadn't happened when they were younger.

His mother had insisted she'd be the perfect wife for him. She was twenty-five already and worldly in a way that would suit Jacob. In light of his career, where he'd traveled the globe and encountered every kind of person, he wouldn't have liked a fussy, immature debutante.

When his mother had proposed the union, he couldn't have argued that he wasn't prepared to wed. He was thirty after all, so he couldn't persist with his delays. Roxanne was beautiful and sophisticated. She was very independent too, so if he didn't retire from the navy and was gone for long periods, she'd be fine without him.

But would he like to have a wife who was fine without him? Wouldn't he like a bride who was a little less self-sufficient? If he shackled himself to a woman who never missed him, what was the point?

He went down a rear hall and exited onto the verandah. He leaned on the balustrade and studied his surroundings. Cattle grazed in a pasture, and horses frolicked in a meadow. Servants bustled to and fro, carrying out their chores.

The sight was verdant and soothing, like a scene a painter might have rendered to capture rural England on a summer afternoon, and he tried to let the exquisiteness sink in. He should be reveling in his ownership, in his prosperity, but the sad fact was that he didn't perceive much of a connection to any of it.

He'd left for school at age seven, and during holidays, he'd visited friends or boarded in the dormitory. Then, once he was sixteen, he'd joined the navy and had never looked back. He returned only on the rarest occasions, then he quickly departed, wondering why he bothered, but he was about to marry.

He'd soon have a wife to consider, so would he stay away forever? Was that his plan? Why wed if he would never be around? It made no sense.

On the other side of the park, a dog was running on the edge of the woods, and when he focused in, he recognized Mutt. Could his mistress be far behind?

He waited for her to emerge from the forest, but she didn't. Not being inclined to dissuade himself, he marched down the steps. Could Mutt take him to her? He supposed so, and at the notion, he couldn't keep from smiling.

He was anxious to talk to her again, but he couldn't figure out why. Maybe he was simply eager to assess her auburn hair in the daylight.

Mutt saw him, and he rushed up, tail wagging ferociously.

"Where is Miss James?" he inquired.

Mutt seemed to understand what he'd asked. He actually motioned with his snout and hurried off. Jacob followed at a brisk pace, while he struggled to deduce his purpose.

He was the biggest snob in the kingdom, and he was a great believer that diverse individuals shouldn't fraternize. The Good Lord had created different sorts of people, and in England, they all had their places and remained in them.

He wasn't sure who Miss James was or *what* she was. It sounded as if she was a nurse or midwife, and Kit had conveniently neglected to explain why she supplied duties that warranted lodging in a cottage.

Somehow, she'd managed to fascinate him, and he hated to dawdle at Ralston Place. He was a man of action and adventure, and he was easily bored. Miss James might provide a pleasant diversion that would help to pass the dreary hours.

He and Mutt continued on for a lengthy distance, then Mutt led him off the trail and down a rocky path. They ended up at a stream he couldn't name and hadn't known to exist. Miss James was sitting on the bank, her basket next to her and filled with flowers.

Her shoes were off, her skirt tugged up to her knees, her toes dangling in the water. Her bonnet was laying on the grass, so her hair was visible, and it wasn't red or auburn, but somewhere in between those two shades. The base was more of a chestnut color, with strands of gold and red woven throughout.

She was pretty as a picture, and it was the strangest thing, but his heart leapt under his ribs, as if it had swelled with gladness.

Mutt barked softly, and she said, "There you are, you naughty dog. Where have you been? What if I'd needed you?"

She glanced over her shoulder, expecting it to be her dog. As she noted him too, she grinned a grin he felt clear down to his toes.

"Captain Ralston! Why are you out in the middle of the woods?"

"I could ask you the same, Miss James."

"I'm gathering flowers."

"For a bouquet?"

"No. I brew medicinal tinctures with them. This is a good spot to find blossoms."

"You brew tinctures? Are you a witch?"

She scoffed. "Everyone has agreed, Captain, that there are no witches. It's just a story invented by frightened, pious men to make children shake in their boots."

"Yes, and witches are ugly crones, so you couldn't possibly be one."

He walked over and plopped down beside her. He sat much closer than he should have, so his thigh and arm were pressed to hers. She didn't scoot away to put space between them, and he was delighted to learn she wasn't squeamish.

He studied her keenly. She was older than she'd seemed the previous night. She was so petite that, initially, he'd worried she was a girl out alone in the dark, but no, she was definitely a woman. She was very refined, her movements graceful and elegant, but it was her eyes that riveted him.

They were big and green and brimming with merriment, as if she relished the day and was always happy. What would it be like to be so free and comfortable in the world? Even though he was from a rich, prominent family, he'd always felt as if he had a foot off the center of the line.

His upbringing had left him moody and prone to sulks, and it was exhausting to keep harkening back to his horrible rearing, but he was too reflective. It was a reason he never came home. His mother had been awful, his sisters miserable, and his father ...

Well, his father had been such a tawdry, sorry man that it was mortifying to describe him. Yet Jacob was his son, so he couldn't really ever stop pondering him. His great hope was that he'd never exhibit any of his father's immoral traits, and in fact, he'd once sworn to his mother that he would never behave so reprehensibly.

Most of the time, he lived up to that lofty vow.

"Would you do me a favor?" she asked.

"It depends on what it is."

"Would you please never mention I'm a witch when you're talking about me?"

"I was joking."

"I realize you were, but there are plenty of people in this country who don't like to hear about a woman brewing medicine or practicing the healing arts. I like it at Ralston, and I wouldn't want to ever upset anyone where I might have to depart."

"I like to think our neighbors are modern and educated. They don't truck with much superstition."

"It's a rural locale, and nonsense can spread quickly and without warning."

"I suppose that's true, but I wouldn't let you be hurt of insulted."

"How, precisely, would you prevent it? I could hardly contact you for assistance when you were on a ship in the middle of the ocean."

He patted her knee. "Don't fret about it. Not on such a lovely afternoon."

"I'm not fretting. I just wouldn't like to stir any anger."

"I don't see how you could. You're much too meek and fetching to cause any trouble." He pointed to the stream. "Is the water cold?"

"No, it's very refreshing."

"Will you faint if I shed my boots and stick my feet in too?"

"I'll try to bear up."

He yanked off his boots, his stockings too, then he plunged his feet in, but the temperature was frigid, and he grimaced. "You scamp! It's icy."

"You'll get used to it."

She was correct; his skin adjusted rapidly, and he rested his elbows on his thighs and scrutinized the area. The scenery was bucolic, and it was embarrassing to acknowledge how often he complained. He had to cease being so negative about his home.

He peered over at her and said, "Would it surprise you if I admit I wasn't aware this stream was here?"

"No. You've never tarried much at Ralston."

"How could you know that?"

"I know all sorts of things about you. I've been at the estate for a whole decade, remember?"

She smiled a smile that was probably similar to the one Eve had flashed at that poor sap Adam, and alarm bells rang in Jacob's head. She exuded a calmness and serenity that drew him in, so he was eager to linger in her company.

He could envision himself growing besotted as a green boy, but she was a maiden, living under his protection, and she was some kind of healer, so she was very far beneath him in class and station. Any attention he paid her would be wrong, and she would misconstrue it, but even as he recognized those issues and scolded himself, he stayed right where he was.

Evidently, he was content to make any number of mistakes with her.

"I was talking to Kit Boswell about you," he said.

"I hope he didn't tell you anything too horrid."

"No, nothing horrid, but nothing truly relevant either."

"What would you consider to be relevant?"

"Where are you from? How did you wind up at Ralston?"

"I came with my Aunt Pru. We resided in a village near Telford, but her benefactor passed away, and the property was sold. We didn't have anywhere to go."

"She was a healer too?"

"Yes, and a renowned midwife. She was famous in many circles, and she delivered hundreds of babies in her life."

"Hundreds? My goodness."

"She sent out letters, requesting a new situation, and a friend invited us to Ralston. Eventually, after she'd proved her worth, Mr. Boswell let us have our cottage. He claimed she was a *blessing* to the ladies in the neighborhood."

"Kit Boswell said that? He must have been drunk."

She smirked. "Maybe he was, but after he sobered up, he didn't evict us. Will you? Now that you've learned about it? Promise me you won't. I'm happy there, and I have my niece, Clara, to raise."

"No, I won't evict you. Besides, you're nursing my sister, so she'd kill me if I tried."

"Thank you. I'm grateful."

"Would it surprise you again if I confess that I had no idea about you or your cottage? I can't picture where it's located."

"It's off the beaten path."

"You'll have to show it to me. You must realize that."

"I'm not showing you my cottage."

He huffed with feigned offense. "I'm lord and master on this estate."

"Just barely," she muttered.

"And if I demand you oblige me on any topic, then you must."

She scowled at him, and there was the cutest frown line between her eyes. He could hardly keep from reaching out and rubbing it away with his thumb.

"You're a man who could become a bother," she said.

"A bother!"

"Yes, and if you find out where I live, you'll be popping in constantly, and I really can't have it."

"You are the strangest woman I've ever encountered. Who doesn't like to have visitors?"

"I don't sit around embroidering towels and curling my hair. I'm very busy."

"With your potions and your healing?"

"Yes, and don't you dare make fun of me."

"I wouldn't dream of it," he said, but his tone was very sarcastic.

"I provide a valuable service, but I'm sure you think my life is silly."

"You're correct. I think you are extremely silly."

He smiled at her, his gaze warm and even a tad affectionate. In his mind, he understood he was treading on dangerous ground, but he couldn't rein in his fascination. She was charming, and he was charmed.

She blew out a heavy breath. "Why am I letting you waste my time?"

"I'm not wasting your time. My arrival is the most intriguing thing that's happened to you all day."

"Or maybe the most annoying. Don't you have chores at the manor? You've been away for ages. There must be ledgers to review or tenants to harass."

"I'll be home for a few months, so there will be plenty of opportunity to review ledgers and harass tenants."

"Have you chatted with your sister yet?"

"No. She doesn't appear too excited that I'm back."

"I'm sorry to hear it. I'm meeting with her in a bit; I'll drag her out of her room to converse with you."

At the news that she would stop by the manor, he was much more thrilled than he should have been.

"Do you call on her often?"

"If I'm nearby. I've advised her it's pointless to mope and brood."

"We're Ralstons. We're skilled at moping and brooding."

"*You* don't seem very morose."

"I hide it better than her." He shrugged. "It was difficult for us, growing up here."

"How could it have been difficult? You're rich and landed, and your father was a famous mariner. You don't necessarily comprehend the meaning of the word *difficult*."

"You could be right. Perhaps I shouldn't whine so frequently or flog myself so much."

"Perhaps not."

She stared at the stream, at the sky, relishing the quiet tranquility, and again, he was struck by her beauty and poise. His sense resurfaced that his rural sojourn might be more interesting than he'd expected. *She* would render it more interesting.

She pulled her feet from the water, and though he glared avidly, she ignored him and tugged on her stockings and shoes. He couldn't irritate or rattle her, so he did the same.

"Are we leaving?" he asked.

"*I* am leaving. I can't speak for you."

He rose, then reached down to help her up too, but she gaped at him as if she'd never seen an extended limb before.

"Don't tell me you're squeamish about clasping my hand," he said. "I'll never believe it."

"I don't usually . . . ah . . . hold a person's hand."

"I'm not trying to *hold* your hand. I'm trying to lift you up."

He didn't wait for permission, but grabbed on and yanked her up, but then . . .

The eeriest experience occurred. For an instant, their palms were fused together, and she studied him with a look that delved down to his tiniest pore, as if she was rummaging around in his veins.

Time seemed to halt. The wind in the trees ceased blowing. Birds silenced their cawing. Even Mutt quit breathing, and Jacob was rocked by the oddest perception that she was digging into details about him she shouldn't. He yearned to order her to desist, but he was frozen like a statue, his tongue unable to form any remark.

Then she blinked twice, and the peculiar episode abruptly terminated. She jerked away and stepped back. Before he could recover his wits, she'd scooped up her basket and was hurrying away, her dog trotting at her heels.

He physically shook himself, as if he'd been momentarily turned to stone, and he called to her, "Miss James!"

She glanced over her shoulder. "Yes?"

"What just happened?"

"Nothing, Captain."

"You're a terrible liar. What was that?"

"Don't work yourself into a lather over it."

"Our hands were . . . we were . . . you were . . ." He couldn't describe what had transpired. Was she a sorceress? "You were assessing me—from the inside out."

"I couldn't possibly have been."

"It feels as if you're still in there, probing where you shouldn't be."

"I wasn't aware that you were prone to flights of fancy."

"Where are you going?"

"As opposed to you, I have chores to complete."

He was suffering from the most potent notion that they had much more to discuss, and he shouldn't allow her to flit away. "Forget about your chores for once. Let's stroll in the forest. You can show me some of your favorite spots. I ought to learn more about my property."

"It can't be me. If you're curious, you should ask Kit Boswell. Or Mr. Sanders." Geoffrey Sanders, Sandy, ran his stables and tended his carriages, carts, and wagons. "He knows more about Ralston than anyone. He'd be delighted to give you a tour."

"I don't want to trudge about with a boring, tedious male. I want female company, and I demand you entertain me."

"Despite what you imagine, I am not very entertaining."

"I would beg to disagree. I find you thoroughly fascinating."

"I can't fathom why."

"When will you visit Margaret?"

"I'll be there when I get there." She could be so exhausting!

"Which is no answer at all. How am I to guess when to expect you?"

"You shouldn't ever expect me."

"You are a nuisance, Miss James."

"So I've been told, Captain. It was lovely chatting with you, but I really must be off."

She whipped away and continued on, acting as if he was a person of no account, and he was incredibly annoyed. He was a navy captain who'd commanded underlings for the past fourteen years. He said *jump,* and they asked, *how high?* They didn't argue. They didn't refuse to obey. They understood their place in relation to him, and they behaved accordingly.

It was the same at Ralston Place. He was recognized as the lord and master, but he stumbled in so rarely that people tripped over themselves to please him. Yet she wasn't impressed in the slightest. Nor did she comprehend their disparate positions.

She should have been eager to conduct herself in any manner he requested. She should have been flattered to have the chance to tarry with him, and the fact that she wasn't was galling and bewildering.

He was absolutely enthralled by her. What might she do next? What might she say next?

A shiver slithered down his spine. He felt bewitched, as if she'd shoved an odd burst of energy into his anatomy. He peeked down at his palm, fully assuming she'd have left a mark on his skin, but there was no indication of her mischief.

He scoffed at his foolishness, then headed off too. He wouldn't lurk in the forest, fretting over an insane woman. He had ledgers to read, a fiancée to charm, and a sister with whom he needed to become reacquainted. What ailed her? He definitely had to inquire so he could pitch in to improve her condition.

He was as busy as exasperating, snooty Miss James. Or, at least, he could pretend to be busy. He stomped off, and he decided he wouldn't watch for her at the manor. He wouldn't gaze out the windows, wondering if she was about to arrive. He wouldn't obsess over her!

But even as he warned himself to ignore his fixation, he was reviewing every comment she'd uttered, and he was anxiously excited to bump into her again—and soon.

Chapter

3

Joanna strolled down the lane, headed for her cottage. Clara was with her, which was always enjoyable. With her white-blond hair and dark black eyes, her slender physique and pleasing manner, she was very fetching. She was nine already and growing up so fast.

She attended school in the village, with seven other girls. Her teacher was an older widow, and three of them boarded with her. Clara went four days a week, and occasionally, she stayed overnight when there was a birthday or other event to celebrate. Joanna was keeping track of the years they had left together, and they were passing much quicker than she liked.

Clara had come to live with them as a newborn. Aunt Pru had delivered her, and it had been a difficult and very secretive birthing, to a young and unwed mother, the father not named.

The grandmother had been so incensed about the situation that Pru had worried over Clara's fate. She'd offered to take Clara, to *dispose* of her so she'd never be found, and she'd often tormented herself over what Clara's relatives had assumed she'd meant to do with the child.

Had they thought she'd kill Clara? Had they thought she'd dump her in an orphanage? Had they thought she'd smother her, then bury her in the forest?

She'd brought Clara home, and Joanna was raising her. Clara's grandmother had given Pru a purse of gold coins to buy her silence. The money paid for Clara's schooling and clothes, so she didn't have to stagger about like an orphaned pauper.

There would be a bit of it remaining when she decided to marry, so she'd even have a small dowry to entice a local boy into matrimony.

"What is your opinion about Captain Ralston?" Clara asked her.

"He's vain, bossy, and very set on himself."

"You would say that about any man."

Joanna chuckled. "Probably."

"Is he handsome?"

"Yes, he's very handsome—but he knows it too."

Everyone was talking about Captain Ralston. He was so rarely at the estate, and speculation was rampant as to what he was like. Clara and her fellow classmates were particularly intrigued.

"He's betrothed to his cousin," Clara said.

"Not quite yet, but he will be soon."

"Have you met her?"

"No. I haven't had the chance."

Thank goodness, Joanna silently added. She had no desire to discover what sort of gorgeous creature had tantalized him.

"She's incredibly beautiful," Clara said. "That's the rumor anyway. I hope she's worthy of him."

Clara and her classmates had gossiped about Jacob Ralston to an exhausting degree. They viewed him as a prince who'd been searching for a princess, but Joanna had heard depressing stories about his cousin—stories she shouldn't have heard—in the kitchen at the manor. The servants didn't like her. She was snooty, rude, and never satisfied with any service they provided. She was also swift to lash out verbally if they failed to rise to her exacting standards.

Once she was the Captain's bride, she'd take charge of the household, so it would become a very different place, and Joanna couldn't abide awful behavior. She understood that England was a country of status and station, but she could trace her lineage back a thousand years—on her mother's side *and* her father's—and she didn't feel as if she should have to bow down to anyone.

It was a dangerous attitude to have though, so she spent as much time as she could around common people and none around the more exalted. It was best not to tempt Fate and get herself into trouble by being too uppity.

They left the lane and walked down the path toward their cottage. It was an old gamekeeper's hut where the lord's men had watched for poachers and brigands. The woods surrounding it were thick and dark, and unless a person was specifically shown where it was hidden in the forest, it was hard to find.

The house was cozy and snug and a perfect haven for her. There were three rooms on the main floor—a kitchen, a parlor, and a work room—and two bedrooms up above. There was a white fence to enclose the yard, and flowerboxes under the windows. The thatch was thick, the walls sturdy, and the windows blocked the wind and the rain.

It seemed like an enchanted spot, one where a virtuous maiden might be imprisoned under a wicked spell. She liked to envision herself as the virtuous maiden, but she was in no hurry to escape.

They didn't have many visitors though. If there was a knock on the door, it was because a baby was coming or because there was sickness or an accident. Or it might be a forlorn woman, requesting more nefarious aid: for a baby to be washed away, or a baby to attach to a womb, or for an enemy's fortunes to plummet, or to halt a man's roving eye so he'd remain faithful.

She could assist with all of those problems, but she never did. She didn't trust people to be circumspect, and she never engaged in ill-wishing. Her ancestors had suffered through the ages, and even though it was a more modern era, she was always careful.

"Oh, look," Clara said as they approached the gate, "someone's here. Who do you suppose it is?"

A horse with a fancy saddle was tethered to the fence, munching on a bush, and she sighed with aggravation. "I'm fairly sure I know who it will turn out to be."

"Who?"

"Let's go inside, and we'll see if I've guessed correctly."

"Might you have to leave?"

"No, I promise."

When Joanna had to rush out for an emergency, Clara tarried in the village with her teacher until Joanna was finished, but this wasn't one of those times. They entered the house, and Clara was almost jumping with excitement.

"Hello, Miss James," Captain Ralston said from over on her sofa. "I didn't think you'd ever arrive."

"Hello, Captain. May I inquire as to your purpose?"

"I was bored so I decided to stop by."

"How did you discover where my cottage is located?"

"I asked Kit Boswell."

"I imagine it's futile to mention that this is my home, and I don't appreciate you barging in like this."

"Yes, it's futile, but you should learn to lock your door. You're living in the middle of nowhere, and it's not safe to be so trusting. It borders on negligence."

"It's not necessary for me to lock my door. I don't own anything that's overly valuable. If a rogue is so desperate that he needs an item of mine, he can have it."

"What a bizarre reply, but it's precisely what I should have anticipated from such a peculiar female."

He'd lit a fire in the fireplace, and he'd helped himself to a glass of wine, which meant he'd snooped in her cupboards. She couldn't determine whether she should be annoyed or flattered by his interest. A bit of both emotions flared.

He stood and bowed to Clara. "Who is this? Will you introduce me?"

"This is my niece, Clara," Joanna said. "Clara, this is Captain Ralston. You've been dying to meet him and now you have."

Clara gave him a curtsy he didn't deserve. "I'm very pleased to make your acquaintance, Captain."

"And I'm very pleased to make yours. Why have you been dying to meet me?"

Clara smiled as if he hung the moon. "The girls at my school have been talking about you."

Joanna explained, "They heard you were handsome and dashing, and I haven't been able to convince her that you're not."

He winked at Clara. "Don't listen to her. You may tell your classmates that I am as amazing as you suspected."

"Oh, botheration . . ." Joanna grumbled under her breath.

"You have very pretty manners, Clara," the Captain said. "You must not take after your aunt at all."

Clara couldn't figure out how to respond to the comment, and Joanna said, "Don't pay any attention to him, Clara. He enjoys being a nuisance."

Mutt was loafing on the floor next to him, reveling in the heat from the fire. The Captain had let him in, but he wasn't usually allowed inside, and he knew it. She glared at him, and he peered back woefully, begging to be forgiven.

She clucked her tongue, then whipped the door open. She pointed out, but Mutt gazed at Captain Ralston, visually pleading with him to intercede.

"Can't he stay?" Captain Ralston asked.

"No, and you are presuming on me horridly."

Clara grabbed Mutt's collar. "Come with me, boy. Don't get yourself into trouble."

"Play with him," Joanna said, "while Captain Ralston and I chat. I must find out what he needs, so we can send him on his way."

"Can't he join us for supper?" As Clara posed the suggestion, she cast such an adoring look at the Captain that it was embarrassing to witness it.

"He's much too busy." Joanna was feeling gravely put-upon. "With his just being home from the navy, they'll be expecting him to dine at the manor."

Clara hesitated, waiting for the Captain to disagree, but thankfully, he kept his mouth shut. She left with Mutt, and once the door closed behind her, Joanna focused her irate frown on him. But he had no shame and couldn't be cowed.

She yanked off her bonnet and shawl, then sat in the chair across from him. He was grinning, delighted by how he'd irked her, but she wasn't irked exactly. She simply didn't like how he'd blustered in, yet the cottage belonged to him, and she wasn't charged any rent to live in it. If he wanted to strut in, she had no authority to tell him he couldn't.

The prior afternoon, he'd clasped her hand and lifted her to her feet before she could tuck the appendage out of sight. She had an odd power in her palms, and when they touched some people, she could see details she shouldn't. As a result, she tried to never hold anyone's hand. It could be risky to possess certain information.

Unfortunately, she'd firmly connected with him, and the episode had stirred an awkward situation. She was brimming with knowledge she shouldn't have acquired: He was an angry man, an unhappy man, a proud and exhausting man. He was conflicted about his path, about his choices—about his pending engagement.

Most disturbingly, Joanna appeared to have a destiny binding her to him, and it would unfold over the next few weeks.

She'd perceived it clearly. Not the specifics of what would occur, but she understood the general drift. Her presence in his life would provide him with something he desperately required, and until he discovered what it was, he wouldn't leave her alone.

She wanted to be irritated by that prospect, but she couldn't be. He was rich, handsome, and interesting. Why not bask in a bit of fraternization? Her days were nearly always the same. She worked, she brewed her medicines, she delivered babies, and she nursed those who were ailing.

It was a rare occasion when her routine varied. Why not wallow in the distraction he would supply?

There was a reason she'd met him. It seemed inevitable. It had begun when her Aunt Pru had moved them to Ralston, the home of Captain Miles Ralston who'd rescued Joanna in the Caribbean.

He'd been deceased for many years, but Joanna had a fond place in her heart for him. During their final conversation, she'd begged him to watch over her forever, and he'd sworn he would, so she viewed her relocating to his estate as having been engineered by him from the other side.

Jacob was his son, and she supposed their burgeoning friendship was part of his father's plan too. From how sparks erupted when they were together, it was obvious they shared a very potent physical attraction. Might it ignite into a romance?

A relationship might turn out to be the best thing that ever happened to her. Or it might turn out to be a catastrophe. The cards—that she kept carefully hidden—were practically shouting at her to learn how it would evolve, but she absolutely would not read them.

"I asked you this when I first arrived," she said, "but you didn't answer. Why are you in my parlor?"

"I told you. I was bored, and I decided you should entertain me."

"I've explained to you that I'm not a woman of leisure. I always have chores, so I don't have a minute to waste on you."

"You don't have to ignore your chores. I'll simply follow after you and quietly observe, and I'll be completely entranced. You never cease to astonish me."

"You're being silly."

"I've been accused of having many peculiar traits, but being *silly* is not one of them."

"How about annoying then? How about pompously aggravating?"

"I've heard that too." He gestured around the room. "Do you like living here? Does it suit your needs?"

"Yes, I like it."

"I thought I should check. I am your landlord after all, but I have to say—now that I've met you and Clara—I don't like you being so isolated. I could easily envision a despicable character sneaking in with felonious motives."

"Who would wish to harm me? And we have Mutt to guard us."

"He's the nicest dog ever. What type of protection could he furnish?"

"He's only nice because he likes you, but he's ferociously loyal. If he judged you to be a fiend, he wouldn't let you within a hundred feet of me."

He snorted, then downed the remnants of his wine. The bottle was on the table in front of him, and she stood and refilled his glass. Before she could pull away, he grabbed her wrist and ran a finger up her arm.

She remained very still, watching him, curious as to what he intended. She could have clasped his palm and gotten a clearer idea, but from his hot look, it wasn't much of a mystery. She'd piqued his manly instincts.

She'd never had a beau, so his attention was producing many heady sensations. She could have dawdled all afternoon and allowed him to ogle her, but she wasn't a frivolous debutante seeking a flirtation. She yanked away and sat down again, and he studied her as if he were a wolf and she a rabbit he was stalking.

He had wicked goals with regard to her, and she suspected he'd be able to coax her into all sorts of conduct she shouldn't permit. The notion made her smile and recall her mother, Belinda, who'd had a lengthy affair with Joanna's father.

He'd been an earl's fourth son, a gambler and wastrel with no money or prospects, but he'd been wild for Belinda and wouldn't stay away— despite how she struggled to tamp down his ardor. He would never have married her, both because he'd been too top-lofty to consider it, but also because he'd already been married.

Their passionate amour had outraged his lawful wife, and eventually, she'd grown tired of it. Belinda had fled England to escape her wrath.

Joanna's father had declined to intervene and help them, which had led to the shipwreck, which had led to Joanna and her mother being marooned on a deserted island, which had led to Belinda dying there and leaving her alone with Caro and Libby, which had led to her being rescued by Captain Miles Ralston, which had led to her being returned to England and hailed as a *Lost Girl* of the Caribbean, which had led too . . .

"Why are you smiling?" he asked. "I swear, you constantly resemble Eve in the Garden. I'm sure that's exactly how she smiled at Adam as she lured him to his doom."

"I was thinking about my mother."

"Why would a conversation with me bring your mother to mind?"

"I was pondering how Fate guides our steps."

"I don't believe in Fate."

"You should."

"I don't."

"How about omens and magic?"

"No."

"How about ghosts?"

"Definitely not."

She wondered if that was true. She frequently felt his father's ghost hovering. Had he ever noticed the same? Perhaps his father's spirit was only attached to the estate, and since his son was rarely on the property, he never sensed his presence.

"You're a sailor," she said. "Aren't all of you incredibly superstitious?"

"The enlisted men usually are, but I like to imagine I'm smart enough to know fact from fiction."

"If you don't believe in Fate, how can you explain being in my cottage?"

"I have absolutely no idea."

He appeared so bewildered that she laughed. "You poor boy. What if your fascination grows until you're wandering in circles?"

"I'll try to control myself. Who was your mother?"

He'd switched subjects so fast that she was practically dizzy. Normally, she didn't discuss her mother, but she answered him. What could it hurt?

"Belinda James."

"Is she still with us?"

"No. She died many years ago."

"Who was her family?"

"No one of any account. I'm descended from a long line of spinsters who work as midwives and healers."

"How utterly bizarre. Why are you spinsters? You must hate men. Is that it?"

We don't hate them, but they drain our power and waste our energy, but she would never admit it. She chuckled instead. "We don't hate men."

"It sounds as if you do."

"My kin have a tendency to be bossy and independent—it's an inherited trait—so it's hard for men to put up with us. It's hard to have a successful marriage when we're so insistent about having our own way."

"Yes, I can see where a fellow would be completely emasculated by you. Was your mother's hair red? Is that where you got it?"

"Yes, she had very pretty red hair."

"And do you look just like her? Was she as striking and beautiful as you are?"

"Yes, she was very beautiful, and was that a compliment? If you're not careful, you'll be spouting poetry about my eyes."

"Gad, I will be, won't I? You have the strangest effect on me, and I can't figure out what's causing it."

"Maybe Fate is driving you. Maybe you should start believing in it."

"Who was your father? Who was his family?"

She clucked her tongue with offense. "You are so nosy. Why are you so intrigued by my past and my relatives?"

"I've never met a woman like you, and I'm anxious to deduce what kind of people could have created such an odd female."

As with discussing her mother, she never mentioned her father. She was reticent about her mother because she'd nearly been swept up as a witch. Her father's wife had urged a vicious priest to harass her, and he'd been dangerously thorough. Joanna lived far from the town where it had happened, and she doubted anyone would remember the incident, but she would never rekindle old, perilous stories. Nor would she focus a lens on her own habits.

During her mother's ordeal, her father had refused to intercede, and Joanna blamed him for her mother's ruin. Belinda had been young and naïve, and he'd coaxed her into the illicit liaison. Her reward had been his total disavowal of their affection—and of Joanna's existence.

Joanna liked to pretend she'd been hatched from an egg, with no man ever planting a seed to make it transpire.

"You still haven't confided in me," he said. "Who was your father?"

"He was a scoundrel who used my mother badly, and I was the result."

"Oh."

"Is that enough information to satisfy your morbid curiosity? Or will you force me to provide details? I hope you won't. It would embarrass me, and I don't like to talk about him."

"Just tell me this: Was he a nobleman?"

She blanched. "Why would the prospect even occur to you?"

"You're so extraordinary. I can't picture you being sired by a commoner."

It was a sweet flattery, and in appreciation, she threw him a bone. "Yes, he was from an aristocratic family."

"Will you ever confess his identity?"

"No. Never."

"But you know who he is?"

"Yes, Captain Ralston, I know who he is. I wasn't a foundling, left on the parish church steps." She was weary of his interrogation, and she rose to her feet. "Are we finished? Is there anything else you need?"

"Am I being tossed out?"

"Yes. I'm busy—which you never deem to be possible."

He studied her, then frowned. "I've upset you."

"As we are barely acquainted, you couldn't have."

"Was it my inquiring about your parents? If so, I apologize. I didn't realize it would be such a difficult subject."

"There are . . . issues from my childhood. They distress me."

It was on the tip of her tongue to admit who she was. She'd never boasted about being a *Lost Girl* at Ralston Place, so the Ralston family wasn't aware of her connection to Captain Miles Ralston. She always protected her mother's memory, and she wouldn't ever explain why they'd fled England in such a hurry. There was never a benefit in declaring her mother had been accused of witchcraft.

If she spoke up about her link to Miles Ralston, what might Jacob Ralston say? She decided she'd tell him someday, but not *that* day. If she mentioned it just then, she'd never get rid of him.

He hadn't taken the hint that he should go, and she glared at him, debating how she'd react if he declined to depart. It wasn't as if she could pitch him out bodily.

His questions had stirred painful recollection that fueled her apprehension and claustrophobia—any reference to the shipwreck always did—and in order to calm down, she had to occupy her mind and hands with other tasks so she wouldn't reflect on it. She opened the door and gestured outside, rudely indicating he should leave.

"I want to come to supper some night," he said from over on his chair. "Clara invited me, and I demand you honor the invitation."

"I have no kitchen skills, so I wouldn't dare cook a meal for you."

"Don't you have a servant? Are you that poverty-stricken in your finances?"

"I have two servants."

One helped her mix and deliver her remedies, and the other prepared their food and tended the house. They didn't reside with her, but stopped by during the day.

"It means you employ a cook," he said. "You don't deal with it yourself, so you fibbed right to my face." He grinned his devil's grin. "For shame, Miss James."

"Would you go?"

Finally, he stood, but he was in no rush. He sauntered over to her, and as he neared, so many raucous sparks ignited that she was surprised she didn't catch on fire. No wonder young ladies landed themselves in so much trouble. Who could resist such a sly seduction?

Before she knew what he intended, he dipped down and kissed her. It was just a light brush of his lips to her own. She hadn't expected it, so she hadn't grasped that she should ward it off.

It was quick and dear, and her anatomy rippled with such excitement she was amazed her heart didn't burst out of her chest. As he drew away, he looked cocky and assured, as if he'd been testing her in some fashion. Had she passed the quiz he'd been administering?

He straightened, and like the conceited ass he was, he pronounced, "I always thought I was partial to blond women, but it appears I like redheads better."

It was a ridiculous comment, and she laughed. "You are a menace, Captain. Haven't you tormented me enough for one afternoon?"

"I suppose I have. Will you walk me out?"

"If you promise to behave. I can't have you kissing me in my front yard."

"Why not? It's not as if there are any people around to see."

"Clara is in the woods with Mutt. I wouldn't want her to think we're friendly."

He raised a brow. "Are we friendly? Is that what's happening?"

"There's no other word to describe it, and I won't try."

"I have several more salacious terms I'd use, but probably none I could utter in your presence."

"Thank you. I'm a very modest person, and I appreciate your reticence."

They exited the cottage, and it was only a few short steps to the gate and the fence where his horse was tethered. She petted the horse and rested her cheek on his muzzle. Captain Ralston scrutinized her in that potent way he had, and when she pulled away, he was scowling ferociously.

"Were you talking to him?"

"Oh, yes," she blithely lied.

His scowl grew even more fierce. "What did he say?"

"He said you are a great master, and he's glad he belongs to you, but his true love is Sandy who takes such good care of him in the stables."

His jaw dropped in astonishment. "He did *not* tell you all of that!"

She laughed even more lustily, being delighted to have flummoxed him. "Of course he didn't. Despite what you imagine, I have no ability to speak to animals."

His cheeks flushed. "If you had such a skill, it wouldn't surprise me in the least. I find you to be odd and absurd and completely extraordinary."

"There you go again with your compliments. If you keep it up, I won't be able to get back inside. My head will swell, and it won't fit through the door."

"I am never a man to dispense flattery, so you must be working some strange magic on me."

"It's that Fate you mock. It seems there's a destiny brewing between us."

"Yes, it does."

Their conversation lagged, and he stared down at her. The most precious sense of affection flared, and she let it flow over her like a gentle rain.

"When will you be at the manor again?" he asked, breaking the special moment into a thousand pieces.

"I'm not sure."

"When you visit, you must have me apprised. Don't you dare ever slip in and out without my being informed."

She smiled, but with exasperation. "To what end, Captain? What possible reason could there be to inform you?"

"I told you, Miss James. I can't deduce what's driving me, but whatever it is, it's very powerful. I doubt I can fight it and win."

"You act as if we're in some sort of war."

"No, not a war precisely. We're . . . we're . . ." He cut off and scoffed.

"Don't listen to me. You have me totally befuddled. Have you cast a spell on me?"

"I wouldn't have the faintest idea how to cast a spell."

"I'm betting that's the biggest lie you've spewed in my presence so far."

He dipped down and stole another kiss. This one was more desperate, more urgent, and she jumped in and participated enthusiastically. How could she not? If it had been up to her, she'd have begged him to continue until dark.

"I'll ride over tomorrow," he said like a threat.

"I might actually be looking forward to it."

He tried to grab her hand and squeeze it, but she wasn't about to let him. Who could predict what she'd discover?

She eased back, giving him the space he needed to mount his horse. Then, from up above her, he asked, "What is your Christian name? Is it Joanna?"

"Yes."

"I'm calling you Joanna from now on."

"I guess it would be pointless to request that you not."

"And you will call me Jacob."

"I'll think about it."

He yanked on the reins and trotted off. She watched him depart, and her yearning was palpable, like a besotted girl mooning over her first beau. Once he vanished in the trees, she blew out a heavy breath and turned toward the cottage, wondering how their relationship would unfold, how it would conclude.

He would be at the estate for several months, so she'd have plenty of opportunity to get herself into all kinds of trouble. Plus, he was about to become engaged to his cousin, and he was hosting a huge betrothal party in September.

Since he was about to bind himself, he had no business flirting with her. It definitely had her worried over what type of man he was deep down. She'd assumed she knew, but she might have misjudged.

She missed him already, and she had to buck up and refuse to dally with him, but she likely wasn't strong enough to order him away. What woman could?

As she reached the door, Clara and Mutt skipped around the side of the house.

"I was spying on you with Captain Ralston," Clara said.

"I should probably scold you."

"Are you in love? Will you marry him?"

"No and no."

"But you were kissing!"

"That's all it was. A *kiss*. Captain Ralston is very fond of me."

"He certainly is!"

"Promise me you won't tell anyone what you witnessed." Clara didn't reply, and Joanna said, "I'm serious, Clara. People at the manor wouldn't like us to be so close. I'm too far beneath him, and they'd be angry."

"Your lineage is more elevated than his," Clara huffed.

Joanna chuckled. "We'll keep that opinion to ourselves, and can we please drop the subject? He overwhelms me, and I hate that you saw me misbehaving."

"I thought it was very romantic."

"It was very romantic, wasn't it? I have to agree."

"Will he visit us again?"

"He claims he will."

"I can't wait. Can you? I like him very much."

Joanna sighed. "Unfortunately, I like him too."

"I'm glad he's sweet on you."

"He's not sweet on me. He's ... he's ..."

Joanna couldn't describe what he was. She simply went inside, but the afternoon and the parlor were both boring and much too quiet with him gone.

Chapter

4

"THERE YOU ARE. I'D about given you up for dead."

Margaret glared at her brother, Jacob, and said, "Very funny."

"Who's being funny? I haven't seen you in five years."

"Seven."

"What?"

"It's been seven years since we last saw each other."

He frowned. "Has it been that long?"

"Yes."

They were in the dining room, a pair of footmen hovering, but other than that, they were alone. The only other person who might have strolled in was their cousin, Roxanne, but she never rose early, so there was no chance of her putting in an appearance, for which Margaret was grateful.

She hadn't decided if she liked Roxanne or not. When they were younger, they'd occasionally socialized with Roxanne's side of the family, but once they grew to adolescence, Roxanne moved to Italy and stayed there. She was mostly a stranger to them.

Margaret had been at Ralston Place for two months, and Roxanne for three. Margaret had slithered home from Egypt, after her husband, Mr. Howell, had passed away from a heart seizure. Roxanne had slithered home from Italy.

Due to their extensive traveling in foreign lands, she and Roxanne probably had a lot in common and should have bonded immediately. They could have sealed their friendship by jumping into the arrangements for Jacob's betrothal party in September, but Margaret couldn't muster any enthusiasm for the celebration, and Roxanne was content to handle the details herself.

On the few occasions Margaret had attempted to help, Roxanne had ignored her every suggestion, leaving Margaret with the distinct impression that her assistance was neither needed nor necessary.

Now that Roxanne had barged in and assumed control of the manor, Margaret would have a difficult time fitting in with Roxanne as her sister-in-law. Margaret had staggered to Ralston Place with naught to show for her ten years of marriage to Mr. Howell. She felt like a poor and very unwanted relative. Roxanne already pictured the house to be her own, and she hadn't been particularly welcoming.

After she became Jacob's wife, she could ask Margaret to depart, but where would Margaret go?

She was fairly certain Jacob wouldn't allow Roxanne to evict her, but he was rarely in England. If she and Roxanne quarreled, and Roxanne ordered her to pack her bags, it wasn't as if Jacob would be standing nearby to counter her edict.

Margaret had been having a quiet breakfast when Jacob had blustered in. It was eight o'clock, and she was finished eating and on her way out. He was just sitting down to begin. He looked annoyingly chipper and eager to face the day, while she was exhausted, irritated, and wondering why she'd come downstairs. There was quite a bit of comfort to be found in her old bedchamber.

"I've met Joanna James," he said. "She tells me you're morose and she's been tending you because of it."

"Maybe Miss James should be a little more circumspect about my private business."

"What does that mean? You're not morose? She's not tending you?"

"I've been a tad down in the mouth. You needn't worry about it."

"Why are you so glum? Was Egypt terrible? Was it Mr. Howell? I warned you he was a pompous prig and it would be a grave mistake to wed him."

"Mother didn't give me a choice, Jacob. Could we please not rehash ancient history?"

Jacob motioned to the footmen, and they tiptoed out and shut the door behind them. Not that she cared if the servants eavesdropped. They unraveled every secret and, no doubt, were fully aware of the cause of her woe.

Jacob studied her meticulously, and he appeared genuinely concerned, which was a novel development. He was thirty, and she was twenty-eight, and with their being so close in age, they should have been fond siblings, but the sad fact was that they barely knew each other. He'd left for boarding school when he was seven and had scarcely returned for visits after that.

Their mother, Esther, had been so unlikable, and Margaret had envied him for being able to pick up and flee. She hadn't escaped until her mother had sold her to Mr. Howell. When Margaret had been introduced to him, she'd cried for three days and had sworn she'd never wed him, but Esther had prevailed in the end.

Esther had contracted the match when Margaret was seventeen. She'd been vivacious and spirited, and Esther had constantly raged that she'd inherited her father's low morals and would ultimately wind up just as dissolute. Mr. Howell had been fifty, a twice-widowed government official who'd never sired any children.

He'd been a stern, pious, and petty man, so in Esther's view, it had made him a stellar husband for a girl as vibrant and silly as Margaret had been.

Her friends had counselled her to look on the bright side: She'd get to travel the world with Mr. Howell, and she'd never have to slink back to her mother or Ralston Place unless she chose to. She'd taken the advice to heart, and she'd proceeded without argument.

For a decade, they'd resided in Egypt, where his job had been to arrange grain shipments to England. She'd had a lovely villa on the Nile and loads of British acquaintances, so her public life had been exotic and interesting, but her personal life had been grueling and despicable.

He'd finally died, and she hadn't mourned or missed him.

Her brother asked the strangest question. "Do you blame me for not stopping your wedding?"

"What an absurd thought. Why would I have?"

"I should have put my foot down. I've always been sorry that I didn't."

"That's some consolation, I guess."

In the past, she *had* blamed him for the disaster. She couldn't remember why, and it didn't matter now. He hadn't even been in England when Esther had forged ahead. How could he have intervened? How could it have been his fault?

"Did he bequeath anything to you?" Jacob inquired.

"No. I haven't a single farthing to my name. It's why I've staggered to Ralston Place. I didn't have any other option."

"Your dowry is gone too?"

"Yes."

"The bastard."

"Before I could even bury him, his creditors swarmed to inform me he was bankrupt. Evidently, he wasn't adept at managing his money."

"The grain merchant didn't understand money? How absolutely ironic."

They shared a smile, and Jacob said, "Are you home to stay?"

"If you'll permit me to."

"Of course you can stay—forever if you like. I hope you didn't fear I'd mind."

"I had no idea what your opinion would be. You're about to wed, so it's the worst time to have your destitute sister trudge in and beg for shelter."

"This mansion is more yours than mine. You're always welcome."

"What if Roxanne disagrees with you? It will be *her* domain as a new wife. She might not be too keen to have me underfoot, and I've been fretting about it."

"She won't be allowed to object."

"Thank you."

Tears flooded her eyes, and he seemed disturbed to witness them. "You really are despondent, aren't you? I didn't want to believe it."

"It's just been an eternity since anyone was kind to me."

"Oh, Margaret . . ."

He stood and rounded the table. He grabbed a napkin and dabbed at her eyes, then he clasped her hand and patted it.

"You'll be fine," he said. "I'm certain of it. Will I sound horrid if I declare that I'm not lamenting Mr. Howell's death? I'm not grieving over Mother's either. I'm glad we're here and they're not."

She chuckled, but miserably. "Please keep that to yourself. We might be struck by lightning for leveling curses."

"You should rest and heal. It's your only task. You'll be better soon."

"I'm already better."

"You mustn't hide yourself away. I'm sure if you get out and about more often, you'll improve quicker."

"I think so too. It's what Miss James advises."

"She's correct, and we'll begin tonight with you joining me for supper. Apparently, Roxanne has invited the vicar and some of the neighbors. I can't face them alone."

"I wouldn't be that cruel. I'll be there with bells on."

It was odd to have him being attentive and sympathetic. It was like having a stranger walk up and furnish assistance. She didn't know how to accept it, and she pulled away and left him to his breakfast.

She went to the foyer and considered heading up to her bedchamber again, but for once, she didn't. The more she locked herself away, the smaller her room felt. She sat in the window seat, staring out at the park and reliving the awful moments of her marriage. It simply increased her sense that she'd been wronged by life.

Why hadn't she ever grown a spine? Why hadn't she said this or done that? Why had she been such a milksop about every tiny issue?

Well, Mr. Howell was deceased, and there could be no rewriting the past, so how was her morbid rumination helping?

She had to stop focusing on what had been bad and unbearable. Nothing was bad now. Yes, she was poor, but other than that, she was a healthy, beautiful young widow. She was safe in her brother's home, and he was eager for them to establish the bond that had never developed when they were children.

Wasn't it time to start over? She was no longer Mr. Howell's beleaguered wife. She could shuck off that yoke and become someone else, perhaps the woman she was meant to be.

Who was that woman? What would she be like? She couldn't imagine, but she supposed she ought to find out.

"COULD YOU SPARE ME a few minutes this afternoon?"

"Not with Jacob just arriving. I'm terribly busy, so whatever the problem, it will have to wait."

Geoffrey Sanders, called Sandy by everyone, watched Kit Boswell saunter away. He bit down on the comments he'd like to hurl at the lazy, incompetent prig. Sandy came from a lengthy line of men who'd served the Ralstons for generations, and he'd learned his lessons from them.

The snooty family wasn't like a normal family. They were rich and important, and they pictured themselves as being far above the lowly serfs who toiled away on their behalf. They liked sycophants who would stroke their massive egos and tell them they were brilliant—despite how foolish they were being.

Kit wasn't a Ralston, but he pretended he was, and he was the worst of the lot. He'd been brought to Ralston as a boy and had been reared as if he were a sibling. With Jacob bestowing the job of estate manager, he deemed himself protected in his spot and was positive he'd never lose it.

Sandy figured he wouldn't. Jacob was never present, and when he was, his visits were so brief that he didn't delve into matters affecting the property. He wasn't aware of how useless Kit was, and Sandy wasn't about to apprise him. He valued his own job too much.

Officially, he ran the stables, but unofficially, he ran everything outside the house. He supervised the employees, dealt with the tenant farmers, handled the ordering, deliveries, and payments to merchants. Kit did very little at all, except eat, drink, and travel to London frequently to gamble, carouse, and buy new clothes.

Sandy always grimly reflected, if he ever dropped dead, the entire place would cease to function, but the instant he pondered that dreadful notion, he'd remind himself to count his blessings.

There were few men in his situation who possessed such authority. He was respected and esteemed, and people recognized Kit's shortcomings. They knew who really managed Ralston Place, and he took special pride in his achievements, all of them carried out to make Jacob Ralston thrive.

He was in the barn where he'd accosted Kit as he'd saddled up for a morning ride. It had been a surprise to see him out and about before noon, so he was probably hoping Jacob would notice and be impressed.

Unfortunately for Sandy, there were several problems that needed to be addressed, and Kit had to approve some of the solutions Sandy would like to implement. It was tricky to get Kit to focus, and with Jacob in residence, he'd have even more excuses to shrug off his responsibilities.

Sandy could forge ahead without Kit's permission, but if he experienced difficulties later on, he'd be in trouble. Kit was an expert at wallowing in the triumphs, but blaming others for any calamities, so Sandy had to be extremely careful.

He was a widower, with two sons to raise. His position provided a good salary and a fine house, and he would never confront Kit and jeopardize his sons' security.

He exited into the sunshine, and he stared across the park, relishing the smell of the green grass, the freshness of the summer sky. He let his fury at Kit float away. He was lucky and happy, and he had to remember he was.

He'd intended to stroll in the meadow and chat with his favorite horses, but as he rounded the corner of the building, he literally bumped into Margaret. They collided so hard that she staggered and nearly fell. He leapt to steady her.

"Oh, Sandy!" she said. "I was marching along, lost in thought, and I wasn't paying attention. I'm sorry."

"I wasn't paying attention either. Are you all right?"

"I'm grand."

She smiled a tight smile, as he quickly and furtively assessed her condition. With her blond hair and blue eyes, she was still beautiful, but she was much more slender than she'd been previously. According to the housemaids, regret and remorse were gnawing at her.

Sadness was written all over her face. It was so clear to him. He'd once known her better than anyone, definitely better than her awful, elderly husband, and she'd never been able to hide her emotions from him.

Since she'd returned to Ralston Place, he hadn't talked to her. He'd constantly expected she would seek him out, but she hadn't, and he'd convinced himself not to be aggrieved over the slight.

The members of the Ralston family were not a mystery to him. They were snobs, and they couldn't help being pompous. Why wish for them to change their habits? It was like asking a cow not to moo.

When she'd decided to shackle herself to Bernard Howell, she'd been very blunt as to how she viewed Sandy. Although he'd loved her for years, he was a humble farmhand, and therefore, far beneath the sort of man she would choose as her husband.

She'd explained it kindly, but he'd often wondered if she'd ever realized how her remarks had devastated him. Probably not. In certain areas, she was blindly oblivious.

Back then, they'd been very young and stupid, and Esther Ralston had been such a shrew. Margaret hadn't been strong enough to stand up to her. Sandy had been vain and proud, and he'd truly assumed that he and Margaret could have run away together and lived happily ever after.

It was humorous, at age thirty, to recall how naïve he'd been. She'd wed Howell and had traipsed off to Egypt with him. Sandy had wed a local girl, a farmer's pragmatic, sensible daughter who'd been from his same reduced station in life.

They'd both moved on, but now, Howell was deceased. Esther too. Sandy's wife had passed away—several years earlier. He and Margaret were widowed adults who were free to behave however they pleased. There was no one to complain if they were cordial.

On her first arriving, he'd believed they might rekindle their prior romance, but with her never bothering to knock on his door, he'd been forced to accept that she wasn't reflecting on the past as he'd been.

She was still a Ralston daughter, and he was still a laborer who worked for her brother. He couldn't wrap their disparate circumstances in a pretty bow.

They stared at each other, and he recognized that he ought to tender a polite comment to smooth over the awkwardness, but he didn't. Previously, when he'd been much more imprudent, he might have kept the conversation going merely so he'd have an excuse to tarry by her side, but any fraternization could never be on his terms. They always had to be on hers, and he wasn't willing to be roped into her world again.

There was no advantage to any association.

"How have you been?" she asked.

"Fine. And you?"

"I've been better. I've been home for awhile."

Seven weeks, three days, twelve hours. "I know."

"I apologize for not calling on you, but I couldn't decide if I should or not."

"There was no reason to bestir yourself."

He sounded incredibly petulant, and she frowned. "I deserved that, I suppose."

"I didn't mean to seem surly. I'm glad you're back. How long will you be visiting?"

"I'm not visiting. I'm staying—for good."

She'd confirmed the rumors circulating. Apparently, Bernard Howell had left her so destitute in Egypt that she'd had to beg pennies from her fancy friends in order to book passage to England.

Sandy was trying not to gloat over what an idiot Howell had been. He, Sandy, wasn't the brightest fellow in the kingdom, but he wouldn't have treated his dog that shabbily.

"Well . . . I'm sure this is a perfect ending for you," he said like a dolt.

"Jacob told me I could remain. I've been fretting over whether he'd let me or not."

"Why wouldn't he have let you?"

"He's marrying, so I doubted his bride would be keen to have me on the premises."

He chuckled; he couldn't help it. "You always worried about the silliest topics."

"Yes, and I haven't changed a whit." Suddenly, she asked, "What's your opinion of Roxanne? You've had a bit of time to watch her, and you're such an excellent judge of people. Will she make Jacob happy?"

He loathed Roxanne Ralston, and the man who shackled himself to her would wind up miserable for all eternity. She was petty, conceited, and impossible to please, but she was also exceedingly beautiful, but in an icy, aloof sort of way.

He couldn't predict if that type of female would appeal to Jacob or not. Top-lofty families pursued strange motives in arranging their marriages, and Sandy was the very last person who would comment about it.

"I haven't met her yet," he lied, "so I haven't reached any conclusions."

She scoffed. "Which I don't believe at all. You know every detail about the estate."

She hesitated, expecting him to agree, expecting him to supply her with detrimental gossip about Roxanne, as he would have when he'd been young and infatuated, but he was stoically silent. When she realized he wouldn't play her game, her shoulders slumped.

"Did you need something?" he asked her. "Would you like to have a horse prepared?"

"Yes, I'd like a horse. I haven't been out much lately, and I'm craving some fresh air."

He went into the barn and hollered for a stable boy to ready a mount. He stopped an older boy too who would accompany her as a groom. Then he returned to her and said, "You're all set. Give them a minute, and they'll take care of you."

"You won't be coming with me?"

"I can't. I'm busy this morning."

"I understand."

"It's good to see you up and about. I hope you'll ride more often. I concur that fresh air can be very beneficial."

He walked off, and he could sense her glaring at him, her gaze beseeching him to announce he'd escort her after all. What was wrong with her? In the past, he'd loved her more than life itself, but she'd tossed off his affection, crushing him with the admission that she had to stick to her own kind.

He'd moved on, had picked a bride who'd been part of his small world and a much wiser choice. His wife had been a worker, a striver, and she'd shared his view that their simple existence suited them just fine. It was a path Margaret could never have comprehended.

He had his two sons who'd tend him when he was old and grey, so he'd never be alone. In contrast, Margaret had birthed no children, and rumor had it that she was barren, that Howell had nearly divorced her over it.

As he and Margaret aged, he'd have his sons. What would she have?

Like a besotted swain, he thought about hiding and spying on her as she trotted away, but that would be foolish and ridiculous. And he'd been over her for years.

It didn't matter how she stared up at him with those pretty blue eyes of hers. It didn't matter how beaten down she looked, how forlorn and dismayed. He'd never been her savior. On that point, she'd been very clear, and nothing between them had changed in the slightest.

He had chores, and he whipped away and got on with his day.

"THERE YOU ARE!"

Roxanne grinned at Jacob as he entered the room. She'd comman-deered a rear parlor, making it into an office so she could have a quiet spot to plan their engagement party.

"You've been such a hermit," she told him, "that I was beginning to suppose I'd imagined you being in residence."

"I am really here."

She'd had the servants bring a desk down from the attic. She was seated at it, and as he plopped onto the chair across, she said, "I feel like we're about to commence an employment interview. Will you show me your references?"

"Definitely not. If you learned too much about me, I might not be offered the position."

She chuckled and studied him, recalling—with a great amount of relief—that he was very handsome. It wouldn't be difficult to be his bride, and the biggest advantage would be that he was rarely home and wasn't retiring from the navy any time soon.

She'd wed him, then he'd sail off into the sunset. She was very fussy, and she liked to be in charge, so she'd hate to have a husband around and underfoot. She wouldn't like to have him counting every farthing and berating her over how she spent his money.

She waved a stack of papers at him. "I'm working on the party."

"So I heard. I thought I should pop in and see if I could assist you. Are you overwhelmed?"

"No, I'm managing. I figured a two-week fete would be best. Is that all right with you?" She didn't wait for him to respond. "I assume you'll give me a budget."

"I don't need to. Just don't beggar me. I'm not too keen on pomp or ostentation, so try not to over-do. As long as we entertain in moder-ation, I won't have any complaints."

"I should check the guest list with you. I nagged at Kit until he suggested acquaintances and cousins he insisted you'd like, but is there anyone I shouldn't invite?"

"I can't think of anyone to omit, but there are three people I'd like you to add."

"Who are they?" She dipped a quill in the ink jar, the tip poised to write.

"Don't faint," he said, "but I'd like to include my half-brothers and their guardian, Sybil Jones."

Her jaw dropped in surprise. "You want to invite Caleb and Blake Ralston? And Miss Jones? Seriously?"

"Yes."

"Your mother will be spinning in her grave."

He shrugged. "It's the saddest aspect of dying. You're not around to tell the living how to behave."

"You are horrid, Captain Ralston."

She snickered with amusement, then jotted down the names, but her mind was awhirl as she struggled to deduce how she felt about it. She'd have to warn Margaret. Depending on Margaret's assessment, they might have to dissuade Jacob.

Miles Ralston had been Jacob and Margaret's famous father, but he was also father to Caleb and Blake Ralston. To the astonishment of the entire family—most especially Jacob's mother, Esther—Miles had been a bigamist.

During the years he'd been posted to the Caribbean, he'd had a second wife. No one in England had been cognizant of the disgraceful predicament until after Miles had passed away. Caleb and Blake had lost their mother shortly afterward, and their vicar in Jamaica had sent them to their British relatives.

Miss Jones had traveled with them, and she'd been a vicious sentinel, intent on protecting their interests. If it had been left up to Esther, the two boys might have starved on the streets. As it was, she'd promptly escorted them off the property, then had refused to convene with them again.

Miss Jones had marched directly to the navy and had demanded Ralston support for Caleb and Blake and that it be commensurate to their station as Miles's sons. To keep Miss Jones quiet, the navy had brokered an agreement with Esther where she'd paid for their schooling, then their navy commissions when they'd turned sixteen.

In exchange, everyone had promised to refrain from ever mentioning the thorny dilemma.

But Esther was dead now, and Jacob was head of the family. If he wanted to establish a relationship with his half-brothers, it probably wasn't any of Roxanne's business. Or was it? On the spur of the moment, she couldn't decide.

"Are you certain about this?" she asked him.

"No, but I'm doing it anyway. The involved combatants—the two wives and the one husband—are deceased. There's no reason for their children to carry on the fight."

"That is a very generous attitude."

"Or maybe I'm going mad in my old age."

"Maybe."

They smiled, and it occurred to her that she'd enjoy climbing into his bed. With his being a sailor, he'd know his way around a mattress. She wouldn't have to teach him any tricks.

"I have a question," she said, "and you don't have to answer immediately. You can think about it."

"What is it?"

"We're announcing our betrothal in September, then we're to wed the following spring when you're in England again, but it's silly to delay that long. What if we moved up the date and wed before your current furlough ends?"

"We'd proceed right after the engagement party?"

"We could hold the wedding the last day of the party—while the guests are here." She kept her expression carefully blank. "It's just a thought. I can't convince myself that we must wait until next spring. It was your mother's plan, but as you pointed out, she's not present to tell us how to act."

His expression was blank too, so she had no idea how he viewed the suggestion. Ultimately, he said, "It might work. Let me ponder it."

"No hurry, no worry."

He stood and started for the door, but he peered back and said, "I spoke to Margaret this morning. Mr. Howell left her penniless, and she's been fretting about her situation."

"She told me. I wish he was still alive so I could wring his neck."

"She's been afraid I'd kick her out. More specifically, she's been afraid that *you* might be opposed to her tarrying, but I assured her she's welcome to stay at Ralston Place—forever if she'd like. I assume you don't have a problem with that notion."

He stared at her in a steely manner, as if he was administering a test, and her reply was simple. "I love Margaret. How could I have a problem with her staying?"

It was an easy lie to spew, and he swallowed it, then he strolled out. She listened as his booted strides faded down the hall. Once it was silent again, she blew out a heavy breath.

She liked Margaret, but the house was Margaret's childhood home, so she felt a poignant attachment to it. But Roxanne was about to be mistress of the manor, so she and Margaret would get on fine—if Margaret continued to mope in her bedchamber. If she began to complain about Roxanne's management, then they'd quarrel.

Margaret would accede to Roxanne's demands, or Roxanne would make her so miserable that she'd leave. About that pertinent fact, Roxanne had no doubt at all. She was finally at the spot she'd been meant to occupy, and she wouldn't be thwarted over any issue.

From the time she was a girl, there had been talk of her marrying Jacob, but at fifteen, she'd committed a blunder that had wrecked her chance. She'd spent a decade in Italy, and now, she had the opportunity to rectify her prior mistake.

Over the winter, when his mother, Esther, had contacted her and offered the match, Roxanne had shuddered with relief and had fled Florence in an instant.

She and Jacob were plodding along at the slow schedule Esther had set prior to her death, but Roxanne couldn't follow it. There was a huge scandal dragging after her from Italy—namely two lovers dueling over her—and she had to have Jacob's ring on her finger before it caught up with her in England.

After they tied the knot, if he heard any stories, she would vehemently deny them. And if he refused to believe her? She'd be his bride, and it would be too late for him to do anything about it.

<hr />

Kit Boswell lurked in the doorway of the parlor Roxanne had turned into her office. There was a mirror on the wall, and he wasn't surprised to find her preening in front of it. She was absolutely fixated on her looks.

She was as strikingly beautiful as she'd been when they were adolescents, but the years had added a maturity to her features so she appeared even more exotic. She had white-blond hair and coal-black eyes that shouldn't have blended in a pleasing way, but on her, they were mesmerizing. He'd certainly thought so when he'd been younger.

She was willowy, possessed of a feminine figure that caused men to stop and gape when she walked by. She knew it though, and she enjoyed tormenting the oafs who danced to her tune. He'd never be one of them again.

Esther had completed the betrothal without informing him. If she had, he'd have had a few comments to share that might have prevented it, but his opinion hadn't been sought.

Roxanne had waltzed in before he'd realized she was scheduled to arrive. He'd been stunned to see her, but he'd swiftly regrouped. She had no secrets from him, and he wondered how he could use them to his own benefit.

"Well, well," he said, his tone taunting, "if it isn't Captain Ralston's glowing fiancée."

She whipped around and glared. "Why are you pestering me, Kit? Don't you have herds to tend or trees to prune? Surely there's a chore to occupy you."

"I'm totally at leisure, so I decided we should chat."

"You may not be busy, but I am. Why don't you scurry off to some other parlor? There must be someone in this house who would be glad to fuss with you. I'm not sorry to report that it isn't me."

"You're awfully rude—when you so desperately need my help."

"Don't flatter yourself into thinking you're indispensable to me."

"I've made myself indispensable. Jacob and I are like brothers. If you're not nice to me, what link can you boast that will keep you safe with him?"

"I'll be his wife, which will put me quite a bit higher on the ladder than you. Best watch yourself."

He snorted with amusement and sauntered into the room. There was a brandy decanter tucked behind a vase. She liked to act as if she was modest and retiring, but she had more vices than any female in the kingdom. A passionate taste for liquor was just one of her many bad habits.

He poured himself a glass, then went over to the window to gaze outside.

"I didn't offer you a drink," she testily protested.

"I don't care."

She huffed with offense, then sat down at the desk. She sifted through her papers, pretending to ignore him, but she couldn't.

"Miss James is coming across the park," he said. "Could she be a witch? It's the gossip among the stable boys."

"Honestly. There's no such thing as witches. Don't be absurd."

"Apparently, she can cast spells and brew magic potions. You should have her tell your future. Or might you be too afraid of what you'd learn?"

"If anybody should be afraid, it's you."

"I don't like her constantly showing up here," he said. "Why is she? She's unwed and much too fetching. It simply stirs up the male servants."

"Margaret must be having another fit of the vapors."

"Now, now," he snidely chided, "don't be snotty about your sister-in-law. She had a terrible marriage, and she's struggling to recover."

"I can't abide weak, trembling ninnies. Nor can I understand how a woman would let herself be abused. Mr. Howell has dropped dead, so she's free. She should quit whining and celebrate."

"Were you aware that Jacob visited Miss James at her cottage?"

He peeked over his shoulder, delighted to see Roxanne freeze. She feigned nonchalance with him, but she wasn't very good at it.

"He visited her? So what?"

"It's just her and her niece. He was worried that it might be dangerous for them, living in such an isolated spot."

"Again, Kit, so what? Why mention it to me?"

Miss James was fascinating and bewildering, and she exuded an air of vulnerability so a man wanted to protect her. Roxanne was the exact opposite. She didn't comprehend how to persuade a man to need her. She simply blustered forward toward her goal, shoving dolts out of her path, and he was curious how she'd fare with Jacob.

Kit predicted it would be like a grueling carriage accident, and of course, he'd wedge wrenches into their relationship. When he detested her so vehemently, it was the least he could do.

"How are the party plans progressing?" he asked.

"You're not interested in the party, and I'm not discussing it with you."

"I'm Jacob's devoted agent. I have to be interested in every facet of the estate."

She blew out a scoff. "Pigs might fly someday, I suppose."

"How is the guest list? Will we have any intriguing people joining us? Or will it be a bunch of stuffy Ralston aunties and cousins? You two have such tedious kin."

"If you must know, Mr. Estate Agent, Jacob is inviting Caleb and Blake Ralston."

He blanched with astonishment. "You're joking."

She smirked. "No, I'm not."

"Gad, Esther will be spinning in her grave."

"That's what I told him."

"Will you send them an invitation? Or will you claim you forgot?"

"I can hardly forget. He specifically requested I handle it." She leaned back and raised a brow. "Here's some news that should distress you. We've talked about moving up the wedding date. I may be Mrs. Jacob Ralston much sooner than you were expecting."

"Why the rush, Roxanne?" He cast a contemptuous glance at her belly. "Is there a little bun in the oven? And if there is a *bun*, how are we to be sure Jacob is the baker?"

"There's no *bun*, as you so crudely put it."

"What's driving you then? Why am I suspecting there are rumors trailing after you from Italy?" Most times, she was unflappable, but at his comment, her cheeks heated, and he realized he'd hit on the truth. "You must be anxious to get a ring on your finger before your antics there are exposed. Is that it?"

"Shut up, Kit."

He downed his brandy, walked over to the desk, and slammed down the glass. "The scandal must be hideous—if you can't let Jacob find out. Is it another baby? Will you spit out a second bastard that must be concealed from the world?"

She bristled ferociously, then grabbed a letter opener and leapt to her feet. She poked the tip into his chest so deeply that it would leave a small tear in the fabric of his shirt.

"If you ever breathe a word about that again, I'll murder you," she said. "I won't hesitate. You think you're smarter and more important than me. You think you have a huge secret to hold over my head, but I hold the same secret over yours."

"It thrills me to envision telling Jacob some of your sins. He truly has no idea what sort of person you are. Shouldn't he be apprised?"

"I wonder how he'd view some of *your* sins," she tossed back. "What if he discovered what we'd done all those years ago? Your cozy job wouldn't last very long. If Jacob threw you out, you lazy fiend, who else would have you?"

She pushed him away and plopped down on her chair. She glowered at him, her loathing clear, but his was clear too. Their malice oozed out, and he had to give her credit. In any battle, she was a worthy opponent.

"*Touché,* Roxanne." He nodded. "It seems we are to be conspirators in guaranteeing Jacob is happy with his choice of bride."

"He'll be happy with me. I've been waiting since I was a girl to have this marriage happen, and nothing will prevent it."

"If your marriage is spoiled, it won't be because of me."

"You better hope not."

"You'd better too."

It wasn't the pithiest parting remark, but she'd exhausted him. He spun on his heel and marched out.

Chapter

5

"Hold it right there, Miss James!"

Jacob trotted up behind her, relieved to see that she halted. She was such an impertinent wench that it wouldn't have surprised him if she'd continued on, despite his sharp command. He wedged his horse in very close, blocking her way so she couldn't skirt on by.

"Hello, Captain."

"Where is your dog today?"

"He ran off, but I expect he'll be back. He never vanishes for long."

"You were just at the manor."

"Yes, I brewed some tinctures for the housekeeper. She likes to have them available for when your servants are feeling poorly."

"So I heard. I also heard that, while you were there, you stitched a cut, treated a cough, and tended my sister whose fever is plaguing her. Have I neglected to mention any of your antics?"

"I don't believe so, but why are you glaring at me? Should I have *not* treated them? Will you order me to stay away?"

"Don't be ridiculous. I'm happy to have you helping people. Just promise you won't kill anyone."

She rolled her eyes. "You can be so absurd. Is that all you came to say? I should try not to *kill* anyone? I'm busy, as usual, and you're not. I have chores."

"You seem to have forgotten our prior conversation. Did I—or did I not—ask you to inform me whenever you visited?"

"I didn't suppose you were serious."

"I'm always serious. You are *not* to ever stop by without pausing to chat with me."

She frowned. "Why are you so insistent about it?"

"I have no idea, but you'll oblige me anyway."

"Fine. On future occasions, I'll have you summoned."

"That's more like it. Where are you off to? It appears you're headed to your cottage. Climb up, and I'll give you a ride."

"I'm not letting you take me home."

"Why not?"

"First off, I don't like horses. They're big and . . . big."

"You liar. You love them so much that you can talk to them."

"And second, I don't understand why you're pestering me. There must be others who can entertain you. Why must it be me?"

"If I ever determine the cause of my obsession, I'll apprise you as to what's fueling it."

He wedged his horse a bit nearer, and he leaned down and extended his hand. She stared at it, but didn't reach for it.

"Coward," he taunted.

"I didn't think I was afraid of anything, but I might be afraid of you."

"What a ludicrous comment. Why would you be afraid of me?"

"You have wicked intentions. Are you a scoundrel? Is that your reputation?"

"No, but you're spurring me to behave in new ways."

"I don't want to be friendly with you."

"I don't care, and my opinion is the only one that matters."

He'd been telling the truth when he'd claimed he didn't understand his fascination. In his stultified world of naval officers and upper-crust families, everyone carried on pretty much the same. She was the sole person he'd met in ages who provided any variety.

At least he was pretending that was the basis for his fixation. He refused to accept that he was desperately attracted to her. A man of his station never fraternized with a woman of hers. There was no position for her to occupy except that of mistress, but an immoral liaison had to be pursued in the city where rural sensibilities weren't considered.

He could never trifle with her in the country where gossip abounded about his every move. He was pushing his luck simply by trotting after her.

Due to her odd skills and independent style of living, she was already a strange creature who generated stories. If he coaxed her into a scandal, she'd be crushed by the weight of rumor and innuendo. He would never be able to repair any damage, even if he vigorously defended her.

He'd about given up on escorting her, figuring she'd stomp off in a huff, when she grabbed his wrist. With a quick lift, he had her seated in front of him on the saddle.

He bent in and ruffled his nose in her beautiful hair, saying, "You smell so good. Like flowers and sunshine."

"It's probably because I'm so often out-of-doors."

"It's not a special perfume you produce to entice men?"

"No."

She laughed, her voice sweet and sultry in a manner that tickled his innards. He dipped in and kissed her. He couldn't help himself. Since he'd kissed her the previous day, he'd yearned to repeat his folly. He'd told himself the prior embrace had been committed in a moment of temporary insanity. If so, what was his current excuse? Could there ever be one?

There were always people in the woods, so there could be witnesses to his foolishness, but he wasn't concerned. Why was that exactly?

He had a fiancée lodged in his home. She was busy, planning their engagement party. She was eager to speed up the schedule, to rush the wedding, yet he was loafing in the forest with another woman.

What was wrong with him? Was he hoping he'd be discovered? Was he hoping Roxanne would find out and cry off?

It couldn't be that. He was fully prepared to become her husband. Or was he? Every time he pictured himself speaking the vows, his anxiety would spiral, and he'd feel as if he couldn't breathe.

He had a sneaking suspicion that it was his guardian angel warning him to back out. Did he believe in guardian angels? He was fairly certain not.

When he drew away, she looked extremely exasperated, and she said, "What shall I do with you, Captain?"

"Why would you have to *do* anything? And it's Jacob, remember?"

"You can't keep kissing me. What, precisely, are you expecting to achieve by it?"

"It makes me happy. Must I have more of a reason than that?"

"I suppose you always get your way."

"Of course. What would be the point of life otherwise?"

He urged his horse forward, and the animal lumbered off at a slow pace. She relaxed into him, her petite frame nestled to his much larger one. He liked how she fit against him, as if she'd been created to sit right where she was and in no other spot in the world.

They rode along in a companionable silence, and he studied their surroundings, trying to recollect any fond experiences as a boy. There had rarely been other children at the estate—not any with whom his mother would permit him to socialize anyway—so there had been no building of forts, no swimming in the streams, no playing of Robin Hood and his merry band of criminals.

As a sea-faring man, if he'd been pressed to supply his view of the property, he'd have declared it landlocked, so it couldn't appeal to him in the slightest. But it was a balmy summer day, and he had a fetching temptress snuggled on his lap. The interval was as perfect as it could be.

They reached her gate, and he lifted her down, then dismounted himself. He tied the reins to the fence, and she said, "I assume you're coming inside."

"Yes, and you should be a tad more gracious about it. I doubt you have many visitors, so you should be glad I've bothered."

"Have I told you that you're a menace?"

"I'm sure you have."

"I wasn't joking."

She started up the walk, and he followed like a puppet on a string.

"Where is Clara?" he asked.

"She's at school. There's a widow in the village who teaches a group of girls."

"You have money for that?"

The nosy question popped out before he could swallow it down. She wasn't offended though. "Her grandmother left it to us, to pay for incidentals."

"Who was her grandmother?"

"I don't know."

He scowled. "I thought she was your niece."

"I tell that story about her, but she's not a relative. My Aunt Pru attended her mother at the birthing. The family didn't want her, so we kept her."

"Why didn't they want her?" he inquired like a dolt.

"I'll let you ponder the answer. I'm positive you'll deduce it without too much heavy contemplation."

"Oh. I'm guessing her mother was young and unwed."

"You'd be guessing correctly."

They entered the residence, and he was annoyed to see that the door was unlocked.

"How long will I have to nag at you about this situation?" he asked. "It's not safe for you to be so trusting."

"It's futile to badger me about it. I'm very stubborn, so I would never listen."

"I understand why you have no husband. What man would tolerate such blatant disrespect? Weren't you ever informed that men are your masters? You're required to heed them in all matters. It even orders it in the Bible."

"I have to confess to being a terrible sinner. Most every man I've ever met is a fool."

"What about me? Am *I* a fool?"

"You're the biggest one of all."

"Why would you believe that? Everyone agrees that I'm a brave, industrious, and smart fellow. Why is your opinion so different?"

She didn't reply, but yanked off her bonnet and shawl and hung them on a hook. Then she lit a lamp and tugged open the curtains. The cottage was tucked away in deep woods, so there was never much sunshine to filter through the trees. Even though it was the middle of the afternoon, it felt like dusk was about to arrive.

Finally, when she had the room adjusted, she spun to face him. "You're engaged to be married, Captain. Your fiancée is ensconced in the manor and planning your betrothal party, and you should be helping her, yet you're here with me instead. When is the wedding to be?"

He'd been wondering if she'd heard, and he coolly fibbed, "Next year, so you see, Miss James, I remain very much a bachelor."

"What would she think if your mischief with me was exposed?"

"My activities are none of her business."

"Spoken like a true cad." She gestured to the door. "Would you go?"

"No. I'm too amused by you to consider departing."

"How about if I feed you? Might you then have your fill of me?"

"You already admitted you can't cook, so I'm not keen to accept your offer."

"I can't cook, but I can pick blackberries. My servant baked me a pie."

She went to the kitchen and drew out a chair for him. He sat down, and he watched her as she bustled about, pulling out plates and dishing up two slices. She put them down, then seated herself across from him.

They didn't dig in immediately, but were content to stare, and he was irked to find himself drowning in her pretty green eyes. It occurred to him that he might be in a great deal of trouble with her.

There appeared to be something he wanted, something he needed her to give him. Until he discovered what it was, he probably wouldn't be able to leave her alone. What would it turn out to be? How much mayhem would he stir before he settled on the answer?

She began to eat, and she ignored him completely, which was interesting to witness. He simply took up too much space in any room, and he was always the center of attention.

"What will happen between us?" she asked after they'd finished.

"I can't imagine. What do *you* expect?"

She rested her elbows on the table, her chin on her hand, and she studied him in an absorbing manner, as if she could peer down to his tiniest pore. It produced the strangest sensations, as if she was creeping through his veins, and he didn't like it one bit. He wouldn't tell her that though. Nor would he let her realize she was having such a deleterious effect on his equilibrium.

He was much too manly to be undone by a *look*.

"Why are you studying me so intently?" he asked.

"I'm trying to figure out your purpose."

"So am I." He motioned around the kitchen. "When I was waiting for you yesterday, I snooped in your cupboards and drawers."

"You poured yourself a glass of wine too. You are so rude."

"This is the most intriguing little house, and you are the most intriguing person."

"I'm not really. You're just bored, so you're imbuing me with traits I don't possess."

"You have jars of herbs and flower blossoms and plant roots. Your workroom could belong to an apothecary, and it's obvious you boast of many bizarre skills. Where did you learn them?"

"From my Aunt Pru."

"And where did she learn them?"

"From her mother."

"Why didn't your own mother teach you. Have you skipped a generation?"

"My mother died when I was very young, so she didn't have the opportunity to teach me. Aunt Pru had to step in."

"How old were you when you were brought to live with your aunt?"

"Five."

"Are you part of a secret society? Are you a sect of pagans or are you witches or—"

She cut him off. "You're not uttering that word around me. You promised, remember? The women in my family have simply accumulated an enormous amount of ancient wisdom, and we pass it down from one daughter to the next."

"How far back can you trace your lineage?"

"A thousand years."

He chuckled, certain she was jesting. "It's impossible to track that far."

She smiled coyly. "I might have exaggerated just a tad."

"Would you do me a favor?" he asked.

"That depends on what it is."

"You have those magical cards. The Taro cards? I'm curious about them. Would you read them for me?"

It was the type of exploit one might engage in at a fair or with a gypsy at his roadside wagon. He'd seen sailors using them. Elderly matrons occasionally displayed them too, as parlor entertainment. They were made for sport, so what could be the harm?

"I never read them for anyone," she said.

"Why not?"

"It's a kind of divining, where we can learn how our path will unfold. Some people find it threatening."

In explaining her reservations, she was so serious, as if she actually assumed she could predict his future. Could she? And if she could, should he let her? Should any man know his future?

Even as he debated the issue, he scoffed. He didn't believe in pre-destiny or that a man's fate was written in the stars. He especially didn't think a few colorful cards could tell him anything relevant, but he was eager to discover what she might say, to watch her slender hands as she fussed and contemplated.

She hesitated, and the wheels were spinning in her head as she tried to devise a reason to refuse. He raised a brow. "Will I have to call you *coward* again?"

The taunt was too much for her. She pushed back her chair, marched into her workroom, and returned with the deck. She kept them in a wooden box that had strange symbols carved on it. She removed them and gently placed them face down, as if they were fragile or perhaps even hot to touch. Then she went through the house, closing the curtains and shutters so no spies could peek inside.

She lit a candle and put it on the table, then she sat across from him. Shadows danced on the walls, and she appeared eerie and ethereal—as if she was about to wield great power. Her furtiveness made the whole endeavor seem illegal and perilous.

"I will oblige you this one time," she said, and she was very somber, "but you have to swear you won't ever talk about it. If you can't swear, I won't proceed."

"Why would it matter if I talk about it?"

"Can it be our secret or not?"

She was so earnest that he could only say, "Fine, Joanna. I swear."

She must have been reassured because she nodded and shoved the deck over to him. "Rest your palm on them, then shut your eyes and ponder the question you'd like to have answered."

"Out loud or to myself?"

"To yourself—and be precise or you might have a different question answered, and the reply will confuse you."

He was glad he didn't have to speak his query aloud, for he'd have been incredibly embarrassed. His approaching marriage wasn't a topic he should mention in front of her.

As she'd instructed, he shut his eyes and thought, *Will I be happy in my marriage? Should I go through with it? Or will I be miserable forever?*

It was three questions rather than one, but what the hell? It was a circus game, so no pertinent information would be revealed.

He'd decided to wed that year, but he hadn't felt competent to select a candidate himself. His mother had arranged the match—practically on her deathbed. She'd picked Roxanne, as had always been the plan, and Roxanne had traveled from Italy to bring it to fruition. He should have been ready to walk to the altar, but he couldn't picture it.

He eased away, and Joanna shuffled the cards, then pulled out six of them and laid them in a line. They were peculiar, but mesmerizing, awash with vibrant patterns and characters that were probably demonic.

The first was titled, *The Lovers.* That was a good sign, wasn't it?

There were others though, filled with swords and violent scenes that seemed to indicate it would involve strife and conflict. The final one showed an imperious woman sitting on a throne and staring out arrogantly. She had red hair that curled over her shoulders, and it took him a moment to realize she looked exactly like Joanna.

A shiver slid down his spine.

She studied the display, and he studied her, and the tension was nearly unbearable. He broke the silence. "If I didn't divulge my question, how can you know what my answer should be?"

"The cards will tell me." It was a response that made no sense. She pointed to them, clarifying their general purpose, then she said, "I recognize that you're a very masculine man, so what I'm about to say will sound odd, but the main message being delivered is that you're about to fall madly in love. She will be the woman you've waited for all your life, the one created just for you. There will be enormous struggle and jeopardy as you battle to win her, but in the end, you'll wed her and be happier than you ever imagined."

"Huh . . ." Another shiver slithered down his spine.

"Do you understand what I've told you? Have you received your answer?"

His cheeks heated. He wasn't about to admit that his inquiry had been about his pending marriage. She'd just insisted he'd be fantastically happy with Roxanne. Somehow, he didn't see that conclusion winging toward him with her as his bride.

Roxanne was aloof and beautiful, but they were both detached and reserved. It was the Ralston blood flowing in their veins. They simply weren't affectionate. How could two such stiff, taciturn people find the sort of contentment Joanna had described?

She had no idea what he'd asked, so it couldn't be a trick she'd performed to make him believe she was very astute. He'd probed for advice about a private nuptial matter, and the reply was spot on to the subject he'd raised, but it felt completely in error too.

Him? Roxanne? Madly in love? The notion boggled the mind.

"I must have done it wrong," he fibbed. "I wasn't curious about . . . ah . . . *love,* but about a different issue entirely, so your comments might be gibberish."

"Would you like to try it again? You could reflect for a bit, then reword your query."

"I think that will be my one and only attempt at the occult."

"It's not the occult." Her tone was scolding. "These cards are ancient and prophetic. They've been utilized for hundreds—perhaps thousands—of years so human choices are clearer."

"So you say. As for myself, I won't claim to be impressed."

Appearing dubious, she scrutinized him, then she pushed away from the table. She bustled about, opening the shutters and curtains, blowing out the candle. Order was restored, the perception of sorcery vanishing as light flooded in.

She tucked the cards into their box, then took them to her workroom. He followed, leaned on the doorframe and observing as she put them away.

She came over to him and said, "Have I entertained you sufficiently for one afternoon? Clara's classes are almost finished, and I walk to the village to meet her."

"I suppose I can declare myself sated."

It was a bald-faced lie. He'd likely never have enough of her. She'd ignited a fire in him that he couldn't quell. He had no desire to quell it.

He wrapped an arm around her waist and drew her close. He liked that she didn't skitter away, that she didn't pretend offense, and it had him speculating as to whether she was still a maiden. She was so independent, and she carried on far outside the bounds of society. Maybe she'd had lovers in the past, and he was tantalized by the prospect.

If she was loose with her favors, it would solve several problems for him. A gentleman couldn't seduce a maiden, but once a lady had shed that badge, it produced a route to all kinds of wicked conduct.

He wasn't such a rude oaf that he'd pressure her about it, and he had to hope—as they were better acquainted—she would provide a hint about her condition.

He dipped down and kissed her, which was becoming a habit. She jumped in with delightful enthusiasm, and the embrace quickly spun out of control. To see her was to want her. How could he ignore such an overwhelming impulse?

She was young, pretty, and alone in the world. She exuded a confident air that was enticing, but she seemed very vulnerable too, as if she needed a strong man by her side.

You could be that man . . .

The remark wedged itself into his head, and he shoved it away, being determined to focus on the moment and naught else.

He simply kissed her, then kissed her some more. He didn't unbutton any buttons or untie any laces, but salacious thoughts were pelting him. A potent animal lust was pounding in his veins, and he caught himself yearning to throw her down on the floor, to ravish her without consequence.

The urge was so gripping that he forced himself to slow down and ease away. Their lips parted, and she gazed up at him, her expression tender, but exasperated too.

"I can't resist you," she said.

"You shouldn't resist me. Why would you?"

"I can list a thousand reasons."

"Name one."

"How about your engagement and marriage?"

"I told you: I won't be wed for over a year. It means I am very much a bachelor."

"I could argue the point, but I won't. I'll merely state that *you* feel free to dally, but I am unwed, so I don't have the luxury to pursue a romance with you."

He grinned. "Is that what this is? Are we pursuing a romance?"

"I can't settle on the appropriate term to clarify what's occurring."

He tried to link their fingers, but she wouldn't permit it, and he remembered the day by the stream when that odd surge had flowed from her into him.

"Why won't you allow me to hold your hand?"

"I have power in my palms," she said, "and I'd rather not waste it on you."

"You have *power* in your palms? What kind of power?"

"I'm positive you'll laugh, but my hands heal people, and it requires an incredible amount of my energy."

"You *might* use them for healing, but you use them for other things too. You definitely used them on me—for something."

"Did I? I can't imagine to what you refer."

She looked innocent as a nun, and he smirked with derision. "You are a rolling ball of fabrications and outright lies. Do you ever tell the truth?"

"Usually."

The blithe comment made him laugh. "At least you admit you're a partial fraud."

"It's not always beneficial to be brutally honest. Depending on the circumstance, it's not harmful to round the edges a bit."

"You have an answer for every facet of your mischief, don't you?"

"It's not mischief, and if you're going to stand there and insult me, I don't have to listen."

"I'm not insulting you. I'm critiquing you. You should devise better anecdotes to explain yourself."

"You are not simply critiquing me. You deem me to be very peculiar, and if I'm not careful, you'll soon be counselling me as to how I can conform my behavior in order to be just like everyone else."

He nodded. "You could be correct, so I'm being an ass. I wouldn't want to change a single detail about you. You are absolutely fascinating, and I'm sure—if you attempted to conform to any of society's rules—you would fail miserably."

"I'm sure of it too."

She scooted away and went to the front door. He dawdled, feeling horribly besotted. He was anxious to tarry, but that was idiotic.

No doubt his lengthy absence had been noted at the manor, so he'd have to invent a few alibis.

He followed her, and she continued on outside and proceeded through the gate to where his horse was tethered. She nuzzled with the animal, leaving Jacob with the distinct impression that they really were chatting.

"Are you and my horse conversing again?" he said as he sauntered up. "What's he complaining about today?"

"He's tired of waiting for you to depart, and he's afraid you'll be very late getting home. He hopes you won't blame him for your being tardy."

"I won't even ask if that's true or not. It probably is."

He kissed her a final time, and this one was more urgent and desperate, and to his great disgust, he was hastily calculating how quickly he'd be able to see her again.

He pulled away, and he assessed the dark woods. They seemed sinister. "I worry about you and Clara living so far out of the way. If I could find you a house nearer to some neighbors, what would you think of that? Or maybe even in the village?"

"I appreciate your concern, but I wouldn't like to move. I'm happy here, and I'm grateful for what's been provided. I don't need more than what I have."

"I'll stop by tomorrow. I don't know when, so it will be a surprise."

"I suppose it would be futile to tell you you shouldn't."

"Yes, it would be futile, and if you visit the manor, you're aware that I must be notified."

"I shall inform you of my presence, so we can . . . what?"

"I'll let that be a surprise too."

"Should I remind you that your sister and your fiancée are at the manor?"

"I haven't forgotten."

"Yes, you have. What, precisely, will we *do* after I accost you?"

He stood very still, struggling to deduce his reply. He pictured himself picking her up, racing up the stairs to his bedchamber, and debauching her for hours on end, and he chuckled, deciding he was a smitten fool.

"I have no idea what we'll do. We'll figure it out as we go forward."

He stepped away and mounted his horse, and as he stared down at her, there was such a perception swirling that he'd arrived exactly where he was meant to be, but that was an insane sentiment.

He gave her a mock salute, then he tugged on the reins and trotted away. As he hurried off, he was eager to glance back, to wave, to discover if she was watching and waving too, but he forced himself to look straight ahead.

For pity's sake, he'd see her the next day. He had to cease his obsessing, but he missed her already, and he had to physically prevent himself from turning and cantering back to remain by her side.

⌒〜⌒

JOANNA LOAFED BY HER gate until he was swallowed up by the trees. He'd stayed much too long, so Clara would have to walk part of the distance by herself. The lane from the village was safe, but Joanna liked to show up and accompany her. Before she could depart though, she had to check one little detail.

She dashed into the cottage and proceeded directly to her workroom. She retrieved her cards, and she laid them on the table, shuffling them, filling them with energy.

She debated whether to inquire about her own situation, but it was pointless to divine her fate. Most times, her future was shielded.

Instead, she had to learn something about the Captain. She wasn't positive what his query had been, but she had her suspicions, and the response he'd received was absurd. It was blatantly evident that he was about to marry the love of his life, but she didn't understand how that could be even remotely true.

She'd finally been introduced to Roxanne Ralston, and Miss Ralston was a vain, conceited shrew who berated and intimidated the servants. She was unpleasant and unlikable, and Joanna couldn't imagine why any man would wed her. She definitely couldn't fathom how the Captain would find even a modicum of contentment with her.

Joanna placed her hand on the stack, and she posed her question aloud: "Is Roxanne Ralston the love of Jacob Ralston's life? Will she make him happy forever?"

She selected a card, and it was titled, *Death*. She selected several others—just to be certain—and on observing how they arranged themselves, she grinned with satisfaction.

There was no doubt that Jacob Ralston was about to wed, and it would be to the bride who was destined to be his partner. That message had been quite plain. But it wouldn't be Roxanne Ralston, so he was in for a few wild months.

He wasn't the sort who liked upheaval though, and she'd garner enormous amusement as events unfolded and pummeled him in a manner he'd never expect.

She tucked the deck away, then grabbed her shawl and bonnet. She rushed off to meet Clara, and she smiled all the way.

Chapter 6

"My brother mentioned that he's met you."

Margaret studied Miss James, thinking she was so pretty. What had Jacob thought of her?

Despite the fact that Jacob's engagement was about to become official, he was still a bachelor. He was home, where he was always bored, so it probably wasn't a good idea to have him bumping into such a tempting siren.

Should Margaret cancel Miss James's visits?

"Your brother and I have conversed," Miss James said.

"I'm aware that you discussed me with him. In the future, please don't."

Miss James's cheeks heated. "I apologize. He heard I was tending you, and he demanded to know why you were ailing. It was incredibly difficult to deflect his nagging."

"He is very impressed with himself."

"He definitely is," Miss James agreed, and they smiled a conspiratorial smile.

Margaret pondered for a moment, then jumped in with both feet. "We're having a party on Saturday night. We'll have a buffet supper, and there will be dancing afterward. Would you come?"

Miss James froze, as if the request was a riddle she had to unravel. "Are you certain you'd like me to?"

"I wouldn't have asked you if I wasn't serious. Why are you frowning?"

"I've lived in the area for years, and I've never previously been invited to a social event at the manor."

"That's because my mother was a great snob. She wouldn't have deemed it proper to include you. I'm much less set on myself, and you're the only interesting person I've encountered since I returned. If you attend, I'll have someone to chat with who won't bore me to tears."

Miss James chuckled. "After an explanation like that, how could I decline? It would be cruel of me to refuse, and my niece is attending a party of her own on Saturday, so I'm free that evening."

"You have a niece? What's her name?"

"Clara. She's nine."

"Every time I talk to you, I learn new information."

"Her parents couldn't raise her, so my Aunt Prudence and I took her in."

Margaret was swamped by a wave of self-pity, wondering why every woman in the world seemed to have children but her. Even unwed Miss James had a girl of her own. Motherhood was so easy for others. Why had it been impossible for Margaret?

She'd tried her best to give Mr. Howell a son, but she'd failed. It was the sole task that really mattered for a wife, and Mr. Howell had never forgiven her. Not that she cared, but her lack still stung.

They were in Margaret's bedchamber, in her sitting room. Her health was fine, so she hadn't needed Miss James, but for some reason, it was soothing to dawdle with her. She exuded a serenity that made Margaret yearn to linger in her presence.

She was so assured and confident, while she, Margaret, had always perceived herself as being on the wrong side of a wall, that there was a better life on the other side, and she simply had to cross over to it. She could never manage the leap though, but continued to wallow where she didn't wish to be.

Miss James gathered her supplies and left, and Margaret tarried in the quiet, feeling anxious, as if something was supposed to happen. But nothing ever did.

It was late afternoon, and supper wouldn't be served for hours. Roxanne wouldn't let them eat at a decent time, but forced them to pretend they resided in a London mansion and were surrounded by posh aristocrats who reveled until dawn.

Roxanne was running the manor, having arrived from Italy prior to Margaret arriving from Egypt. Since Roxanne wasn't Jacob's bride yet, or even officially his fiancée, Margaret should have yanked the reins of authority away from her, but when she'd staggered in, she hadn't had the energy.

Initially, she'd been content to have Roxanne assume the duties, but now that her condition had improved, she'd like to step in, but she couldn't figure out how. It would stir a quarrel between them, and where Roxanne was concerned, Margaret had already recognized that she'd have to pick her battles.

She wandered over and stared out the window, and on the edge of the park, she could see the roofs of two houses. Kit lived in the larger, fancier one, and Sandy in the smaller, more modest one. She was distressed by Sandy and their brief meeting out by the barn. He'd been cool and aloof, but his detached attitude was her own fault.

She'd been home for weeks, but she hadn't sought him out. She should have, but she hadn't been able to decide what to say. A decade earlier, when she'd acceded to her mother's commands and had agreed to shackle herself to Mr. Howell, she'd abruptly severed her affair with Sandy.

He'd wanted to marry her, and she'd convinced herself that it could transpire. On one very unpleasant occasion, she'd discussed the prospect with her mother, but Esther had been so enraged that she'd almost suffered an apoplexy. Esther's reaction had been to move up the wedding and to whisk Margaret away from the property—and from Sandy.

Before she'd departed, they'd had one fraught conversation where he'd begged her to stand up to her mother, to refuse Mr. Howell. He'd truly believed they could elope and live on love. His last words to her had been, *If you wed him, you'll be sorry forever...*

It was humiliating to admit how right he'd been, but he was too kind to ever rub it in. After she'd sailed for Egypt, she'd never heard any gossip about him, so she had no idea how his life had unfolded without her.

In her more morbid moments, she liked to imagine he'd never stopped pining away for her, but she doubted that was the case. He'd been a handsome boy, then a handsome young man, and the years had added maturity and strength to his features. His shoulders were broad, his body lean and strong from physical exertion.

With his blond hair, blue eyes, and tanned skin, he resembled a bronzed god an artist might have painted on a church ceiling.

Should she try to talk to him again? Would he like that?

She had to find out, and she dashed out of her room, down the rear stairs, and out of the manor. He'd likely have completed his chores for the day and—like any sane person—would be having supper, so she proceeded to his house.

It occurred to her that she was being very rash, but she hurried on, determined to speak with him and not lose her nerve.

She rushed up his walk, having to knock twice before footsteps sounded. As she waited, she noticed how the residence had been enhanced. Was it by feminine hands? Shutters had been attached, and there were flowerboxes under the windows. Rosebushes had been planted along the front.

When she'd parted from Sandy, he'd been nineteen, a bachelor with a good job and a house, so he'd been quite a catch among the local girls, but he'd only ever been enticed by her. She hadn't paused to wonder if one of them might have snagged him for a husband.

What if one of them had? What would she do? She had to be glad about it, didn't she?

A boy opened the door. He was eight or so, and with his being blond and blue-eyed, he was a little version of Sandy. Her heart dropped to her shoes.

Was he married? In her time away, she'd never pondered whether he might be. Was his wife inside? Would Margaret have to be introduced to her and feign cordiality? She nearly spun and slunk off, but she wasn't a coward.

"Is Sandy at home?" she inquired. Then she changed her question to, "I mean Mr. Sanders?"

"Yes. Shall I fetch him for you?"

"Would you?"

He raced off, calling loudly, "Pa! Pa! It's Miss Ralston!"

Sandy replied to his son, "Are you a barbarian, Tim? Why are you shouting? And why would Roxanne Ralston be here? Is there an emergency at the stables?"

"I didn't think to ask," the boy said.

Margaret entered the parlor without being invited, and she tried to recollect if she'd ever been in the house, but if she had, she couldn't remember.

Sandy strolled in, the boy dogging his heels. He was holding a towel, as if he'd been drying the supper plates in the kitchen. His coat was off, his sleeves pushed back. It was such a cozy domestic scene that she could have wept.

"Oh," he said on seeing her. "Margaret! I was expecting your cousin. May I help you? What's amiss?"

"Everything's fine. I . . . ah . . . I just wanted to chat, but it's obvious you're busy."

"We're done eating. I'm not busy."

Another boy popped in too, and Sandy said to her, "Have you met my sons?"

She shook her head. "No."

"This is Tim who answered the door—and who was so rude about it. He's the younger, and this is Tom. He's the older."

"Hello, Tim and Tom."

They didn't respond to her greeting, but gaped at her as if she had purple skin or five legs.

Sandy's affection for them was clear. He snorted with fond exasperation. "Have you two idiots been struck dumb? Haven't you been taught how to act when we have company? You make me look as if I'm rearing a pair of heathens."

In unison, the boys chirped, "Hello, Miss Ralston."

"That's more like it," Sandy grumbled, "but she's not Miss Ralston. She's Mrs. Howell."

They murmured her married name, as if tasting it on their tongues, then Sandy gave his towel to Tom. "Finishing cleaning up while I talk with Mrs. Howell."

"May we have pie?" Tom asked.

"One slice each."

"Am I in charge while you're away?"

"No one is in charge. I won't be gone that long."

Sandy gestured outside, and they went out together. She distinctly noted that he hadn't been keen to have her tarry in his home, and she couldn't decide if she was irked by his attitude or not. With his sons there, they couldn't have discussed much that mattered, so it was probably better that they'd left.

He led her out into the park where there was a bench positioned under a rose arbor, but they didn't sit on it. The interval was very awkward. They trudged forward like strangers, or if not strangers, then as if they didn't like each other very much.

They turned to face one another, squared off like pugilists in the ring.

"Are you married?" she asked.

"I was. I'm a widower."

The admission cut through her like a knife, and she scolded herself. Of course he'd have wed. He was thirty, and she'd been away for over a decade. What woman wouldn't have grabbed hold when he proposed?

She was the only one who'd been conceited enough to refuse.

"I didn't realize," she said.

"She died several years ago. I'm raising the boys on my own."

"It's just the two of them?"

"Yes, and they're a handful."

"Did I know her?"

"No."

"What was her name?"

"Actually, it was Margaret, but we called her Maggie."

"Was she like me at all?"

"No, she was nothing like you."

There was scorn in his voice. Had she been insulted?

"When did you start courting her?"

He studied her, his expression irritated. "I can't have this conversation with you."

"Were you happy?"

His reply was very brusque. "What is it you need, Margaret? I don't mean to be rude, but my day begins very early, and I have a ton of chores to complete before my evening is over."

He was glaring as if he'd never been her dearest companion, as if he was a servant—which he was. But she'd never thought of him that way, and she'd never treated him that way, except for that terrible night when she'd parroted her mother's condescending words to inform him that she had to wed according to her class and station.

Obviously, he hadn't forgotten the comment. Nor had he forgiven her for it.

"You're so upset with me," she said, "and I don't blame you. I've been back for two months, and I should have sought you out sooner, but I was confused about what to say."

"What is there to say? And what would be the point of saying it?"

"I've been so despondent."

"I appreciate that you have been. I hear plenty of gossip, and I hate that your road has been so bumpy, but I can't help you. If you require some healing, I can send for Miss James."

"Weren't we friends in the past? I assumed we were. Could we be friends now?"

He scoffed with derision. "We weren't ever friends, Margaret. You're rewriting our history."

"We *were* friends. Don't you dare claim we weren't."

"I was a passing fancy, but you moved on. I moved on too. It's futile to look on that period with any nostalgia."

"Even after Jacob marries Roxanne, I'm staying at Ralston Place. Can you stand to have me strolling around the property, but to pretend you don't notice me? Is that a viable option for you?"

"I doubt our paths will cross very often. I don't ever come to the manor, and you ride so rarely. Why would we be forced to fraternize?"

"Wouldn't you like to ... to ... fraternize?"

Her cheeks heated, and she felt like a needy beggar. Why, precisely, had she visited him?

She didn't want to rekindle their amour. She was twenty-eight, a widow who wasn't grieving her husband, but who was definitely grieving her marriage. She wasn't in the market for a beau, yet she craved things from him she couldn't identify.

"I can't bear for us to carry on as if we're strangers," she said.

"Well, we *are* strangers. How can you fail to comprehend that fact?"

"You used to know me better than anyone."

"We were children, Margaret!" He threw up his hands in frustration. "We believed we were so smart. We believed we could bend the world's rules, but we couldn't. You're home, and I'm still here, but so what? What are you hoping to have happen? For the life of me, I can't deduce what it is."

"I can't figure it out either. I'm just . . . just . . ."

Tears swarmed to her eyes and dripped down her cheeks. He appeared stricken, as if she'd hit him with a club.

"Don't you cry on me," he said. "I can't deal with it."

"I'm sorry! I shouldn't have wed Mr. Howell! You warned me, but I didn't listen, and I hurt you, and . . . and . . . and . . ."

She stopped talking, thinking—if she didn't shut her mouth—she might vent so much woe that she would flood the entire kingdom. She was that forlorn.

She saw now why she'd bothered him. She needed him to fix what was wrong. She couldn't fathom how to repair it on her own, and he was so strong and capable. He had sturdy shoulders, the kind a woman could lean on when she was alone and in trouble, but he wasn't interested in being her knight, and she shouldn't have prevailed on him.

It was the height of presumption for her to have assumed he should oblige her. It had been the problem during their prior amour. She'd viewed him as a sort of toy, a sparkly object she could utilize to entertain herself. The minute he'd become inconvenient, she'd cast him aside.

She yearned to revert to the spot where they'd been previously, to ignore the intervening years, no husband for her, no wife for him. She'd like to forget that she'd tossed him away as if he didn't matter.

She was so embarrassed, and she would have skirted around him and run off, but before she could move, he pulled her into his arms.

"My poor, poor Margaret," he murmured. "You've always been such a pest, and I can't ever swat you away."

"Please forgive me! Let me apologize, and tell me my apology is accepted. Don't act as if you don't know me."

"I can't act that way."

"Neither can I," she wailed quite miserably.

He laughed, sounding miserable too, then he was kissing her and kissing her. She was cradled to his broad chest, and her body relaxed against him, and for the first time in over a decade, she felt safe and cherished.

She couldn't guess how long they continued, but it was long enough that the sun set and dusk arrived. They didn't chat, didn't pause to consider their wild conduct. They simply held each other like survivors of a shipwreck.

Finally, one of his boys called, "Pa! Where are you? It's late."

He drew away and chuckled. "It's been difficult for them since their mother passed away. They can't bear to be parted from me."

"I'm sure you're the best father ever."

"I have to get back. Will you come with me?"

She stared at the manor, where lamps were being lit. "I probably shouldn't. I'm a distraught mess, and your sons would realize I've been crying. I would hate to have to explain why I'm so sad."

"I'll see you tomorrow." He squeezed her hand. "Maybe you could join us for supper."

"I can't wait until evening. I'll be too impatient. I'll visit the stables in the morning. Early!"

"I'll look forward to it."

She gazed up at him. Silhouetted as he was against the lavender sky, he was perfectly magnificent. He delivered another stirring kiss, then he started off.

He hadn't gone ten steps when he peered over his shoulder and said, "I miss you already."

She sighed with gladness. "I miss you too."

She sank down on the bench, feeling relieved, feeling as if something good might happen for a change. With this fabulous turn of events, how could it not?

"Hello, Miss James. Fancy meeting you here."

"Hello, Captain."

At encountering him, Joanna's pulse raced, which was incredibly infuriating. He was intertwined in her life in a manner he shouldn't be, and she couldn't keep it from occurring. She could command him to stay away, but he was such a vain oaf. He'd never heed her.

They were in the front foyer of the manor, and they'd bumped into each other as she'd come downstairs from conferring with his sister. He'd insisted she have him apprised whenever she was on the premises, but she'd been debating whether to have him informed.

She'd just decided she wouldn't have him notified, but he'd appeared. Like magic. Evidently, with Fate observing their antics, there could be no avoiding him.

"What brings you by this time?" he asked. "Are you healing the sick? Performing miracles? Making my footmen fall madly in love with you?"

"I was talking to your sister."

"How is she?"

"She's well."

In Joanna's view, Margaret was merely grieving and lonely. Her tropical fever could be an annoyance, but it wasn't critical. Margaret didn't seem to have any friends, and Joanna popped in often, simply hoping she'd feel less isolated.

"Are you headed home?" he asked.

"Yes."

"We have guests tonight so I can't escort you."

"I wouldn't expect you to."

"Will you let me send you in a carriage?"

"No, thank you. It's much quicker if I go through the woods. If I went in a carriage, it would take forever."

"I don't suppose you'd allow me to supply you with a cart and a horse. You could keep it at the cottage. It would ease some of your burdens."

"What would I do with a horse?"

"Feed it? Ride it? Have it pull your cart so you don't have to walk everywhere?"

She tsked with exasperation. He was so silly, and they were so different. She wasn't about to have him giving her gifts. "I like walking."

"At least permit me to guide you out to the verandah."

"There's no need. I can find my own way."

"Of course you can, but if I see you out, I get to spend a few minutes with you."

It was pointless to argue, and she proceeded down the hall that led to the rear door and the verandah. He marched behind her, a towering, irksome, and fascinating presence she couldn't ignore.

Suddenly, he grabbed her and lifted her into a deserted parlor and, with no warning, kissed her soundly. And with his fiancée and sister both in residence!

She would have scolded him, but she didn't have the chance. He simply winked, then gestured for her to continue on. She glared ferociously, but he was a cad who couldn't be cowed. He grinned and took her arm, and they strolled on as if nothing odd had transpired.

Once they exited the manor and were down in the grass, she said, "You have nefarious designs on me."

"Maybe."

"I'm very virtuous, and I was raised by my very prudish, very moral aunt who regaled me with sad tales about great lords seducing their scullery maids. If you plan a similar fiendish ploy, you should be advised that it won't work on me."

"I have no idea what I plan, remember?"

"I don't believe that for a second."

Mutt bounded up—to the Captain, not to her.

"Traitor," she muttered.

"He likes me better than you." The Captain petted and hugged the dog, as Mutt peered up at him adoringly. "If Mutt is with you, I won't fret so much."

"Why would you ever fret? The path is perfectly safe, whether Mutt is with me or not."

"You're too trusting, and I'm too jaded. You assume you'll be fine, but I see catastrophe around every corner. I will always worry about you."

There was the sweetest affection in his eyes, and it rattled her. She'd never had a man gaze at her as he did, and she was beginning to think she might not be able to live without his delicious attention.

She had told Clara they might take a holiday to Bath someday, and she was wondering if it might not be time to depart for a bit. If she vanished for several weeks, she was sure his ardor would cool.

"I have a question about something I might like to do," she said, "and I'm curious as to what your opinion would be."

"If it means I can do it with you, then I'm all for it."

"Your sister invited me to your party on Saturday night."

"I'm stunned."

"Why would you be stunned? Is it that I won't fit in?"

"No, it's that Margaret is a snob. In that, she's like our mother. I can't imagine her asking you, so she must have changed while she was away. As for me, I'm delighted she's included you, and I would love to have you come."

"You wouldn't mind?"

"Mind? Are you mad? Can you dance?"

She snorted with amusement. "I'm not completely unsocial."

"Then if you promise to dance with *me*, I shall be waiting with bated breath for you to arrive. In fact, I'll send a carriage to convey you to the manor. I can't have you traipsing through the forest in your best gown and slippers."

"I might accept your offer. Let me reflect on it."

"That furnishes me with an excuse to stop by your cottage so I can learn what you've decided."

"You're starting to seem absolutely besotted."

"I am, aren't I? I guess I should be ashamed of myself—but I'm not."

"I'll see you . . . when? Tomorrow?"

"I'll bring some ribbons for Clara to wear in her hair. I'll bring some for you too. I'll say they're for her, but they'll be for both of you."

"You are not to give me any gifts!"

"Don't tell me what I can and can't do. It's a waste of energy."

She smiled up at him. He was handsome, dashing, and amazing, like a comet streaking across the sky. For some reason, he'd noticed her, and she was being bowled over by his obsession. She supposed this was how her mother had become embroiled with her father. He'd pushed and pushed for an affair until she'd relented and had joined in. The end result had been that she'd wound up with a babe in her belly.

It wasn't surprising that her mother hadn't been able to resist. Joanna had never experienced anything comparable to what Jacob Ralston was inflicting, and she was alarmed over how she might ultimately respond. Her mother's blood sang in her veins, coaxing her to behave exactly as her mother had behaved.

He stared down at her, and for a chilling instant, she was afraid he would lean down and kiss her goodbye, but they were right out in the open, and there were servants everywhere.

She motioned to her dog. "Come, Mutt. If we're not careful, the Captain will tempt us to linger forever."

She hurried off, but Mutt loafed, looking as if he'd rather stay with the Captain than accompany her. He only raced to her side when the

Captain ordered him to go, and she scoffed at how men wielded so much more power than women. It was exasperating.

She walked across the park, and she didn't glance back until she reached the path into the woods. She turned, and he was still there, but he'd climbed onto the verandah so he could have a better view of her as she got farther away.

She waved, and he waved, then she continued on, feeling lighter than air.

My, oh, my, but wasn't she in trouble?

⌒〜⌒

ROXANNE WAS HAVING A brandy in her office, enjoying a quiet interlude before she went up to her bedchamber to dress for supper.

When Jacob's mother, Esther, had been alive, she hadn't arranged proper meals in the evenings. She'd been so unlikable that she'd never had visitors.

Once Roxanne had sailed in from Italy, and with Esther deceased, she'd immediately begun fixing Esther's missteps. Supper was served every night at nine, and they carried on as was appropriate for people with their status and breeding. She was determined to be the premier hostess in the area, so they always had guests.

She stood and stretched, then meandered over to the window, and she was a tad disturbed to find Jacob in the garden with Miss James. Normally, she wouldn't have cared or watched them, but they were huddled together in a way that was extremely vexing. They were much friendlier than they should have been, and sparks were practically visible in the space around them.

Jacob had been home for just a few days. How had he grown so cordial with the little strumpet? Why would he have considered it? Had he no regard for Roxanne and how she might view such a blatant amour?

Miss James was very pretty, and with her being so exotic in her habits, Roxanne could appreciate that he'd be enticed. There was no doubt that his manly interest had been piqued.

After an annoying bout of flirting, Miss James finally left. Roxanne lost sight of them, but she avidly pondered the encounter, struggling to deduce what it indicated. Should she be concerned about it?

She couldn't decide. She was about to betroth herself to Jacob, and she wasn't so naïve that she'd expect him to be faithful, but she wouldn't tolerate carnal mischief occurring right under her nose. No wife should have to.

Surely he must realize how disrespectful that would be, but if he didn't, she couldn't mention it to him. So what to do?

Her anger flared. She was very possessive, and if Miss James imagined she could seduce Jacob without consequence, Roxanne would have to set her straight. And Miss James wouldn't like to learn how ruthless Roxanne could be.

Chapter

7

A KNOCK SOUNDED, WHICH was a very odd occurrence, and Joanna froze. She was in the rear of the house, tidying up her workroom, but not particularly busy, and she wondered who had arrived.

It was rare when she had a visitor. Most neighbors requesting her assistance stopped her when she was in the village. The lane running near the cottage was a sufficient distance away that she couldn't hear a carriage passing by, and the path outside was hidden by foliage. Anyone who'd traveled in a vehicle had to stop and walk the rest of the way. A horse could be ridden down the path, but a carriage wouldn't fit.

Her maid had already left for the day, and Clara was at school, so there was no one to answer the summons. She sighed and shouted, "Hold on! I'll be there in a minute."

She removed her apron and headed to the door, and just as she reached for the latch, the knock sounded again. This time, it was more impatient. She smoothed her features, wanting to look welcoming and kind, when she wasn't feeling very spry.

She opened the door, and when she realized the identity of her guest, she couldn't completely conceal her consternation.

"Hello, Miss Ralston," she said to the Captain's fiancée and cousin. "I must admit I'm surprised to have you call on me. What brings you by?"

"Your residence is so difficult to find that it could be located up on the moon."

"It's an old gamekeeper's lodge," Joanna explained, "where men watched for poachers."

"It appears absolutely wretched to me. How can you stand these dark woods? Don't you worry you might be attacked by wolves?"

Joanna chuckled. "As far as I'm aware, there are no more wolves in England."

"How about wicked elves then? It seems exactly the sort of spot where they would make mischief you couldn't deflect."

"I'm sure there are no elves either. What did you need? How may I help you?"

"I'm told you have private consultations. I should like one."

Joanna should have declined, but she wouldn't antagonize the awful woman. Miss Ralston had swiftly garnered a reputation as a harpy. People crossed her at their peril.

"I'm happy to talk to you," Joanna said. "You can tell me what aid you seek, and we'll discover if I can supply it. I may not be able to furnish what you're hoping."

"Your comment is perfectly ludicrous. Without knowing my mission, how can you be so confident you'll fail me?"

Joanna nodded. "That's a very good question. Please come in."

She pulled the door wide and stepped back. Miss Ralston marched in as if she owned the place, and her meticulous gaze swept over the parlor, assessing every chattel, as if she was cataloguing the value so she could sell them later.

Joanna gestured to the sofa. Miss Ralston sat down, then Joanna seated herself on a chair. She couldn't imagine Miss Ralston's purpose, and she wasn't about to start the conversation. She was adept at waiting, at letting the other party apprise her of the situation.

Miss Ralston was no different. "I expect this chat to be confidential. You will not mention that I was here. Nor will you reveal what we discussed."

"No, I won't. You have my word."

"You're treating Margaret Howell who will soon be my sister-in-law."

"I am."

"For melancholia and fevers." Joanna didn't reply, unwilling to provide specifics, and Miss Ralston said, "She speaks highly of you."

"I'm flattered. I'll have to thank her."

"She brags about how you've improved her condition. Are you a trained apothecary? You're a female, so how could you have obtained such a skill?"

"The women in my family are healers, and we've developed many recipes that are beneficial. I share them with those who are feeling poorly."

Miss Ralston scoffed in a derogatory way. "Are you a gypsy? Is that how you acquired your tricks?"

"No, ma'am. I'm merely supporting myself and my young niece through diligent effort—and with no man in the picture."

"I'm dubious about your claims of modest endeavor. The housemaids insist you cast spells."

"I can't fathom where they'd get that notion. I just grow herbs and brew them into curative tonics."

"They also insist you dispense magic charms."

"No. I don't believe in magic, and I have no idea how it works."

Miss Ralston frowned, so clearly, Joanna wasn't giving the correct answers.

There were many enchantments she could perform, but she would never display any of them for Miss Ralston. If she gleaned the slightest information about Joanna, she'd use it to Joanna's detriment.

Plus, she was positive Miss Ralston would like to engage in some ill-wishing, but Joanna would never direct negative energy toward anyone. Life was hard enough without the added burden of harmful thoughts being piled on.

"Don't be coy with me." Miss Ralston clucked her tongue with offense. "I should like to purchase a potion."

"What type of potion?"

"There is a fiend vexing me, and I should like him to vanish, but he refuses to disappear. I would be delighted to spur him along."

Joanna could barely keep from blanching. She hoped Miss Ralston wasn't trying to be rid of the Captain! She wasn't even betrothed to him yet.

"I'm sorry, but I can't make a person disappear. I simply birth babies and distribute tonics to people who are sick. I have no mysterious abilities."

"I'm certain you're lying. How much would you charge for a spell to be cast? I'll pay double your price."

"I have no *price* for such a thing, and this isn't about Captain Ralston, is it? He's my benefactor, and I would never consider bad behavior that involved him."

"Oh, for pity's sake. It's not Captain Ralston. He's about to be my husband. No, this is a snake in the grass who's overstayed his welcome. I am a woman who is gravely in need of help, and you *help* women all the time. Why won't you assist me?"

Joanna wondered who Miss Ralston detested so vehemently, and she would worry about him. She wondered too what it would take to persuade the horrid shrew to leave.

Miss Ralston was growing impatient, and she stuck out her hand. "Can you read palms? Surely it won't kill you to admit to that small talent."

Joanna hesitated for an eternity, then she clasped Miss Ralston's wrist, being careful their palms didn't connect. There was no detail about Miss Ralston that she wanted disclosed, and she couldn't forget how the Captain's cards had shown he wouldn't be marrying her. Joanna had to be wary lest she divulge a hint of that dicey news.

She scrutinized the appropriate lines, then asked, "Is there any topic in particular you were anxious to have addressed?"

"Will I have a long life?"

"Yes," Joanna fibbed, figuring she would falsify through the whole appointment.

"Will I be happy?"

"Mostly. You can't be happy constantly. Fate doesn't let our paths unfold without occasional difficulties."

"How many husbands will I have?"

Joanna didn't see any. "Two."

"How many children?"

Without thinking, she said, "Well, you've already had the one, and I—"

Miss Ralston yanked away. "What are you talking about? I've never been married, and I have no children. What sort of charlatan are you?"

Joanna was rattled by what had been exposed, and she inhaled slowly, determined to calm her raging pulse. "I was probably wrong. I don't perform readings that often, and obviously, I'm out of practice. Would you like me to look again?"

"No, thank you. I've found out what I came to discover, which is that you are a fraud, but I wouldn't like it to spread that I'm ungrateful for any service provided to me." She opened her reticule and placed a coin on the table.

"You don't have to pay me," Joanna insisted. "I haven't really done anything."

"That has to be the truest words you've ever spoken."

Miss Ralston stood, so Joanna stood too. Joanna was very petite, and Miss Ralston was quite statuesque. She towered over Joanna, so she felt vulnerable to attack. Joanna never bowed down or cowered, so the irksome sentiment was annoying.

"Since I've revealed your failings," Miss Ralston said, "I am duty-bound to tell you that you will suspend your visits to Margaret. She's about to be my sister-in-law, and when her mood is so desolate, it would be easy for a swindler to take advantage of her. I demand you break off contact. Do it however you like, but do it immediately."

"I will," Joanna lied. She would behave as Margaret Howell requested, and Miss Ralston's wishes wouldn't be considered in the conclusion that was chosen.

"I shouldn't have to meet with you about this again. We don't need you inflicting yourself on the gullible wretches at the manor. If you persist, I'll have to confer with Captain Ralston about the wisdom of your residing on the estate. Don't make me, for I can guarantee you won't like the ending I orchestrate."

"I understand."

Miss Ralston whipped away and left, and Joanna followed her out. She blew out a heavy breath, hating that she'd been threatened and hating too that her presence would cause problems at the manor.

Mrs. Howell wouldn't agree to have Joanna's visits cease, and there was the party on Saturday night to which she'd been invited. If she attended after Miss Ralston had warned her away, they'd become enemies. Yet if she didn't attend, the Captain would demand to be apprised as to the reason, and she didn't suppose he'd like to hear about Miss Ralston's edict.

What a quagmire!

She loitered on the stoop, observing as Miss Ralston stomped away. As she reached the gate, Clara was skipping down the path toward the cottage. It was too early for her to be home from school, and Joanna frowned, curious as to why she'd been dismissed.

Clara saw Miss Ralston, and she stopped and stared. Miss Ralston stared too, and as the pair came face to face, the eeriest pall settled over the forest. For an instant, it felt as if the world had quit spinning on its axis so the universe could note their encounter.

Joanna hadn't noticed it previously, but Miss Ralston and Clara looked exactly alike: white-blond hair, coal-black eyes, a willowy physique. They were so similar that they might have been mother and daughter.

It was the black eyes that linked them the most. Many women had blond hair, but they rarely had such dark eyes. It was a striking feature that was very unusual.

Clara broke the awkward interval. "Hello, ma'am."

Miss Ralston didn't respond to Clara's greeting. Her tone sharp and rude, she simply said, "Who are you?"

Clara was startled by the brusque query, but she was a polite girl. "I am Clara."

"How old are you, Clara?"

"Nine."

"Who is your mother?"

"I'm sorry, but I don't know. She died when I was a baby."

Joanna hurried out to the gate. "This is my niece, Miss Ralston. She's home from school earlier than I expected. I should get her settled."

"Your niece?" Miss Ralston scathingly asked. "Clearly, you're confused. If she was your niece, you'd be able to tell her that her mother was your sister."

"We took her in after her mother passed away, and we've always viewed her as family."

"Where was she born?"

"I'm not certain of the village," Joanna fibbed. "My Aunt Pru— God rest her soul—was midwife at the sad event."

At Joanna mentioning Pru, Miss Ralston blanched, and she was about to unload a slew of questions about Clara, but Joanna wouldn't discuss any of them. She recalled the line on Miss Ralston's palm, the one that had plainly shown she'd birthed a child. Could it be . . . ?

No . . . she scolded herself. *Don't even think it.* It would raise so many insurmountable issues, and she didn't want to deal with any of them.

Clara skirted by Miss Ralston and dashed over to hide behind Joanna. Joanna urged her up the walk.

Once Clara was inside, Miss Ralston said to Joanna, "Remember my command: Stay away from the manor. Find some other victim to fleece. Leave Mrs. Howell alone."

Joanna dipped her head, as if to comply, then she watched Miss Ralston disappear down the path. Then Joanna went into the cottage, and Clara was in the front parlor, peeking out the curtain.

"Who was that?" she asked.

"It was Roxanne Ralston. Captain Ralston's fiancée?"

"I didn't like her."

"Neither did I, but we'll keep that opinion to ourselves."

———

"I'VE BEEN COMPLAINING FOR months that this would happen. Now it has."

"My answer is still the same."

"Their kin have lived here for over a century!"

"How is that my problem?"

Jacob was bound for the estate office at the rear of the manor when he heard two men quarreling. He recognized Kit's voice, but he wasn't sure who the other one was.

"It's a widow and six children. Have you any concern for their fate?"

"None," Kit said.

"What should I tell them?"

"Tell them what I've already told them: We aren't running a charity."

"Maybe not, but have we a Christian duty to those less fortunate?"

There was a tense silence, then Kit said, "Are you finished? You've exasperated me beyond my limit, and I need to dress for supper."

"Yes, I'm finished." The other man muttered, "I don't know why I waste my breath."

Jacob was about to bluster in and pretend he'd just arrived, when Sandy stormed out. His cheeks were flushed, his eyes spitting daggers, but as he noted Jacob lurking, he smoothed his expression.

"Hello, Captain. Were you hunting for me? I'm on my way to the stables."

"I'm looking for Mr. Boswell."

"He's inside."

Sandy marched off, and Jacob listened to his furious strides fading away, then he entered the office.

Kit was loafing in his chair at the desk, drinking a brandy. The liquor tray was by his elbow, and he pointed to it and said, "Will you join me? It's late enough in the afternoon for us to start imbibing without our feeling like sots."

If he was dismayed that Jacob had overheard a portion of their argument, he didn't show it by the slightest twitch of a brow.

"Yes, I'll have one." Jacob eased onto a chair and reached over to accept a glass after Kit had filled it. He leaned back, sipping his beverage, then he casually said, "I didn't mean to eavesdrop, but when I was walking down the hall, you two were having quite a row. What's wrong? Why is Sandy so enraged?"

Kit waved a hand as if their harsh words had been trivial. "He constantly has a bee in his bonnet about some topic or other. He's never liked how I run things, and we don't ever agree on methods or solutions."

"That much was obvious."

"He disrespects me repeatedly, and I'm weary of his tantrums. I don't suppose you'd let me fire him."

"For speaking his mind? Isn't that a valuable trait in an employee?"

"Not always. Am I in charge or aren't I? One of these days, you should determine whether you've granted me full authority or not."

"How long has his family served us? Hasn't it been a thousand years or more?"

Kit smirked. "Yes, probably."

"And he's good at his job. You don't have any criticism about his managing the stables, do you?"

"No. It's just that he's surly and impertinent. If he talked to you a single time with the contempt he regularly displays to me, you'd send him packing."

Jacob shrugged. "I'm more tolerant than you are. I can scold him if you'd like. I can order him to cease his insolence."

"Don't you dare! I'm not a baby, and you don't have to hold my hand." Kit scowled. "What did you need? You can't have wandered back here for no reason."

"I'd like you to get the estate ledgers together for me."

Was there the briefest hesitation on Kit's part? "What for?"

"I'd like to remodel the south wing of the manor, so I'll have to borrow some money. I'd like to have a clearer idea of where I stand financially."

"I can explain the numbers to you."

"I've hired a London accounting firm. They've promised to give me a report in plain English—one I can read and comprehend without my eyes glazing over."

"Will you take them now? Or would you like me to post them to London for you?"

"I'm traveling to town next week, so I can deliver them myself. Just gather them, so when I'm ready to depart, we're not scrambling about, searching for lost documents."

"Your wish is my command."

Was there condescension in Kit's tone? If so, Jacob ignored it.

Kit had grown up with them, and he'd been raised as if he were a Ralston. They'd paid for his upbringing and schooling, but he had a chip on his shoulder. No matter what they'd provided, he'd never believed it was sufficient.

Jacob had tried to persuade him to enlist in the navy when they were sixteen, but he'd been content to tarry at Ralston Place. Eventually, the chance arose for him to become the manager, but occasionally, Jacob wondered if he was regretting his decision. Jacob had spent the prior fourteen years exploring the globe, fighting in battles, and having adventures. Kit had sat in the country, carrying on pretty much as he had when Jacob had first sailed away.

Was Kit bitter? Was he chafing that he hadn't picked a different path?

Jacob wasn't prone to deep reflection, so he wasn't keen to contemplate those questions. Men made choices, and Kit had made his. Jacob wasn't his nanny, and it wasn't his burden to guarantee Kit was happy.

He finished his drink and put the glass on the desk. "I should be going. I guess we're dressing for supper now."

"It's what your fiancée tells me, so I have to get moving too or I'll be late."

Jacob opened his mouth to comment, then he abruptly closed it. "Gad, I was about to say I preferred the routines we had when Mother was alive."

Kit shuddered with mock dread. "Perish the thought. I realize I shouldn't speak ill of the dead, but I can't claim that I miss her."

"You are a master of understatement—as always, Mr. Boswell. You stayed and dealt with her, so I didn't have to. For that favor, I will be eternally grateful."

"I should be awarded some type of medal, don't you think?"

"Courage under fire?"

"Yes, definitely."

Jacob snorted with amusement, stood, and left. He should have proceeded to his bedchamber to change his clothes, but as he reached the stairs, he spun away and headed for the stables. He wasted a bit of time snooping, checking the stalls to see if they were clean, the tack to see if it was oiled and in good condition.

The place was spotless, but then, he'd supposed it would be. The men of the Sanders family had supervised the horses and equipment for decades, perhaps even centuries, and they were sticklers for doing a thorough job.

Finally, he stumbled on Sandy, which had been his goal, but he hadn't wanted it to appear as if he'd been chasing after the man. He was leaned on a fence, watching the horses frolic, and Jacob dawdled too, watching Sandy watch the animals.

The sun was in the western sky and would begin to set very soon. The air was so fresh, the grass so green. He felt lucky all of a sudden—and very glad to own such a magnificent property.

The powerful swirl of emotion was surprising. Usually, he couldn't care less about the estate, so maybe he was maturing. Maybe someday, he'd shuck off his unpleasant memories and start to be proud of what he had.

Sandy noticed him and waved, and Jacob used the gesture as an excuse to bluster over and stand beside him. He could never figure out how they should interact. When they were very young, they'd been playmates of a sort.

Not often though. His mother had been too much of a snob to let them socialize, but despite her best efforts to separate them, they'd been chums, little Jacob and Sandy, two rascals who'd snuck away to rollick in secret mischief that he still fondly recollected.

But adulthood and their disparate stations had erected barriers he wasn't sure how to surmount. They'd once been little Jacob and Sandy. Now they were . . . what?

Only the strictest formality was appropriate.

"It's a lovely evening, Captain," Sandy said. "Nice to be out in it."

"I'm away from England so much. I never really view it like this."

Their conversation lagged, and the encounter grew awkward. Jacob couldn't deduce how they were to chat, and ultimately, Sandy said, "I ought to be going. I have to get home to supper with my sons."

"I hadn't heard you were married. Who is your wife?"

"You wouldn't ever have met her, but I'm a widower." Sandy's tone indicated he wouldn't discuss her, and Jacob shouldn't pry. "My boys are greedy about seeing me at the end of the day. Since their mother passed away, they cling tighter than they should, but I don't have the heart to be aloof with them."

"What a refreshing style of parenting."

Sandy scoffed. "Before I head off to join them, may I assist you with anything?"

"You know Miss James, don't you? The healer who's been tending my sister."

"Everybody knows her."

"It's not safe for her to be walking around the neighborhood on her own. What would you think if we loaned her a cart and a horse? It would ease some of her burdens."

Sandy chuckled. "I've already offered them, but she's too stubborn. Her exact words were, *What would I do with a horse?*"

Jacob chuckled too. "That sounds like her, so I guess it's not in the cards to provide them. We can't force her to accept our help."

"It's kind of you to ponder her though. She's alone in the world—she and that niece of hers—living in the woods like that. She's content out there, but I fear for them constantly."

"Maybe one of the local boys will fall in love and wed her. A husband would solve many of her problems."

"They're all afraid of her. They claim—if you were her husband and tried to boss her—she might ..." He cut off the remark. "I like her, and I shouldn't be crude. Don't listen to me."

"Tell me what they say."

"Well ... ah ... that she can cast a spell and shrivel a man's private parts."

Jacob blew out an annoyed breath. "People are such idiots."

"I agree."

He turned toward Sandy and said, "Why were you and Kit quarreling?"

Sandy gazed at the horses forever, debating his reply. In the end, he chose, "If you're curious about it, you should ask him."

"I did ask him, and now, I'm asking you."

"I wouldn't like to have a dispute arise between Mr. Boswell and myself."

"What's this spat about?" Sandy still didn't explain, and Jacob said, "Are you scared to confide in me? Why would you be? We've been acquainted for three decades. I like to imagine I wouldn't fly off the handle with you."

"I have my job and my sons to consider."

"Your job is safe. Your sons too. Short of embezzling from me, I can't envision you enraging me sufficiently to where I'd fire you. So I'd appreciate it if you'd be candid."

"Do you know Widow Barnes?" Jacob shook his head, and Sandy continued. "Her husband was a tenant farmer. He was killed last summer in a threshing accident, and she has six girls to raise on her own. Their roof collapsed, and I've been anxious to repair it, but Boswell doesn't feel we should waste the funds. He thinks they should move on, but they don't have anywhere to go."

"What can it cost to repair a widow's roof? It won't beggar me, and why would *you* be the one to worry about it or to fix it? Isn't it a chore far from your usual duties?"

Sandy glared at him, and Jacob sensed a huge wave of umbrage boiling just below the surface. It was obvious Sandy yearned to divest himself of many heavy issues, and the notion left Jacob incredibly weary.

He never focused much of his attention on the property. When he'd handed the reins to Kit, he'd been delighted to have the load lifted off his shoulders. His interest was and always would be his career in the navy, and during his brief visits at home, the place seemed in fine shape to him.

In the past, he'd never fretted about it, but he should probably start. If he gave Sandy the slightest opening to vent his frustrations, what might he confess?

"I may remodel the south wing of the manor next spring," he said.

"While you're at it, I hope you'll let me convince you to rebuild the chimneys. They've needed to be re-bricked for ages."

"Thank you for pointing it out. I only mention the remodeling because I'll be in London next week. I intend to show the estate ledgers to a new team of accountants. What is your opinion about that idea?"

Sandy was so eager to expound that he physically bit down on his bottom lip so no words would escape. Finally, once he was more in control, he said, "I believe that might turn out to be money well spent. Goodnight, Captain."

He hurried away before Jacob could ask any other questions.

Chapter

8

"I have a gift for you."

Clara's eyes lit with merriment. "A gift! How splendid!"

Captain Ralston gave her a small package, wrapped in silver paper, and Clara ripped it off in a frenzy. Inside, she found the ribbons he'd told Joanna he'd buy.

Joanna wasn't a pauper, but they didn't exactly have funds to purchase frivolities. Except on the rarest occasions, such as Christmas, Clara didn't get many presents.

"These are so beautiful," Clara gushed, and she smiled at him, providing plenty of evidence of the beauty she'd grow to be when she was an adult.

"I couldn't decide which color would look prettiest in your hair," he said, like the worst flirt, "so I purchased them all."

"I shall keep them forever!" Clara was wearing her pink dress, and she pulled the pink ribbon from the pile and offered it to Joanna. "Would you put it on for me?"

"I would be delighted."

Joanna yanked off the old ribbon and attached the new one. She tied a bow on the top of Clara's head, so she appeared very fetching.

"Is it perfect?" Clara asked.

"Yes, it's perfect," Joanna assured her.

"I must see it for myself. May I be excused?"

"Yes, you're excused, and while you're preening in the mirror, I'll escort the Captain out to his horse. How about if you tell him goodbye before you go to your room?"

At hearing he'd depart, Clara was crestfallen. "Must you leave so soon?"

"I'm afraid I must."

Clara peered over at Joanna. "Could he stay for supper this time?"

"It's not for hours yet," Joanna replied, "and I'm certain he's too busy to tarry."

Clara turned to the Captain and curtsied to him. "Thank you, Captain. Please visit again when you can. We enjoy having you as our guest."

He bowed over her hand, and she was so charmed Joanna was amazed she didn't swoon. Then she flitted away and raced up the stairs.

As the energy from her exit settled, he disturbed her by saying, "She reminds me of someone, but I can't figure out who."

"I can't imagine who it might be." Joanna was determined to never discuss the topic of *who* Clara resembled. "Let me walk you out."

"You're always in such a hurry to be rid of me."

"That's because I have no idea what to do with you when you arrive. Once you step into my parlor, I can't breathe."

"I could stay to supper."

"You could not. How would we entertain you all afternoon?"

"I could just sit in a corner and watch you at your chores. I'd be fascinated."

"When you shower me with such mesmerizing compliments, it makes me want to like you."

"You should like me."

She was staring up at him like a besotted girl, proving she was as smitten as Clara, which was embarrassing. She liked to assume she had better sense, but maybe she didn't.

She opened the door and left the cottage, not checking if he followed her or not. He was so stubborn. If he refused to obey her, she'd never be able to pry him away.

They went to his horse, but he didn't immediately mount the animal. He studied the woods as if they concealed numerous villains.

"I'll never be comfortable with you living here," he said.

"This has been my home for a whole decade, and I've never had any problems. I wish you wouldn't fret about it so much."

"Wasn't your aunt alive for much of that time?"

"She died four years ago."

"So you had an adult residing with you. Now it's just you and Clara."

"*I* am an adult, Captain. I'm twenty-four."

"Yes, but you're such a tiny little thing. You look as if you're ten."

"I don't know if that remark should flatter or annoy me."

He dipped down and kissed her as she'd been hoping he would since he'd sauntered in.

He'd shown up without warning, and it had been a thrilling surprise. He was quickly training her to pine away for his sudden appearances. Anymore, she could barely concentrate. She constantly thought about him and wondered if he was thinking about her just as intently.

"Could I ask you a question?" he said.

"You can ask me, but I can't swear I'll answer."

"What is your opinion of Kit Boswell?"

"Should I be candid? Or should I lie?"

"Your response matters to me. I'm at Ralston Place so rarely, and when I am, people fawn and fib to make me happy. I'm never positive I'm receiving a clear picture of what's occurring."

"I understand, and no, I don't like Mr. Boswell, but don't you dare tattle to him. I wouldn't want to ever be on his bad side. He can be very spiteful, and I wouldn't ever like his malice directed at me."

"He's malicious?"

"Yes, as well as lazy, pompous, and unlikable. He's probably corrupt too."

He gazed up at the sky, her words sinking in, and she regretted being so frank. Then he said, "What is your opinion of Sandy?"

"I love Sandy. He's kind, generous, and incredibly diligent. He's actually the one who runs the estate for you."

"What does Mr. Boswell do?"

"Drink? Loaf? Chase trollops?"

He smirked with aggravation. "Perhaps I shouldn't ask you questions. That might be more information than I truly sought."

"Sandy works, and Mr. Boswell takes the credit. It's the rumor circulating anyway, but isn't that the way it always is with men?"

"I suppose." He kissed her again, leaving her even more bewildered about her conduct and choices, then he said, "What about the party on Saturday? Shall I send a carriage?"

It was the topic she'd been dreading. "No, no carriage. I've been pondering your invitation, and I shouldn't rub elbows with your snooty friends."

"My snooty friends are in London. Saturday at the manor will be a collection of neighbors, and I predict you'll be acquainted with every guest. You'll fit right in."

"I never fit in, so I shouldn't join you."

She'd like to bluster in merely to poke a stick at Roxanne Ralston's pride and audacity, but she had no desire to quarrel with the vicious termagant. Miss Ralston was the type of vengeful person who would get even, and her methods would be devastating and impossible to fight.

"Will I have to enlist my sister to nag at you?" he asked.

"I'm not easy to persuade or dissuade. When I settle on a course, it's hard to convince me to change my mind."

"You're being ridiculous. The carriage will pull in around seven. You'll have to walk out to the lane though. My driver couldn't maneuver a vehicle through the foliage to your door."

"You're being a bully."

"How am I being a bully? Margaret and I tendered a perfectly valid invitation, and *you* are being a snot to claim you're not interested."

"If I came, what would be your plan once I arrive? Would you flirt with me the entire evening? Would you hover by my side until we stirred gossip? I'd rather not endure such a hideous debacle, and you shouldn't provoke it either."

"By refusing to attend, you'll be saving me from myself?"

"Basically, yes. I'd be saving *me* too. I don't want to ever be a spectacle."

He assessed her, and he was much too astute. "What is this really about? We discussed it previously, and you didn't have any reservations. What's happened?"

"Could I just not explain?"

"No. What is it? And again, please be frank. I don't like to tiptoe on the edge of an issue. I like to delve to the heart of a problem and solve it."

She stood very still, yearning for a hint of inspiration to drop onto her tongue.

From reading his cards, she'd discovered that Roxanne Ralston wouldn't be his bride, but she wasn't always correct in her estimations. What if she told him about Miss Ralston, and he wound up wed to her? Joanna would have created an eternal enemy.

Or what if her reading was accurate, and he didn't wed Miss Ralston? Was Joanna meant to be the wrench that was thrown into that situation? Was she the catalyst that would tear them apart?

Unfortunately, wisdom and insight were never conveyed when she desperately needed them.

"Will you promise not to become angry?" she inquired.

"How can I promise that when I can't imagine what you're about to tell me?"

She decided to leap into the inferno. "Your cousin visited me."

It took him a moment to deduce which cousin. "Roxanne was here? Why?"

"She pretended it was to buy a potion, but in reality, she ordered me to stay away from all of you. She believes I'm a charlatan, a fake, and a fraud, and I shouldn't be treating your sister."

"Roxanne doesn't speak for me or Margaret, and it appears I have to bluntly clarify that she doesn't."

Joanna winced. "You can't talk to her about this! If you breathe a word, she'll realize I complained to you. I would hate to ignite her enmity, for I can guarantee I wouldn't like how it would rain down."

"I'm trying to figure out why she felt free to harass you."

"People are compelled to harass women like me. It's why I live quietly and separately from everyone else."

"You're being absurd. You make Margaret happy, and if you ceased caring for her, I'm certain her condition would deteriorate."

"Maybe."

She was particularly glum and kicking herself for mentioning Roxanne Ralston. What had she been thinking?

"Don't be sad," he said.

"I'm not sad. I'm furious over her gall. I'm not a weakling, and she's lucky I didn't turn her into a toad."

He laughed. "Can you do that?"

"I'll let you wonder."

He dipped down and kissed her, then he pulled away and mounted his horse.

"You're coming to my party," he announced from up on the animal's back. "The carriage will pick you up at seven. You'll revel until midnight, as if you're Cinderella, then I'll have you delivered home."

She bristled with frustration. "You're not listening to me."

"Well, you're being silly, so why would I listen?"

"I'm never silly."

"You are to me. I doubt I'll be able to stop by before Saturday. If not, I'll expect you to be ready when my driver arrives. Don't disappoint me."

"You are mad, Captain Ralston."

"Yes, I've heard that about myself occasionally."

He grinned his devil's grin, tugged on the reins, and trotted away.

She watched him depart, and she was scolding herself for being such a milksop. She hadn't agreed to the arrangement, but when his carriage rolled up to fetch her, she was positive she'd climb in.

To her great disgust, he'd become important to her. She wanted to please him, and she couldn't tamp down the impulse.

She whipped away and went inside. Clara bounded down the stairs, and she asked, "Is the Captain gone?"

"Yes, and guess what? He and his sister, Mrs. Howell, have invited me to a party on Saturday night."

"My goodness!" Clara clapped her hands with glee. "That's the prettiest news we've had in ages."

"It is, isn't it? It's been such a long time since I've been dancing."

"I have my own party with my classmates that night, so you won't have to worry about me. This is meant to be."

"I'll keep telling myself that it is."

She crept into her workroom, and she debated forever, then she walked over to the chest in the corner where she had several locked boxes. Some of them contained ancient recipes. Some contained lists of herbs and the remedies they produced.

One was stuffed with private papers. She withdrew an envelope her Aunt Pru had left, and she sat down at the table and studied it, struggling to decide if she shouldn't relent and read the message.

She'd given it to Joanna when she'd been ailing, her body preparing to pass away. *It's about Clara,* Pru had said. *It's about her parents. In case you ever need to be apprised.*

Aunt Pru had been sworn to secrecy about Clara's birth, and she'd taken the vow seriously, but Pru had recognized too that Clara's lineage might be an issue in the future. For example, if there was a boy who wished to wed her, Joanna had to verify they weren't related. So Pru had written the letter.

Yet she'd counselled that not all secrets should be revealed. If Joanna didn't ever have to know, she shouldn't look.

Finally, she broke the seal, and she froze for an eternity. She wasn't surprised by the mother's name, but the father's name was definitely a shock.

"Oh, Aunt Pru," she whispered, "if you were aware of this dilemma, why move us to Ralston Place? Of all the spots in the kingdom, why here?"

There was a fire lit in the hearth, and she glared at it, figuring she should toss the damning page into the flames. But in the end, she didn't. Who could predict how a path might unfold? It might be wise to have the note as proof.

She put it back in the box, but first, she resealed the envelope with her own wax, so no one could snoop. She was extremely disturbed by what she'd discovered, and hopefully, she'd never have to open it again.

JACOB GLANCED AROUND THE ostentatious parlor. He'd bumbled down to supper a few minutes early, so he was alone.

Roxanne had altered their nightly meal into a grandiose extravaganza, where everyone dressed as if they were headed to the theater. There was a constant stream of guests, and he was conflicted in his opinion about the situation.

When his mother had still been alive, supper had been a grim affair, where she'd either stewed in silence over unspecified grievances or she'd quarreled viciously over petty complaints. Jacob was glad that era was over, but he wasn't persuaded that he liked Roxanne's plan instead.

Surely there was some middle ground, where the family could dine quietly and pleasantly without a table of strangers drinking all their liquor.

Roxanne had returned to Ralston Place before Jacob or Margaret had managed to stagger in. Once they'd arrived, she'd been in charge, as if she and Jacob were already married. Margaret hadn't been in any condition to take over, and Jacob was never even in England.

Was there a reason to protest the arrangement? She'd soon be Jacob's wife, and the manor would be her kingdom. What did it matter if she'd started running things prior to the wedding being held?

Margaret strolled in, and she stopped by the sideboard to have the butler pour her a glass of wine, then she came over to Jacob.

"You're looking much better," he told her.

"Thank you. I am much better."

"Miss James must dispense miracle tonics."

"It's not her tonics so much as her encouraging me to quit moping. I've been raging over stupid topics. I'm home now, and I need to focus on that and let the past fall away."

"It's a terrific attitude to have, and I should have my lawyers harass your husband's family for a bit. You were notified that he was bankrupt, but I'm betting he'll have stashed away some assets. If his kin are hiding them from you, you should be entitled to claim a widow's stipend."

"I would like to torment them—merely so they realize I'm not a helpless baby. Mr. Howell died suddenly, and I was so stunned that I didn't stand up for myself in a single argument. I even permitted them to have the rings on my fingers."

"You were by yourself in a foreign land. It had to have been hard to handle his death on your own."

"It was very hard."

"I have a secret I've been meaning to share with you," he said, "but you've been so morose, I didn't inform you. You've improved, so I'm debating whether it might send you into a relapse."

"What is it? And if it's horrid, how about if you keep it to yourself awhile?"

"It's not horrid. I simply can't imagine what you'll think. I'm quite resolved about it, so even if you're opposed, you won't be able to dissuade me."

She scowled ferociously. "Tell me quick—or I'll be envisioning dire scenarios."

"It's this: I'm having my engagement party in September, and I'm inviting Caleb and Blake."

"Caleb and Blake . . . Ralston? As in our half-siblings, Caleb and Blake?"

"Yes. What is your opinion of the insane notion?"

"Mother will be rolling in her grave."

"That's the sole comment I hear. Will you welcome them? Or will you have to flee the property for two weeks so you won't have to be sullied by their presence?"

She scoffed with offense. "I like to hope I'm not so thin-skinned that I'd avoid them, but we've hated them for so long. I can't decide how I should view their waltzing into the house."

"You and I never hated them."

"Speak for yourself." She pondered, then said, "I suppose, with Mother deceased, it's silly to continue loathing them. It wasn't their fault Father was a bigamist and liar."

"My feeling exactly. I'd like to have a cordial relationship with them."

She gulped her wine down to the dregs. "Gad, I need a stronger libation. I've been recuperating, but you're making my nerves flare."

"There's one other thing too."

"Will it be better or worse than your news about my half-brothers?"

"You've invited Miss James to the party on Saturday night."

"I have, and . . . ?"

"I seconded the invitation, but Roxanne cancelled it. Apparently, our cousin doesn't like her tending you, and she's warned her to desist."

"How ridiculous. I'm twenty-eight years old. I'm competent to select who will nurse me and who won't. Would Roxanne rather I had a drunken surgeon bluster in to bleed and purge me."

"Probably. Don't mention this to her. I'll deal with it, but I figured you should be apprised."

"Are you sure you should go through with your betrothal?" Margaret uttered the question without much reflection, and the instant the words were out of her mouth, she blanched. "I can't believe I said that. I'm sorry, but Mother arranged the match. Should you trust her choice?"

"I was glad to have her manage it for me. I couldn't see me wandering London drawing rooms and searching for the perfect girl on my own."

Margaret chuckled. "You definitely would have been awful at it. Who could guess what sort of idiotic debutante you might have dragged home? You'd have been ensnared by the first pretty face you encountered, with no thought to any other attribute."

"You're correct, but our problem is that Roxanne is here, and she's seized control."

"She certainly has." Margaret sounded aggrieved.

"I haven't put any limits on what I'll permit, but I will. Don't fret over it."

Margaret might have offered some other frank comments that he ought to have heard, but Roxanne sauntered in.

She always dressed like a rich princess, her wardrobe expensive and flattering. Her jewelry was expensive too, and it occurred to him that he had to have a conversation with her about their finances. She had a suitable dowry that would be his after the wedding, but it appeared she had an allowance from somewhere too, and she spent it lavishly.

He prayed she wasn't charging to his accounts on the promise she'd be his bride and he'd cover the bills later. His income was mostly generated by his being a navy captain as well as a gentleman farmer. He was thrifty with his money and never saw reasons to waste it.

The notion of talking to her, of explaining to her about frugality and moderation, was too exhausting to contemplate.

Margaret whispered, "Your destiny awaits."

"I find myself braced for any ending."

"Did you enjoy supper?"

"It was excellent."

Roxanne smiled at Jacob. She didn't usually worry about how others viewed her, but she felt as if she was on a perpetual employment interview. The engagement wasn't official yet and wouldn't be until various papers were signed.

They were plodding along according to his mother's schedule, but Roxanne had suggested they dump it and move up the wedding date. He'd agreed to mull the possibility, but he hadn't mentioned it again, so she wouldn't dare mention it either. She wouldn't want him to think she was too assertive.

She watched the road every minute, anxious that no mail be delivered of which she was unaware. She was terrified gossip from Italy would sneak in when she wasn't paying attention. People could be so petty, and he had acquaintances around the globe. No doubt one of them would delight in informing him about her sordid history there.

She'd had several paramours in Italy, and two of them had even dueled over her. She refused to be ashamed over how she'd thrived, but she didn't suppose Jacob would welcome the truth, and she was determined he never learn it.

They were on the rear verandah, leaned on the balustrade and staring out at the sky. It was a cloudy night, so there were no stars to see. The meal was over, their guests chatting inside. There would be no dancing or other amusement. Those would occur at the larger event that was scheduled for Saturday.

She'd been eager to catch him alone, so she'd been furtively observing him. Once he'd gone outside, she'd waited a bit, then had followed him. She'd been keen for it to seem as if she *hadn't* followed him, as if she'd stumbled on him by accident.

"I'm thrilled that you were pleased," she said.

"I was, but you don't have to try so hard. In fact, we don't have to have such a feast every evening. It's fine with me if we just dine with family."

Was that a criticism? "I like to host big suppers. I hope you don't mind if I continue."

"I don't mind. I simply don't need constant entertainment, but you're used to being in Florence. I'm sure this is very quiet by comparison."

"It is quiet here, and it took me awhile to settle in, but it's lovely to be back in England. I was away for most of a decade."

"I'm always away," he said, "and when I initially arrive, it takes me forever to adjust too. About the time I've calmed down, it's time for me to depart again, so I never get my feelings in the right spot."

"We have that in common."

"Have you written to my half-brothers? About the betrothal party?"

"Yes, but I have no idea where to send the letters."

"I have to travel to London next week. I can bring them."

"Good. It means I won't have to hire an investigator to track them down. Are they in England?"

"Caleb is. He owns a business in town."

"He left the navy to become a merchant? If your father wasn't already dead, that news would probably kill him."

Jacob smirked. "Most likely."

"Why did he quit?"

"He landed himself in some trouble. It was all very hush-hush, so I never found out what happened, but he had to muster out."

"How about Blake?"

"Last I heard, he was still a sailor."

The conversation lagged, and she thought he'd head inside, but he turned to her and said, "I have to talk to you about an awkward topic."

Gad, was it Italy? He looked so serious that her pulse raced with dread. "What is it? From how you're glowering, you're scaring me. Have I offended you in some fashion? If I have, I most humbly apologize."

"Am I glowering? I'm sorry; I didn't realize I was." He laughed and physically shook himself. "I don't know you very well."

"Maybe that's beneficial," she blithely retorted. "I'm not entirely convinced that a man and woman should share too many details before they marry. If they discover each other's faults, they might never proceed."

"True." He stared out at the sky again, as if conflicted about what to reveal.

"Spit it out, Jacob. It can't be that difficult. I'm a sturdy female. I can bear up."

"I don't want you to take this the wrong way."

"I swear I won't."

"You arrived at the estate and immediately began running things. I'm grateful for it. After Mother died, the manor was adrift and required a steady hand."

"But . . . ?"

"This is my and Margaret's home, and we will need time to get used to you being here."

"I understand."

"It's odd to have you in charge, to have you making choices that are different from what we would make ourselves."

"I'm renowned for being very bossy. When I walked in the door, it seemed natural for me to grab the reins."

"I figured that was the case, so be patient with us as we acclimate. We may have some bumps in the road, but I'm positive we'll work through them with minimal upheaval."

"I'm positive we will too." She blew out a heavy breath, relieved that the subject hadn't been much worse, but just when she assumed they were finished, he continued.

"That said, I have to mention this predicament. Margaret is very close with Miss James, and Margaret's condition is much improved because of Miss James's devoted attention. We're glad she's been tending Margaret, and we've both invited her to the party on Saturday."

"Oh."

Roxanne didn't add a comment. She merely gaped at him, her expression blank as she valiantly fought not to show a hint of her rage.

"I was apprised that you had cancelled our invitation," he said, "but I have reissued it. I'm sure that won't bother you and that you will graciously welcome her to the festivities."

His gaze grew steely, giving her no opening to complain.

"How did you hear that I had rescinded it?" she asked.

"It doesn't matter how, but it appears to me that you led a very independent existence in Italy. I believe that's a good trait in a navy wife, but you must remember that I will be your husband, and *I* will decide what will occur and what won't. If you have questions with regard to any situation, you should discuss it with me prior to responding. I regret to inform you that *my* opinion will always prevail over yours."

"Of course it will, and I'm distraught that I've upset you."

"I'm not upset. As I explained, we don't really know each other, and we're staggering forward like a pair of blind people."

"Still though, I must clarify my dealings with her. There are awful stories circulating about her being a charlatan who delivers false hope, and I was worried about Margaret's burgeoning attachment. With her being so despondent recently, I was afraid Miss James might take advantage of her."

"It's kind of you to fret about Margaret, but Margaret will pick her own companions, without any concern over what you and I might think of them."

She nodded. "Your message is received loud and clear, and I shouldn't have butted in. I was only trying to help."

"I realize that fact." He studied her, then frowned. "You shouldn't fume about this or attempt to retaliate against Miss James in some fashion."

"I never would!" Roxanne huffed.

"I wouldn't want any discord to erupt."

"Honestly. I'm not a school girl, bent on vengeance. You've embarrassed me to the marrow of my bones."

"Then it's my turn to apologize."

Her shoulders slumped, and he clasped her hand and gave it a supportive squeeze.

"This conversation was very awkward," he said, "so can we go in and forget we talked about it?"

"Certainly."

"When we enter the parlor, we must be smiling or our guests will imagine we've quarreled. We'll be the focus of gossip, which I hate."

"I hate it too."

He offered his arm, and she grabbed hold and allowed him to guide her in, but all the while, she was contemplating Miss James and how Jacob had been flirting with her in the garden.

Apparently, the little tart had tattled to him, and her audacity had stirred enormous problems—for Roxanne.

She'd already been stewing about Miss James's niece, and she'd been struggling to devise a method to learn more about the child. But with Jacob warning her away from Miss James, she didn't dare call on them in the future. She didn't dare inquire about several thorny topics that had to be addressed.

Evidently, Miss James had a relationship brewing with Jacob, but it couldn't be pursued or permitted. Not right under Roxanne's nose, so what was Roxanne prepared to do about it? *Could* she do anything? And when and how should she do it?

Chapter
9

"What are you doing here?"

"I was bored."

Sandy pulled the door wide so Margaret could step into his front room. His son, Tim, was nowhere in sight, but Tom had fallen asleep by the hearth. Sandy had been seated on a chair next to him, reading a book, and drinking a glass of wine.

It was such a homey scene that it brought a sting of tears to her eyes.

He laid a finger to his lips, urging her to silence, then he lifted Tom off the floor.

"Is it morning?" Tom drowsily asked.

"No, my young wolf. It's time for bed. Let me tuck you in." He glanced at Margaret and whispered, "Tim already went up. I'll put him down too."

He walked off, Tom dozing against his chest. As he exited, he nodded to the chair he'd just vacated, indicating she should sit down. She nodded that she would, and he continued on.

She helped herself to Sandy's wine, listening as he walked around overhead. It was so quiet she could hear the soft murmur of their male voices, then he tiptoed down.

He marched over and delivered a stirring kiss, then he said, "You have a mansion full of guests. Why would you sneak over to my paltry house? Aren't you supposed to be the hostess? You'll be missed."

"I thought you'd attend. I had to find out why you stayed away."

He frowned as if it was the strangest comment ever. "Why would I have attended? I wasn't invited."

"Roxanne didn't ask you?"

"No. Nor would I have expected her to."

"Kit is there, bold as brass."

"Well, Kit is . . . Kit. Why wouldn't he be there?"

"And *you*, being a lowly employee, didn't warrant an invitation?"

"I'm sure this will come as a huge surprise to your grand self, but I've never been to a party inside the manor. Not in thirty years."

There was no rancor in his tone. He was simply stating a fact of his life.

"We sound like such snobs."

He grinned. "You are snobs. All of you, but you seem to have climbed down off your high-horse a bit."

"I'm trying anyway."

His gaze roamed down her torso. Although she was a poverty-stricken widow, her outfit provided no signs of her penury. She was wearing a sapphire gown that enhanced the blond of her hair and the blue of her eyes. Her jewelry wasn't real, but it was expensive enough to appear as if it was. She even had a tiara in her hair, the fake diamonds glittering in the firelight.

He made a circling motion with his hand, so she'd spin for him and he could see the whole ensemble. She felt like a silly, flirty adolescent again, and the sensation was thrilling and welcome.

"Very nice, Mrs. Howell. You could be an heiress."

"Wouldn't that be lovely? Were you aware that Mr. Howell died bankrupt? I was left so destitute that I had to borrow money from acquaintances in order to purchase my ticket to England. In case you were thinking I returned rich, I didn't."

"I wasn't thinking that. I was thinking you staggered home poor, miserable, and looking as if you'd lost your last friend. And when we manage to steal a few minutes together, could we please not talk about your deceased husband? He was a fiend, and I don't believe it's healthy for you to dwell on your marriage. It merely dredges up the bad memories."

"It's what Miss James keeps advising, but I've never mentioned my lean history to anyone. It's cathartic to tell you my secrets."

He reached out and linked their fingers. "What's wrong?"

"I'm upset that you weren't at the party."

"We're from different worlds, Margaret. It was our problem when we were children, and nothing's changed."

"Could I have supper with you some night? You suggested it, remember? The three of you are so happy. Some of it might rub off on me."

"I've decided supper isn't a good idea. How would I explain your presence? You're Mrs. Howell. You're the Captain's sister. You live in the manor, and we live here. I tend the horses."

"So . . . ?" she retorted like the worst spoiled brat.

"Don't pretend to be confused about it," he told her. "There's the issue too of me bringing a female into the house. My boys were very attached to their mother, and they took her death very hard. If you wedged yourself into our small family, they'd like you too much, and I can't have them growing fond when you won't stay around."

"I don't want our situation to be like this."

"Unfortunately, my dear, we don't get to choose the restrictions that rule us."

When she'd observed the cozy tableau—Sandy drinking wine and watching over his sleepy son—she'd felt such a terrible yearning to step into the montage and become part of it. A vision had flared, of herself as Sandy's wife and mother to his boys. In a bout of temporary insanity, she'd pictured herself fitting in with no trouble at all.

She was barren, so she'd never have any children of her own. Why couldn't his sons be *her* sons? The image had been so clear, so perfect, but he had the most annoying way of yanking her back to reality.

"You could describe us as friends," she said. "They'd understand that."

"A man like me can never be friends with a woman like you, and I won't have them assuming it's possible to smash the barriers that separate us. They shouldn't ever pine away over a female they can't have—as I've pined away over you. It's futile."

"Did you really pine away?"

"For an entire decade, and that's the one and only time I intend to ever admit it."

She wished she could be angry with him. Or maybe she'd like to insist there were no barriers, but he was correct in every word he'd uttered.

She sighed. "What will happen to us?"

"I haven't the vaguest notion."

"I can't act as if you're not nearby."

"Yes, you can. You used to be adept at it, and you're much older now. You've had more practice at how to behave."

She snorted. "If I begged prettily enough, would you change your clothes and come over to the party?"

"No. I can't leave my boys alone, and I would never show up where I wasn't welcome."

"Miss James is there."

"Then she's braver than I am. Boswell would hate to have me stroll in. Miss Ralston would too. I have no doubt she would deem me to be putting on airs, and I'd just as soon never have her notice me."

"What do you think of her?" Margaret asked.

"I don't plan to ever offer an opinion about her—not even to you."

"I went out on a limb and urged Jacob to cry off from the betrothal. When he loathed Mother's attitudes on every subject under the sun, I pointed out that perhaps he should question the match she arranged for him."

"What was his response?"

"He said he was content to proceed, that it was better than searching on his own for a vacuous debutante."

Sandy smiled. "Thank the Lord he didn't drag home one of those."

"I heartily concur."

He pulled her close and kissed her for an eternity, and it was the most romantic interlude she'd ever endured. He made her feel special and adored, which was lovely.

Eventually, he drew away, and he seemed perched on the edge of a profound remark. She braced, excited for what it might be, but he simply said, "You need to return to your party."

"It's Roxanne's party. Not mine."

"Still, you shouldn't be loafing over here. Your mother may have passed away, but it doesn't mean we're free to dally. If you were discovered in my parlor, I can't predict what sort of upheaval would ensue. I could probably weather it, but you're in no condition to be pushed into a scandal, and I won't be the cause of any negative gossip about you."

"I suppose I'll depart—but quite grudgingly. You're a beast for kicking me out."

"It's for your own good, and you know it too."

"That was always your admonition to me in the past."

"My prior chastisements are as apt now as they were back then."

A spurt of recklessness flooded through her, and she said, "What if I snuck in later?"

"To do what?"

"To ... to ... join you in your bed."

It was a shocking proposition, and she'd never previously been so risqué. Luckily, he didn't laugh or scold her.

"First of all," he said, "I'm up at the crack of dawn to get to work, so I can't engage in the type of nocturnal antics I enjoyed when I was younger. And second of all, if you tiptoed into my bedchamber, I'd likely die of an apoplexy."

She grinned. "I shouldn't risk it then."

Their conversation dwindled, and he gazed down at her, his expression tender and even a tad lustful. He'd claimed he wasn't interested in a carnal tryst, but her lewd suggestion had altered something between them.

She wasn't partial to marital conduct. She'd suffered enough of it during her marriage, but she yearned to lie next to him in the quiet hours of the night. He would cradle her in his arms and whisper in her ear until dawn.

Those were the kinds of passionate moments she'd dreamed of experiencing as a girl, but that could never have been achieved with cold, brutal Mr. Howell. With her tossing the prospect of a physical relationship out into the open with Sandy, new possibilities might be blossoming.

He led her to the door, then he dipped down and stole a final kiss.

"Go," he said.

"I don't want to."

He chuckled. "Go anyway. You have to."

He peeked out, saw no one, and gestured for her to creep off. She paused for an instant, filling her eyes with the sight of him, then she hurried away.

He didn't linger in the threshold to watch her, and she thought she heard him set the latch to bar intruders, as if he suspected she might actually sneak in and climb into his bed.

Would she ever dare?

Now that she'd planted that seed in her head, it sounded like a terrific idea. Why not try it? Why not indeed?

JOANNA WAS SEATED ON a bench in the garden behind the manor. She was staring at the house, liking how the windows shone against the black sky.

Inside, dozens of revelers were milling, dressed in their finery. They were chatting, drinking, playing cards. In one parlor, they were dancing. She, herself, had participated until she became so overheated that she'd had to cool down.

She was acquainted with many of the guests, and everyone had been polite. If they were disturbed to have her sharing in the merriment, they'd kept that opinion to themselves.

The attendees were mostly neighbors, as well as the more important merchants from the village, so it wasn't odd for her to have been invited too. She had suitable gowns for a fancy party, so she hadn't looked out of place. She hadn't *felt* out of place either.

She never did. She was perfectly content in any social situation. Her father was an earl's dastardly son, so she had a high, if dissolute lineage, and she thrived in any circumstance. But she never forgot the stratifications that ruled their lives. People weren't aware of her ancestry, and she never informed them. They simply viewed her as a healer who birthed babies and dispensed tonics.

She was delightfully happy the Captain had demanded she come. It was so rare when she was included in a jubilant event, and it had been a splendid experience. It was just after eleven, and soon, she'd leave for home. When she arrived, she would jot down every detail in her journal so she could show them to Clara later on.

The Captain appeared on the verandah. He leaned on the balustrade and peered out at the sky. He was drinking liquor, and he sipped it slowly, giving her a lengthy chance to study him.

She hadn't been able to predict how they'd interact during the festivities, but he'd been a gracious host, being no more cordial with her than he was with anyone else. With him keeping his distance, she'd observed him in his element. He was funny, charming, and obviously well-liked.

It made her sad though because it had starkly underscored their differences. His friendship with her was so wrong, and so inappropriate, that he couldn't display his fondness out in the open where others might witness it. She wasn't a member of his world, but hovered on the fringe of it, flitting around like a moth that he occasionally noticed.

Through much of the evening, he'd stood with Miss Ralston, greeting guests and introducing her to those she didn't know. They were a handsome couple, and their binding connection was recognized by all.

So Joanna was *what* to him precisely? Where did she fit in that scenario?

Nowhere, was the only answer to that question. Why was she encouraging him? Why was she allowing herself to be ensnared in his web? And how would she extract herself without too much drama or damage?

She wished her Aunt Pru was available to provide some wise counsel. There wasn't another female with whom she could discuss the dilemma, but one thing was very clear: She had to buck up and figure out where she was going.

He finished his liquor, then headed over to the stairs and walked down into the garden. The bench where she was sitting was under an arbor, so she was hidden in the shadows, and he didn't see her.

She was debating whether to announce her presence when he glanced over and said, "Joanna! There you are. I was worried you might have left without a goodbye."

"I was so hot from dancing. I needed some fresh air."

"It's so stuffy in the house. I'm used to being on my ship. I can't abide being stuck indoors."

He plopped down next to her, and of course, he wedged himself much too close, their bodies pressed together all the way down. She didn't move over, and she sighed with exasperation. Hadn't she just scolded herself about her behavior with him? Hadn't she just tabulated how little they had in common? Hadn't she just recollected how she had to erect some barriers and keep them in place?

"Why are you sighing?" he asked.

"Before you came outside, I was thinking how I have to try harder to avoid you."

"What a ludicrous notion. Why would you avoid me?"

"This party has reminded me of our disparate stations, but I conveniently ignore them."

"Normally, I'd nod like a dunce and say, *Yes, Joanna, I'm so far above you. Why am I even speaking to you?*" His tone was teasing, but there was an incredible amount of truth in the comment. "But I will only be in residence until the end of September, then I'll traipse off across the globe again, so I'm determined to enjoy myself while I'm here."

"I'll miss you."

"You'd better."

"Do you wish you were out on your ship right now?"

"I always wish that. Have you ever been out on the ocean?"

"Once—when I was a girl. I didn't care for it overly much."

Considering that the vessel she was traveling on had sunk in a violent storm and everyone had perished except her and her two friends, Libby and Caro, it was the understatement of the century.

"Well, then," he said, "if you don't care for ships and sailing, why have I bothered with you a single second?" He flashed a grin that was wicked and seductive. "Are you having fun?"

"Yes. I'm glad I attended."

"You didn't dance with me."

"You didn't ask."

"I didn't dare. I was afraid I'd gaze at you so fondly that I'd light us on fire."

She chuckled, and he surprised her by dipping in and stealing a kiss. As he drew away, he looked mischievous, as if he was a miscreant who'd pulled a prank.

"We're not kissing in your garden." She sounded prim and fussy.

"Why not? No one can see us in the shadows."

"We can't be sure of who might be spying on us, and your fiancée is inside." He appeared as if he'd protest her referring to his cousin as his fiancée, and she hurried to add, "I know, I know. You're not betrothed yet. You're an unattached bachelor."

"Now we're getting somewhere," he said, "and by the way, you are very beautiful tonight."

"Thank you."

"You're the most glamorous woman in the room."

"That's not true, so stop trying to charm me. You have dubious motives toward me, and it doesn't take much calculation to deduce what they are."

"Am I a scoundrel at heart?"

"Yes."

"A month ago, I would have huffed with offense at the allegation, but since I met you, I've been forced to conclude that I'm a cad after all."

"I stand warned, Captain Ralston."

"Where is Clara? Who's minding her?"

"She's staying in the village. Her teacher is hosting a birthday party for one of the students."

"The timing was lucky for me then. It meant you could attend *my* party."

He touched her throat, sending a shiver down her arms. As her sole piece of jewelry, she'd tied a ribbon around her neck, and there was an ivory broach pinned in the center. There was a woman's face carved in the ivory.

"Who is the woman?" he asked as he traced a finger across it.

"My mother."

"Tell me more about her."

"I don't remember much. I was four when she died, but my Aunt Pru claimed we were just alike."

"Was she from a common family?"

"Yes."

"But your father was quite high. Who is his family? You can't keep it a secret from me forever."

"Why can't I?"

"Your refusal to admit his name has fueled my curiosity. I won't cease hounding you until you confide in me."

"I realize you won't believe me, but I'm much more stubborn than you are. You can nag to infinity, but it won't garner you the information you seek."

"Why be so furtive about it? Most people who have a grand sire are happy to brag."

"If I told you who he is, I'm certain—when you next bumped into him—you'd engage in an entire conversation about me, and I would never give you that sort of ammunition."

"You've indicated he's someone I might actually know."

"It wouldn't surprise me. You top-lofty men live in a small world, and you all seem to be acquainted."

"Have you ever met him?"

"Never, and I have no desire to. He was horrid to my mother, and there's not a single topic he and I could ever discuss that wouldn't infuriate me."

"Why didn't he marry her? Was she too far beneath him? Was he a snob about it?"

"If you must be apprised, he couldn't marry her because he was already married."

"Oh." His cheeks reddened with chagrin.

"His wife was extremely enraged about their affair, and my mother and I suffered greatly because of it. He was a coward who wouldn't lift a finger to protect us. Why would I boast of a connection to a cretin like that?"

"How did you and your mother suffer? What did his wife do to you?"

Joanna studied him, wondering if she should confess to being one of the *Lost Girls* who'd been rescued by his father in the Caribbean.

As a child, she'd been notorious for a bit—until Aunt Pru had arrived to claim her. They'd carried on quietly after that, with Pru determined that Joanna's infamy slide into obscurity. Their home had been located near the estate of Joanna's father, and Pru had constantly worried his wife might learn that Joanna had returned to the area.

Pru hadn't necessarily expected the woman to lash out at Joanna, but she hadn't been willing to risk it. When Pru had gotten the chance to move them to another part of the country, she'd jumped at it.

Through the years, Joanna had grown accustomed to burying the past. There was no point in mentioning she was a *Lost Girl.* It simply generated attention she didn't care to have focused on her, and because of her odd quirks, she had to be cautious.

Why talk about it anyway? It left her anxious and edgy, and it dredged up enormous melancholia, both about the tragedy itself, but also about the trauma of being separated from Libby and Caro. She'd start to have nightmares, so it wasn't worth the cost.

"I can't describe that terrible period," she said. "It haunts me, and I can't bear to rehash it. Please don't ask me to."

Her old anguish must have been visible because he didn't press. "I'll let it go—for now."

"You'll never pry out any details you shouldn't discover."

"Would you do me a favor?"

"That depends on what it is."

"Would you hold my hand again? Palm to palm?"

"Why would you want that?"

"You have some strange skills, and they fascinate me. Can you see the future?"

"No one can see the future. It's not set in stone, and humans have free will."

It was the accepted answer, intended to keep pious vicars satisfied, but she had many disturbing talents. She just didn't summon them very often.

She debated forever, then thought, *Why not?*

He was eager to have it occur, and she was intrigued too. Before she could dissuade herself, she raised her hand and laid it to his. They sat very still, their gazes locked. Her power stirred, heat flowing from her to him, then a myriad of images flooded into their minds.

She saw him at his wedding, standing at the altar and waiting for his bride. He looked handsome, dashing, and very happy. She saw him a few years later, with two young boys—his sons. He'd bought them a pony and was teaching them to ride.

Then, without warning, the perspective shifted from him to her, and she was immersed in the shipwreck. The wind was howling, the ship sinking. There were people in the water, and they were screaming and praying. Her mother was gripping a log, clutching Joanna around the waist as a wave crashed over their heads.

"Hold on, hold on . . ." her mother was urging, but the tempest whipped her words away.

Joanna couldn't abide the deadly scene, and she yanked away. She was breathing hard, her heart hammering so raucously she was amazed it didn't burst out of her chest.

"What the bloody hell was that?" he asked. "Were we viewing the same things?"

"Most likely."

"How is that possible?"

"I can't explain it. I am possessed of several unusual gifts over which I have no control."

"How do the visions originate?"

"I can't guess."

"Did that incident really happen to you? Were you the girl in the waves?"

"Yes, and with me receiving such a vivid picture of it, I expect I'll have nightmares for a month."

He snorted at that. "It's why you don't like ships and sailing."

She shrugged. "That's putting it mildly."

"When was that? Where was that?"

"I can't and won't discuss it!" She was keen to change the subject. "I saw you at your wedding, and I saw you with your children. I think you'll have at least two."

"I saw them as well, but was it a prophesy? Will it come true?"

"I would never claim it will."

He eased away, as if she'd grown too hot to touch. "You are dangerous, Miss James."

"I'm sorry."

"Don't be sorry. I meant it as a compliment. I'm just flabbergasted. I understood you to be peculiar, but my goodness! Apparently, I had no idea."

"Could you promise not to tell anyone about this?"

"How long have you had such an odd power?"

"I was born with it. I inherited it from my mother."

"I can certainly comprehend why your father was so captivated. Did she cast a spell on him? Is that how he was ensnared?"

There was a teasing note in his comment that aggravated her. With her mother's voice still ringing in her ear, she was in no mood to have her denigrated.

"My mother didn't practice any magic on him." Her tone was irked.

"My father was a spoiled roué who seized whatever he craved. My mother was foolish enough to oblige him, and I was the result."

He was scrutinizing her as if he'd suddenly realized she had a disease that was catching, and she could have clouted him alongside the head.

"Stop staring at me as if I'm a madwoman," she said.

"I don't believe you're mad. In my view, you're the most astounding creature in the kingdom. When I was standing at the altar, were you able to see my bride?"

"No."

"I felt so happy."

She wondered if he'd ask her about his marriage, but she wouldn't parlay over his impending nuptials—that evidently wouldn't include Roxanne Ralston. She wouldn't clarify why she suspected that conclusion, and she definitely refused to play a role in what happened among the Ralston family members.

She merely wanted to slink to her cottage, live quietly with Clara, and hide from any trouble or adversity.

"What time is it?" she asked.

"It has to be nearly midnight."

"I should proceed to the manor. If my carriage hasn't already pulled up in the driveway, it will be there shortly."

"Why don't you tarry? There is no rule declaring you must go at midnight."

"Aren't I Cinderella for the evening? If I don't flit away before the clock strikes twelve, I might turn into a pumpkin."

"I spent the entire party furtively watching you. If you waltz out the door, my fun will waltz out with you." He scowled. "Are you sad? You can't be."

"I'm not sad. I don't like to hear that you deem me to be odd. It's a burden I carry, and I'd rather not carry it."

He kissed her urgently, and when he drew away, he said, "Does it feel to you as if we were supposed to meet? Do you ever get the impression that Fate has orchestrated some sort of destiny where we're concerned?"

"Fate always provides a destiny."

"What will ours be? Can you read your Taro cards, then tell me what you discover?"

"I never try to divine my own path. I'm content to travel down whatever road opens for me. I don't need special guidance to find the route."

She eased away and stood. "Thank you for inviting me."

"Don't leave yet."

"I have to. I've overstayed my welcome."

"You're being absurd."

He was loafing on the bench like a lazy king, grinning, his legs stretched out, appearing as if he hadn't a care in the world. And he didn't really.

"Shall I walk you out?" he asked.

"No. I can't have us observed together. Let me slip into the house, then you can follow in a few minutes."

"I'll visit you tomorrow."

She didn't bother to protest. It was pointless. She hurried away without a goodbye. She went to the verandah, dashed up the stairs, and rushed in to locate the butler so she could inquire about her carriage.

All the while, she sensed him studying her intently. He was lusting after her in a thrilling way, and she was anxious to go home and calm down so she could brace for when he next arrived.

Clearly, she had no ability to avoid him or to protect herself and, for once, she wished she wasn't quite so averse to learning her future. If the universe chose to give her a tiny hint of what was approaching, she wouldn't complain.

Chapter
10

Joanna sat on a chair in front of the fire. A candle burned on the table next to her. It was very late, but she couldn't sleep. Her attendance at the party had enlivened her to where it was impossible to relax.

She'd dined and danced and had even been kissed by a dashing rogue under a rose arbor in the garden. After such a perfect evening, who could rest?

Clara was gone to her own party, so Joanna was alone in the cottage. She didn't mind being alone, but she missed Clara's energy pulsing in the rooms.

She froze, thinking she'd heard a horse's hooves on the gravel outside. Mutt lay by the warm hearth, and when she glanced down at him, he woofed softly to say, *It's fine. Don't fret.*

Ever since she'd arrived home, it had been raining steadily. Lightning flashed occasionally, and every once in awhile, there would be a loud crack of thunder that made her cringe. There was an eerie perception in the air that almost felt like an enchantment.

She heard a sound outside again, and she was sure it was the gate opening and closing. She looked at Mutt, but he barely raised his head, not even when there was a knock on the door.

"Some guard dog you are," she complained, but he simply stood and stretched, his tail wagging ferociously.

She tiptoed over and peeked out the curtain, and to her great astonishment, the Captain was there. He was wet and bedraggled, and she rushed over and pulled the door wide.

"You ridiculous man!" she scolded. "Why are you riding about the countryside in the dark and the rain?"

"I missed you."

"You deranged fool! Come in, come in."

She grabbed his wrist and led him over to the fire. She pushed him onto a chair, and Mutt hovered at his feet, appearing delighted. She tossed on a log to get the flames burning hotter, then she hurried to the kitchen and returned with a towel and a bottle of brandy.

She fussed over him, removing his coat and boots, drying his face and hair, pouring him a glass of liquor and urging him to drink it. There was a knitted throw on the sofa, and she draped it over his shoulders.

"Better?" she asked.

"Definitely."

He clasped her arm and tugged her onto his lap, and she nestled with him, the throw folded around them both so they were wrapped in a cozy cocoon.

"Why are you here?" she asked.

"I told you: I missed you."

"I missed you too, but not enough that I'd have ventured out in a storm to see you again."

"After you departed, the weather worsened, and the guests fled. In practically the snap of a finger, the manor emptied, and it seemed so quiet. I couldn't bear it."

"I don't suppose it would do any good to warn you about catching a chill. Or are you too tough to be felled by a little illness?"

"I'm much too manly to ever be sick."

She scoffed. "I should chastise you for visiting me, but this is a very nice surprise, so I won't."

"Why are you still up? On the trip over, I was calling myself a fool. I was certain you'd be in bed."

"It was such a lovely party, and I couldn't calm down afterward. The thunder and lightning aren't helping. I keep jumping and cringing."

"What time is it?"

"I can't imagine. Three? Four?"

"Dawn will break in a bit."

"Let's enjoy ourselves until it sneaks up on us."

He kissed her then, and she leapt into the embrace, feeling wicked and emboldened, and she was starting to want things from him she couldn't precisely describe. But she wanted them anyway.

Because she was ready for bed, she was wearing only her nightgown and robe, a pair of floppy wool socks on her feet. The belt on her robe was securely tied, so she was covered from chin to toe, which meant the situation wasn't exactly risqué, but it wasn't exactly proper either.

They were secluded in her cottage, and they might have been the last two people on Earth, and the rules about propriety had flown out the window.

She'd assumed she was content with her life, but he brought an exhilaration to her small existence that she couldn't ignore. As she was fully aware, this was how unwary maidens landed themselves in trouble, so she was trying to deduce her purpose. She wasn't about to ruin herself, as she was positive he'd request, so what was she planning?

For the moment, she would simply wallow in the pleasurable interlude and not worry about what else might happen.

Her hair was down and brushed out, and he riffled his fingers through it, then roamed over her torso, touching her everywhere, as if he was imprinting her shape into his palms. Each stroke of his hand was electrifying.

His tongue was in her mouth, her breasts crushed to his chest, the embrace growing wilder and more passionate by the minute. She began to fear they might ignite from the thrill of it all. Finally, when it seemed that they couldn't possibly keep on, he slowed and drew away. He pressed his forehead to hers, their breath mingling, their hearts beating at the same elevated speed.

"Gad," he murmured, "what will become of me?"

"I don't know."

"Would you take me up to your bed?"

"I couldn't do that."

She chuckled, but miserably. She'd been expecting that very question, and she was fortunate he wasn't the sort of rogue to force her there, despite her refusal.

"I realize it's horridly rude of me to inquire," he said, "but are you still a maid?"

"Yes, it's rude, but I'll answer truthfully: I'm still a maid. I live an odd life, but it's a moral, modest life."

"I'm a cad to have mentioned it. I apologize."

"You're hoping to entice me sufficiently that I'll provide you with what you should never have."

"Maybe."

"If I succumbed, have you pondered the ending? You'd be wed, then gone on your navy ship, and I'd be here, badly used and perhaps even with child. That can't be the conclusion."

"I would never dishonor you that way."

They snuggled for a bit, his body warming and relaxing. It was an unusual night, what with Clara being away. Joanna caught herself wishing she was a tad more dissolute. She would love to give him what he sought.

In a very short period, she'd turned into a woman who might be willing to commit any sin for him. Where would she be when he was finished with her?

"I don't want to get married," he suddenly said.

This was a bog she didn't dare enter. "What do you want to do?"

"I thought I was prepared to proceed. Before my mother's health failed, I had her find me a bride, and I never fretted over her choice."

"Is it Miss Ralston who's rattled you? Or have you found you're a dedicated bachelor?"

"I believe I'm ready to be a husband, and I'm not necessarily opposed to Roxanne. She's beautiful, educated, and competent."

As well as cruel, petty, and all wrong for you, Joanna added, but silently. Instead, she asked, "Then why are you vacillating?"

"When I was riding over here, I was so excited to see you. I was debating how I'd react if you were asleep. I was thinking I'd have to hurl rocks at your bedroom window until I awakened you."

"You'd be my very own Romeo?"

"Yes, so it occurred to me—if I could feel so happy about you—I must not be as eager to wed as I presumed. I'm the type of man who exerts my best effort at any endeavor. If I can't be totally resolved, why would I forge ahead? It would be so unfair to my wife."

She was biting her tongue so hard that she was amazed it wasn't gnawed bloody. She yearned to share what she'd learned about Miss Ralston, but if she blurted it out, she'd be interfering in his relationship with the awful shrew.

Joanna couldn't be the catalyst that broke them apart. If Fate intervened, so be it, but Joanna shouldn't involve herself. She sensed it to the marrow of her bones.

For a brief instant, she wondered if *she* might be the bride Fate intended for him. They possessed such a potent bond, and they had their unrevealed connection to his father. Might his father's ghost be pushing them together?

Over the years, she'd waited to notice Miles Ralston hovering, but she never had. Was he finally pitching in so she'd wind up with his son? She'd never quit expecting he'd follow through on the vow he'd made while she was still on his ship. What if he gave her the most perfect gift of all? What if he gave her Jacob?

She'd confessed her father's elevated lineage to Jacob. If her father had wed her mother, Joanna would have been much higher in rank and station than Jacob. Had he grasped that fact?

She was sure he hadn't. Nor had he deduced that she could be his wife. In order for it to transpire, he'd have to overlook her parentage and peculiar talents, but she comprehended British men and how they viewed the world. He'd never realize she was a viable candidate, and—with her being a female—she couldn't point it out to him.

Yet even if he proposed, would she consent to have him? It went counter to the historical view of her ancestors. Yet despite their teachings, she thought, for *him,* she might agree. If she could have him as her husband, matrimony might be worth it.

"You keep reminding me that the engagement isn't official," she said. "Could you postpone it so you can contemplate your path?"

"I can't imagine doing that. Roxanne traveled from Italy, due to my promise. It would be callous of me to demand a delay."

Joanna frowned. "Could we not talk about this? I understand you need a confidante on the topic, but it can't be me. I'm very fond of you, and I can't bear to discuss your betrothal or your marriage. It's painful for me."

He snorted with disgust. "Gad, I'm an ass, aren't I? I was so anxious to vent my frustrations that I never considered how difficult it might be for you to listen. I'm sorry."

He snuggled her down, and she rested against his chest, soothed by the sound of his heart beating under his ribs. It was such a splendid interval, and she must have dozed off because, next she knew, he was whispering, "Joanna! Wake up."

She flinched and glanced about, requiring a moment to figure out why she wasn't in her bed. Then she exhaled a nervous breath and sank down.

"Was I sleeping? I didn't mean to."

"The rain has stopped and dawn is upon us. I should go."

She sat up and ran a hand through her disheveled hair. "Am I a mess?"

"Yes, but you're an adorable mess."

He drew her in and kissed her, and they both sighed with pleasure.

"I will be very greedy," she said, "and ask when I'll see you again."

"I'm not certain when it will be."

Panic surged, but she tamped it down. "That can't be your response. You're like a bad habit. You can't simply avoid me. I'd miss you too much."

"I'm off to London for a few days. I have business to conduct."

"I'm glad you told me. If I hadn't been apprised, I'd have been glued to my window, staring out to discover if you were strolling up my walk. I'm growing that used to having you around."

"Can I tell you of a task I've scheduled?"

"Of course."

"It's a tad shocking, and no one in my family likes to admit it, but did you ever hear that I have two half-brothers? Their names are Caleb and Blake."

"Yes, I have heard that."

"When my mother was alive, I wasn't able to be friends with them, but I can make my own choices now. I've been thinking I should establish a relationship with them. While I'm in town, I intend to visit Caleb and invite him to Ralston Place."

"What a pretty idea."

"Really? Everyone else believes it's an insane notion."

"I'm all alone in the world—except for Clara—so it's lovely that you'd want to expand your family. You absolutely should befriend them."

"The minute I'm back, I'll call on you to report how it went."

"Are you leaving tomorrow?"

"Yes, so I'll be home next Sunday."

"Will you be at church this morning? I could grin at you from the rear pews."

"No. I'm a dedicated heathen."

"I am not, so I'll be there with bells on."

She always attended services. She would never let others suppose she wasn't a Christian. It was a warning passed down by her female kin.

He shifted her off his lap and stood her on her feet. She helped him up too, then she assisted him as he donned his coat and boots. He was gazing down at her with such a serious expression on his face. She braced for him to offer a profound comment, but in the end, he didn't.

He dipped down and kissed her again, then he practically yanked himself away.

"I have to get going," he said. "You entice me so thoroughly that I feel as if you've attached fetters to prevent my escape."

"I have no fetters to ensnare you, but I will declare myself ecstatic that you spent part of the night with me."

"I'll miss you every second while I'm away."

"I will very brashly confess that I will miss you too."

"The ground is too wet," he said, "so stay in here."

"All right, I will."

"But watch out the window as I depart. Will you? I'll wave goodbye."

"I must inform you that you're very close to spouting poetry. You must flee before you completely embarrass yourself."

"I'll see you in a week."

"I can't wait."

He left, and Mutt scooted out with him.

"Can he come outside?" he asked.

"Yes. He can even follow you to the manor if he wishes. He knows the way back."

Jacob nodded, then hurried out. She tarried until he appeared on his horse that he must have hobbled in the shed behind the cottage. He trotted past the front, and Mutt was loping along with him.

Just when he would have been swallowed up by the trees, he reined in. She waved enthusiastically, and it made her feel as if he was *hers,* that he lived with her, that he was merely off on an errand and would return shortly.

It was a thrilling thought, and she let it sink in so it would keep her smiling all day.

***

"If it isn't Roxanne, the new mistress of Ralston Place."

"Sod off, Kit."

Roxanne glared at Kit, but it was impossible to shame him. When she'd agreed to betroth herself to Jacob, she hadn't realized he was Jacob's land agent, but she *should* have realized it. After all, he'd been raised at the estate and had been too lazy to ever leave. It had been a huge shock to show up and bump into him.

Jacob's mother, Esther, had written to her about the engagement, and it would have been nice if Kit had written too. He could have warned her of his presence before she accepted, but he was too much of a prig to consider anyone but himself.

She had to get rid of him, but she wasn't sure how. She knew his secrets, but he knew hers too. If she moved to ruin him, he'd run to Jacob and tattle. If he couldn't save himself, he'd be delighted to drag her down with him.

They were in the dining room, and she'd risen much too early. With the bad weather ending the party so abruptly, she'd tossed and turned, worrying that the soiree had been a failure—and that Jacob would blame her.

"Why are you eating in the manor?" she asked Kit. "You have your own house and your own servants. I'm positive they can scramble an egg and put it on a plate. Why must we feed you?"

"I've always eaten breakfast here. Esther and I began our day together."

"She was an obnoxious shrew, so I'm not surprised to learn you were chums."

"I flattered and cajoled her, so she adored me."

"In your deluded mind maybe. She didn't like anybody."

She dug into her food, and he stood and meandered over to the sideboard to dish up another helping for himself.

"Oh, look," he said, his voice dripping with sarcasm, "there's Jacob coming home. Where could he have been?"

Kit was adept at needling her, and she should have ignored him, but she couldn't stop herself from inquiring, "What are you talking about?"

"He just rode into the yard."

Kit was staring out the window, but whether Jacob was out there or not, it was hard to predict. Kit loved to torment her.

"It's not even eight o'clock," she said, "and the roads will be muddy from the rain. Why would he be out and about already?"

"It appears to me that he's wearing the same clothes he had on last night."

"You're a man," she scoffed. "As if you'd have noticed what he was wearing. As if you'd remember it later on."

"If I had to guess, I'd swear he hasn't been to bed yet. At least he hasn't been to the one up in his bedchamber. He must have slept somewhere else."

There was a footman hovering in the corner, and she said to Kit, "Would you shut up?"

"Aren't you curious as to where he's been? I certainly am. If I asked him, I wonder if he'd whisper the name of the lucky girl."

Roxanne peeked at the footman, and his eyes were wide as saucers. She waved him out, then she rose and walked over to stand beside Kit. And . . . ?

There was Jacob, skulking across the garden toward a rear entrance, and Kit was correct: He was wearing the clothes he'd had on the night before.

The bastard!

There was a mongrel dog with him, and as he neared the verandah, he petted the animal, then he pointed to the woods. The dog barked, then raced off, and Jacob continued on into the house.

Kit smirked. "Aren't you his dearest betrothed? I would hate to imagine he's cheating on you so soon, but then, he *is* Miles's son."

Concealing her fury, she sauntered back to the table and resumed eating, but she casually said, "Whose dog is that?"

"I believe it belongs to the little witch who's treating Margaret— and I use the term *witch* literally."

Roxanne tamped down a blanch. "I doubt she's a witch. I begged her to read my palms once, but she insisted she had no ability for that sort of endeavor."

"That's not what the stable boys tell me. They claim she can make a man's private parts stop working. If she can make them stop working, she can probably make them *start* working, wouldn't you suppose?"

"For pity's sake. Be silent."

"Should we fear that she's cast a spell on Jacob? How can we explain his being so enthralled? Perhaps she wants him for herself, and she's luring him away from you."

"Gad, you are so aggravating. Have mercy and let me finish my meal in peace."

"If it's not magic, how can an amour have flared so quickly?"

She threw down her napkin, leapt to her feet, and marched for the door.

"What's wrong?" He was innocent as a choirboy. "Have my remarks upset you? Don't mind me; I'm just babbling aloud."

"I can't wait for the day I skewer you with a sharp sword and spread your innards on the barn floor for the dogs to devour."

"You have such a picturesque way with words. Is Jacob aware of your violent tendencies?"

She halted and said, "Miss James has a young girl living with her who she pretends is her niece. Do you know anything about her?"

"No, I haven't a clue."

"She's nine or so. White-blond hair, very black eyes. Her name is Clara."

"Why would that news interest me?"

"Figure it out, Kit. I'm betting you can."

Their gazes locked, her message resonating, rattling him, then she whipped away and left.

She was desperate to escape his vile presence, and the best place to mope and fume was in her bedchamber, but she didn't dare climb the stairs. If she met Jacob in the hall, it would be blatantly obvious that he was sneaking in from a tryst, and it had to have been with Miss James, didn't it?

Roxanne's blood boiled. Clearly, her suspicions about the pretty tart were valid. Did Jacob imagine Roxanne wouldn't care about a dalliance?

It wasn't the dalliance so much as his pursuing it right under her very nose. A rural estate was such an incestuous spot. Everyone knew everyone else's business. Did he think he could keep an affair a secret? Did he think Roxanne would never find out? Wasn't he concerned about her finding out? If that was his attitude, what kind of marriage would they have?

She'd thought he was an honorable fellow and that he'd at least attempt to practice monogamy—but no man could. Just look at his dastardly father! In her view, she'd expected he'd be mostly faithful, but when he trifled with a paramour, he'd go to great lengths to hide it. She wasn't even his wife yet, and he was already indifferent to her feelings. How was she to deal with such disregard?

And what about Miss James? Roxanne was about to be Jacob's bride. How could Miss James assume she would be allowed to reside at Ralston Place after Roxanne's wedding? Why would she assume Roxanne would be content to have her close by and available for Jacob's mischief?

The wench had to vanish, and she had to take her niece and her mongrel dog with her. The sooner the better. The only problem to resolve was how to have it happen with clean hands so Roxanne could never be blamed.

Roxanne would ultimately be shed of her. Of that fact, she had no doubt at all.

Chapter

11

Joanna walked down the lane toward her cottage. She was lonely and at loose ends. Clara was at school, and Jacob had gone to London. It was foolish to mope, but she didn't like him being so far away. Nor did she like it that he wasn't around to surprise her. She'd gotten accustomed to having him bluster in unexpectedly.

Suddenly up ahead, a man was standing by the path that led through the woods to her gate. It was obvious he was waiting for her, and she halted and studied him. He was dressed like a bank clerk or maybe a secretary to an important gentleman—brown suit, bowler hat, spectacles—and he seemed harmless enough.

"Miss James?" he asked. "Joanna James?"

"Yes, I'm Miss James."

He hurried over to her, removed his cap, and bowed. "I am Mr. Howard Periwinkle. I'm a newspaper reporter for the London Times."

"My goodness, what a thrilling remark. I always thought it would be so exciting to write for a living. You love your work, don't you? I can see that you do."

"Well, yes. Yes, I do love it."

"You're quite a distance from the city, but you're not lost. What brings you to my neighborhood?"

"I was looking for you."

"For me! My goodness again. I'm flattered. What is it you need from me?"

"I've been searching for you," he told her. "Aren't you a Mystery Girl of the Caribbean? You were in a shipwreck when you were little. You survived with your two companions, Libby and Caroline."

"Yes, I was a Mystery Girl. You sought me out over that? How very odd."

"The three of you are famous."

She chuckled. "*We* are famous? I find that very hard to believe."

"No one has ever stopped talking about you."

She knew he was correct, but she pretended he wasn't. "You're pulling my leg. I'm convinced of it."

"No, no, it's true! Why, Libby is in London right now, appearing on the stage to gushing audiences. She regales them with stories about the tragedy."

She knew about Libby too, knew she was famous on the stage, but she said, "You're joking."

"No. People were agog when you were returned to England years ago, and they still are."

"I had no idea," she lied.

"It's the reason I'm here—because it's the twentieth anniversary."

"So it is. The time has passed so quickly."

"My newspaper would like to print a retrospective about the three of you."

"What kind of retrospective?"

"We'd like to draft a few articles about how your lives unfolded after you were claimed by your relatives."

"Who would be interested in that?"

"Everyone?"

"I doubt that very much."

"I guess I've failed to explain how popular you've been."

"Mr . . . Periwinkle, is it? I can't think that *popular* is a word I would use to describe my life."

"How was it then? Was it scary? Was it horrid? Were your relatives cruel? Did they mistreat you? Our readers are eager to know how you've fared."

"Again, sir, I doubt that very much."

She was about to continue on, so he hastily added, "We'd like to arrange a reunion too. For you, Libby, and Caroline. Would you like that? Would you like to see them?"

It was an electrifying suggestion. She'd constantly yearned to communicate with them, and she was haunted by how they'd been immediately separated upon their arrival in England.

Her Aunt Pru had understood how devastating the split had been, and they'd incessantly worried about Libby and Caro. They'd occasionally checked the cards for both girls, so they'd been aware they were suffering, and they'd wished there had been a way to help them.

Pru had tracked down Caro's family. She'd written to them, asking if she and Joanna could visit, but she'd received such a nasty reply from Caro's grandfather that she hadn't pestered him again.

Libby had traveled with performing troupes, so it had been trickier to locate her. They'd attempted to see her on the stage once when she'd been advertised at an area theater, but when they'd attended the matinee, Libby hadn't been there. They'd inquired about her after the show and had been apprised that she'd traipsed off to a bigger engagement.

After that, she'd never appeared anywhere near to where they'd resided, so there hadn't been a second opportunity.

A reunion? What a splendid notion! Perhaps Mr. Periwinkle could organize what Joanna had never managed.

"I would like that," she said, "and if you could arrange it, I would be happy to participate. I've missed them so much."

"I've heard that you were closer than sisters."

"Yes, I suppose that's true."

"And that you were ripped apart, without having a chance to say goodbye."

"It was a trying situation. The authorities weren't sure of what was best for us. They had difficult decisions to make, and I shouldn't judge them."

"Would you like to confide in me about those terrible days? How was it difficult?"

She sighed. "That, Mr. Periwinkle, is none of your business at all."

Deeming the conversation to be over, she circled around him.

She wouldn't dredge up the past. It left her sad and anxious, and she didn't want him delving into details about her father or why she and her mother had been on the ship to Jamaica in the first place. Why stir that controversy?

"I'll write you," he called to her. "As soon as I've conferred with Libby and Caroline, I'll contact you about the plans for the reunion."

"I shall be waiting on pins and needles until then," she called back.

She kept on to her cottage. Once she went inside, she proceeded directly to her workroom, with Libby and Caro front and center in her mind.

They'd had painful lives. She, Joanna, was the only one who'd had a stable existence and a kindly caregiver. With Mr. Periwinkle mentioning them, she was concerned about them again.

She pulled the curtains, then retrieved her cards from their box. She shuffled them, then asked about Libby and Caro, about whether they were about to meet, and it definitely seemed as if they were. It seemed too as if Libby might be about to wed.

"Libby getting married," Joanna murmured to the quiet room. "What a pretty thought."

She tucked the cards away and smiled with gladness—and satisfaction too.

———

JACOB SAT WITH FRIENDS at the theater. Miss Libby Carstairs, billed as the famous Mystery Girl of the Caribbean, was performing a monologue, and the audience was riveted on her story. He couldn't deny that he was riveted too.

It was the twentieth anniversary of her rescue, so people were gossiping about the shipwreck, and his father, Miles, was the main character in any reminiscence. Miss Carstairs had spent the prior decades earning money from the tragedy. She toured the kingdom, and it had made her notorious to the public.

He'd never seen her previously, but evidently, she had dozens of soliloquies and ballads she used to describe what she remembered of the incident. According to his acquaintances, she shared a different tale every evening, so a person could never be certain what narrative would be supplied.

She and her two companions had been the sole survivors, and they'd been dubbed the little *Lost Girls*. No one could explain why or how they'd survived. They'd been so young when it had happened that it had been hard to glean much information. If their families had pried out subsequent facts, he hadn't heard about it.

Miss Carstairs was twenty-five and stunningly beautiful, but she was a talented actress too, so it was easy to forget she was an adult. Currently, she was attired in an unadorned white shift, her blond hair tied with a strip of leather, her feet bare, so she looked like an orphaned waif. A single lamp illuminated her.

She was talking about the day Captain Miles Ralston had sailed into the bay to save them. She told the event from the perspective of a child: how large the ship had been, how scary to watch the sailors rowing ashore, how big and gruff Jacob's father had seemed.

It was a bit like having his father whisper from the grave, and shivers kept racing down his spine. He viewed himself as a very manly man, and he was surprised to find that a theatrical scene could have such an effect on his equilibrium.

He blamed his response on his father, which was an excuse he frequently utilized. He harbored so many conflicting opinions about Miles Ralston. He'd been a brave, brash navy captain, but he'd also had two wives and two families.

Jacob and his half-brother, Caleb, were the same age of thirty, proving Miles had been an immoral dog. Jacob often wondered how his father had dared, how he'd coped with the pressure.

Of course, his wife, Esther, had been in England, and his wife, Pearl, had been in Jamaica, so the distance had helped to hide his mischief. Had Miles possessed nerves of steel? Or had he tossed and turned at night, terrified his bigamy was about to be exposed?

Miles's rescue of the *Lost Girls* was his most famous exploit, so for once, Jacob forced himself to ignore his father's many failings and simply revel in Miss Carstairs's recitation of the incredible feat.

She waxed on about what a hero Miles Ralston had been, how he'd saved her life. Jacob had considered him a hero too—until Caleb and Blake had knocked on their door. Since then, his memories had been quite a bit darker.

The monologue wound to a close, and Miss Carstairs took her bows. The audience came to its feet, hooting, hollering, and throwing flowers and coins at her. She dashed away from the ruckus, and the play resumed. It was a half-hearted comedy that wasn't funny, and after it ended, his friends escorted him backstage. They all knew Miss Carstairs and had promised him an introduction.

Every gentleman in the city was hoping to coax her into becoming their mistress, and when he discovered how many dandies had rushed to speak with her, he was embarrassed to be one of them.

He'd missed his chance with her though. By the time he elbowed his way into her dressing room, she'd already departed, and he couldn't determine if he was relieved or not. For years, he'd pondered tracking her down and having a conversation about his father, but he'd been afraid of what she might confide.

Clearly, she had only a fond recollection, so he'd have to try again in the future, but he wouldn't lurk backstage. He'd have a clerk investigate her situation, and he'd send her a letter to request an appointment. It's what he should have done.

His companions were heading off to gamble, and he pleaded fatigue and left them to their merriment. It was an odd decision. In the past, London had never exhausted him. He'd loved the camaraderie and wild escapades, but to his great bewilderment, he was weary and bored.

Earlier in the evening, he'd stopped by Caleb's gambling club. They'd had a civil chat—the first one they'd ever managed—and Jacob had extended an invitation to his house party in September. He'd conveniently neglected to mention that it was a betrothal party too, and he was struggling to figure out why.

Why hadn't he been able to confess the truth to Caleb? Had he changed his mind about the engagement to Roxanne?

He stood on the busy street, watching as the theater emptied, as people jumped in their carriages and rolled off to other venues. Everyone was going somewhere except for him, and it dawned on him that he wished he was at Ralston Place.

Actually, he wished he was with Joanna so he could tell her about his discussion with Caleb, as well as his attempt to meet Libby Carstairs. Joanna had quickly wedged herself into his thinking and life, but he shouldn't have let it happen.

It was so wrong for him to have befriended her. What good could come from it? He was behaving very badly, and he would break her heart in the end. He had no doubt about it. He might even wind up ruining her reputation in the neighborhood.

If word of his infatuation leaked out, no one would believe it had been an innocent romance. She'd be vilified, while he would board his ship and sail away. Yet even knowing all that, even admitting all that, he missed her desperately.

There was no reason to loiter in London. He'd scheduled a week's visit, but it was merely because he'd assumed he needed to flee the estate for a few days. But he simply wanted to be at Ralston Place instead.

He rippled with astonishment. Imagine that! When he could be with Joanna in the country, why tarry in the city? It made no sense so . . .

Apparently, he was leaving in the morning.

⁘

MARGARET WAS SITTING IN the garden, loafing on a bench. It was a beautiful afternoon, and she hadn't felt warm since she'd sailed from Alexandria. England's gloomy grey skies weighed her down. If she wound up with a sunburned nose, it was a tiny price to pay for several minutes of decadence.

One of Sandy's sons walked by, but he didn't notice her. He was peeking over his shoulder, as if he was involved in mischief and hoping not to be observed.

"Hello, Tim," she said. "Or are you Tom?"

At the sound of her voice, he jumped and whipped around. "Oh, Mrs. Howell! I didn't see you there."

"I've only met you boys once, so I can't tell you apart. Which one are you?"

"I'm Tom."

She patted the spot next to her on the bench, and he hesitated, glancing down the path, then he joined her.

"Who are you hiding from?" she asked.

"My brother. I'm supposed to be minding him, but sometimes, I'd rather not."

"If you're not watching him, who is?"

"No one, I guess. We have chores, but I told him to finish them on his own. The weather is too nice, so I'm going swimming."

"You're a truant."

"I have to be or I might choke."

"I'm hiding too," she said, "and dawdling in the peace and quiet. I lived in Egypt, and it was hot and sunny there. I miss it."

"Have you seen a pyramid?"

"I saw tons of them."

"And the Nile river?"

"I had a house that was on the banks of the Nile."

"You're so lucky. Pa says it's not our lot to leave the estate and that we should be happy where we are, but I'd like to travel everywhere."

"I don't blame you. Now that I've traveled myself, Ralston Place seems very small."

"Pa wants me to run the stables when I'm an adult, but I can't imagine it."

"What would you like to try instead?"

"I'd like to be a pirate or an explorer."

She chuckled. "I'd encourage you on the idea of being an explorer, but pirates are criminals who usually end up being hanged. It might not be such a good career choice."

"Probably not."

His shoulders slumped with dismay, and she said, "What if you enlisted in the navy when you're a bit older?"

He grinned, a charming, miniature version of Sandy. "I would love that!"

"I think you can sign up when you're fourteen."

"Pa says I have to attend school until I'm sixteen."

"It's not that many years away, and it will pass quicker than you expect."

"I'll likely go mad here, waiting for something to change."

"I'll mention your interest in the navy to my brother. He can give you some advice about it."

"Would you?"

He looked so delighted that she grinned too. "The navy is his favorite topic, and he'll talk about it until you reach a point where you'll be begging him to desist."

He sighed. "My mother thought I should be a sailor. Her brother joined, and he liked it, but Pa claims I should stay at home where I belong."

"Parents typically pick the right path for their children, but not always." She was referring to her own mother who'd forced her to marry Mr. Howell. "I can discuss it with your father."

"Would you, Mrs. Howell? I tell him my plans, but he simply scolds me for being a dreamer. He says I need to come back down to Earth."

"That definitely sounds like your father."

They enjoyed a companionable silence, then Margaret couldn't resist asking, "Do you miss your mother?"

"Every day, ma'am. She was the best person ever."

"It's too bad she's not around to persuade your father."

"It was easier when she took my side. He can be a stern fellow."

"I know that about him. He and I have been friends for a very long time."

"He told us that you were."

She smiled, liking that Sandy had spoken of her with his sons. It made their furtive affection seem a little less forbidden.

From far off, they heard his brother calling, "Tom! Tom! Where are you? I'm not about to finish this by myself! If you don't help me, I'll tell Pa!"

Tom bristled. "There's Tim. He can be such a tattle."

Margaret waved him away. "You better go then. You shouldn't get in trouble because you were loafing with me."

"Can we chat in the future? I'd like you to describe those pyramids you saw."

"I would like that. I'll find you some afternoon when you're not busy."

His brother hollered again, and he jumped up and marched off, calling back, "I'm coming, I'm coming. Stop caterwauling or you're like to wake the dead."

She watched until he vanished, then she relaxed and pondered the world and her place in it.

She reflected on Sandy and his boys. They were three males who'd lost the female they'd needed to balance them, and it was so unfair that Sandy had been given two sturdy, healthy children, but she hadn't managed to birth a single one.

Did he realize how fortunate he was? The question answered itself: Of course he realized it. His luck at life left her incredibly jealous.

It seemed as if she'd chosen every wrong road, while he had everything he'd ever wanted. She had nothing really. Not a husband. Not a home of her own. Not a penny to her name. Not a son or daughter upon whom she could dote. Would she ever have any of those things?

Well, not if she kept moping and never implemented any action to improve her condition. What would it take for her to feel she was moving forward? Where did she hope to end up?

She tarried for hours, debating where she'd like to be in a few years. She refused to stagger around at Ralston Place as Jacob's unwanted, tedious sister. He'd insisted she was welcome, but she couldn't bear to be under Roxanne's thumb and constantly having to remember that she was the poor relative.

That miserable existence wasn't an option, so what was?

When the afternoon began to wane and she headed inside, she was certain she had it all figured out.

"HELLO, MISS CLARA."

Clara glanced up and recognized Miss Ralston who was Captain Ralston's cousin and fiancée. She had stepped out of the milliner's shop when Clara was strolling through the village, on her way home from school.

"Hello to you too, Miss Ralston." She curtsied to her even though she wasn't certain a curtsy was appropriate.

"Why are you alone?"

"I attend school, but classes are finished for the afternoon."

"You attend school? Aren't you lucky? Are you a good student or are your studies boring?"

"I'm a very good student."

Clara's cheeks heated. She shouldn't have offered such a vain comment. Joanna always urged her to be more modest.

Miss Ralston smirked. "You're not humble, are you?"

"I shouldn't have bragged. I apologize."

She wasn't sorry though. She liked being smart, and she was glad she was. Joanna was very smart, and their Aunt Pru had been smart too. Clara wanted to be like them when she grew up.

Miss Ralston gestured down the block to where her carriage was parked. "I'm heading in your same direction. Shall we walk together?"

"That would be fine."

They started off, ambling side by side, but it was very awkward. Miss Ralston seemed very stuffy, very posh, and Clara couldn't think of a single topic that might interest her.

"How do you like living out in the cottage with your Aunt Joanna?" Miss Ralston asked.

"I like it very much. It's perfect for us."

"How long have you been there? I don't recall what your aunt told me."

"We moved to the area when I was a baby, so it's been almost ten years."

"You're nine?"

"Yes."

"You weren't born here?"

"No."

"Where were you born?"

"I'm sure you've never heard of the town."

"Tell me anyway." Miss Ralston's tone was very sharp.

Clara peeked up at her. The woman's lips were pursed so tightly that Clara wondered if she'd been impertinent, and she was suffering from the strongest perception that she shouldn't provide the name of the spot, but she said, "It was Telford."

"Telford!" Miss Ralston practically spat it out.

It was obvious she yearned to pry out other information, but Clara peered down the street, and Joanna was coming toward her. She sighed with relief.

"There's Joanna," she said. "I have to go."

She rushed away, and when she reached her aunt, Joanna appeared very worried.

"What were you chatting about with Miss Ralston?" she asked.

"Nothing. I bumped into her by accident."

Joanna glared at Miss Ralston, and Miss Ralston glared back, her expression scary to witness, then she whipped away and climbed in her vehicle.

"I don't think she likes us," Clara said.

"I don't think she likes anyone. It's not just us."

"She looks like me. Did you notice?"

Joanna blanched. "No, I didn't notice. It's your blond hair making you seem similar."

"Mine is prettier than hers."

Joanna chuckled. "You need to work on your humility."

They headed for home, and it was Clara's favorite part of the day—when she had Joanna all to herself.

"Miss Ralston is so grouchy," she said, "and Captain Ralston is so nice. Will he like being married to her?"

"We probably oughtn't to speculate about it. Their life at the manor isn't any of our business."

"Do you know what I wish would happen? I wish he'd marry you."

"Why would you even ponder such a peculiar notion?"

"He's sweet on you," she said, "and I saw you kissing. He wouldn't kiss you unless he was very fond."

"We're not ever mentioning that, remember? Besides, he has a path that's quite different from mine."

"I bet he'd be much happier wed to you than her."

Joanna stopped and stared up at the sky, as if she was searching for guidance from the heavens. Ultimately, she said, "Could we not talk about him?"

"I like talking about him, but we don't have to."

"Let me tell you something much more interesting. It's a fun surprise."

"Ooh, I love surprises."

"I met a man on the lane by our cottage. A Mr. Periwinkle? He's a reporter for a London newspaper. He is writing a story about me."

"About your healing or your clairvoyance?"

"About the shipwreck! It's the twentieth anniversary, and people are curious about how I've fared over the years."

"There will be an article in the newspaper? Are you positive you'd like that? Your past won't be buried then."

"He claims their readers have fretted over how my life unfolded, if I've been safe and cared for, and I'd like to assure them that it's been grand. I'm tired of hiding my identity."

"I've never understood why you were so wary. If I'd been a *Lost Girl,* I couldn't have been silent about it."

"Guess what else."

"What?"

"He's planning a reunion—for me, Caro, and Libby!"

Clara had frequently heard about the three of them, how they'd been rescued by Captain Ralston's father. She thought it was the most thrilling tale ever, and it was so hard to bite down on the truth. She was forced to keep many secrets about Joanna, but her being a *Lost Girl* was the most difficult one of all.

"After it's in the newspaper," Clara said, "will I be able to discuss it?"

"Yes."

"Finally," Clara mumbled.

She could never figure out why it was such a huge issue. It concerned Joanna's mother leaving England in such a hurry, and the memory distressed Joanna. Clara had hated to conceal it from Captain Ralston. During his visits, Clara could barely stop herself from blurting out, *Don't you realize how Joanna is connected to you?*

"Can we confess it to Captain Ralston now?" she asked. "He'll be excited, don't you think?"

"I'll tell him about it next time I see him. He shouldn't read about it in the newspaper without having advance warning. He might faint and hurt himself."

Clara laughed. "When is the reunion?"

"It's not scheduled yet. Mr. Periwinkle will write to apprise me."

"May I attend with you?"

"Absolutely," Joanna said. "And I was debating whether we should have a holiday. I promised you a summer trip to Bath. What if we went there for a few weeks?"

"To Bath? Really? I can't imagine how marvelous it would be."

"I assumed that would be your opinion. Maybe we'll investigate the prospect. We'd have to determine where to stay, and how much it would cost, in order to decide if we can afford it."

"What if Mr. Periwinkle contacted you while we were away? What if you missed the reunion?"

"Believe me, I won't let that happen."

Chapter
12

SANDY WAS ABOUT TO bank the fire in the hearth when a knock sounded on the door. It was soft and furtive and, without checking, he could predict who it was.

His initial instinct was to ignore her. What good could come from answering?

The boys were in bed, and it had been a long day, but then, they were all long days. An enormous amount of effort was required to run the estate, and he was exhausted. He had to do his own job, plus Kit Boswell's, so he was always overwhelmed.

The knock sounded again, a bit louder, and he sighed with resignation. He was thirty and a widower, yet it felt as if he hadn't matured a whit from when he'd been sixteen and had first fallen in love.

As if a magic spell was pulling him over, he went to the door and eased it open. Margaret was standing there, and they exchanged a hot look, then she murmured, "Well? Will you invite me in or not?"

"I shouldn't."

"But you will."

She smiled the smile he'd never been able to resist, and he grabbed her wrist and dragged her inside.

"Are your sons asleep?" she asked.

"Yes."

"Perfect."

He wasn't sure what she wanted this time, but she was an expert at torturing him. During her prior visit, she'd suggested they sneak upstairs to frolic. He'd been stunned by her proposition, but he was also kicking himself for refusing. It had been the only proper reply, but oh! Just once, he'd like to push them to an outrageous conclusion.

"To what do I owe the pleasure of your company, Mrs. Howell?" His tone was very sarcastic.

"I searched for you all day, but you are so adept at hiding. I couldn't find you anywhere, and we have to have a serious chat."

She'd brought a satchel, and she held it out. He took it from her and asked, "What's this?"

"Champagne and chocolates."

"What are they for?"

"We have an important issue to resolve, then we'll celebrate."

"What will we be celebrating?"

"You'll figure it out shortly."

Obviously, she planned a surprise, but he couldn't bear her surprises.

They were still trudging down the road they'd walked when they were adolescents. She was a Ralston, and he was a Ralston employee. He was a servant who *served* her family. There were so many obstacles separating them that she might have been living up on the moon. Their circumstances were that far apart.

When he'd heard she was a widow and coming home to stay, he'd told himself they were older and wiser, so their youthful impulses would have fled, but after he'd kissed her, he couldn't deny that he was more besotted than ever, which had him worried about his sanity.

Wasn't it a sign of madness to keep doing the same thing over and over, but expecting a different result? If he wasn't careful, he'd wind up committed to an asylum. His warped relationship with her would drive him to that sort of bad ledge.

He tossed a log on the fire to get it burning again, then he emptied the satchel. There were two chairs by the fire, a small table between them, and he put the champagne and chocolates on it. She'd even included glasses and plates.

As he fussed with the treats, she removed her cloak and hung it on the hook by the door, and he noted that she'd dressed as if she was off to attend a fancy party. Why would she have? He wouldn't try to guess.

In many ways, he knew her better than anyone, but in many other ways, she was a complete mystery.

Her gown was a pretty blue color, and the shade set off the blue of her eyes so they were particularly striking. Her hair was intricately styled, with braids and curls and a jaunty feather dangling in the back. Her slippers and fan matched her gown, and he was a tad unnerved by the display.

She sauntered over—yes, she definitely sauntered—then she pointed to one of the chairs and said, "Sit down."

"Uh . . . all right."

"I'm going to talk for a bit, and you're going to listen. Then when I'm finished, you'll give me the correct response."

"I hope I'll be able to."

"I have no doubt about it. You've never failed me in the past, and you're not about to fail me now."

He sat as she'd commanded, and he stared up at her, terrified over what she was about to convey. He prayed it wouldn't be a hideous request. She was horridly spoiled, and it wouldn't occur to her that she might seek a favor he didn't dare supply.

She studied him tenderly, as if he was greatly adored. He melted when she looked at him like that. No one else ever had. Not even his deceased wife who'd been fond, but who'd possessed no heightened affection.

"How long have I known you, Sandy?" she asked. "Twenty-eight years?"

"Yes, if we start counting from the day you were born."

"When did we first become friends?"

"I remember it so clearly. I was five and you were three. You fell and skinned your knee in the garden. You'd snuck away from your nanny and were outside when you weren't supposed to be. I helped you up and escorted you to the manor."

"Really? Is that it? I don't recall the incident. How old would you say I was when I initially realized I was in love with you?"

He shifted uneasily. "You loved me?"

"Don't be daft, my silly man. It probably flared when I was about twelve. That was when I noticed you in a whole new way."

"Well . . ." He couldn't deduce a reply, so he added nothing further.

"My mother demanded I wed Mr. Howell, and I thought I would die of a broken heart for the loss of you."

In his opinion, she'd gotten over him quickly enough, but he didn't mention it. "It was a difficult period, and you were always destined to be a bride for an oaf like him. Your mother wouldn't have made any other choice for you."

"Even then, even when I devastated you with my disregard, you were steadfast. Yet I took you for granted."

"I didn't mind." He halted and frowned. "Let me retract that statement. I minded, but I understood your reasoning. You had to obey your mother."

"Yes, I behaved like the dutiful daughter I'd been raised to be. I didn't wish to ever be compared to my sister, Pamela. She eloped rather than heed my mother, and she's been cut off from us ever since. I couldn't have lived like that."

"Pamela was more reckless than you, and after she'd caused such a furor, you couldn't have done it too. It might have killed your mother to have both of you elope on her."

"I agree, so I married Mr. Howell. It was my only genuine option, but I want you to comprehend that I paid for my sins against you. Every day I was wed, I paid."

"Don't share that kind of information with me. It's too depressing."

She squared her shoulders and shook off her moment of melancholy, then she said, "I'm a snob and an ingrate, and I constantly fret over how others view me. I have shrugged off your affection, and I have received much more devotion from you than I deserve."

He smirked. "That's all true."

"I don't have any money. My dowry was squandered by Mr. Howell, and I've come home to my brother with my hat in my hand like the worst beggar."

"You're lucky he opened the door to you," he facetiously said.

"Ha! I slithered in before he arrived, and he was too polite to kick me out."

"Where is this going, Margaret?" he inquired. "What are you trying to tell me?"

"I'm trying to tell you that I have loved you all my life. I've never stopped, and I'm an adult woman who can make her own choices. This is what I choose: Geoffrey Sanders, will you do me the honor of becoming my husband?"

He scowled ferociously, positive he'd misheard. "What did you just ask me?"

"Will you marry me?"

"Absolutely not."

"Can't you contemplate it for a minute? Why must that be your immediate answer?"

"Because it's impossible."

"Says who?"

"Says . . . everyone?" He was startled and completely flummoxed.

"When we separated years ago, we were little more than children. I obliged my mother by wedding the candidate she selected for me, but I've grown up, and my parents are deceased. No one will be allowed to pressure me ever again. *I* will decide, and I have decided that you should be my husband."

"But . . . but . . . what would people think?"

"I don't give two figs for any opinion but yours."

"What about your brother? You may have determined that you'd like to shackle yourself to the hired help, but he would never let you."

"He'd like me to be happy, and *you* will make me happy."

"What about his fiancée? She's more of a snob than you've ever dreamed of being. She most especially wouldn't like it."

"Of all the individuals in the world who get to order me about, she is so far down the list that she's not even on the list."

He chuckled, but miserably. It sounded so simple, as if they could flaunt society's rules and finally be together, and it was amusing to realize how their stances had changed from when they were adolescents.

Back then, Sandy had begged her to run away with him, and initially, she'd promised she would, but reality had crashed down on them. He'd have been fired, and she'd have been disowned, so she'd submitted to her mother. Now here she was espousing his prior arguments.

It would have been humorous if it wasn't so sad.

Yes, her parents were dead, but he couldn't see that much else had been altered. Eons earlier, it had been declared that dissimilar people shouldn't wed. There were too many obstacles to prevent a cohesive existence, but he hated for that to be true.

He yearned to marry her more than he'd ever wanted anything. Why couldn't he have her? He'd loved her forever, and he supposed he would until he took his last breath. But so what? The fact that he loved her had no bearing on any aspect of it.

To his great consternation, she dropped to one knee and clasped hold of his hand, which stunned him. It was the man's required role, but he was sitting like a bump on a log as she grew more absurd than she'd ever been.

"My dearest Sandy," she said, "will you marry me?"

"Oh, Margaret..." He winced. "Don't do this. It will kill me to refuse you."

He attempted to pull away, but she simply tightened her grip. "Then don't refuse. Why would you? A decade ago, we were boxed in by issues beyond our control, but we're not now. We're both widowed, and you have two boys who need a mother. I heartily toss myself at your feet and request that you let it be me."

He hadn't thought about his boys. Yes, they needed a mother, but how could it be her? He struggled to picture her at their table, checking their schoolwork or listening to stories about their day.

He couldn't imagine it.

"The wheels are spinning in your head," she said, "as you conjure up a thousand reasons why we shouldn't, but I will not permit you to obsess in your typical negative way. Stop it."

He snorted. "I'm trying to envision you eating supper with us, but I can't fathom it."

"Well, *I* am trying to envision myself up in your bed. That's a much more interesting scenario."

"You've turned into a vixen without my noticing."

"Maybe I was always a vixen, and with me being a widow, I don't have to hide it. Just think how *you* will be the beneficiary of my newly-discovered dissolute tendencies."

He didn't respond to the comment. He couldn't.

There were so many emotions swirling that he felt dizzy. After she'd crushed him with her disavowal, he'd spent the intervening period, reminding himself to stay where he belonged, to never reach for more than he'd been given.

He was a modest, ordinary man, and the agony of dreaming—when those dreams were dashed—could be so devastating. Yet she was offering him exactly what he wanted. In his view, she had very much to lose by wedding him, but she'd decided she didn't care. She was eager to forge ahead and damn the consequences.

He'd assumed he was smarter and braver than she was. Was he? If she could cast off the fetters that had bound them in the past, why couldn't he?

"You're mad," he said, but kindly. "You know that, right?"

"Yes, I know."

He lifted her off her knee and sat her on the chair opposite. Then he shifted his own chair so he was facing her.

"How would you expect this to unfold?" he asked. "You seem to have the matter all planned out. Would we remain at Ralston Place? Would you move in with us? Could you be content in this small house and in our small life?"

"Yes, we'd remain at Ralston, and I'd move in with you. And *yes*, I'd be very content with that ending."

"What if you ultimately determined you didn't like my sons or being a mother? What if you started to hate that you'd wedged yourself into my family?"

"What if humans could sprout wings and fly like birds?" She tsked with offense. "You worry about the silliest things. You always have."

"Your brother might have a fit, and we'd be back where we were with your mother. He'd kick you out, and he'd fire me. I have my boys to consider, so I can't risk that happening."

"Jacob isn't my mother."

"Thank goodness."

"In the beginning, he might be a tad disconcerted, but he likes you. We'll drag him 'round to our way of thinking."

"It's impossible for me to tell you *no*."

"You shouldn't tell me that." She grabbed his hand and linked their fingers. "It will be fine, Sandy. It will be perfect. Don't fret so much."

"One of us should."

"What is our other option? Will we fritter away the years, avoiding each other and pretending we've never been in love? We'd drive each other insane."

"You're probably correct."

She was so confident, and he foolishly yearned to provide her with whatever she sought. She was his weakness. Why couldn't he glom onto her optimism? Why must he be so pessimistic?

He knew the answer to that: He'd learned through bitter experience that catastrophe could strike without warning. She'd been shielded from a lot of anguish by her family's money and position. At his level, calamity hit with a vengeance and there was no money or power to cushion the impact.

"You're so positive this could work," he said.

"Yes, I am, and I need you to be too."

He pondered forever, then he blew out a heavy breath. "I will agree to it on two conditions."

"What are they?"

"First, you have to swear you'll never suffer any regrets. You have to swear it and mean it."

She scoffed with derision. "As if I could ever regret being your wife. I've wanted it since I was twelve! Don't talk as if I'm fickle."

"It's simply that I'm afraid it won't turn out as you're hoping. My world is just this house, my job, and my sons. We'd have to live on my salary, so if you grew bored, there would be no jaunts to London or trips to the seashore to enliven your mood."

She laughed. "I don't have a penny to my name, so I can't whine about how little you have as opposed to me. I have the clothes on my back and that's it. I don't even have dishes or linens to bring to the union.

I had to leave all of it in Egypt because I couldn't afford to lug it home, so I must point out that *you* are the one assuming the burdens. You'll be saving me, and I'll always be grateful."

"You can't ever forget how you feel at this moment. Once reality settles in, you can't wish our life could be different. What I offer is all there is with me."

"I won't ever regret. I swear. What is the second thing?"

"I have to ask your brother for your hand. Unless and until I have his permission to wed you, I couldn't proceed."

"He'll give us his blessing. I promise."

"I will keep my fingers crossed."

She smiled a sly smile. "So . . . can we declare ourselves to be engaged?"

"Yes, I think we can view it as being official."

She slid over and snuggled onto his lap. She kissed him sweetly, then, as she pulled away, she was smirking. "I was certain I could convince you. I had no doubt."

He sighed, praying it would be all right in the end. "I never could resist you. I told you that you can't ever regret this, but don't ever make *me* regret it either."

"I shall be the best wife ever, and you will be happy all your days. Now wipe that frown off your face and open the bloody champagne!"

❦

MUTT HAD BEEN DOZING by the fire, when suddenly, he leapt up and gave a soft woof, the one he used for friends.

Joanna was relishing a quiet moment before she called it a night. Clara was already asleep, so Joanna was alone in the parlor. It was just after ten, so it wasn't exactly late, but it was late enough that no one should be walking through her front gate.

"Is it Captain Ralston?"

From the frantic wagging of his tail, she had to think it was, and she raced over and opened the door without peeking out first.

"What are you doing on my stoop?" she asked him. "You're not scheduled to return from London for several days. Are you all right?"

"I'm fine."

They froze and stared, a thousand delicious sentiments sizzling, then they moved at the same instant, practically falling into each other's arms. He kissed her as if he'd been gone for years, as if he'd been drowning and she'd thrown him a rope.

He drew away, and without another word exchanged, he clasped her wrist and marched her up the stairs. She didn't protest or drag her feet. It was occurring so fast that her mind couldn't catch up with her body.

Her *body* was delighted to follow wherever he led. But her mind was shouting warnings—to remember herself, to slow down—but she didn't really want to slow down. She might have been hovering up above, watching as some other woman behaved precisely as she shouldn't.

It was a small house, and there were only two bedrooms. He glanced in the one on the right, saw Clara, and pulled her door shut. Then he went into the other one, and she went with him. *She* closed the door.

There was no key though, so she couldn't lock them in. She didn't imagine Clara would wake up and interrupt, but what if it happened?

Joanna would never be able to explain his presence.

He proceeded to the bed and flopped down onto the mattress. He tugged her down with him and rolled them so he was stretched out atop her. She'd never lain with a man before, so it was a heady, dangerous experience. She was being pummeled by sensations, all of them thrilling and hazardous to her equilibrium.

He kissed her forever, his fingers in her hair, his palms roaming over her torso. Occasionally, he caressed her breasts, and it produced such giddy joy that she was surprised she didn't expire from happiness.

She was still wearing her clothes, and he hadn't so much as shed his coat, so they were both covered from chins to toes, yet they might have been naked. The sparks they ignited were that potent.

Down below, she could feel his hardened phallus, and it indicated his lust was running hot. He was eager to mate with her. His hips were working with her own in a perfect rhythm that was like nothing else in the world. The ecstasy was overwhelming, and her resolve was slipping.

What if he pressed the issue a bit farther? Would she succumb?

She was terribly afraid she might.

Ultimately, he eased away, and he smiled down at her with such affection that it disturbed her. What was she supposed to do with that smile? How had she lived without it in the past? How would she live without it in the future, after he tired of her?

He started to chuckle, and she joined in.

"You've driven me mad, Joanna James," he said. "You realize that, don't you?"

"I have no idea why you'd accuse me. In my view of our relationship, I've scarcely encouraged you. I can't fathom what's fueling this desire."

He slid onto his back, and she was draped over his chest, her ear directly over his heart.

"Please assure me that Clara sleeps like a rock," he said.

"She does, but I have no key for my door. If she waltzes in, she'll catch us."

"I can't apologize for this. Even if we're caught, I won't be sorry."

He sighed with contentment, and she nestled with him, listening as his breathing slowed.

"Why are you home so early?" she asked.

"I missed you too much to stay in town. Can you believe it?" He laughed as if the admission was embarrassing. "I attended the theater with some friends, and after the play ended, they rushed off to carouse and gamble. They urged me to accompany them, but for once, that sort of revelry held no appeal whatsoever."

"Maybe you're finally growing up."

"That's one excuse, but the pathetic fact is that I wanted to be here with you, and I couldn't figure out why I was there with them instead. It seemed as if I was mixed up about what mattered."

"I'm glad you're back."

"Did you miss me too?" he asked.

"I've been absolutely bereft without you."

She peeked up at him, grinning, and he scoffed. "You liar. You might have missed me just a tad, but I simply can't picture you devastated over any situation."

Her grinned widened. "You might be correct."

He snuggled her down, and she closed her eyes and catalogued every detail so she'd never forget any of them. She couldn't predict how many times she'd be with him like this, and she had to consider that each meeting might be the last one.

He could become bored with their dalliance, or fixated on another lucky girl, or be recalled to the navy without notice. She had to cherish each moment they could manage to sneak off together.

"What have you been doing while I was away?" he asked. "Describe every single minute."

"My days are all the same, so there's very little to tell. I brewed potions and delivered them. I walked Clara to and from school. I tended my garden and toiled away in my workroom. Has my tedious recitation put you to sleep?"

"No. How is my sister?"

At the question, she scowled. "Haven't you been home yet?"

"No. I stopped here first. I was that excited to see you."

"You rat. You can't behave like this. What if you were observed riding by, but you never arrived at the manor? They'd sound an alarm."

"I'll go in a bit. I passed by your cottage on the way. You can't wish I'd have trotted on by."

"I'm extremely delighted, you bounder. There! You've forced me to admit it." She popped up again and said, "Tell me what *you* did in town. I'm sure your activities were much more interesting than mine."

"Well, I visited my half-brother, Caleb. We had a cordial discussion, and I invited him to Ralston Place. I *think* he agreed to come, but I'm not certain."

She smiled. "I'm so relieved that you talked to him. I was afraid you might change your mind."

"He and I have been acquainted for years, but out of respect for my mother, I didn't feel I could befriend him. He and I are the same age, and we have the navy as a common bond. We even look alike, although he has my father's blond hair and mine is black. It's the only genuine difference between us."

"You are siblings after all. I'm not surprised that you'd be similar."

"Can I share a secret about him and me? Actually, it's about our father, Miles."

She'd love to have him speak about his father, and she said, "Of course you can share a secret."

"You likely won't believe it, but he was a bigamist."

"What?"

She pulled away and sat up. He remained relaxed on the pillow.

"We buried that scurrilous truth," he said. "When there are whispers about me having half-siblings, it's assumed they're my father's natural sons, but he married their mother—when he was married to mine."

Her jaw dropped with astonishment. "I had no idea!"

"The navy hushed it up. My father was such a notorious person, and they didn't want rumors to spread that would tarnish his reputation."

"How did you find out about it?"

"Caleb and Blake lived in Jamaica, and after they were orphaned, their vicar sent them to their English kin, but the man wasn't aware that Miles had a wife in England."

"Oh, my goodness! I said I'd enjoy you sharing a secret, but maybe I didn't mean it."

"They traveled with their guardian, Sybil Jones, and she was a veritable tiger on their behalf. She shamed the navy into negotiating with my mother to provide some assistance to them. We paid for their schooling and navy commissions, and in return, they promised to never reveal my father's conduct. They're not bastard sons. They're a bigamist's sons, but I doubt there's a name for that."

"You're not angry about the money your mother spent on them, are you? To me, it seems like a fair resolution."

"I was angry when I was younger, but I viewed the dilemma from my mother's perspective. Now I simply wonder what my father was thinking. How could he have imagined he'd get away with it? I remember him as being very arrogant. Perhaps he deemed himself to be invincible and would never die, so the facts would never be exposed."

"I'm at a loss for words."

"Don't tell anyone. Please? As I mentioned, people know I have two half-brothers, but they're not cognizant of the true situation. Both women are deceased, but still, I would hate to have gossip disseminated."

"I will never tell a soul. I swear."

"Thank you."

"How was your conversation with Caleb? You claimed it was cordial, but what did you discuss?"

"At first, he was grouchy to have me stop by, and I can't blame him. We weren't very kind to him and his brother. In the past few years, he's grown very rich. He owns a successful gambling club, and I felt he was worried I was about to beg him for a loan. After he realized I was merely there to chat, he calmed down. We talked about our parents—all three of them."

"I'm so glad. I like everyone to get along."

"That was my chief adventure in town, but when I attended the theater, it was so I could see Miss Libby Carstairs. Have you ever heard of her?"

She smirked. "Yes, I've definitely heard of Libby Carstairs."

"She's one of the *Lost Girls* my father rescued from that deserted island. She's celebrated for performing stories about him."

"She certainly is."

"I've always wanted to meet her, but I never have, so I went backstage, but she'd already left." He chuckled, as if embarrassed. "I'm perplexed over what I was hoping to have happen. I just thought it would be interesting to confer with her. She and I have quite a connection."

He'd given her the opening she needed, and she gestured to him. "Would you sit up for me? You've confessed a secret about yourself, and now, I should confess one about me."

He studied her, then he scooted up so they were facing each other on the mattress.

"Gad, you look so serious all of a sudden," he said. "What is it? I can't bear to be informed that something awful has occurred."

"No, it's not that. It's amazing and intriguing, and I predict you'll be stunned."

He was wary, tentative. "Let's see if you're correct."

"Libby Carstairs is the most famous *Lost Girl*, but were you ever told the names of the two who were rescued with her?"

"One of them was...ah...Caroline Grey? My brother, Caleb, crossed paths with her recently, and he liked her very much."

She raised a brow. "Did he?"

"And the other one was...ah...Joanne, but I've never learned her surname."

"It wasn't Joanne. It was Joanna—and *James*. Joanna James."

She hadn't exactly been clear, so he didn't immediately grasp what she'd imparted.

"I'm confused," he said. "Is this some sort of riddle?"

"*I* am Joanna James. I am a *Lost Girl* who was saved by your father. I consider Libby and Caroline to be my sisters."

He was completely flummoxed. "You are not one of those girls."

"I am. I really am."

"But ... but ... why didn't you ever admit it here at Ralston? Why didn't you confide in *me*? Why hide it?"

"It's tied up in the reasons my mother and I fled England. My father's wife had threatened and tormented us, and once I was returned by the navy, my Aunt Pru refused to stir that hornet's nest by having my father's relatives discover I was back. She was always afraid his wife might cause trouble for me."

"*You* are Joanna James? Seriously?"

"Yes. Over the years, we got in the habit of concealing it. It's been difficult for me to change my thinking about it."

"Does Clara know?"

"Yes, and it's been killing her to remain silent, especially with how you've befriended us."

"Why tell me now?"

"Well, there is an odd event that transpired. I was visited by a news-paper reporter from London."

"Whatever for?"

"It's the twentieth anniversary of the shipwreck."

"The vision you and I shared? That was *the* shipwreck, wasn't it?"

"Yes. It's why I try to never recollect any details. It haunts me, so my mind has protected me by blocking most of it."

"I can certainly understand why."

"Anyway, the newspaper is planning to write an article about the three of us."

"You're joking."

"No, and they're scheduling a reunion. I agreed to participate, so my past won't be a secret much longer. I thought I should apprise you so you didn't read about it first. I would hate to make you faint."

"I can't believe this!" He physically shook himself. "A shiver just rushed down my spine. There is the eeriest sense in the air, as if Fate is playing with us."

"Or your father's ghost."

"Have you felt him hovering?"

"Recently, yes. He's definitely been hovering lately."

"Another shiver just flitted down my spine."

"The last time I ever talked to him," she said, "I asked him to watch over me, and I'm of the opinion that he guided me to you."

"What do you suppose it means?"

"I can't guess."

"Would you come to the manor tomorrow?" he inquired. "Would you spend an hour or two with Margaret and me so we can discuss my father? We were so young when he died, and he was never in England. We barely knew him, and our memories are warped by our finding out about his second family. Would you do that for us?"

She wasn't keen to ever visit the manor again. She was in no hurry to bump into Roxanne Ralston, but she comprehended his yearning to hear what she recalled about his father.

"I will stop by. When would be convenient for you?"

"How about in the afternoon? Around four? You could join us for supper."

"I'll meet with you at four, but I'll have to reflect on supper. Despite how you constantly forget that you have an *almost* fiancée, I haven't forgotten. I can't sit at the dining table with her. It wouldn't be appropriate."

He laughed off her prim attitude, and he looked happier, as if she'd lifted a burden off his shoulders. "This is such a wild story. My head is spinning. I may grow so dizzy on the trip home that I'll fall off my horse."

"I'm glad I told you about it. I've been biting my tongue so hard that I've practically gnawed it off."

"You are such a scamp. I keep thinking there were some deep corners with you, but apparently, I had no idea."

"I'm very different from everyone else. I can't deny it."

"That, my dear Joanna, is the understatement of the century." He blew out a heavy breath, then said, "I should be going."

"Yes, you should."

"I shall tell myself that my father's ghost dragged me to you. If I'd tried to gallop on by, I couldn't have. It felt as if a magnet was drawing me in."

He pulled her onto his lap and delivered a stirring kiss. It was awkward, and they were off balance, and they giggled with merriment.

"Would you get out of here before we wake Clara?" she said. "I can't fathom how you wound up in my bedchamber, and I have no desire to explain it to her. It is not a conversation I ever intend to have."

He smirked, then slid off the bed. She climbed down too, then they tiptoed out and down the stairs. Mutt was loafing by the fire, and he cast a jaundiced eye in their direction, as if informing them they weren't fooling anybody as to how they'd been misbehaving.

"Don't come outside," he said.

"Let me walk you to your horse."

"No. Just wave from the window again. I like that." He enjoyed a final, urgent kiss. "Bar the door after I'm gone."

"I will."

They gazed over at the dog, and he said to Mutt, "Will you run with me?"

But Mutt simply sank down, indicating he wouldn't leave his warm spot.

"Lazy dog," Jacob muttered, then he smiled at her. "I'll see you tomorrow. At four."

"I can't wait."

He marched out, and she went to the window to watch him depart. She waved as he'd requested, and long after the darkness stilled, she reached out to him with her mind. She observed him riding through the woods, turning onto the lane, proceeding to the manor. She continued to focus on him until she sensed he'd arrived safe and sound.

Goodnight, she murmured, her silent message winging out. *Sweet dreams...*

He flinched and straightened, as if he'd heard her clearly. Then she chuckled and headed back to bed.

Chapter

13

"How was your trip to London, and why are you back early?"

Jacob grinned at his sister. "I missed the estate so much I couldn't bear to stay away."

"You were always the worst liar," Margaret replied. "You've never spent much time here, and when you did, you never liked it."

"Maybe I'm changing."

"Ha! If there's one thing I've learned about Ralston men, it's that all of you are stubborn as mules. You never change."

"Should I apologize and try to be more spontaneous?"

"That would be like asking the grass not to grow. It's just your nature to be obstinate; you can't help it."

They were in the dining room at the manor, having a late breakfast. He enjoyed these quiet conversations with her, and he found himself liking her much more than he had when they were younger. Back then, their home had been filled with bickering and strife due to their mother's erratic temperament.

He hadn't bonded with Margaret or Pamela, and he'd escaped most of the discord by leaving for boarding school at age seven. Pamela had escaped when she'd eloped at eighteen. The minute their mother had started naming possible husbands for her, she'd glommed onto an old beau and had fled the country.

Margaret hadn't had the wherewithal to run away, but had meekly shackled herself to Mr. Howell as their mother had demanded. When the betrothal was announced, Jacob hadn't even been in England, and he'd only arrived to attend the wedding.

He'd instantly and vehemently detested Bernard Howell and had warned Margaret to cry off, but she hadn't been brave enough. Nor had Jacob known how to intervene. He'd always feel guilty that he hadn't stopped it.

"I've brought two pieces of news that will amaze you," he told her.

"Are either of them horrid? If so, please wait until I'm finished eating so you don't spoil my meal."

"They're not horrid; they're quite incredible. Well, *I* think they're incredible anyway. I saw Caleb in London."

"Has he accepted your invitation to visit?"

"Not yet. He doesn't like us anymore than we've ever liked him."

"Smart man."

"Did I tell you he retired from the navy and he owns a gambling club now?"

"I'd heard that somewhere, but I'm not sure if it was from you."

"The enterprise is thriving, and he's obscenely rich."

"Good for him. If I begged him for a loan, do you imagine he'd give it to me?"

He chuckled. "During our meeting, I received the distinct impression that he was braced in case I was about to ask him for money. Once he figured out it was simply a social call, he relaxed and was cordial."

"Are you certain we're destined to be friends with him? Is that what you want? I'm terribly afraid you haven't assessed the ramifications."

"What can it hurt?"

She shrugged. "I just view it as . . . *wrong*, I guess. We hated them for so—"

"We've been through this, Margaret. *We* didn't hate them."

"What's he like?" she inquired.

"He's very much like me: tall, broad-shouldered, and very handsome."

She scoffed at that. "Is he modest like you too?"

"No. He possesses all the vanity."

"Does he look like us?"

"He could be my twin, except that he has blond hair and I have black. You realize, don't you, that he and I are a few months apart in age?"

"Gad! Don't tell me that. Father was such a rutting dog!"

"Speaking of Father . . ."

"Must we?"

"My other tidbit is about him."

"He didn't have a third wife, did he? If so, I'll have to find a cliff and throw myself off it."

He chuckled again. "No, it's nothing like that. I was talking to Miss James."

He halted, recognizing he'd nearly said *last night*, but he didn't suppose he should mention that fact.

"Joanna was here? It's so early. I didn't see her."

"No, not this morning." He ignored the notion of *when* they'd talked. "You will not believe what I've discovered about her."

"She has to be the most intriguing female in the kingdom, so whatever it is—no matter how odd—I won't be surprised."

"Yes, well, this might make you fall off your chair."

Margaret frowned. "What is it? I like her very much, so if it's scandalous or humiliating, keep it to yourself."

"It seems, dear sister, that Joanna James is one of the *Lost Girls* rescued by Father on that deserted island."

"That can't be true."

"I'm serious as a heart seizure. She is coming by this afternoon at four to chat about it."

"But she's lived on the estate for a whole decade, and she's been tending me ever since I arrived from Egypt. Why has she been silent?"

"Do you know much about her past?"

"No. We don't have that kind of relationship."

"There was a private issue with why she and her mother had left England in the first place. Her mother died in the shipwreck, and when Miss James was returned to England, she was claimed by an aunt."

"Yes, Prudence James. She moved to the neighborhood after I departed. I've heard of her, but I never met her."

"Miss James was traumatized by the ordeal, so they were careful not to stir any nightmares."

"Why is she openly declaring her connection now? Why after all this time?"

"It's the twentieth anniversary of the rescue, and she was contacted by a newspaper reporter from London. They are writing a retrospective about it, and she decided she should inform me—so we'd have some warning."

"My goodness," Margaret said. "I'm . . . I'm . . . speechless."

"I thought it would be interesting to have her share what she recollects about Father. We have such negative opinions of him, and it would be nice to have someone paint a fonder picture."

"Those girls were so little when he stumbled on them. Are you sure she has any valid memories?"

"We'll find out at four o'clock."

"I'm actually looking forward to it."

"So am I."

He tossed down his napkin and stood. "I should be going. I have a hundred tasks to complete before we talk to her."

"How could you possibly be busy? Aren't you an absentee landlord? You have Kit to manage things for you."

"I have Sandy anyway. Let's not give Kit more credit than he deserves."

"I'm glad you've noticed who's really in charge."

"It took me awhile, but I'm not totally blind. I've been thinking I should be a tad more involved in how the property is run. I'm eager to learn about it."

She scowled. "You want to *learn* about the estate?"

"It's mad, I know."

"Who are you and what have you done with my brother?"

"Will you please order some refreshments for our appointment with Miss James? She may stay for supper too. Would you apprise the housekeeper?"

"Miss James won't stay. I'm still trying to figure out how we coerced her into attending our party last week."

"I wore her down with my significant charm."

Margaret might have launched an interrogation into how he'd gotten so friendly with Joanna, so he walked on. As he reached the door, she said, "I had hoped to discuss an important topic with you."

"What is it?"

"Just my . . . ah . . . future and what I'd like to have happen."

"You must be feeling better."

"I am, and it can wait."

"Are you certain? If it's vital, I don't have to rush off."

"Miss James is visiting later, so how about if we focus on that? We have plenty to contemplate for one afternoon."

"All right, but we'll make time tomorrow. I promise."

He continued on, and there was a lightness in his step that hadn't been there previously. But even as he pranced along, he was scolding himself.

His happiness was due to his reveling with Joanna. If he'd had any sense, he'd have found a thousand reasons to avoid her, but instead, she was coming to the manor at four, and he was giddy as a schoolboy.

He went to the foyer and was about to climb the stairs to his bedchamber when, from the landing up above, Roxanne said, "There you are! My maid notified me you were home early. May I flatter myself and claim it's because you missed me?"

He felt as if she'd dumped a bucket of cold water on him, and he forced a smile. "I was bored and restless in London, so I left."

She sauntered down, and as he watched her, his mind was awhirl over the miserable prospect of their pending engagement. Was he ready for it to be official or wasn't he?

In Joanna's presence, he suffered such delightful affection, and when he was with Roxanne, he suffered no heightened feelings at all. In fact, whenever he bumped into her, he was temporarily confused, as if he couldn't deduce why she was there.

Love and deep regard had no bearing on matrimony, but shouldn't there be a tiny bit of elevated sentiment? If there wasn't, was it wise to proceed?

He wished he had an older uncle with whom he could debate the issue. His closest chums were in the navy and away on their ships, so he couldn't confer with any of them. One of his good friends was Luke Watson who'd mustered out after his brother had died. He'd ascended to his family's title and had become Lord Barrett.

Jacob wondered if he shouldn't ride to Barrett and have Luke set him straight.

Or what about Caleb? A man who owned a gambling club had to have a shrewd assessment of human nature. Caleb might provide excellent advice that would send Jacob in the right direction.

He was illicitly dallying with an inappropriate girl, and it was skewing his perception. He wasn't the first dolt in history to immerse himself in such an unsuitable, but fulfilling fling, but it was spurring him to sever a perfectly rational betrothal. It was a betrothal his mother had arranged before she'd perished, so it seemed to carry more weight than it might have otherwise.

Roxanne had traveled from Italy to be his bride, so how could he ponder reneging? What did it say about his character? Why should the match be more imperative merely because it was organized by his deceased mother? What was his duty toward her? What was his duty toward Roxanne? What was best?

He had absolutely no idea, and he was incredibly flummoxed over how to resolve it.

She arrived at his side and took his arm. "I was about to have breakfast. Have you eaten?"

"I just finished."

"Will you tarry with me while I eat too? I'd like to hear about London. It's been ages since I was there."

He hid a grimace. "I have two interesting tidbits to share. Let me join you so I can tell you what they are."

She grinned, so he had to grin too, and they headed to the dining room where he would have to pretend to be a devoted fiancé.

⌇

MARGARET WAS DRESSED TO go down to supper, but her attire wasn't nearly as fancy as it had been on recent evenings.

For once, there were no guests coming. Roxanne had exhausted every person in a ten-mile radius who could round out a guest list, so it would be just Jacob, Roxanne, Kit, and Margaret. She didn't like Roxanne, and Roxanne and Kit didn't like each other, so meals with them were never pleasant. They bickered constantly and spewed innuendo Margaret didn't understand.

With her proposing to Sandy—and his accepting—she was happier than she'd ever been, but until he talked to Jacob to receive his blessing, she had to swallow down her secret. Sandy wanted to pick the moment when he would approach her brother, so she was nervous as a cat in a lightning storm.

She had no doubt Jacob would be amenable. He'd known and liked Sandy since they were children, and Sandy was the glue that cobbled the estate together. It definitely wasn't Kit who kept things running smoothly, but the delay was so difficult to endure! She wished Sandy would get on with it.

She wandered over to the window and stared down into the garden. It was dusk, and she could see across the park to the woods on the other side.

To her amusement, she noticed a couple snuggled in the shadows under a rose arbor, and she focused in, curious as to who was flirting. From how furtive they were being, she suspected the amorous pair shouldn't have snuck off.

When she recognized who it was, she gasped with dismay and muttered, "You idiot. You blithering, negligent idiot."

She watched in horror as Jacob dipped down and kissed Miss James. What was he thinking? What was he doing?

He wasn't free to seduce Joanna James—or any other woman for that matter. He was about to engage himself to Roxanne, and while Margaret wasn't keen to have him wed their cousin, it was a plan that had been in place for over a year.

That very instant, Roxanne was in her own bedchamber and dressing for supper too. Margaret wasn't sure of the view Roxanne had out her window, but she hoped to God it wasn't the same angle provided to Margaret.

She forced herself to observe until the ardent couple separated, then she whipped away, not anxious for Jacob to glance up and see her spying. Her pulse was pounding, her temper soaring, and she was brimming with regret too.

She didn't really know her brother all that well, but she liked to suppose he was different from their dastardly father. They'd repeatedly sworn they would never behave so despicably toward anyone. They'd learned too painfully how immoral conduct could devastate a family, but she was suddenly terribly afraid that he was a cad.

They'd just spent two hours with Miss James, where she'd regaled them with stories about her time on the deserted island after the shipwreck. Throughout the whole conversation, Margaret had concentrated on Miss James, so she hadn't bothered to note how Jacob was absorbing her information. Had he gazed at her like an obsessed swain?

Margaret dithered and debated. If he was fond of Miss James, was it any of Margaret's business? If his affection skewed his attitude about Roxanne, might it push him to cry off? Would Margaret care if the betrothal fell apart?

Miss James was gorgeous, smart, and fascinating. She had peculiar habits and intriguing talents, so it was easy to comprehend why Jacob would be charmed. But he couldn't have any honorable intentions. She had no parent to protect her, offer guidance, or warn her to be wary, and while she seemed too astute to be trapped in a romantic quagmire, shrewd females constantly landed themselves in trouble with men.

Margaret blew out a heavy breath, then exited her room. She marched down the rear stairs, and she got lucky, bumping into her brother as he was coming in from the garden.

"Is it time for supper already?" he asked. "Gad, I'm so late."

"We still have a few minutes. Could I talk to you? Alone?"

"Of course."

They tromped back up the stairs, and his bedchamber suite was closest, so she led him into the sitting room. He shut the door, as she went over to the table in the corner where his valet kept a stocked liquor tray. She poured them both a whiskey, and he took his glass from her. They clinked the rims together.

"Here is to Miss James," he said, "for painting such a splendid picture of Father. He's been denigrated so often in this house that I can't remember when any of us had a good word to say about him."

"Her comments were so interesting. I've always wanted to see Miss Carstairs on the stage to hear how she'd describe him, but this was even better."

"I agree."

He downed his liquor and refilled his glass, then he asked, "What did you need? Can we deal with it quickly? I have to change my clothes." He grinned. "Roxanne can't abide tardiness. She might rap my knuckles with a ruler."

Margaret sipped her drink more slowly, studying him, worrying about him. She was probably in no position to butt her nose in, but she was his sister, and there was no one else who'd dare.

They'd had little moral teaching in their life. Their father had died when they were children, and their mother had been a shrew who had liked to shout, hit, and throw things, so they'd practically raised themselves, having to figure out on their own how to be responsible adults.

"I have to discuss an awkward topic with you," she said. "Promise you won't get upset."

"I doubt I will. I don't have much of a temper. In that, I try to never act like Mother."

It was a paltry assurance, but she accepted it and forged ahead. "I was looking out my window a bit ago, and you were in the rose arbor with Miss James."

"Oh..."

"Would you like to clarify what that was about?"

"No."

"Are you flirting with her?"

"No," he said again.

"What should I take that to mean? You were kissing her, so has it progressed beyond flirting? Have you seduced her? Is that it?"

"No, I haven't seduced her. I ... I ..." He cut off his remark, appearing bewildered. "I can't explain what's happening. I ... ah ... like her. That's all."

She snorted with derision. "A man like you can't be friends with a girl like her. You're aware of that."

"I know."

"What does *she* believe is happening?"

"I haven't asked her."

"Shouldn't you—before this goes any farther? I can guarantee she assumes you're about to tender a commitment."

"She would never assume that. She's not like other females. She doesn't sit on pins and needles, wondering if a proposal is about to be voiced."

"If you've convinced yourself of that, then you're an idiot. All women are the same—when they're in love. Is she in love with you?"

"Gad, no."

"What about Roxanne?"

"What about her?"

His tone was caustic, as if it was out of bounds for Margaret to inquire, and her aggravation ignited. He was being deliberately obtuse, deliberately mocking, and she reminded herself to stay calm, to wade through the conversation without quarreling.

"Roxanne is expecting to marry you, and she's so eager that she's hoping to move up the wedding date to September."

"She told you that?"

"Yes."

"She shouldn't have. I'm not rushing the date."

Margaret frowned. "Have you decided not to wed her? Is it because of Miss James?"

He didn't reply, but glared mutinously, and she couldn't read his expression. Was he reneging? Was he still reflecting? Had he reached no conclusion? What?

"Mother arranged this match for you," she said, "and Roxanne traveled from Italy on your verbal agreement. At this stage of the game, wouldn't it be breach of promise?"

"I'm not about to cry off."

"Then what are you about to do? And don't lie to me. This is too important."

He shrugged and stepped away from her. They'd been huddled by the hearth, murmuring quietly, and he addressed her from across the room.

"My relationship with Joanna has spurred me to evaluate my intentions with regard to Roxanne."

"You're that fond of her?"

"It's not that I'm *fond* precisely. It's that—if I could grow so besotted—why would I marry Roxanne? Might it not be better if I remain a bachelor? I haven't answered that question."

"In the interim, you can't suppose it's appropriate to carry on an affair with Miss James. Not right under Roxanne's nose. The neighborhood is too small, and she'll find out. No bride should have to put up with such disrespect."

"You're not telling me what I haven't already considered."

"Will you marry Miss James instead of Roxanne? It's not that, is it? She's very pretty, and I like her very much, but she's so far beneath you."

"I understand that, and I'm *not* picking her over Roxanne."

"Are you certain about that? Your conduct is terrifying me. Evidently, you have quite a bit more of Father's blood flowing in your veins than I ever imagined."

"I'm nothing like Father," he vehemently claimed.

"Aren't you? I am sick at heart over this discovery."

"I met Miss James after I arrived home on my furlough. We simply have . . . a spark, I guess, and it's altered my view of Roxanne. I have no spark with her at all. It's dawned on me that I don't want a wife with whom I share no affection."

"Isn't it a little late to realize that?"

"Probably." He looked incredibly forlorn. "I have no idea how to proceed."

"First off, you must stop lurking in secluded arbors with Miss James. It's stirring your desire for her, so it can't be helping matters."

"No, it's not helping."

"I can't believe I'm suggesting this, but maybe you and Roxanne should take a trip together. Go to Bath or to London for a week or two. If you spent a private interval with her, it might reorder your assessment."

At the prospect, he actually shuddered. "I couldn't abide the notion of loafing in Bath with her. It's why I'm vacillating."

"I wish we had some competent adults to advise us. I'd like to confer with an older, wiser person who could yank you to your senses."

"If I was *yanked*, where would I end up? Are you encouraging me to wed Roxanne all of a sudden? I could have sworn you weren't keen on the match."

"My opinion about Roxanne is irrelevant. *You* made a commitment to her. I grasp that it's not official yet, but she deems it to be. I've always assumed you were an honorable man, and I can't accept that you'd treat her this way. And have you thought about the problem you're creating for Miss James?"

"What problem?"

"She's been here since she was a child. If you marry Roxanne, how could Miss James continue in residence? If she's your paramour—"

"She's *not* my paramour," he testily insisted.

"You can't guarantee that will be true in the future. If your liaison grows any hotter, she'll have to move away from Ralston once you have a bride in the manor. Could you force that conclusion on her? Could you ruin her life like that?"

"This will sound stupid, but I feel as if I have a destiny with her."

"What sort of . . . *destiny?*" She spat the word as if it were a curse.

"With her being a *Lost Girl*, it seems as if she and I were meant to cross paths." More wretchedly, he muttered, "It seems as if Father's ghost is hovering and urging me to involve myself."

"You're correct: It sounds very, very stupid. We barely knew Father, and he's not guiding your steps. Don't imbue this situation with justifications that don't exist. You're lusting after Miss James. You shouldn't ascribe a higher motive to it."

He whipped away and went over to the window to stare outside. She'd lit a fire to his temper, and she could practically see heat wafting off his rigid shoulders.

Ultimately, without glancing around, he said, "Could we consider this conversation finished? I have to dress for supper."

She threw up her hands. "How can we sit at the supper table with Roxanne and Kit while this contentious issue is floating between us?"

"We're British and we're Ralstons. We can keep a stiff upper lip through the entire meal. I'm sure of it."

He peered at her over his shoulder, and she scoffed with disgust. "So that's it? Our discussion is over? What about Miss James? Will you leave her alone? If you won't promise me, I'll be so afraid for her."

"Don't be absurd. I would never hurt her."

"Spoken like the scoundrel you appear to be. What about Roxanne? If you don't intend to engage yourself, how long will you dangle her on your hook? You don't appreciate how thoroughly she's wedged herself into the running of the manor. It's clear—whatever you're thinking—she's not on that same page. If you tossed her over, what would become of her?"

"I haven't thought that far ahead. For the moment, all I can focus on is that you've stuck a knife in the middle of my affection for Miss James."

"Someone should have. You're being an absolute idiot about her."

"You're making my relationship with her seem sordid and wrong, but it's not."

"I'm sorry then—for you *and* for her. I'm sorry for Roxanne too, and I don't even like her."

He chuckled miserably. "We can talk more later, but for now, I can't dwell on it."

They glared forever, then she sighed with defeat. "All right."

"You go downstairs. I'll follow you in a few minutes."

"Don't you dare mope up here. You can't abandon me to Kit and Roxanne. They fight like two gladiators in the ring, and I can't be their referee."

"I'll be there shortly. I swear."

She hesitated, then left, and as she marched away, she decided she had to have a humiliating chat with Miss James, and in fact, Miss James probably shouldn't ever visit the manor again. Margaret would have to be the one to tell her the awful news. How would she bear it?

Chapter
14

"JACOB AND I HAD a little chat before he left for town."

"And...?"

Margaret had just come in a rear door and was approaching Kit's office when she heard him talking to Sandy. She paused, eager to reveal her presence, but debating whether she should. She'd never been fond of Kit, and Kit and Sandy had the status of boss and employee.

She figured she should tiptoe away, but she hadn't spoken to Sandy since she'd proposed. After her quarrel with Jacob about Miss James, she was feeling extremely anxious, and she wanted their engagement to be announced. Sandy had claimed he would confer with Jacob when the time was *right*, but when would that be?

Her nerves were spent, and she couldn't bear much more delay.

As usual, Kit was complaining. "Evidently, we're repairing that stupid roof for Widow Barnes and her brats."

"Oh, good," Sandy replied.

"I could have sworn I told you we wouldn't waste the money or supplies. Jacob is all hot and bothered about it."

"Someone should be. Her husband died, serving the Ralston family. A new roof is the least of what she's owed."

"Would you like to explain how Jacob learned of the situation?"

"I mentioned it to him," Sandy admitted. "He asked me why you and I were arguing, and I wasn't about to lie."

"You know," Kit said, "I don't have to employ you, and Jacob's never even in England. If you antagonize me, you shouldn't assume he'll be around to protect you."

"You and I should discuss my future with him then. I'll track him down and schedule an appointment so we can debate the issue."

Margaret was kicking herself for listening, but she was bristling with offense too. The men of Sandy's family had managed the stables at Ralston Place for generations. She couldn't imagine the estate without them, and Kit was an ass.

She marched over and strutted in. Kit was seated at the desk, leaned back in his chair, his feet up. He was drinking a glass of liquor, even though it was the middle of the afternoon. Sandy was standing across from him, visibly bored, as if this was simply another spat in a lengthy line of them.

"Hello, Margaret." Kit exhibited no embarrassment. "Did you need something?"

"I have to borrow Sandy for a few minutes. May I?"

"Sandy is his own man." Kit's tone was very snide. "Far be it from me to tell him what he can and can't do."

She smiled at Sandy and said, "Can you help me?"

"I'm at your service," Sandy responded.

He joined her, but she didn't continue on immediately. She glared at Kit and said, "I've always thought you were an arrogant prig."

"And I've always thought you were a frivolous ninny. Your tenure in Egypt didn't seem to have mended that problem."

She ignored the jibe. "As long as I'm alive, Sandy will have his job here. You shouldn't ever think you could counter that decision."

"I'll keep that in mind."

He toasted her with his drink, and she was so irked by his insolent attitude that she nearly stormed over and smacked it out of his hand. She might have, but Sandy grabbed her elbow and dragged her away.

They hurried off, and they were silent as he guided her down the hall and up the stairs to an empty guest bedchamber. Once they shut the door, they giggled like naughty children.

"Ooh, I loathe him," she said. "I loathed him when I was a girl and he used to pull my hair and tease me about my clothes, and I loathe him even more now that he's an adult."

"Thank you for acting as my champion, but your intervention probably made matters worse for me."

"I don't believe he likes you."

"He never has. Even when we were youngsters, I was better at every endeavor. He's the type who bears a grudge."

"Is he always so awful to you?"

"I rarely see him, so our animosity doesn't flare very often. He mostly revels in London, so he's not ever home. For the moment, he's stuck in the country because Jacob is on furlough. He's trying to pretend he's actually in charge."

"The estate looks in fine shape to me, but then, I'm not much of a farmer."

He chuckled. "No, you never were."

"Your efforts keep things running smoothly, and everyone is aware of that fact. Except maybe my brother."

Sandy was too polite to comment. His answer was a simple shrug. "I can't gossip about him with you."

"Why? Because I'm his sister?"

"Of course because you're his sister, and Kit is like a member of your family. If a feud developed between us, it would put Jacob in a difficult position of having to take sides. I won't force him into that sort of predicament."

"What about Kit?"

"I'll stay out of his way. That's how I normally deal with him."

He kissed her soundly, and when they drew apart, they both sighed with gladness.

"I've been so busy," he said. "I haven't seen you anywhere."

"You haven't panicked, have you? We're still getting married?"

He didn't jump to assure her, but said, "I'm inviting you to supper after all. I'd like you to spend a few hours with us, so you have a clearer idea of how small our life is. I'm terribly afraid—after you view it up close—you won't like it."

"You are such a nuisance. I'm going to be your wife. You can't talk me out of it."

"I'm concerned that you haven't thought it through."

She rolled her eyes with exasperation. "Would you stop worrying?"

"I will bite my tongue—for now."

"I'd appreciate it, and I will absolutely come to supper. If I survive the experience, will you please speak to Jacob? I can't keep this a secret much longer. I'm about to bust."

He snorted with amusement. "Yes, if you survive supper, I will speak to Jacob. I promise, but have you pondered what we'll do if he refuses?"

For an instant, her heart squeezed with alarm, but she shook off her fear. Jacob wanted her to be happy, and she would be so happy with Sandy, so she assumed it would be easy to garner his blessing. Yet she'd just quarreled with him over his budding affection for Miss James. They'd discussed how inappropriate it was for him to dally with a person who was so far beneath him in class and station.

Would he deem Margaret's situation with Sandy to be the same?

Well, it *wasn't* the same. Margaret was a widow who'd obeyed her family and married the man they'd picked for her. She'd done her duty, but that era was over, and she would make her own choice. Sandy wasn't some stranger they barely knew. He was a valued employee, and she had always loved him.

Jacob wouldn't disappoint her. She wouldn't consider that he might.

"Jacob won't refuse," she staunchly insisted.

"From your lips to God's ear. Now then, I can't waste time with you. I have to return to work."

"You're so serious about your job."

"And *you* have never had a job, so you can't possibly comprehend the issues that plague me."

"Your life will be simpler after you're my husband."

He laughed. "You have never uttered a more ridiculous remark."

"Why is it ridiculous?"

"Because you are a spoiled brat, and you always have been. I will run myself ragged, satisfying your every whim."

She grinned. "Aren't I lucky then?"

"You will be, and don't you forget it." He swatted her on the rear. "Let's get out of here. I'll see you tonight. We eat at seven."

He went to the door, peeked out, and rushed away.

Very soon, perhaps by the very next day, she would be betrothed. She couldn't abide the delay of having the vicar call the banns. It would mean they couldn't wed for another month.

She'd have to have Jacob apply for a Special License so they could wed right away. Before the week was out, she would be Margaret Sanders rather than Margaret Howell. She would shed the despised surname and adopt Sandy's for her own.

She couldn't wait.

"Well, well, if it isn't Roxanne."

Kit sneered at her. He couldn't help it. He didn't like her, and they couldn't interact in a civil manner.

When Jacob's mother, Esther, had still been alive, she'd once asked Kit his opinion about Roxanne being Jacob's bride. Kit had practically choked, swallowing down the derogatory insults that had begged to spill out. He'd controlled himself enough to blandly explain why she'd be a very bad choice.

Esther hadn't mentioned the notion again, and he'd figured she'd listened to him and heeded his advice, so it had come as a shock when Roxanne had sauntered in, bent on matrimony. Matters had careened downhill ever since.

It was late in the afternoon, and they were in the village. She'd just exited a shop, and he'd nearly bumped into her.

He'd been going mad at the estate and had needed to escape. He'd argued with that pompous ass, Sandy, and Margaret had eavesdropped, then scolded him as if she were a princess and he a serf. The entire episode had left him so aggrieved that he'd snuck away, eager to drink himself silly in the local tavern.

But who should he stumble on immediately but Roxanne? Was there no safe place where he could be alone for a few bloody minutes?

"Are you following me, Kit?" she asked. "I swear, every time I turn around, you're standing there."

"Did you hear the news from London? Were they talking about it in the shop?"

"Why would these provincial dolts be babbling about London?"

"The whole kingdom will be buzzing about it shortly, and I guess we're peripherally attached."

"What happened?"

"You remember Libby Carstairs, don't you? The theater actress?"

"Isn't she one of the girls Jacob's father rescued on that island?"

"Yes, and it's being reported that she's Little Henrietta Pendleton."

The *Little Henrietta* saga had rocked the nation two decades earlier. Henrietta had been Lord Roland's baby daughter, and his deranged ex-wife had absconded with her. Though he'd searched for ages, he'd never found them. Ultimately, he'd accepted that Henrietta had to be dead, but her fate had remained a puzzle that intrigued the masses.

"Libby Carstairs is Henrietta?" Roxanne asked, and she scoffed. "Here's a tidbit you should realize about me. I couldn't care less about those stupid girls *and* they seem to be crawling out of the woodwork all of a sudden, starting with that fraudulent tart, Miss James."

"You don't think she's one of them? Why not? Jacob and Margaret were certainly persuaded."

"She's a conniver who scams fools out of their hard-earned money."

Kit smirked. "Miss James is very beautiful, so I detect a note of jealousy in your comment."

"I want her gone—to a spot far, far away. How much of a bribe must I fork over so you'll get rid of her for me?"

If Roxanne wanted Miss James to vanish, then Kit would like her to stay right where she was.

"Now, now," he said, "Jacob and Margaret are very fond of her. Why would I help you evict her?"

Across the street, a trio of girls walked by, and they had school books under their arms, as if class had just been dismissed. They were ten or so, laughing and chatting. Kit glanced over at them, and when Roxanne glanced over too, she blanched.

"See the one in the middle?" she asked him. "Her name is Clara. Miss James tells people Clara is her niece, but they're not related. Clara was delivered by Miss James's aunt. Prudence James?"

"Ah, yes, I knew her well."

"When Clara was born, her mother paid Prudence a substantial amount to make her disappear."

"That's a very touching account, Roxanne. Your point?"

"They came here—from Telford."

"Oh."

Telford was the town where Roxanne had grown up. It was where her family's estate had been located—before her father had gambled it away, then killed himself with vice and liquor. It was also where Kit had visited his own kin in the summers, where he and Roxanne had engaged in a quick, torrid affair.

She'd been too young to have the sense to avoid their misbehavior—and deep down, she was a slattern—so she'd wound up with child. She'd spent years running and forgetting that dark period.

"Take a good look at her, Kit," Roxanne said. "She is nine, almost ten. She was born in Telford. To a mother who couldn't and wouldn't raise her. The midwife was Pru James."

He assessed the girl, the white-blond hair, the coal-black eyes, the willowy figure. He felt as if he'd been transported back in time and was studying Roxanne when *she* was ten. Comprehension settled in, and he sucked in a sharp breath of astonishment.

"It occurs to me that you have finally grasped the problem," Roxanne said.

"I believe I see it clearly."

"I have asked Jacob to move up the wedding date, but he hasn't given me an answer. To my great horror, he's befriended Miss James—and Clara resides with her."

"I don't imagine this would be the moment to mention that there's gossip about you in London."

"There couldn't be. I carried on like a nun in Florence."

He snickered derisively. "You are such a bad liar. The rumor involves two lovers. And what were they doing?" He pretended to reflect, then said, "Oh, that's right. They were dueling over you. Would you like to explain the incident to me?"

"I've told you this before, and perhaps you should heed me: If this betrothal falls apart, I will drag you down with me. You'll lose your cozy job, income, and house. If Jacob ever cut you loose, who else would hire you? Are you willing to risk it?"

"I'm so sick of you threatening me."

"I'm not threatening you. I'm simply being very blatant about what I want."

"Which is what?"

"I want Jacob's ring on my finger as soon as possible, so I need you to urge him to speed matters along."

He scoffed. "You talk as if I have some control over him. We're not a pair of debutantes who wax on about our marital prospects."

"You have to find a way to influence him. You also have to persuade Miss James to leave the area. There is no reason for her to dawdle in this neighborhood. Can you think of any?"

"No, I can't think of a single one."

"Let me know when you've formulated a plan to be shed of her. I'll assist you however I can."

She stomped off and climbed in her carriage, while *he* peered down the street, watching the girl who was most likely his daughter as she strolled with her friends. He wished he'd scrutinized her face more meticulously. He'd like to recollect the details, but then, she lived on the estate.

No doubt he'd cross paths with her again before he chased her away.

"I WAS HOPING IT would be you. Come in, come in."

Joanna grabbed Jacob's wrist and pulled him into her cottage.

"I'm glad you're awake," he said.

"I was about to call it a night."

"Is Clara in bed?"

"Yes, she has school in the morning, so we have to be up early."

"Since it appears we're alone, I should give you a more personal greeting."

He drew her close and kissed her, and he reveled in the embrace.

"I'd scold you for being out on the roads so late," she said, "but you wouldn't listen."

"I was anxious to speak with you, and I couldn't get away until now."

She must have noted his despondency because she said, "What's wrong? Has something happened?"

"Why would you automatically assume something happened?"

"I wouldn't have to be clairvoyant to realize you're dejected. You're not enigmatic at all. You wear your heart on your sleeve."

He feigned mock offense. "I do not. I'm completely stoic and reserved."

"If you say so."

"I have a surprise for you."

"A good one or a bad one?"

"You don't ever read the London newspaper, do you?"

"Rarely, why?"

"There are some amazing articles today that will astound you. They're about Libby Carstairs."

Joanna frowned. "Is she all right?"

"I suppose that depends on your definition."

She led him over to the chairs by the hearth, and they sat down.

"Remember the *Little Henrietta* scandal?" he asked. "You would have been a baby when it occurred."

"Isn't she the nobleman's daughter who was kidnapped? I've heard people discuss it."

"Yes, and Lord Roland was the nobleman. He'd divorced his wife for madness and desertion, and they had a child together: Henrietta. His ex-wife stole her and fled England."

"The details are coming back to me."

"It seems that Libby Carstairs is Henrietta."

Joanna's jaw dropped. "What? No!"

"Her mother, who died in your shipwreck, was Lord Roland's ex-wife. When Miss Carstairs was rescued by my father, she didn't recall her true name or position, and apparently, her mother had filled her head with lies about who she really was."

"I'm stunned. How could she have learned about this?"

He handed her the copy of the paper he'd brought with him. "Here. Read for yourself."

She glanced at the first story and said, "Look at that! It was written by Mr. Periwinkle! He's the reporter who visited me."

"Did he mention Libby when he spoke with you?"

"Only that he would arrange the reunion. He certainly didn't breathe a word about her being Henrietta!"

They tarried quietly, and she perused the enthralling information. He watched her, cataloguing every expression that crossed her beautiful face. He could stare at her forever and never grow weary.

He recognized when she reached the most riveting story. Once news had spread about Miss Carstairs being Henrietta, Lord Roland had had her arrested for fraud.

"Libby is in jail!" Joanna fumed. "What is Lord Roland thinking? He ought to be celebrating, not having her imprisoned. With him publicly declaring her a liar, how will they ever bond as father and daughter?"

"I feel she's connected to you and me in a powerful way, so I was wondering if I shouldn't ride to London and post her bail. It doesn't say anyone has, and I hate to picture her languishing in a cell."

"Would you post her bail? And after she's released, if she doesn't have anywhere to stay, you could bring her here." She waved the paper at him. "May I keep this? I'd like to show it to Clara."

"Yes, of course you can keep it."

The fire in the hearth flared, illuminating her, and for just an instant, she was enshrouded in a golden halo of light. Then he blinked and the peculiar aura vanished.

She put the newspaper on the floor, then she turned to him and said, "I notice you didn't drag me up to my bedchamber the moment you walked in. I should likely thank you for your reticence, but I can't decide if I'm glad or not."

"I'm trying to mind my manners."

"You're so morose. I sense that you arrived with a purpose other than to give me the newspaper."

"I guess I have."

He couldn't force himself to start though, for when he did, he'd set in motion a series of events he didn't care to imagine. Yet how could he *not* proceed?

"Confide in me, Jacob. It can't be that hard."

She used his Christian name for what had to be the first time ever, and it imbued him with the fortitude he needed to begin.

"My sister and I talked about you."

"Why am I betting it wasn't a flattering conversation?"

"We both adore you."

"But . . . ?"

"She happened to glance out her window and saw us in the garden."

"You kissed me under the rose arbor. I warned you not to."

"I didn't listen."

"Now we're found out. What has she urged you to tell me?"

When she posed the question, she was totally serene, as if his answer didn't matter to her in the slightest. He felt as if his innards had been squashed in a vice. How could she be so blasé?

"We simply chatted about my intentions toward you."

"I hope you insisted you don't have any."

"It's not that I don't have intentions," he said. "It's that they wouldn't be honorable ones."

She chuckled. "Is Margaret worried that I'm praying for you to toss over your cousin and wed me instead?"

"Well . . . ah . . . yes. She believes I'm leading you on when I shouldn't be. I couldn't deny that she was correct."

"I will admit to suffering a few spurts of whimsy where I dreamed of us marrying, but I'm not an idiot. I'm not the sort of wife a man like you needs by his side."

The statement was exhaustively true, but he hated for it to be. She could never be the bride a man needed, but what about her being the bride a man *wanted*? He suspected he'd never have a dull day with her. She'd always surprise and delight him.

"You're pretending I haven't overstepped with you," he said, "but I've behaved badly and raised your expectations. Despite how you claim otherwise, I'm certain you've painted a hundred mental pictures of the future you envision with me."

The remark sounded incredibly arrogant, and she scoffed with derision. "I'm sure it will put a huge dent in your massive ego, but I've mentioned this before. The women in my family don't wed. Men are too much of a bother—as you're proving right now."

"You've told me that, but I've flirted with you outrageously, and I'm positive it's caused you to consider walking to the altar with me."

She tsked with exasperation. "You are so vain, but I like you anyway."

"I can't decide if that's an insult or a compliment."

"Will this be your last visit?"

"It has to be. I've let a relationship flare between us, but it's impossible."

"Yes, probably."

"I have many personal issues to address this summer. I can't have you distracting me and befuddling my thought processes."

"Are you befuddled? You seem quite lucid to me."

"Every second I'm away from you, I obsess constantly and wish we were together. I definitely view that as a distraction."

"Will you stay away from me? Is that your plan."

"It has to be."

"Are you predicting time and distance will snuff out your fascination?"

"Yes."

He'd mope and pine away, but for pity's sake! He was Miles and Esther Ralston's son. He was a navy captain who guided a ship around the globe. He would break off their friendship, and he wouldn't ponder her, wouldn't stop by, and in a few weeks, his bizarre attraction would wane.

"Would you notify your sister for me," she said, "that I won't be able to attend her anymore?"

"We don't have to be that dramatic. If she's feeling poorly, you should tend her."

"I can't. I'm finished nursing people at the manor."

A wave of alarm washed over him. What was he doing? Would he really never see her again?

"Margaret's condition has improved," he said, "but what if she suffers a relapse? What if she needs one of your tonics?"

"I sell them at the mercantile in the village. She can buy them there."

Her cool attitude was setting a spark to his temper. He was bereft, as if he was making every wrong choice, but she was so calm. They might have been discussing the weather.

He shook his head with disgust. He'd just bluntly informed her that he was severing their amour, and she'd agreed to his edict without argument or tears, so he could hardly complain that she wasn't weeping.

Then she said the very worst thing: "You'd better go."

Was there any reason to refuse? "Yes, I suppose I should."

"Please don't come again. This will hurt me for a bit, and I'll have to reconfigure my world without you in it."

It was a poignant declaration, and exactly the kind he'd been dying to hear from her, but as she uttered it, she was completely preoccupied, as if she'd already moved on to more important concerns.

"I won't pester you in the future," he said. "I swear."

"Thank you. I appreciate it." She scowled. "You won't force us to leave, will you? You won't kick us out? I've been fretting about that. Once you're married, it wouldn't be appropriate for me to remain here."

At the prospect of her departing, his heart actually seized in his chest. "No, don't be silly. You won't have to ever leave."

"That's good to know."

She stood and went to the door, and he dawdled on his chair, staring at the fire. A voice in his head was shouting, *Are you an idiot? Are you a fool? Don't do this! Not when you're so happy with her!*

But Margaret was correct: It was cruel and immoral to trifle with her.

He stood and walked to the door too. He couldn't bear to depart without kissing her goodbye, but when he would have tried, she stepped away, providing the distinct message that he shouldn't dare.

Mutt had been loafing by the hearth, and he said to the dog, "Will you accompany me?"

Apparently, the dog was over him too. He slunk down on his paws, indicating he'd rather not.

He trudged out without another word. After all, what was there to say?

As he climbed onto his horse, she closed her door, and he tarried for a minute or two, thinking she'd peek out the window, but she didn't. He sighed with regret, with remorse, then he yanked on the reins and trotted away without looking back.

❦

"THIS IS THE MOST fantastic story ever!" Clara gushed. "It's like a fairy-tale in a book."

"I thought you'd like it," Joanna said. "Grab your cloak and bonnet. We should be going."

They'd just had breakfast, but they'd delayed so Clara could read the articles in the newspaper. If they didn't hurry, she'd be late for school.

"Can I tell my classmates about it?" she asked.

"Yes, but they'll probably already have heard. I bet it's spreading like wildfire."

"You haven't seen Miss Carstairs since you were returned to England. Don't you miss her?"

"I've missed her every second since we were parted."

"I hate to imagine her being in jail."

"I doubt she'll be there for long. I'm sure someone will post her bail. She's England's darling, and everyone loves her—"

"Except Lord Roland!"

"Yes, except for him, so she won't languish."

Clara frowned. "Should we travel to London? Should *we* help her?"

"That is a splendid suggestion, but I have no idea how to post a person's bail after she's been arrested."

"When did Captain Ralston bring the newspaper?"

"Last night, after you were in bed."

"Drat! I didn't get to talk to him. Will he stop by today? He may have learned more details about Miss Carstairs."

"He won't be stopping by."

Clara must have noted a somber tone in her comment because she asked, "Today or ever?"

"Not ever again. It's why he called on me last night. He and I have become too cordial, but it isn't fitting."

"He kissed you!"

"Yes, and I shouldn't have let him. It was shameful for both of us to misbehave so flagrantly."

"I guess this means you won't be marrying him."

Joanna snorted. "It would *never* have happened, and it's a mystery to me why you were so certain."

"It might be impossible, but I can still wish for it."

"True, but as with many other of my secrets, please don't discuss my relationship with him. There are several people who would be upset about it, and we shouldn't make them angry."

They bundled up, then they went to the door and walked outside. As they started off, Clara said, "I don't understand adults. Why can't he be friends with you? Why is it so wrong?"

"We were a bit more than friends. That was the problem, and we couldn't solve it."

"Why is it a problem?" Clara mulishly asked. "You're pretty, nice, and smart. He'd be lucky to have you as his wife."

"I'll keep telling myself that."

Mutt came up and nuzzled her fingers, sensing her woe in a particularly potent way. She laid her palm on his head, having him absorb some of her anguish. He never minded. He was good at whisking it away from her.

The Captain had been so morose when he'd sat in her parlor. She didn't suppose he'd really wanted to end their liaison, and it was galling to discover that his sister had demanded it—and he'd immediately complied. Joanna had assumed Mrs. Howell liked her, that they'd established a bond, but what had she expected from someone who viewed herself as being so exalted?

If Joanna's awful father had wed her mother, she'd be perched at a very high level and able to snobbishly glare down on Mrs. Howell and Captain Ralston. They never realized it though, and she never mentioned it.

He'd actually had the temerity to lecture her about how she was growing too attached. He figured she was like the silly debutantes of his acquaintance, that she would simply die of heartbreak if he didn't marry her. But she was too tough to rue and regret, and she would never allow a man to make her feel inferior. She especially wouldn't allow Jacob Ralston to do it.

She was one of the three *Lost Girls* who, against all odds, had survived a shipwreck in the Caribbean when she was four. It had imbued her with a strength Captain Ralston had never previously encountered.

He thought he was marvelous and that she was fortunate he'd deigned to notice her. Well, the joke was on him! He was fortunate she'd noticed *him*. The women of her ancient line had taught her that conceit.

The males of the species sucked up too much energy from the females in their lives, and she didn't have the patience to put up with his pompous posturing.

She would give herself a week to mourn the loss of him. She would fondly reminisce over their furtive meetings, but she'd also remember that those meetings had been so clandestine he couldn't talk about them aloud. He deemed her to be that disreputable.

Yes, she'd recall him fondly, and she'd sigh whenever a memory surfaced, but she'd move on without glancing back. There wasn't a man in the world who could devastate her, and Captain Ralston definitely couldn't.

Mutt nudged her hand again, and he stared up at her. He appeared to be frowning, as if he knew she was lying to herself, but she forced a smile and continued on, as if she was leaving Jacob Ralston far behind.

Chapter 15

"WHY DON'T YOU MARRY her and get it over with?"

Jacob glared at Kit and asked, "Why would that ridiculous idea have occurred to you?"

Kit shrugged. "It was just a suggestion. There's no need to bite my head off."

"I won't have you conspiring with Roxanne to coerce me. I'm perfectly capable of picking the date for my wedding without any help from you."

They were in the library, having a brandy before they left to dress for supper. He was seated at the desk, and Kit was in the chair across. There were guests coming, but he was too grumpy to socialize with people he couldn't abide. He'd expected some liquor would calm his dour mood, but so far, it wasn't working.

"I'm not trying to aggravate you," Kit said, "but I don't see why you'd put it off for another year. I realize it was your mother's plan, but when did you ever listen to her on any topic?"

"Gad, Kit, let it rest, would you?"

"If the nuptial state was winging toward me, I'd hurry to the altar so I didn't have a chance to reconsider."

"Your opinion is noted."

Two weeks had passed since the awful night he'd visited Joanna, and he was grouchy as a wounded bear. He'd agreed with Margaret that he was conducting himself dishonorably, so he'd severed his connection with Joanna, but the decision felt so wrong.

In the meantime, he'd been dancing attendance on Roxanne, struggling to become better acquainted, but it was a losing proposition. They had nothing in common, and their stark differences were irritating him in a manner that was difficult to ignore.

If he staggered into the marriage, the disparities would grow more pronounced. They'd start to hate each other, and gradually, they'd live apart. It was how his parents had carried on, their dislike festering until his father vanished and never returned. They'd hardly known him and had to rely on the likes of Libby Carstairs to hear stories as to what he was like.

Jacob refused to immerse himself in such a debacle, so now what?

On top of his issues with the engagement, he'd received a preliminary report from his accounting firm in London. Huge amounts of money were missing, and Kit had been in charge for over a decade. Jacob wasn't yet ready to accuse anyone of stealing, most especially Kit.

He hoped it would boil down to a case of gross mismanagement, but what was worse? Embezzlement or incompetence?

He and Kit were on the edge of a monumental quarrel he was loathe to initiate. He'd have to level threats and demand improved behavior, but he was simply anxious for things to limp along as they always had, with people doing their jobs so Jacob didn't have to worry about what was happening when he was away.

"I have a question," Kit said, "but with you being so peevish, I'm not keen to pose it."

"Just ask me. Don't be an ass about it."

"I've been pondering the gamekeeper's cottage where Miss James resides."

"What about it?"

"I have a tenant who needs a new house, and she's never paid any rent. The place is so far from the village, and I felt it was worth it to have someone on the premises to look after it. What if I told her she had to move out? Would you mind?"

"Leave her alone."

"I'm regularly deluged with gossip that she's a charlatan who preys on the sick and the weak. Those who are more superstitious, who believe in the old legends, insist she's a witch. Should we be encouraging her to spread her nonsense around the neighborhood?"

"Who, precisely, is gossiping about her? Recently, Roxanne raised the same objections, so it sounds to me as if you're much too cozy with my fiancée."

"Why are you so angry with Roxanne? With each mention of her name, you fly off the handle."

His patience was exhausted for numerous reasons, but mainly, he kept imagining how he might renege on the betrothal. Then what? Her parents were deceased, her family's property and other assets sold a decade earlier when her father went bankrupt. If Jacob set her aside, what would she do?

She'd traveled to England on his promise to marry her. What kind of cad would he be if he backed out?

Kit continued his nagging. "And why are you so accommodating of Miss James? She couldn't survive without our charity. Has she cast a spell on you? She has that effect on men, you know."

"Oh, for pity's sake. I invited you to have a drink because I thought it would be a pleasant way to spend an hour. Why must you constantly annoy me?"

"Have I mentioned how grouchy you are lately? What's wrong? I can't utter a word without you jumping down my throat."

They might have erupted into a full-blown argument, but the butler poked his nose in and said, "Mr. Sanders is here, Captain. He's asking to speak with you privately."

"Sandy is here?" Jacob inquired. "Did he tell you what he wants?"

"No." The butler shot a caustic glare at Kit. "He didn't share his purpose with me. Are you available?"

In all the years since Jacob had inherited, he couldn't remember a single occasion that Sandy had sought an appointment, so it was probably important, but he was in no mood to chat with Sandy—or anybody else for that matter. He'd conversed with Kit, but he'd simply snapped and barked. Hopefully, Sandy would talk about a topic that didn't involve Roxanne or Jacob's skewed engagement.

"I'll see him," Jacob said. "Send him in."

The butler bowed himself out, and an oppressive silence descended. Then Kit asked, "Will you let me stay?"

"No." Jacob scoffed. "What part of *private* conversation didn't you understand?"

"If he has a complaint about me, he ought to disclose it to my face. I bet if I was sitting here, he wouldn't be so quick to tattle."

"Why would you automatically assume his comments will be about you? It's entirely possible he has a whole slew of subjects to discuss that don't include you at all."

"He went behind my back to whine about Widow Barnes's roof."

"He didn't go *behind* your back. I tracked him down on my own. I was grateful he told me the truth, rather than lying. In my view, a man should be allowed to be frank, and he shouldn't be punished for it."

"Bully for you, but this isn't your ship. He's *my* employee, and he works for me. You're never confronted by his insolence."

"I've always found him to be unfailingly polite."

"Of course he's polite to you! To me, he's a pompous, overbearing prick. I put up with him because he's skilled at his job, but where is the line to be drawn so I can recognize when he steps over it?"

Jacob sighed. This was the sort of problem he detested. On his ship, he was the ultimate ruler, and he had complete authority. He was judge, jury, and executioner. He could have a sailor flogged or hanged. He could lock him in the brig on bread and water rations.

No penalty was beyond him. At Ralston Place though, he was an absentee owner. He gave Kit the power to run things as he liked, so he comprehended Kit's pique over his usurping control.

He comprehended it, but that didn't mean Sandy couldn't voice an opinion. In fact, because of the report about the ledgers, he should speak to Sandy more often. He suspected he'd learn many details he definitely ought to discover.

"Sandy can have his meeting," Jacob said, "and if *you* are the topic, I'll apprise you immediately. We'll deal with any issue he raises."

Kit nearly offered a snide retort, but Sandy and the butler were approaching, so he couldn't. He downed his drink and headed out, exiting as Sandy arrived. They bristled, their mutual dislike clear. Sandy hesitated and didn't enter. With Kit being present, he was obviously having second thoughts about proceeding.

"I'm leaving," Kit told him, "but when you and the Captain are finished, you and I should have a long talk. Find me when you're through."

"It will have to be tomorrow morning," Sandy responded. "I'm having supper with my boys in a bit. I have to get home to them."

Kit flashed a glower at Jacob that seemed to say, *See how he sasses me?*

He whipped away and kept on, and Sandy hovered in the doorway. Even though Jacob waved him in, he said, "This probably isn't a good time. Not after Kit was just with you."

"Were you intending to confer about him?"

"No."

"Then we shouldn't be prevented from continuing."

Still, Sandy vacillated, and Jacob irritably said, "Come in, Sandy. Your indecision is infuriating. Stop it."

Sandy gnawed on his cheek and might have left, but he couldn't stomp away with any grace. He marched in, and Jacob was thinking that he'd hate to be Kit and have to constantly bump up against Sandy.

Sandy was competent, steady, and highly respected. Kit was rude, lazy, and disrespected. The two men were like oil and water, and their visible aversion was about to explode—as with so many other problems at the estate.

Suddenly, he was wondering if he shouldn't muster out of the navy. Should he retire? His friend, Luke Watson, had done it recently. How was Luke faring as a veteran rather than a sailor?

Or he could ride to London and question his half-brother, Caleb, who'd landed on his feet in a very lucrative way. Did he ever miss the navy? Did he ever wish he hadn't quit?

Sandy faced Jacob across the desk, and they suffered an awkward moment where Jacob couldn't figure out how to treat him. He shook himself out of his stupor and said, "I'm having a whiskey. Would you like one?"

"No, thank you. I have an important subject to address, and I shouldn't be imbibing of liquor when I do."

"Will you sit?" Jacob gestured to the chair Kit had vacated.

Sandy eased onto it, but he appeared so serious that Jacob's pulse raced with apprehension. Was he about to resign? If he did, it would simply be one more issue that had reached a boiling point.

"What is it you need?" Jacob asked, anxious to tamp down the tension. "You look so solemn. I hope it's nothing awful."

"It's not awful. I'm positive you're not expecting it though, and I'm concerned over how you'll view my request."

"Try me. Let's see what sort of reaction you get."

"That is what's worrying me. You're not in the best mood."

"I will admit I've been better."

"It might be wise for me to return later."

"The longer you delay, the more alarmed I become."

"It's not alarming. I don't deem it to be anyway. I'm here about Margaret."

Jacob scowled. "What about her? She's been in a low condition, but I'm not sure you and I should discuss it."

"It's not that. You were never around much as a boy, so I'm not certain how much you recollect of what occurred."

"It depends on the circumstance. With some incidents, I recall every detail. With others? Not so much."

"Were you aware that Margaret and I were good friends."

Jacob pondered, then said, "I guess I remember that."

"Did you ever notice we were *more* than friends?"

Jacob froze. "What do you mean?"

"When we were adolescents, we were very much in love."

Jacob chuckled—when he shouldn't have. "You were not."

"We were, and my relationship with her was the main reason your mother betrothed her to Mr. Howell. Mrs. Ralston was determined to yank her away so we couldn't behave foolishly."

"Are you claiming you'd have run away together?"

"Yes. We had it all planned out, but in the end, Margaret couldn't proceed. After how your sister, Pamela, had eloped, she decided she couldn't shame your mother. So . . . she married Mr. Howell."

"Why are you telling me this? After so many years have passed, perhaps it should simply fade away."

"Well, that's a bit tricky because I've never stopped loving your sister."

Jacob winced. "Don't confess to that."

"I have to. You should understand the strong feelings I've always possessed for her. When she wed Mr. Howell, I truly thought I'd die from heartbreak. My parents intervened and forced me to move on and heal. I wed a local girl, and I have my two sons."

"What are you saying, Sandy? Would you spit it out?"

"Margaret is a widow, and she did her duty to your family, and she paid dearly for it. I did my duty to mine as well, and my wife is deceased. I'm widowed too."

Finally, Jacob grasped where this was leading. "Could you halt right there? I'm terribly afraid of where you're going, and we shouldn't arrive there."

"I have to. Margaret and I are more devoted than we ever were when we were younger."

"You and Margaret have been pursuing an amour? Are you mad?"

"I don't like that we've been hiding it from you, and it should be out in the open. Margaret and I would like to marry, and I'm asking for your blessing."

"Oh, Sandy..."

Jacob felt as if he'd been punched in the gut. He'd been expecting Sandy to talk about the farm or the horses, about Kit or the estate's many problems. He hadn't expected declarations of love for his sister.

How was Jacob to respond? Sandy was staring in that calm, steady way he had, daring Jacob to be condescending, and it was exasperating to realize that Sandy knew him so well. There were so many snobbish, patronizing comments rolling around in Jacob's throat that he was practically choking on them.

"As I mentioned when I first began," Sandy said, "this isn't a subject you were anticipating, so I've shocked you. A thousand replies will have flooded into your mind as to why you should refuse my request, but I beg you to consider Margaret."

"You've discussed it with her?"

"Of course. She and I have been contemplating this since she was sixteen and I was eighteen. Back then, we bowed to family pressure and stepped away from the brink, but we're adults now. In the past, we behaved as was demanded of us, and we both wound up miserable. We're ready to choose our own path, but I told her we have to have your permission."

"Gad, you're putting me in an untenable position."

"Not really. Why would you care if she and I wed? You're rarely here, and she's been despondent for years. You've never been particularly close to her, so you can't appreciate how difficult those years have been."

The remark was galling. "I don't need a lecture from you about my relationship with Margaret."

"I'm not giving you one. I'm merely pointing out that this is what she wants. It's what she's always wanted, and it would make her so happy. Can't you find it in your heart to furnish her with the thing she's always desired? Your mother wouldn't, but how about you?"

It seemed as if Sandy had thrown down the gauntlet and challenged him to a duel. If they were fighting, it was definitely a low blow for Sandy to have dragged Jacob's mother into it. He didn't like to ever be compared to her.

As evenly as he could, he said, "Without ever having had the chance to confer about it with my mother, I can assure you there were many reasons she wouldn't have consented."

"I know. I'm not an idiot. I'm the hired help, and Margaret is a daughter of the manor. She's a Ralston, and I'm the stable manager. It's like a backward version of Cinderella."

"What would people think?" Jacob muttered before he could swallow the words.

"It doesn't matter what they'd think. She and I would like to live a quiet, contented life together. If there are neighbors who don't like it, why would it concern her or me?"

Jacob sat very still, struggling to figure out how to explain his rationale without sounding like a complete ass.

Two weeks earlier, Margaret had relentlessly chastised him for his flirtation with Joanna, so he'd broken it off. He'd been rude, abrupt, and callous about it too.

Every minute since, he'd been kicking himself. He'd nearly saddled up and ridden over a hundred times, but he'd constantly told himself that Margaret was correct. He had to save Joanna by leaving her alone.

Yet while Margaret had been so viciously haranguing at him, she'd been pursuing a secret engagement with their horse trainer!

It would have been humorous if he wasn't quite so angry.

His temper was flaring, and he was loathe to insult or offend, but honestly! Margaret couldn't have thoroughly pondered the ramifications.

The gossips would have a field day. Their relatives would have a fit. Acquaintances would shun them. The servants especially would be furious. There was no more bitter person than a servant who'd had one of their own up-jump to a higher spot he didn't deserve.

Underneath it all, there was Jacob's very British belief that every man should stay where he belonged. The men of Sandy's family had worked for the men of the Ralston family for generations. They didn't slip in a side door and abscond with the master's daughter.

It was a terrible attitude to have, but it underscored how he was guided by the rules of the society that had bred him. How could Sandy assume he'd be amenable? No doubt Margaret had egged him on, and in an odd way, he felt betrayed by her.

She'd placed Jacob in an impossible predicament, having sent Sandy to embarrass himself, so it seemed as if she was deliberately trying to make Jacob hurt her.

How were any of them to escape the morass unscathed? If he didn't allow them to forge ahead, Margaret would never forgive him, and he couldn't imagine how he'd interact with Sandy in the future. He might even quit and move away, but how could that help the situation?

He sighed, being forced into an agonizing choice, as if he were a king in the Old Testament. Unfortunately, he wasn't as wise as those ancient fellows. He had to open his mouth and speak, but despite what words emerged, he would humiliate Sandy and crush his sister.

Sandy was tired of waiting for a reply. "Well? Put me out of my misery, and tell me your opinion. Before you begin, let *me* admit that I have loved Margaret all my life and will love her until I draw my last breath. I hope that will count for something with you."

Jacob rippled with regret. "I'm sorry, but I can't agree to this. My parents would have been mortally opposed, and according to you, my mother already intervened once to stop it. I just can't give her to you."

"Why? Because you're so grand? Because you're Miles Ralston's son? Because you're a naval captain?" Sandy's tone was very snide. "I recognize how far you are above me, but I'm not asking to wed *you*. I'm asking to wed Margaret, and I wish you'd think about her rather than yourself."

"I need to talk to her about this."

"Why?" Sandy sneered. "Will you remind her of how lowly I am? How inappropriate a candidate to be her spouse? It will simply ignite a quarrel. You can't want that."

"I'll clarify my objections. I'm sure she'll understand."

"You've just emphasized how little you know about her."

"I know what kind of husband she should have, and we should end this conversation or we might utter comments we don't mean and can't retract."

"That's probably a good idea, but what now? I told her we had to obtain your permission. You've refused to provide it, so where does that leave us?"

"At the moment, I can't answer that question."

Sandy scoffed with disgust, then rose to his feet. "Just so you're aware, I could have eloped with her—without any warning. But I didn't because it would have driven an irreparable wedge between the two of you. The discord would have killed her, so I couldn't proceed. That's how much I care about her. What can you say? How much do *you* care?"

He whipped away and marched for the door.

"I feel awful about this," Jacob called to his retreating back.

"No, you don't."

"I hate that the world is like this. I wish it were different."

Sandy halted and glared. "Save your lies and justifications for your sister. I'm not gullible enough to swallow them."

He stormed out, and Jacob slumped down, sick at heart and filled with dread. How would he ever explain himself to Margaret?

⌒⌒⌒

"You bastard!"

As Margaret slammed into Jacob's bedchamber, she hurled the derogatory term for what had to be the first time ever. He was in his sitting room, over in the corner and pouring himself a drink.

She hadn't knocked, but had barged in, and she'd caught him dressing for supper, as if he'd blithely prance downstairs, and they'd have a cordial meal together. His hair was wet, his shirt off, and he had a towel draped over his shoulders.

"Hello, Margaret." He sighed with what sounded like remorse. "I take it you've spoken to Sandy."

"You pompous swine! You dog! You cur!"

"Would you calm down?"

"Why should I? I've been angry for twelve years, and every second of those years, I've had to bite down my fury. I'm finished bowing down to my Ralston relatives."

"I won't discuss this with you when you're shouting at me."

"Won't you?" she mockingly retorted. "You poor baby! You've behaved like a conceited, contemptible ass, and I'm calling you out for it. Oh, the horror!"

He downed his drink in a quick gulp, then smacked the glass down on the tray. His eyes sparked with ire. "You couldn't have bothered to apprise me of what was coming? You couldn't have given me a hint? Why send Sandy to plead your case? You had to realize I'd be opposed. Why would you put me in such a hideous position?"

"Why would you refuse him? I could have sworn you and I were finally becoming friends. I could have sworn you'd want me to be happy."

"Sandy could never make you happy."

"Ooh, you idiot! You say that to my face? He's the best man I know. Don't you dare belittle him!"

"I'm not maligning his character."

"Then what are you doing?"

"I'm just pointing out that disparate people shouldn't wed. It never works."

"Thank you for that stirring pot of wisdom, Brother, but here's a tiny morsel you obviously haven't considered: I was married—at my mother's command—to a dolt from my own rank and station, and it produced the most nauseating union ever contracted. I was constantly criticized for my flaws. I was repeatedly shamed and disrespected. I was ridiculed for being stupid, useless, and lazy. Once in a great while, I was even slapped around for my own good." She was delighted to see him wince. "Perhaps you could find me the same kind of despicable fiend to be my next spouse."

"You're deliberately failing to understand me. Sandy is a fine person, and I like him. I've *always* liked him, but he is an employee, which means he is totally inappropriate."

"According to who?"

"To Mother—who I'm told already declined to allow it. Why should I feel differently?"

"You never gave two figs for Mother's opinion on any topic, and she's dead! Why would you care what she thought a decade ago?"

"In this instance, she was correct, and if you'd climb down off your high-horse, you'd realize that *you* share the same view."

The comment stopped her in her tracks. "What are you talking about."

"Did you—or did you not—recently lecture me about my flirtation with Joanna James?"

"So ...?"

"You were quite adamant that I shouldn't involve myself with her because she was too far beneath me. And I was merely flirting! That's it. Imagine my surprise when I discover that you're not only flirting with the hired help, but you're eager to wed one of them!"

"Miss James was a bit of ... of ... *fluff* who enticed you when she shouldn't have. You were fascinated by her, so Father's wicked tendencies burst out. You would never have married her, no matter how disgracefully you acted. Don't pretend I was wrong about that."

He rolled his eyes, as if she was being hysterical. "Could we not hurl these repugnant accusations? I'm nothing like Father, and I won't listen to you insisting I am."

She ignored him and kept on. "You were trifling with Miss James, curing your boredom at her expense, and in the process, you were perfectly willing to imperil your betrothal. But *I* have been falling in love with Sandy all over again. In fact, I've never fallen *out* of love with him."

"Bully for you," he snottily said.

"We've known Sandy forever. He's loyal and dedicated, and he runs the place for you, but you've never figured that out. You pay Kit an exorbitant salary, but Sandy does all the work."

"That's starting to become clear to me."

"Sandy is the reason you have money in your purse, yet you scoff and claim he's worthless."

"I never said that!" he fumed.

"Didn't you? You strut around as if you and I are so magnificent, but you need to speak for yourself. Not me. I'm twenty-eight, and I've wound up a dispossessed widow who's barren and penniless, but Sandy is willing to wed me anyway. He's willing to supply me with a home and two boys to mother. What is my other option? Shall I never remarry? Shall I spend the rest of my life, wandering the halls in this bloody mansion with only Roxanne for company?"

"There will be other matrimonial choices." He was so ludicrous! "There will be other men—suitable men—who will be glad to have you."

"Suitable men!" she spat. "You actually presume there are men more *suitable* than Geoffrey Sanders?"

"You haven't been in England that long. Why don't you take an extended trip to London? I'll fund it for you. If you'd just socialize a bit, there's no telling who you might meet. Why must you declare Sandy to be your sole option?"

"Will you pay attention for once? Sandy is my great love, and you will not wreck this for me. Mother wrecked it in the past, but I'm not a trembling, terrified girl who can be bossed and threatened. I will not be treated that way ever again!"

She was next to a decorative table, and she smashed her fist down on it. It collapsed and crashed to the floor with a loud bang. They froze, stunned by her vehemence, then the door was flung open, and Roxanne raced in.

"Why are you shouting?" she asked. "What's happened?"

"Get out of here, Roxanne!" Margaret said.

Roxanne didn't listen and wasn't cowed. "I can hear you down in the front parlor. So can the servants. Both of you need to calm down."

Margaret's temper soared to an even hotter degree—if that was possible. "I am having a private discussion with my brother. It doesn't include you. Now go away!"

Roxanne simply turned to Jacob and asked, "What is your quarrel about?"

Jacob smirked scathingly. "Margaret wants to wed our stable manager, Geoffrey Sanders. He asked me for her hand, and I refused to give them my blessing. She's a tad ... *upset* about it."

"Of course you had to decline." Roxanne took Jacob's side immediately. "You couldn't have done anything else."

"Since she's a widow," Jacob continued, "she believes she should be able to marry whomever she pleases."

Roxanne clucked her tongue with offense. "Honestly, Margaret. Mr. Sanders is the hired help. You can't think we'd approve. You've been despondent, but I'm afraid your melancholia has disordered your mental capacities to the point where you're acting like a lunatic."

Margaret studied Roxanne, then she rudely gestured to her and said to her brother, "Is *she* the example of the type of stellar spouse you deem appropriate for us? We're such top-lofty people, aren't we? And she fits right in. Good luck in your own marriage. I'm sure it will bring you exactly what you deserve."

She stormed out, feeling as if she might explode into a thousand pieces that could never be put back together.

Chapter
16

Jacob knocked on Joanna's door. It was late, nearly midnight, but there was light emanating from the inside. He figured she was still awake.

He understood that he shouldn't be at her cottage, but after his brawl with Margaret, he hadn't been able to stay away. Once Margaret had stormed out of his bedchamber, he and Roxanne had gone downstairs and had tried to have a normal supper. A dozen guests had been invited, so he'd had to suffer through the meal and pretend there was no crisis occurring.

But the entire time, he'd been choking with rage. He never liked to fight with anyone, and he especially didn't like to fight with his sister. There had been too much of that sort of vitriol during their childhood. He was anxious to smooth over their quarrel, but with Sandy and Margaret both so angry, he couldn't imagine how he ever would.

The minute the socializing was over, and he could safely escape, he'd snuck away. He'd assumed he was simply riding the country lanes, wandering with no specific destination in mind, but when he'd found himself at Joanna's gate, he shouldn't have been surprised.

He was sick at heart and keen to talk to someone who could provide solid advice. He couldn't discuss the situation with Kit. His solution would be to fire Sandy. Roxanne was already demanding it, but Jacob couldn't envision terminating him. Apparently, Sandy had loved Margaret forever. How was that powerful sentiment an action that should bring about his firing? Yet what was the alternative?

He was at a loss as to how he should respond, and he was eager to forget about it for a few hours. Or maybe he'd like to be told that the circumstances weren't quite as dire as they seemed.

Joanna was the only person he could think of who might furnish any solace. She was kind and pragmatic, and she'd likely have insights he hadn't considered.

That's what he was telling himself anyway, but if he was being brutally honest, he'd have to admit that he was desperate to be with her. Since his last visit two weeks earlier, he'd been horridly adrift. If he could just wallow in her charming company for awhile, he was certain his condition would improve.

He knocked again, and he could sense her listening, hesitating, debating whether to answer. If she didn't, he couldn't predict how he'd behave. Would he kick his way in? He was that determined to speak to her.

Ultimately, she approached, and he breathed a sigh of relief. He wouldn't have to bluster in like a barbarian.

She opened the door and peered out, but she wasn't glad to see him, and she greeted him with, "You're like a bad penny. You keep showing up, no matter how I try to be rid of you."

"May I come in?"

"Why should I let you?"

"Must I state a reason?"

She studied him for an eternity, then scoffed with disgust. "I guess not."

He entered, and they faced each other like combatants on a battle-field. On the journey over, he hadn't pondered what he would say to her, and now that he'd arrived, he couldn't deduce what it should be. What did he want exactly?

Well, he wanted her to fix what was wrong, but she'd have to be a miracle worker to solve any of his problems.

Mutt was lying by the hearth, and he decided it might be easier to reconcile with the dog. He went over and patted the animal, but Mutt didn't rise or wag his tail. He flashed a definite glare that seemed to ask, *Where have you been?*

Jacob turned to her and said, "Is Clara home?"

"No. She slept in the village with her classmates. They're celebrating another birthday."

He warned himself not to be too excited about the fact that they were alone, and like a dunce, he asked, "How have you been?"

"Fine."

"I missed you."

She didn't reply in the same vein. She simply stared, looking impatient and irked.

"Why are you here?" she inquired. "It's obvious you're distraught, but I'm in no mood to soothe your woe. What is it you need?"

"I'd like to chat for a bit."

She bristled with exasperation. "This can't be how we carry on. From the first moment we met, you took advantage of my generous nature, but once our relationship became inconvenient for you, you ended it."

"I was awful to you. I realize that."

"I'm delighted to hear you admit it."

"I've never been very astute."

"That is the biggest understatement ever uttered in my presence."

He snickered. "If we keep conversing, I'm sure I'll spout something even more ridiculous."

"I was hurt when you severed our bond, but I convinced myself it was for the best. There is no benefit for me to be involved with you, so why are you bothering me? You can't flit in and out of my life, depending on your level of boredom. I have no idea why I opened the door to you."

It was clear she was about to toss him out. If he didn't hurry and offer a viable explanation for his appearance, he'd be evicted like the scoundrel he was. Margaret had accused him of harboring their Father's worst tendencies. Was she correct? Would he do any foul thing to a woman, despite the consequences she might suffer?

He was terribly afraid he might. Previously, he'd never believed he possessed unruly passions, but perhaps he did.

She was ready to throw him out, while he was over by the hearth, coaxing her dog to be friends again. Evidently, he needed to expend his energy on the human in the room.

He marched over to her, coming so close that the tips of his boots slipped under the hem of her skirt. She didn't step away, and he liked that about her. She wasn't impressed by him, wasn't cowed or awed.

"I shouldn't have told you we had to part," he said.

"Yes, you should have. It was the logical conclusion. This is a very small area, and there are no secrets."

"I don't want to avoid you. I can't."

"You are such a child, Jacob. A spoiled, coddled child. You demand that the world spin in your direction and that I should gleefully agree to let it. As you are posturing and informing me of what *you* intend to have happen, I should like to apprise you that I don't wish to continue on with our flirtation."

"Liar."

"You think you're very grand, and I concur. You are grand, but I'm quite grand myself—although the prospect never occurs to you. I can trace my ancestry back a thousand years on my mother's side. Can you?"

"No." He likely had a good shot at two hundred.

"And my father is an earl's son. He was a fourth son—and a libertine and spendthrift—so it's not much of a heritage to brag about, but you treat me as if *you* are the superior personage in our association. Well, Captain, it may be that *I* feel the same. I deserve every ounce of respect that is ever shown to me, and I won't tolerate snubs from anyone. Not even you."

She gave a pompous shake of her auburn hair, and it dawned on him that she was the most stunning female he'd ever met. She'd also just delivered an enormously thorough dressing-down. He'd never been so completely put in his place.

The Ralston name was famous throughout the land, producing a lengthy line of sailors who'd valiantly served the Crown for centuries. Women loved them. Fathers sought them out to be husbands for their daughters. Doxies begged to be their paramours.

Only Joanna James wasn't enthralled. Only Joanna James viewed herself as being above him in every way. She lived in a tiny, decrepit cottage and was so poor she wasn't required to pay rent. She brewed potions and supplied them to gullible ninnies like Margaret who needed someone to tell them how to be happier.

She had strange powers, and when no one was watching, she probably cast spells and practiced all sorts of heathen magic that would make any devout Christian ripple with alarm. Had she cast a spell on *him*? Was that why he was so captivated?

The universe had hurled her into his path, and no matter how he tried, he couldn't be shed of her. What was a healthy, red-blooded man supposed to do?

He pulled her into his arms and kissed her. For a second, she remained stiff as a board, acting as if she wasn't interested, but it was a very brief second. She couldn't resist, and she leapt into the fray with incredible enthusiasm.

It was impossible to ignore the sparks that ignited when they were together. She could pretend to be angry, but she wasn't. She was as insanely besotted as he was.

The embrace swiftly spiraled out of control, and he was eager to discover how wild it would grow. He yanked away and headed for the stairs, dragging her up behind him. With Clara gone, they didn't have to be quiet, didn't have to tiptoe.

They were giggling like lunatics who belonged in an asylum, and as they raced to perdition, he was struggling to deduce his purpose. It was dark and they were alone. They rushed into her bedroom and straight to the bed. He tumbled onto the mattress and drew her onto it with him, and he rolled them so he was stretched out atop her.

She didn't complain, didn't scold him or scoot away.

"I hate you," she suddenly said, erasing any confusion as to what she was thinking.

"No, you don't."

"You chase me relentlessly until I decide to like you. Then you break my heart and leave. Now, without any warning, you're back. I'm so incensed."

"You're glad I came. Admit it."

"No, I'm not. I'm disgusted with myself. I typically consider myself to be very strong-willed, but it's obvious I have no spine at all."

"You're mad about me," he said.

"I'm *mad* about something," she caustically retorted, "but I'm too much of a lady to confess what it is."

He chuckled. She was adept at soothing his low mood, at getting him to grin despite how glum he was.

He started kissing her again, and she joined in, but apparently, she was awash with fury. They sparred like brawlers intent on winning their skirmish. They bit and wrestled and scrapped, going on and on and on until he couldn't imagine where it would end.

They were so isolated. They might have been the last two people on Earth, and they could engage in any illicit behavior. Who would ever know?

He felt as if he was outside his body, observing as a stranger carried on precisely as he shouldn't. What was his plan with regard to her? If he kept on, they would wind up fornicating, which would be a horrendous disaster. But wasn't this the road they'd been traveling from the beginning?

He had a destiny with her. Why not let it unfold? Where might he be when it was over? He suspected it would be somewhere fascinating.

Or was that the lust talking? It probably was. If he didn't have her—and soon—he truly couldn't predict how he'd survive the debacle. A man could grow too amorous, and it wasn't healthy to ignore the amount of desire flowing in his veins. It had to be sated.

The interval became more ardent, as he caressed her in places he hadn't previously. His hands roamed over her thighs and bottom, her waist and chest. He massaged her breasts, playing with the nipples, being very rough and not worrying about her tender condition. It seemed as if they were in a war, and they would both be victors when it was over.

She was enjoying his ministrations, her oohs and aahs driving him to new heights of yearning. Gradually, he was unbuttoning her gown, pushing it off her shoulders. She wasn't wearing a corset, but a pretty chemise that had flowers embroidered on the border.

He tugged down the straps, baring her bosom, and she didn't exhibit a stitch of maidenly shyness. Not even when he abandoned her luscious mouth to suck on a nipple. She trembled with pleasure and held him even closer, urging him to feast.

All the while, he was easing the hem of her skirt up her legs, past her shins, her knees. He arrived at her drawers and discovered a lacy undergarment he wouldn't have expected on a woman as modest as he deemed her to be. It might have been a secret gift she'd been hiding just for him.

He slid his hand under the trim and found her woman's sheath. She was wet and ready for him, and as his lips tormented her breast, he dabbed at the special spot at the vee of her thighs where all her sensation was centered. She was a very physical creature, and with three flicks of his thumb, he sent her soaring to the heavens. She spiraled up and up, reached her peak, then tumbled down.

Again, she exhibited no shock or shyness, and her lack of inhibition had him wondering if she was really a virgin. She'd once insisted she was, but now, he wasn't sure he believed her.

He shifted onto his side, and she moved too so they were nose to nose. He couldn't fathom what thoughts were racing in her mind. She wasn't like any other female he'd ever encountered, so he wouldn't hazard a guess, but when she finally spoke, he laughed long and hard.

"I still hate you," she said.

"We've been through this. You don't hate me."

"I used to think I didn't detest anyone, but you've forced me to accept that I have a massive temper."

"It's all that red hair. It's impossible for you to be meek and calm."

She rolled away from him, her back snuggled to his front. He spooned himself to her, his much larger body cradling her much smaller one. She fit next to him perfectly, as if she'd been meant to lie just where she was and nowhere else.

He couldn't resist taking a firm thrust against her bottom, his phallus pressing into her in a manner that was completely unsatisfying.

"You desire me," she said.

"Is that a surprise to you?"

"No. I may be a maiden, but I'm not naïve about masculine drives. I'm a midwife, remember? I deliver babies, and I've had more than a few women tell me how they're created."

"I've figured that out about you."

"What dragged you here?" she asked. "You haven't told me."

"I was fighting with my sister."

"Shame on you."

"It left me very despondent."

"Are you feeling better?"

"Yes. I'm feeling better by the second."

"Why were you fighting with Mrs. Howell?"

It was on the tip of his tongue to confess it, but he couldn't unburden himself. He was loafing in her bed and trying to determine whether he should fornicate with her, so he could hardly admit that he was angry because Sandy and Margaret wanted to marry.

He and Margaret had quarreled over class and station, over what type of person was appropriate for them to love and lust after. He'd hurled plenty of harsh opinions at Margaret, but afterward, he'd rushed straight to Joanna's cottage. What did he actually believe about the issue? What did he truly know about how the world should work?

"Could we not talk about it?" he asked. "I'd rather not dredge it up. It will simply infuriate me."

"Just because you don't talk about it, the problem won't vanish."

"I realize that. I'm merely certain—if I give you a hint of what it was about—you'll scold me for being an idiot. Then *we* will quarrel too, and I've had enough fighting for one day."

"Poor, poor Captain Ralston." She snorted with amusement. "I don't feel sorry for you."

"You shouldn't. I'm a beast and a fiend. I can't deny it."

"I've started to recognize those traits in you."

They were quiet for a bit, and he said, "Do you think I'm like my father?"

"In what way?"

"He behaved hideously toward us. Toward my half-brothers, Caleb and Blake, and their mother too. Can that sort of immoral character be inherited?"

"No. We make our own choices. You can be whoever you wish to be."

"I'll keep telling myself that."

She reached a hand over her shoulder, and he clasped hold and kissed the center of her palm. She pulled it away, and he draped an arm across her waist and nestled her even closer.

With their ardor partially spent, the room was cooling. He tugged a blanket over them, sealing them in a cozy cocoon. He couldn't predict how many more times he'd be with her like this, and he was cataloguing every aspect of the precious moment so he'd never forget a single detail.

Yet he was exhausted, and if he wasn't careful, he'd doze off.

She was so still that he was sure she'd fallen asleep, but she drowsily asked, "Must you go home?"

"No, I don't have to."

"Would you stay the night? I'd like you to. It can be so lonely here by myself."

"I can stay," he murmured in reply. "I can stay as long as you want."

JOANNA STOOD BY THE window in her bedchamber, studying the sky outside. Dawn was just beginning to break.

Jacob was asleep in her bed, and she wasn't aghast to find him there. Her request that he tarry hadn't been a reckless impulse. She'd known he'd return to her cottage—sooner rather than later—so when he'd knocked on her door, she hadn't been surprised.

When he'd fled two weeks earlier, she'd been so hurt that she'd finally read her cards, which she tried to never do. For once, they'd actually supplied her with some clear answers. She and Jacob had a destiny, and until it was realized, he wouldn't leave her alone.

Before they'd dozed off, he'd asked her if she thought a man could inherit his father's low character. She'd placated him, claiming people had free will, but she didn't believe that at all. She believed a person's path was written down at birth in a grand book arranged by Fate. Everyone walked around as if they were tiny pieces on a chessboard.

Jacob Ralston was bound to her through their connection to his father. Joanna had begged the man to watch over her, and with that powerful entreaty hanging over their heads, how could she hope to keep herself separated from his son?

She'd spent hours studying him and figuring out what she was supposed to do for him—and for herself. She wasn't an innocent Miss, and she didn't view her body as shameful. She didn't view sexual play as wicked or wrong. No, she simply considered it to be normal human conduct that created babies.

Her female ancestors had rarely married, but they often had children. They fell in love and behaved as they shouldn't, so they moved frequently to hide their sins from fussy preachers and Puritanical neighbors.

She'd wondered what it would be like to engage in the marital act, and she wasn't worried about a child catching in her womb. There were secret herbs that could prevent it from occurring. They weren't always successful, but they usually were.

As he'd slumbered so deeply, he hadn't noticed when she'd climbed out of bed, when she'd tiptoed around and had taken off her clothes. She was dressed only in her robe, with nothing on underneath. She waited until the sun crested the eastern horizon, then she nodded out to the day.

This was what she wanted to have happen. This was what she picked for herself.

She shook the robe off her shoulders, hurried over, and slid under the blanket. Her hasty arrival roused him, and apparently, he'd forgotten where he was because he glanced about frantically. Then comprehension settled in, and he relaxed down.

He laid an arm across her waist and pulled her to him, and of course, she was naked.

"Joanna James!" There was a teasing gleam in his eye. "It appears to me that your clothes have vanished. What are you thinking?"

She leaned in and kissed him before she lost her nerve. He kissed her back with an incredible amount of enthusiasm, and his obvious eagerness quelled her doubts. It would be all right. She wouldn't contemplate a bad ending.

"I want to do this with you," she told him as their lips parted.

"Are you sure?"

"Yes."

"You might have given me some warning. You've shocked me so completely; we're lucky I didn't suffer an apoplexy."

"Heaven forbid."

"Why me though? You're offering a precious gift you should save for your husband."

"I don't intend to ever have a husband, remember?"

"You constantly tell me that, but I'm not convinced you really mean it."

"And I'm not a debutante. I'm not protecting my virtue so my father can sell me to the highest aristocratic bidder. I'm an adult woman who can make her own choices. I *choose* you to be the one."

He gazed at her fondly, but with enormous consternation too. She could practically see the wheels turning in his mind as he debated whether to oblige her. He was a lusty man who fervidly desired her, yet he was a gentleman too. According to the rules of his world, he wasn't allowed to ruin a young lady.

There were laws against it. The Church declared it a sin. Society deemed it a great moral outrage.

"Don't fret about it, Jacob," she murmured.

"How can I not?" he absurdly replied. "Once we're finished, I won't drop to my knee and beseech you to marry me."

She rolled her eyes. "I'm not expecting that."

"Yes, but what else can I bestow that you might consider valuable?"

"This isn't a situation where we must barter over terms. I merely want to learn what it's like. I've always been curious."

"Do you know what happens? Have you ever been apprised?"

"I've delivered many babies, so *yes,* I have a good picture of how they're created."

"Well, it's two very different things to be told verbally and to actually experience it."

"I understand that it is, and I'd like you to show me how it can be. Please?"

It was horrid of her to add on that entreaty, but it stoked his vanity. After all, how often did a woman beg to be ruined? It helped to persuade him.

Men were very simple creatures. They could be easily led and manipulated so a female could garner what she required from them. The trick was to figure out the best method.

Apparently, his cerebral wrangling was over. "You have to promise me you'll never be sorry."

"I'm the one who suggested this. Why would I be sorry?"

"You're seeking something from me that I'll never be able to furnish. I would hate for you to be disappointed after you accept that I can't supply what you're hoping."

"We should worry more about you than me. I'm clear as to what's transpiring, but I don't believe you have any idea."

He snorted with amusement. "Where you are concerned, I've never had any idea of what I'm doing."

She kissed him again. "Trust me, Jacob. This will make me very happy."

She stared at him, her gaze steady and firm, and he seemed to see what he was anxious to find. He shifted them so she was on her back and he was stretched out on top of her, and she sighed with delight.

There was such naughty joy to be gained by him pressing her down into the mattress, and she reminded herself to pay attention so she'd never forget a single detail.

Still though, he didn't move to begin, and she asked, "What's wrong?"

"I'm so nervous. I'd like this to be special for you, but I'm not certain I'm skilled enough."

"I disagree. You are a randy scoundrel who, I'm positive, has seduced women around the globe. It will be perfect."

He smirked at that, and he dipped in and initiated his own kiss. It was sultry and delicious and brimming with wicked temptation.

He started playing her anatomy as if it were an instrument, nibbling, touching, caressing. All the while, he was whispering endearments, complimenting her, telling her how much he treasured her, how glad he was that she was his. She decided to share his view of the encounter.

She was his, and he was hers, and in the quiet dawn of her small bedroom, the outside world could never intrude.

Their passion swiftly escalated, their hips flexing together in the ancient carnal rhythm lovers relished. He was sucking on her nipples, stroking her between her legs, and with scant effort, he brought on a wave of pleasure that sent her soaring to the heavens.

As she tumbled down, she was sputtering, laughing, scolding him for being such a dissolute cad. She was putty in his arms, and he could goad her to behave in any shocking way.

He eased onto his haunches and tugged off his shirt, giving her her first glimpse of his bare chest. It was broad and smooth, muscled from strenuous endeavor, and she laid her palms on his skin. He hissed with a sort of delectable agony, and she didn't suppose the ultimate event would last very long.

He'd desired her from the moment they'd met, and she'd never assuaged any of the lust she'd stirred in him. His restraint was just about gone.

"It's your final chance, Joanna," he said. "Are you still sure?"

She chuckled, but with exasperation. "Yes! You can't talk me out of this."

"It's just that, if we continue, I can't hold back. If you lose heart, I doubt I'll be able to stop."

"You shouldn't hold back or stop. You must show me how thrilling it can truly be."

"Gad, you'll be the death of me. I just know it."

That was all the conversation he could manage. He leapt into the fray again, and they raced toward a satisfying collision, but to her great frustration, her virginal tendencies kept trying to burst out. She'd catch herself quavering, debating whether she was really certain, and she'd have to physically force herself to relax.

She *wanted* this. She wanted him. She wasn't confused about that.

He was touching her all over, massaging her breasts, as down below, he was opening his trousers. He did everything gradually so she could adjust. There was no need to panic. He widened her thighs, his torso dropping between them, then his cock was placed where it was so desperate to be.

It felt very strange though, and while she comprehended every facet of the mechanics necessary to get the act accomplished, she was overwhelmed and out of her element. She always assumed she was so smart, but not about this.

He wedged in the tip, and she tensed instinctively, but he whispered, "Don't be afraid."

"I'm not."

"It will be over quickly."

"I don't wish it to be quick. I wish it to go on forever."

He laughed at the comment, and she told herself to remember how he looked right then: handsome and determined and overjoyed.

He nibbled on her nipples, and her passion rose again. As it crested, as she flew to the heavens, he flexed—once, twice—and he was fully impaled. She huffed out a soft breath, and he halted and peered down at her with such affection that tears surged into her eyes.

He appeared stricken. "You can't be sad."

"I'm not sad."

"What is it then? Does it hurt?"

She frowned, took stock. "No. I'm ... bewildered and happy."

"Wrap your arms around me. Hold me tight."

"Like this?"

"Yes, just like that."

He started to move his hips, pushing into her, then pulling out. He watched her the whole time, and she watched him too, relishing the sentiments that spread across his face.

His motions were very deliberate, very sure, and she required a few minutes to get the hang of it. When she did, she participated with as much vigor as she could muster, but her enthusiasm propelled him to the brink.

He muttered a curse, then delivered several deep thrusts, and spilled himself against her womb. He was very still, planted far inside her, then he groaned and collapsed onto her. His weight pressed her down, but he didn't feel heavy. He felt welcome and wonderful.

After a bit, he drew away, their bodies separating, and she winced, deciding her inner parts were more tender than she'd realized. For a day or two, she'd probably be sore, but she wouldn't mind. Whenever there was a twinge of pain, she would reflect on *why* she was sore. It was a sensation she would cherish.

"What did you think?" he asked. "And be honest."

"It's was lovely. Truly lovely."

He snorted. "I can't tell if you're lying or not."

He rolled onto his back to stare at the ceiling, with her snuggled to his chest. This was the best piece of it, she thought, this intimate interval afterward. All of it seemed worth it just so they could arrive at this point.

"I have no idea what to say to you now," he told her.

"What would be appropriate? Is there a script written somewhere that is supposed to provide guidance?"

"I wish there was. If I wasn't such a scoundrel, I'd be down on my knees, proposing marriage."

"Why? I have no desire to marry you."

He harrumphed at that. "You understand, don't you, that you have to be the only female in the kingdom who feels that way?"

"I hate to break this news to you, but you're not much of a catch."

"*I* am not?" He clucked his tongue. "I am Jacob Ralston, a renowned naval captain who's descended from a lengthy line of national heroes. Every woman in the world longs to be my bride. What's wrong with you?"

"You're always gone, so your wife would never see you. Your ship is your real bride. What kind of life would a woman have, being wed to you?"

"It's a vexing problem for every sailor."

"It's *not* a problem for any of you. It gives you the perfect excuse to pretend you're still bachelors."

He chuckled. "You could be right."

"I never had a family," she said. "When I was little, it was just me and my mother. Then, when I was returned to England, it was just me and Aunt Pru. Clara joined us later, almost by accident. That's the extent of my kin, and I've chafed at having such a small circle to call my own."

"If you had any notion of how crazed my mother used to be, or how bitterly I just quarreled with my sister, you wouldn't be so quick to assume *family* is so great."

"I'm also not interested in marriage because I'd never let a man boss me."

"No man would dare."

"But *if* I forged ahead, my husband would have to be madly in love with me. He'd have to remain by my side and not be gallivanting across the globe."

"You're a romantic at heart," he said.

"Isn't everyone?"

"Not me. I'm the most pragmatic person ever."

She laughed. He was so confused about who he was, about what he wanted, about where he'd end up.

They were silent awhile, then he glanced over to the window. The sun had fully risen, and he asked, "What time would you guess it is?"

"I can't imagine. Seven or so?"

"Could I tarry with you all day? Could we just not get out of bed?"

"No. You have to sneak out very soon. I have a maid who comes at nine to cook and clean. I can't have her find you here. She'd drop dead from shock. Then I have to traipse to the village at noon to meet Clara. She'll be home after that, and I especially can't have her find you here."

"It seems wrong for me to leave."

"Yes, but we probably shouldn't have done this. If you depart, we'll have a period to ponder our actions—for we definitely didn't ponder them earlier."

"I feel like a green boy, seduced against his will."

She laughed again. "As I remember it, you were quite willing. You didn't voice a word of complaint."

"What now?" He shifted them so they were facing each other. He looked younger than he was, and a tad puzzled. "How should we proceed?"

She was thinking that it was time to flee Ralston Place. She'd arrived at the estate when she was fourteen, so she'd had ten good years in her cottage in the woods.

But since he'd befriended her, she'd been accruing enemies. His sister refused to have Joanna socializing with him, and his fiancée would like her destroyed. There was the brewing danger too of Clara's parents being so close by.

Her biggest concern was her burgeoning affection for him. She was desperately fond, maybe even in love, and she had her mother's blood flowing in her veins. She was already calculating how she could pursue a furtive affair, but there was no such thing as a *furtive* affair. Reckless lovers were ultimately exposed.

She wouldn't carry on as her mother had, wouldn't grow overly attached to where she couldn't pull away to safety. If they continued with their physical mischief, she'd have to constantly take herbs so she didn't wind up with child, but they didn't always work.

She was living proof of that. She couldn't and wouldn't loaf at Ralston Place until her belly swelled and gossip spread about who the father was. She wouldn't humiliate herself like that.

She resided in such an isolated spot. She could pack her belongings and tiptoe away without anyone noticing. He'd simply visit one day, and she'd have vanished.

She wouldn't share any of her musings though because she wouldn't furnish him with a chance to prevent her. Instead, she said, "How should we proceed? Well, I was about to declare that this had to be our one and only dalliance, but I don't imagine it will be possible for us to keep away from each other."

"No, I can't stay away. You're like a disease in my blood, and I can't cure myself."

"We'll have to be careful. Clara can never suspect."

He shook his head with amazement and perhaps even a bit of alarm. "You are the strangest female. You're so blasé about this, while *I* am completely bewildered."

She rested a palm on his cheek. "I'm not blasé on the inside. I'm adept at hiding my feelings."

He kissed her, then he drew away and sat up, his back to her, his feet on the floor. She lounged on the bed behind him, naked and well-used, like a harem girl who'd serviced her master.

"I should get going," he said, but he didn't move.

"I miss you already."

She stroked a hand across his back, which imbued him with some energy. He stood and straightened his clothes, then he snorted miserably. "I deflowered you, and I was in such a hurry, I didn't even take off my boots. I can't deny it now. I'm a cad and a bounder."

"At our next assignation, I shall strip your garments away so I can inspect your delicious male body."

"You talk like an experienced courtesan."

"During birthings, I've heard women say things about men that would light your hair on fire."

"I'll bet you have."

"I'll send you a note when Clara will be away from home, but until I contact you, I wish you wouldn't stop by. I can't have her bond with you."

He scowled ferociously. "Why not? She's very sweet, and I like her."

"Her life is as small as mine, and she'd expect us to begin making plans. I won't raise her hopes."

"I suppose I can consent to that, but you must promise you'll summon me very soon. It can't be too far in the future."

"Clara will be at school on Monday, and I can tell the maid I don't need her. How about that?"

"Three days..." he murmured, then he scoffed. "I guess I'll survive—but no longer than that."

"No longer."

"Gad, I'm totally ensnared." He bent down and kissed her, then he asked, "Will you walk me out?"

"I'm too lazy and I'm not dressed."

"I can't bear to leave."

"I'll see you in three days. The hours will pass rapidly."

She wondered if she could pack and disappear that fast. If not, she could try to accomplish it the following week or the one after that. It wouldn't necessarily be a tragedy if she enjoyed another romp with him before she departed.

"You were so upset when you arrived last night," she said. "Have I soothed your woe?"

"Definitely."

"Why were you fighting with your sister?"

"I'm too embarrassed to admit it."

"Then I absolutely demand to be apprised."

His cheeks flushed with chagrin. "She wants to marry Sandy. He asked for her hand, but I wouldn't give them my blessing. They're furious, and I'm devastated."

"Why wouldn't you give them your blessing?"

She posed the question without considering, but the answer was obvious. He viewed Margaret as being too top-lofty to shackle herself to Sandy, and Joanna was in the same boat with him. He thought he was so accursedly superior.

"You can tell me about the quarrel some other time," she blithely said, as if she wasn't interested in his reply. "I won't wreck such a beautiful morning by discussing your family's problems. I really don't care about them."

At her saving him from having to clarify his reasoning, he looked relieved.

He offered a mock salute, spun on his heel, and left. She flopped down onto the pillow, listening as he tromped down the stairs, as he stopped to pet Mutt, as he opened and shut the door. She turned an ear toward the window, yearning to hear him ride away, but the woods were silent.

A few minutes later, Mutt strolled in and lay down on the floor by the bed.

"I'm in trouble," she told him.

He woofed in agreement.

She peered down at him. "What shall I do about it?"

He thumped his tail on the rug, but had no other response.

She flopped down again and began to cry.

While Jacob had still been with her, she'd pretended indifference over their dalliance, but she was more overwhelmed than she could ever explain. How was she to manage the raucous sentiment swirling inside her?

There were stories about how a virgin's ruination could be a disturbing event, and they were so exhaustingly true. She felt as if her veins had been scraped raw, her emotions pounded to the ground with huge clubs.

She was changed forever. *He* had changed her forever, and nothing would ever be the same.

Chapter

17

"I'M SO EXCITED!"

Caroline Grey turned to Libby Carstairs and hugged her. It was a spontaneous gesture that surprised them both.

They weren't demonstrative women. In light of the manner in which they'd been raised, they'd learned to keep their distance. They tamped down their emotions. They definitely didn't impulsively hug others.

They were standing in the foyer at Barrett Manor, the home of Libby's betrothed, Luke Watson. He was an earl and Barrett one of the finest mansions in England.

After several tumultuous weeks—where Libby had wound up in jail in London and Luke had had to bail her out—Libby was about to wed him. Massive wedding preparations were underway, so the house was in a frenzy. It was difficult to take a single step without having to dodge a servant, tradesman, or crate of nuptial supplies that had just been delivered.

"She'll come, won't she?" Libby asked.

"She can't refuse. When he talked to her previously, she was amenable. I refuse to accept she'd have changed her mind so fast."

"If she has, I'll have Luke send an army of guards to forcibly bring her to Barrett."

They were discussing two people: Howard Periwinkle and Joanna James.

Joanna was the third person in their notorious trio. Twenty years earlier, they'd been dubbed the *Lost Girls* of the Caribbean due to their being the sole survivors of their shipwreck. After the navy had returned them to England, they'd been wrenched apart and given to various relatives.

Libby had been claimed by a friend of her mother who'd pretended to be her uncle. The navy had believed him, but in reality, he'd been a convincing fraud and no kin to her at all. He'd groomed her for a life on the stage, and she'd constantly toured England as the Mystery Girl of the Caribbean.

He'd been sly and cunning, and he'd taught her to be tough and resilient, but to flaunt her attributes too. She was a flamboyant siren, and every man who laid eyes on her fell in love with her. Out of that endless stream of admirers, Luke Watson, Lord Barrett, was the lucky fellow who'd captured her heart.

As to Caroline, she'd been handed over to her Grandfather Walter who'd been a cruel, pious fiend. Under his roof, she'd lived a true Cinderella existence where she'd been maligned and scorned, her spirit crushed in every conceivable way.

She'd escaped that desperate period with her sanity and gentle nature intact, though she couldn't exactly explain how. She supposed it was a tribute to her deceased parents who'd been kind and happy.

She and Libby had never seen each other again until the prior week, and they still hadn't seen Joanna. They didn't know anything about her or her childhood, and they were on pins and needles, waiting to find out.

Mr. Periwinkle was a newspaper reporter who'd written the articles about Libby being Little Henrietta Pendleton, and because of his efforts, she and her father, Lord Roland, were finally together. If the stories hadn't been printed, her reconciliation with her father probably wouldn't have happened.

Periwinkle had tracked down Caroline in London and had conveyed her to Libby at Barrett. When they'd been marooned girls, she and Libby had viewed themselves as sisters, and during the years they'd been separated, they'd never stopped thinking they were. Their reunification was the perfect conclusion, and at the wedding, Caroline would be an honored guest who would sit in the front pew at the church.

They wanted Joanna to sit there too, and Mr. Periwinkle had just left to fetch her.

"If you ordered Luke to ride after Joanna," Caroline said, "would he?"

"Of course. He dotes on me. He can't help it."

Caroline chuckled. "Have you noticed how relentlessly you boss the poor man? You have him wrapped around your finger."

"If he's not willing to spoil me rotten, what would be the point of marrying?"

Libby studied Caroline as if it were a valid question.

Luke was an aristocrat from an ancient, powerful family. He was a retired naval captain and a hero of the Crown, and Libby was an actress and singer, but she deemed herself the superior person in the match. She'd grown up in the public eye, being adored and fawned over. Now, with her being named Little Henrietta too, she was an aristocrat's daughter herself.

People had always loved her, and the revelations about Henrietta had rendered her even more infamous. Luke was handsome and commanding, possessed of a fortune, title, and respected lineage, but next to Libby, he faded into the shadows. Yet he was so besotted that he didn't seem to care.

Libby's half-sister, Penny, bustled up and whisked her away. Penny was Lord Roland's other daughter from his second marriage, and she'd been reared to run a mansion like Barrett. Libby had no talent in that arena, so Penny was planning the wedding, as well as the days of celebration that would be held afterward.

As they strolled off, Caroline went in the other direction to locate her own fiancé, Caleb Ralston. He'd just slithered to Barrett from London or, perhaps, it was more accurate to admit that Luke had dragged him to the estate. When they'd still been in town, he and Caroline had quarreled dreadfully, and she'd pretty much decided they would never wind up together. There had been too many unsolvable issues dividing them.

But during their brief amour, she'd been seduced and ruined, and Luke was a stickler for the proprieties. He'd been adamant that Caleb propose to Caroline *and* that they wed right away. Caleb had complained the entire trip to Barrett, insisting Caroline was too angry to consider it, but Luke was a formidable character who had an annoying habit of getting his way.

So she and Caleb were tying the knot—sooner rather than later—and they intended a small, private event. They didn't wish to detract from Libby and Luke's grand fete. Most likely, they would have Luke obtain a Special License for them so they could proceed immediately, and she was wondering if they couldn't accomplish it just after Libby and Luke spoke their vows.

Why not? The church would be warmed up and the vicar in the nuptial spirit.

Caroline had never been the type to fuss over herself. She simply wanted to have Caleb's ring on her finger as swiftly as possible so he couldn't change his mind. He was a confirmed bachelor, and she couldn't be convinced that he'd ever willingly shackle himself.

In recent weeks, she'd staggered through so many wild escapades that her head was spinning. She'd severed her lengthy betrothal to her awful cousin, then had escaped from her horrid relatives and fled to London by herself. While there, she'd experienced nothing but calamities. Caleb had rescued her from them, but then, he'd promptly ruined her.

They'd fought and parted, then she'd been reunited with Libby. She'd learned she was a rich heiress and her male kin had been stealing from her for decades. *And* she was about to wed. It was too much to abide or absorb.

It took her forever to find Caleb. He was loafing on the verandah, sitting at a table and drinking a glass of wine. *He* had recently endured so much upheaval that his head was spinning too. He'd forced his brother, Blake, to marry her cousin, Janet. He'd saved Caroline's fortune from her despicable uncle. He'd had himself named trustee of her funds so he could protect them for her.

And, merely to make her ecstatically happy—and persuade her to marry him—he'd given his gambling club to his old guardian, Sybil Jones.

He'd served in the navy for years, and after he'd retired, he'd started the club to earn an income. It had been enormously lucrative and enormously debauched, but Caroline had viewed it as an atrocious venture. In order to win her, he'd blithely relinquished it. In the face of such a humbling act, how could she have refused to wed him?

He'd be plenty busy though and never bored. He was a veritable genius with money, and he would manage her vast trust accounts, which meant he would become her *kept* man—with her having all the wealth in the family and him having none. He was greatly humored over such a peculiar twist of fate.

"Where is Libby?" he asked as she approached. "You two are thick as thieves. You haven't been separated once since I first walked in the door."

She pulled up a chair, but he deemed her to be too far away from him. He drew her onto his lap, not caring if she was observed snuggled there.

"Her sister, Penny, pried her away from me," Caroline said. "She has to make some decisions about the wedding."

"She is the most stunning vixen I've ever encountered. The more I watch her, the more I understand the stories I've heard about her."

Libby was charismatic and magnetic, and people stopped and stared when she sauntered by, and Caroline said, "I wish I'd seen her on the stage."

"You may still have the chance. From Luke's many comments, it seems she's not quitting."

"An earl's wife? Appearing in theaters?"

"Luke swears he'll allow her to continue performing." Caleb leaned nearer and murmured, "If he attempted to prevent her, she'd tell him to stuff it. He'll never have any control over her."

"I can just envision the playbill that will be printed: *Libby Carstairs Tonight! Lady Barrett in Person! Little Henrietta Too!*"

"I'm glad you're somewhat normal," Caleb said. "If I had to deal with all that pomp and glamour, or repeatedly chase off a gaggle of male admirers, I'd stumble around in a jealous frenzy that would eventually kill me."

"I shall try to never be glamorous or fantastic."

"Praise the Lord. I like you just the way you are, so don't let any of her flamboyance rub off on you. Or her stubbornness."

"It's too late on the stubbornness," Caroline said. "I can be quite obstinate, remember?"

"Oh, yes, I remember."

He kissed her sweetly, and as their lips parted, they sighed with pleasure.

"Guess what?" she said.

"What?"

"Mr. Periwinkle has left to bring Joanna to Barrett."

"That's wonderful news. The three of you will finally be together. When should we expect her?"

"He promised to have her here for the wedding next week. Guess what else?"

"I'm almost afraid to ask. With you and Libby conspiring, it might be any insane thing."

"Joanna lives on an estate called Ralston Place. Isn't that your father's property?"

"My goodness, yes. It belongs to my half-brother, Jacob."

"I thought that was it."

"What is she doing there?" he asked.

"I have no idea. Mr. Periwinkle didn't share any of her history with me, and I'm not certain he's learned it. He chatted with her previously, but he was there to inquire about a reunion. I don't believe they had much of a conversation beyond that request."

"The eeriest shiver has raced down my spine. What are the odds that one of you *Lost Girls* would reside at Ralston?"

"I couldn't calculate a number that high. Do you suppose she knows Jacob?"

"If she's crossed paths with him," he said, "it would have to be a very recent acquaintance. I just saw him in London, and he claimed he hadn't met any of you."

"Mr. Periwinkle didn't describe her position at the estate, but isn't Jacob the grand and glorious lord of the manor?"

"Don't remind me."

Caleb's father and his estate were sore spots for him. When he was a boy growing up in Jamaica, he'd assumed he was Miles's heir, but ultimately, his mother's marriage had been ruled invalid in the law courts, so he'd been declared a bastard.

Jacob had inherited everything, while Caleb had received a few financial crumbs from Jacob's mother. In exchange, he didn't ever mention Miles's bigamy.

But Esther was deceased, and Jacob had reached out to Caleb, wanting to be friends. He'd even invited Caleb to a house party in

September. Caleb was debating whether to attend, but Caroline had already decided they were going. She simply hadn't informed him yet.

Her greatest dream had always been to be a member of a big, happy family. If Jacob was willing to have them become members of his, she was eager to have it happen.

"Is it possible my father's ghost is haunting us?" he asked. "I keep feeling him hovering over me."

She smiled. "I like to think so. He's been my hero my whole life, and it would please me to picture him guiding our steps from Heaven to guarantee I met you."

"In light of how he betrayed my mother, I doubt he's looking down from Heaven. If he's anywhere, it's probably in a locale quite a bit lower and hotter than that."

"I refuse to accept it. In my view, he's in Heaven."

"Maybe he's trying to wipe away his earthly sins by bringing us together."

"Let's imagine exactly that."

***

"Well?"

Roxanne glared at the kitchen boy she'd had spy on Jacob. It was early morning, and they were huddled in her bedchamber. The door was closed to bar any eavesdroppers.

After the supper party had ended the prior evening, he'd snuck away again. She'd waited hours for him to come back, and when he didn't, it was obvious she had to take action.

Her temper was flaring, and she had to calm down so she didn't initiate responses she'd regret later on. Jacob wouldn't allow himself to be scolded, and after his fight with Margaret, he wouldn't be in any mood to quarrel.

Roxanne had to strategize and handle the debacle in a manner that would deliver the conclusion she required.

She figured she knew where he'd gone, and before the sun was up, she'd sent the boy to Miss James's cottage. He'd just returned.

"I went there as you commanded," the boy said.

"And . . . ?"

The child looked a tad ill. "I'm not sure I ought to tattle, Miss Ralston. The Captain is my master, and it can't be proper."

She slipped him a coin. "In most cases, it wouldn't be, but I will be his wife very soon, so I'll be mistress here. That means it's perfectly appropriate for you to obey me." He was mulishly silent, and she growled with frustration. "For pity's sake. I won't tell him that you helped me—if that's what is worrying you."

"Could I talk to the butler first? He could advise me."

She gnawed on her cheek, breathing deep so she didn't slap him. "How about this? I'll simply ask you a few questions. You can nod or shake your head. You won't actually be speaking aloud, so you're not really confessing anything."

He pondered her suggestion, then shrugged. "I guess that would work."

"Was the Captain there?"

A nod.

"Is he still there?"

A shake of the head.

"Was the sun up in the sky when he left?"

Another nod.

"Did you see Miss James?"

A shake of the head. "The cottage was dark. There wasn't a candle or lamp burning."

"As he mounted his horse, was he smiling?"

A vigorous nod.

Her blood boiled, and she grabbed his ear and twisted it until he winced in pain. "I won't admit to anyone that we had this conversation, but you'd better not either. If I hear you've gossiped about it, I'll have you whipped, then fired."

"I won't say a word. I swear."

"Good. I believe we understand each other. You're excused."

He ran out as if she'd set him on fire. For several fraught minutes, she was frozen in place, then she went to the window and stared across the park to the woods, wishing she had magical eyes so she could peer all the way to Miss James's hovel.

Roxanne was a sophisticated, worldly woman, and she wasn't naïve. She knew men had affairs with pretty girls. She knew that they took vows to remain faithful, but they weren't sincerely voiced. She fully expected Jacob to stray too, but . . .

She didn't have to tolerate such a blatant flaunting of his misdeeds. She didn't have to tolerate his sneaking out of the manor in the middle of the night. It was the very limit of what she could abide.

She wanted to put her foot down, but didn't feel that she could. The engagement wasn't official. What if she demanded he split with Miss James, and he split with Roxanne instead? What if he was that besotted? From how ridiculously he was acting, it was a definite concern.

He wouldn't like Roxanne interfering in his amour. He wouldn't think a dalliance was any of her business. But honestly!

Clearly, it was time for Miss James to vanish, and Roxanne had ordered Kit to deal with the problem. So far, Kit had ignored it, but they couldn't continue to dither. Miss James had to go—and her niece had to depart with her.

And as to Jacob?

Roxanne had to devise the best method to rectify the situation. Why didn't he recognize how he was embarrassing her? Then again, he was a Ralston male, and they were extremely obtuse. Perhaps he'd never been told there were rules about an illicit liaison, the most pertinent one being that you hid it from your wife.

How could she explain that fact to him without raising his ire? There had to be a means to accomplish it, and she'd deduce what it was. Yet she didn't dare bump into him until she'd carefully rehearsed what she was determined to impart. In that sort of discussion, there couldn't be any mistakes.

Chapter

18

"COULD I SPEAK WITH you?"

As Roxanne waylaid Jacob in the hall, he could barely tamp down a wince.

He was back at the manor, bathed and dressed for the day, and bound for the dining room to enjoy a late breakfast.

Roxanne was standing in the doorway to her bedchamber, and she appeared to have been watching for him, which was aggravating. He reminded himself to remember her influential position in the household and to not be so judgmental about how she wielded her power.

He had let her assume control. He could have reined in her usurpation of authority, but he'd always been content to have others run the estate for him. He'd squandered the chance to complain.

He'd agreed to engage himself to her when he shouldn't have, but if he cried off, he'd probably have to start supporting her financially. She'd traveled to England on the promise that she'd have security as his wife. If he withdrew that security, hadn't he incurred a fiscal obligation?

Then again, she seemed to have plenty of money of her own. Might she have? It was the sort of tidbit his mother should have unraveled during the nuptial negotiations, but if Esther had dug into it, she'd never shared any of the information with him.

Roxanne dressed like a princess. Was that because she was flush with income from some unknown source? Or had she purchased a wardrobe on credit, with the expectation that he would pay her bills after she was his bride? If that was what had occurred, how would he handle the situation? Would their first quarrel be a fight over money and how she was frittering it away?

It was an issue a bachelor never considered, and the quagmire it presented was exhausting.

"I'm headed down to breakfast"—he forced a smile—"and I'm starving. We can chat, but I hope I can keep a civil tongue in my mouth. I'm cranky when I'm hungry."

She waved him into her sitting room, and she gestured to a table by the window.

"I realize you haven't eaten," she said, "so I had a tray delivered. It should tide you over for a few minutes."

He saw a pot of tea and a tray of muffins, and he swallowed down a sigh. Evidently, she intended a protracted conversation. Was he about to be scolded for an infraction? If so, it would be audacious conduct on her part, but he had no idea how to avoid the discussion. He went over and pulled out a chair.

She joined him, and she played hostess, pouring his tea and buttering a muffin. She shoved a plate at him, and he tried to begin, but the moment was incredibly awkward. She was studying his every move, and an oppressive silence festered. Eventually, it became too overwhelming.

He put down his knife and asked, "What's wrong?"

She was a steely female, and she said, "I've never been one to beat around the bush, so I'm just going to bluntly inquire about what it is I wish to learn."

"Good. I hate dithering myself, and we'll get along much better if we deal with problems straight-on."

"I shall pray you mean that."

He scowled. "Of course I do. Please explain what's vexing you. Have I upset you? If so—without even being aware of my transgression—I apologize."

"I've been debating for hours whether to raise this topic. I had told myself to ignore it, but I can't. If we don't address it, I'm not sure what will happen between us."

"I can't bear to suppose you've been fretting. What is it?"

She took a deep breath, slowly released it, then said, "I know you're besotted with Joanna James."

He froze, his mind whirring as he struggled to choose a response. Should he deny it? Should he lie? Should he placate her and claim she was being silly?

"Why would you think so?"

"I've noticed your budding attraction for some weeks now, and you spent the night at her cottage."

"You were spying on me?"

It was a stupid reply, and it slipped out without warning.

She didn't admit she'd been spying. She simply stared, her expression unreadable. His cheeks heated with chagrin, proving his guilt. Never in his wildest dreams had he imagined himself immersed in such a hideous encounter. From the instant he'd met Joanna, he'd understood that he was behaving contemptibly toward Roxanne, but he hadn't been able to stop.

"I grasp that your private life is your own business," she said, "but you are acting outrageously and right before my very eyes. I ought to pretend I haven't observed your antics, but in light of your father's treachery with your mother, I can't help but be alarmed."

Jacob was always incensed when his father was yanked into a discussion, and his first impulse was to lash out verbally, but she was trying to have a sane dialogue, and it would be petty to chastise her.

"You don't need to be alarmed," he half-heartedly stated.

"It's easy for you to feel that way. It's a tad more difficult for me. Your liaison with her seems to have spiraled to a dangerous level, and I'm not certain where it leaves me. You just arrived home from the navy, yet you're fully enmeshed in an amour—while I am living with you and planning our betrothal party."

"It's not an amour," he said.

"What is it then? You're so fascinated that you'll sneak out of the manor in the middle of the night to be with her."

His cheeks grew even hotter. "I'm speechless and have no defense."

"Once we're married, what is your plan with regard to her? This can't continue after I'm your wife. I could never tolerate such blatant disrespect."

"I can't give you an answer, except to say that I'm very embarrassed." It was a paltry offering, but he couldn't devise any other remark that might be relevant.

"Fine, you're embarrassed. Are we still proceeding with the engagement? Or should I pack my bags and depart? Is that what you'd like to have transpire?"

She'd furnished the perfect opening to sever the engagement, but he couldn't force out the cruel words. "No, I don't want that."

"Then what do you want?"

The question hung in the air between them. If he could pick any path in the world, he would alter himself into two men. One man would stagger forward with his very tedious betrothal to his cousin and the other would sinfully frolic with Joanna James.

After an excruciating silence, she said, "I should have bitten my tongue, but you're behaving despicably, and I'm at a loss as to how I should deal with it. Can you advise me?"

"I've been very discreet," he idiotically claimed.

"No, you haven't. *I* know about it, and my opinion is the only one that matters."

"I'm sorry. I'm bewildered over how to have a conversation like this. I'm being an ass."

"I traveled from Italy to be your bride. I had a grand life there. The weather alone was reason to tarry, but I abandoned it all. For you."

"I'm grateful."

"Are you?" She scoffed with offense. "It doesn't appear that you're interested in marrying me—if you ever were. Perhaps you've been a bachelor for too many years. Is that it? Be frank with me."

He blew out a heavy breath. "I can't decide what's best."

"I've never assumed you'd fall in love with me, but I can't wed you when you're in love with someone else. It's a recipe for disaster."

"I'm not in love with Miss James."

Thankfully, she didn't call him a liar. She simply said, "I'm not a naïve woman, and I expected you to have affairs."

"I hate to hear it. I'd like to suppose I'm a better man than you've envisioned me to be."

"I think I should go to London for a bit while you figure out your mental position."

"You don't have to go to London."

She shot such a vicious glare that she could have stabbed him with it. "If I remain here, will you promise you won't dally with her again? Will you truthfully promise?"

He was back where he'd been during his quarrel with Margaret. He'd told his sister he would break off his flirtation with Joanna, and he had—for two weeks. He was treating Roxanne so badly, but he couldn't imagine never seeing Joanna again. He couldn't promise because, as he'd proved, he was incapable of staying away from her.

Why was that exactly? Was he in love with her? Roxanne had leveled the accusation, and he'd denied it, but he allowed the prospect to roll around in his mind. He'd never been *in love*, so he couldn't guess how it would feel. If he'd been pressed to state his view on it, he'd have vehemently insisted there was no such emotion.

But if he was that deeply attached to Joanna, how could he and Roxanne trudge forward together? She wasn't even his wife yet, and he'd already betrayed her.

He was stunned to have changed into such a randy, unrestrained rogue. What had come over him? And how could he return to being the steady fellow he'd been before he'd met Joanna James?

"I will dawdle until Monday," she said, "so you can reflect on our future. If you can't give me an answer about her then—or if you won't—I'll head to London for a month so you can sort it out."

"That sounds fair."

"If, in the end, you declare that you're still willing to marry me, Miss James can't continue to reside in the neighborhood. We'd have to move her far away from here, and you could never be apprised as to where that spot was located. You understand that, don't you? I'm convinced you haven't fully considered the consequences of your actions or the steps that will be required to repair this."

He nearly blanched at the notion of Joanna departing, but he managed to calm down. He'd never deemed himself a fool, but maybe he was, and he found himself being very impressed with Roxanne. She'd been brave to raise the difficult subject, to put her foot down with him, but that didn't render any of it easier to bear.

"That's all I had to say," she told him.

He let out a miserable laugh. "It was plenty."

"There is another matter for you to address, but on a different topic." She looked cool and collected, as if she hadn't been discomposed in the slightest by their discussion. "You're probably in no mood to be confronted with this, but Margaret and Sandy have vanished. His sons too."

"What do you mean?"

"A maid mentioned earlier that Margaret hadn't slept in her bed, and evidently, no one's seen her since she fought with you yesterday."

"Uh-oh."

"And a stable boy knocked on Kit's door this morning, wondering if he knew where Sandy was. They had a chore he was to supervise, but he never showed up, which was highly unusual. Kit checked on him at his house, but it's empty."

"Do you think they simply went somewhere? Or might they have . . . eloped?"

His fury sparked. If they had, he'd wring their bloody necks! Starting with his sister! He'd refused their request to wed. Had they ignored him? Had he no authority in his own home?

"I have no idea what it indicates," Roxanne stated. "I'm merely passing on the information that's been presented to me. Now then, if you'll excuse me? This is my bedchamber, and I don't care to have you in it. I shall lock myself away as much as I can until Monday when decisions have to be made."

"You don't have to hide yourself away. We're adults, aren't we? We're cousins? We're friends?"

"I don't *have* to hide. I want to."

She stared him down so scathingly that he felt petty and ridiculous. He sighed with regret, then stood and left.

"I THOUGHT WE'D FINALLY visit Bath." Joanna smiled at Clara and said, "Would you like that?"

"I'd miss my classmates," Clara said. "How long would we stay?"

Forever? Joanna had to swallow down the word.

Clara loved her school, her teacher, and her fellow students, and she would be distressed if they weren't coming back. Joanna couldn't figure out how to explain the situation in a way that wouldn't sound alarming.

If Clara was apprised that they were fleeing, she wouldn't be able to keep it a secret, but Joanna's plan was to quietly vanish. If she didn't, she truly believed Jacob would track her down and demand she return. If gossip spread as to where she was, she'd spend the rest of her days, peering out the window, hoping he'd be riding up the road to fetch her away. She couldn't and wouldn't carry on like that.

She also couldn't ever have Roxanne Ralston or Kit Boswell learn where Clara had gone, and she couldn't fathom why her Aunt Pru had moved them to a spot that would put Clara in such danger. Then again, when Pru had taken custody of Clara, Miss Ralston had abandoned her daughter and sailed to Italy to conceal her disgrace.

Who could have guessed she'd bluster to the location where Clara was residing too?

Had Miss Ralston ever notified Kit Boswell he'd sired Clara? Was pompous, pretentious Mr. Boswell aware he was a father? Or did he assume his child had died at birth? Is that what Miss Ralston had claimed? If he presumed Clara was dead, how might he lash out if he found out she was alive and well and living with Joanna?

Joanna doubted he'd be interested in Clara, but hazard seemed to be swirling around her, imperiling all she held dear. Should she tell Jacob what she'd discovered? Would that be appropriate? Would she feel safer?

Miss Ralston and Mr. Boswell were both incredibly arrogant. If Joanna ruined them, how might they retaliate?

She peeked up at the sky, yearning to scold Jacob's father. If this was Miles Ralston's idea of watching over her from the afterlife, he wasn't doing a very good job.

She was descended from a long line of females who'd had to be adept at disappearing. There had been many occasions when her ancestors had run from angry men, angry vicars, angry mobs. Aunt Pru had taught her the necessary lessons: *in case something happens...in case there's ever trouble...in case you need to hurry...*

In her mind's eye, she was already packing. What would she like to have with her? What would she miss? What was vital? What wasn't?

A woman could get by with very little, but she'd planted roots at Ralston that sank far into the ground. How would she ever pull them out and start over? The whole notion left her terribly weary.

"We should tarry in Bath for a few weeks," Joanna said. "Once we travel such a distance, it would be silly to arrive, then depart immediately."

"Could I bring a friend?"

"I'm sorry, but I don't have the extra money for it. We can barely afford to entertain ourselves, let alone a guest."

"While I'm away, the girls will have parties and suppers without me. I won't be there for any of it."

"Consider this: When you're back, you'll have many amazing stories to share."

"None of them have ever been to Bath. I'll be the only one."

It was Sunday morning. They'd been to church, and they were walking home. The woods were verdant and pretty, with birds chirping in the trees and small animals skittering in the brush. She was trying to absorb every detail so she'd never forget.

They reached the path that led to her cottage, and as they approached the gate, Kit Boswell was standing there and obviously waiting for them. A shiver slithered down her spine. Had she conjured him by pondering him so vehemently?

"Miss James! There you are!" His tone was aggrieved, as if they'd had an appointment and she was late.

"Hello, Mr. Boswell," she said. "This is a surprise."

He didn't respond to her greeting, but studied Clara meticulously, providing stark evidence that he was aware of Clara's paternity. Joanna studied Clara too, thinking she looked like Miss Ralston and not like Mr. Boswell at all. It was as if Miss Ralston had had a miraculous conception, with no man involved in the event.

"She definitely resembles her mother, doesn't she?" He snorted with disgust. "If questions were raised, it would be hard to deny a relationship."

Clara hadn't previously met Mr. Boswell, and at his snide comment, she shrunk away so she was partially shielded by Joanna. She'd never been particularly shy though, and she asked, "Are you acquainted with my mother, sir?"

Mr. Boswell snorted again, and Joanna was afraid of what he might reveal. She was frightened too as to why he'd arrived. In all the years she'd lived in the cottage, he'd never visited, and his sudden appearance boded ill.

She cut off any chance he might have had to answer Clara. "Clara, this is Mr. Boswell. He's Captain Ralston's friend and estate manager." She spun to him and asked, "May I help you? What do you need?"

"Shall we go inside? I have several delicate issues to discuss with you"—he glared at Clara—"and I'd rather not address them out here in the yard."

"That's fine. Please come in."

She urged Clara to continue on ahead of them, then she and Mr. Boswell followed. He leaned in and murmured, "We shouldn't talk in front of the girl."

"Her name is Clara."

"I know."

He smirked in a manner that made Joanna eager to slap him. Mutt had been off in the forest, and he loped up. When he saw Mr. Boswell, he skidded to a halt, and he growled viciously, his hackles up.

Clara rushed over to pet him, and she said, "He doesn't like you, Mr. Boswell, and he usually likes everyone. Isn't that funny?"

"It's absolutely hilarious," he tightly replied.

Joanna wasn't sure Mutt would let Mr. Boswell pass on by. What if he lunged at Boswell? What if he nipped flesh or ripped his trousers?

She said to Clara, "Why don't you play with Mutt for me? Mr. Boswell and I must have a private conversation. I'll shout for you when we're finished."

"I'm never permitted to listen in on adults," Clara complained.

"I'll tell you about it after we're done."

Clara was too polite to quarrel. She snapped her fingers at Mutt and gestured to the woods. The dog hesitated, as if he didn't want to leave Joanna unprotected, and Joanna had to admit she wasn't keen to chat with Boswell.

Whatever he intended to impart, it could never be to her benefit.

"Go," she sternly commanded Mutt, and she motioned to Clara. Clara marched off, and Mutt reluctantly obeyed and trotted after her.

After they vanished, Joanna opened the door and entered the house. She could have guided him into the parlor to the sofa, as if it was a social call, but she was fairly certain there would be nothing *social* about it. She stepped to her left, to her kitchen. She pulled out a chair at the table, indicating he should sit, and she took the chair across from him.

He peered about, scrutinizing the room, as if wondering how much money he could get for her possessions if he sold them.

"I'm trying to recollect if I've ever been in this cottage before," he said. "If I have, I can't remember."

"It's been a good spot for me." Joanna offered naught more. She stared at him, waiting for him to mention his purpose.

He snickered and asked, "How much do you charge to cast spells?"

"I don't cast spells."

"Why can't you oblige me?" he mockingly inquired. "I'd love to have you turn a few people into toads."

She imagined it was his idea of a joke, and she scowled with exasperation. He viewed himself as being very important, but there was no chance his ego would be stroked in her kitchen.

He finally realized it and said, "I'll come straight to the point."

"I appreciate it. I assume your message is dire."

"Not to me, but I don't suppose you'll like it very much. Captain Ralston has been recalled to duty. He departed yesterday."

"Oh."

Somehow, she managed to exhibit very little emotion, but at the news, she was so shocked that he might have physically punched her.

She'd been planning to sneak away from Ralston Place, but so far, it had been mental wrangling. She hadn't accepted the notion that she'd never see Jacob Ralston again. She struggled to hide her distress.

"It was very fast," Mr. Boswell said, "but then, he's a navy man. He's used to a brisk change of circumstance. He thrives on it."

She had to exhibit scant interest in Jacob. "Is there a reason I'm being notified? I'm barely acquainted with Captain Ralston, so his arrangements with the navy are none of my concern."

He laughed in a cruel way. "Yours is a humorous attempt at innocence, Miss James, but unfortunately for you, you have no secrets from me."

"Meaning what?"

"Roxanne Ralston is the Captain's fiancée. You're aware of that fact, aren't you?"

"I dare say the whole neighborhood is aware of it."

"Well, *she* is aware too—of your affair with him." Joanna would have refuted the allegation, but he held up a hand to stop her. "It's futile to pretend. She caught him creeping home at dawn, after he'd spent the night with you. She confronted him, and they had quite a discussion about you and what a trollop you are. I regret to inform you that their comments weren't flattering."

Joanna bristled, enraged that Jacob would gossip about her, but especially with Miss Ralston. "Fine. I won't deny an affair. Why are you here? I wish you'd just tell me."

He didn't explain though. He studied her with lechery in his expression, his rude, prurient gaze roaming across her bosom. "Personally, I couldn't care less if he's dabbling with you, and it's clear why he'd pick you over her. You're sweet and malleable, and Roxanne is hard as nails. Any man in his right mind would tup you rather than her."

She leapt to her feet. "That's enough. I don't have to listen to that sort of disparaging remark in my own kitchen, and I won't be insulted by you. Let me show you out."

He didn't budge though, but waved to her chair and said, "Sit down, sit down. There's no need to fly off the handle. I was complimenting you."

"No, you weren't."

"Sit, Miss James!" he said more vehemently. "I must clarify my purpose."

They engaged in a staring match, and she might have stomped out in a huff, but it was obvious—if she didn't allow him to bloviate—she might never be shed of him.

She plopped down. "Get on with it, and if you abuse me again, this conversation is over."

He sneered with satisfaction, as if she'd behaved precisely as he'd expected, and her dislike for him soared. Over the years, there had been terrible stories about him, and she suspected every dastardly tale was most likely true.

"I've brought a message from Miss Ralston," he said. "As you might imagine, she is not keen to have you loitering on the property and tempting her fiancé."

"I have never tempted Jacob Ralston, and if you presume I could, then you don't know him very well."

"We're not playing semantic games, Miss James. He's besotted with you, but he's about to wed Roxanne. You're not stupid, so I'm sure you understand the problem this creates for her."

"I understand it, and I'm sorry his conduct has upset her. I hope *you* can understand that I have absolutely no power over how he acts."

He nodded. "Yes, Jacob can be very obstinate, but we're not talking about him. We're talking about *you* and how you will fix this fiasco."

"I'll make the situation easier on you and admit that I'm overwhelmed by the Captain's attentions. I grasp that they can never benefit me, so I have already decided to move away."

"Have you? What a nice surprise. We don't have to argue then. When will you depart?"

"In a few weeks. I will tell people we are heading to Bath for a holiday, but we will travel in the other direction."

"Why the other direction?"

"As you mentioned, Captain Ralston is besotted, and he's very stubborn. If I flee without his permission, I'm afraid—on his next furlough—he'll track me down and force me back."

"You're impressing me more by the minute. You know Jacob so well too! You must have spent some time becoming acquainted. It can't all have been rolling around on a mattress. You must have chatted occasionally."

"You've insulted me again. Are we finished?"

"No, for there's an issue with your schedule. You have to leave immediately."

"Define immediately."

"Today. By tomorrow morning at the latest."

"I can't be prepared that fast."

"More's the pity then, for you see, I'm leveling this section of the woods. I'll be torching this meadow at dawn, so if you're not gone, your possessions will be burned to the ground along with the building."

She hadn't wanted to show any reaction, but tears flooded her eyes. She couldn't abide cruelty, and she'd lived in the small house since she was fourteen. It wasn't grand or fancy, but it was her home and had been for ten years.

It represented her connection to her Aunt Pru who'd been wise, kind, and cunning. Pru had taken her in and raised her after the shipwreck in the Caribbean. Joanna had been a bewildered orphan who'd needed a patient, tender parent, and Pru had enthusiastically stepped into that role.

She'd taught Joanna her family's ancient secrets, but she'd also taught her more pragmatic skills: how to persevere, how to thrive in difficult circumstances, how to brace for hardship, and it had arrived.

"I've distressed you," he said, and he smirked. "It's a waste of effort to weep. I have a heart of stone, so it won't do you any good."

"I would never cry in front of you. You'd enjoy it too much."

"I would. Now then, I'll be abundantly clear: You are to leave, and you are to keep going until you are far, far away."

"I will. I swear."

"You are not to slither back. If you suffer adversity in your new locale, you are not to write to Jacob Ralston. You are not to ever contact him for any reason."

"I figured that out on my own."

"Your little *niece* can't remain in the area either. Not with Miss Ralston about to wed Jacob."

"I especially realize that."

"Have you any documents that prove her maternity? Letters? A birth certificate? Anything like that?"

"No," Joanna lied, her gaze firm.

"Have you any information about her father?"

"I know it's you—if that's what you're asking."

"You are a very forthright person, Miss James, which is refreshing. It makes our negotiation so much easier."

"Are we negotiating?" she inquired.

"No. I'm threatening you."

"There's no need to threaten me. I told you I plan to go. You've simply speeded up my schedule."

"Yes, but the wheels are spinning in your head. You're a female, so you're naturally duplicitous."

"I'm sorry you view me that way."

"If you tarry, I shall summon Vicar Blair from over in the next parish. Have you ever heard of Vicar Blair? He's a very pious, very rigid preacher. He wouldn't like to discover that you practice magic. He'd feel compelled to stop you."

"I don't practice magic," she futilely insisted.

"He has a nasty attitude about young women who don't behave as they ought. He'd be delighted to call you out as a witch."

"This is the modern age, Mr. Boswell. Everyone has agreed there are no witches."

"Vicar Blair thinks there is. I'll set him loose on you. Could you bear to have a vicious priest breathing down your neck?"

She inhaled slowly to calm herself. "I see your point."

"Jacob is my great friend—like my very own brother. Every boon I enjoy, I've received from him. If there is ever the slightest hint that I am a father, I will get even."

"The news doesn't surprise me. You have a reputation as a very vindictive fellow."

He grinned, proud of the charge. "You should be advised, if I have to lash out, it won't be against you. It will be against the girl."

"Her name is Clara. If you can brag about how you'd retaliate against your daughter, you should at least be able to speak her name."

He didn't take her bait, didn't jump into an argument about Clara. Instead, he said, "It appears we're in complete accord. Will you depart this afternoon?"

"I have to pack, so it will have to be in the morning."

"It has to be by dawn. At sunrise, I'll be here with men and torches."

"Yes, I'm certain you will be. You're not the sort to jest about it."

She stood, and he stood too, and he leaned in, as if he might touch her indecently. She braced, refusing to lurch away, being positive he was trying to frighten her. But she wasn't scared of anyone.

She glared at him, daring him to proceed, and as she'd suspected, he was a coward deep down. He was the first to look away.

She wanted him out of her house. It was still hers for a few more hours. She marched by him, went to the door, and flung it open. He dawdled in the kitchen, notifying her he wouldn't blithely obey. After he believed she understood his authority, he sauntered over and walked by her.

"Don't linger in the morning." He was determined to have the last word. "I don't wish to fuss with you ever again."

"I have no wish to fuss with you either."

"We tolerated you for too many years, and you've overstayed your welcome."

He would have strolled off, assuming he'd put her in her place, but she never bowed down. Before he realized what she intended, she grabbed his wrist, turned up his palm, and traced several signs in the center with her finger.

He jerked away as if she'd scalded him.

"What the bloody hell was that?" he demanded, and he frowned at his hand as if pagan marks might have been branded into his skin.

"I don't usually level curses," she told him, "but I've made an exception for you."

"You little shit! What have you done?"

"None of your dreams will come true. You'll lose everything because of me: your job, your income, your fancy house. If my magic is powerful enough, perhaps even your life. You'll never have a wife or any other children, but for Clara. Your male parts will shrivel and quit working.

You'll end up poor, alone, and despised, with Jacob Ralston hating you most of all."

She thought he might strike her, but apparently, she'd terrified the big bully. He laughed in her face, but it was a nervous, anxious laugh.

"You're a charlatan." He struggled to sound brazen, but failed. "You prey on the weak and the gullible. No rational person would ever listen to you. I don't plan to."

"We'll see if I'm a charlatan. We'll find out if I have any power." She displayed another gesture, one she invented and that didn't mean anything, and she hurled it as if it could land on him. "Best keep glancing over your shoulder, Mr. Boswell. Who can guess what ill-wind might be blowing in to knock you down?"

"You deranged witch. I ought to sic Vicar Blair on you after all. It would serve you right."

He huffed off, and she went inside and peeked out the curtain, watching as he leapt on his horse and cantered away. She was delighted to note that he was in quite a hurry too. He might scoff and deride her as a fraud, but he was in no mood to discover what else she might do.

She smirked with satisfaction, figuring he'd worry about her curse every minute of every day for the rest of his sorry life.

Chapter

19

CLARA WAS ASLEEP WHEN a loud noise outside awakened her. She popped up on an elbow and glanced around her bedchamber. Was it Mutt? Had he barked a warning? Or had he cried out with dismay? A man might have cursed too.

She cocked an ear toward Joanna's room, but she hadn't stirred, so it must have been a dream.

She drew the covers up to her chin and tried to doze off again, but her mind was awhirl, and she couldn't relax.

After Mr. Boswell had left, Joanna had sat her down, and they'd had a serious, adult conversation about many topics Clara would rather not have had clarified. Over the years, she'd occasionally asked Aunt Pru and Joanna who her parents had been, but they'd always claimed they possessed no details.

But Roxanne Ralston and Mr. Boswell were her mother and father, and to her great consternation, they were demanding she leave Ralston Place. She was faced with their total disregard. It was such a cruel, unfair blow.

Joanna had debated whether to lie about what was occurring, but in the end, she'd decided Clara had to understand the gravity of what had transpired.

They had to be gone by dawn, and they'd spent the evening packing their bags. Joanna had been prepared for just such an event, so she'd known what they needed. It had merely been a matter of grabbing the appropriate items and stuffing them in satchels. It had happened so fast that it didn't seem real.

She must have fallen back to sleep because, suddenly, Joanna was shaking her, panic in her voice.

"Clara! Get up!"

Clara was befuddled and, drowsily, she inquired, "What's wrong?"

Then she smelled smoke. Fear made her pulse race.

"There's a fire in my workroom," Joanna told her. "Come! We have to flee the house—while we still can."

Joanna yanked off the blanket, and Clara leapt out of bed. Luckily, they were dressed and ready to depart, so they wouldn't have to head out in their nightclothes. Joanna handed her her shoes, and Clara plopped down on the edge of the mattress to tug them on, but Joanna clasped her wrist and pulled her up.

"You can put them on in the yard," Joanna said, and they ran out to the hall and down the stairs.

As they reached the bottom, the smoke was thick and heavy. Her eyes watered, and she began to cough. She couldn't see the door. It was dark and hazy, and she was completely disoriented, but somehow, Joanna led her over to it.

It was an effort to wrestle with the security bar, to lift it off and toss it away, then they staggered out. Joanna guided her to the gate so they were a safe distance away, and when Clara turned to stare, the roof was ablaze. Flames were visible in the thatch.

"Stay here," Joanna said.

"Where are you going?" Clara asked with alarm.

"I have to fetch our satchels or we'll have nothing. Don't worry. They're right in the parlor."

"I don't think you ought!"

Joanna didn't heed her though. She simply dashed away.

The fire lit up the sky, so it was easy to observe the entire spectacle. Joanna pushed inside, and after an anxious minute or two, she threw out three bags, then carried out a fourth. She dragged them away from the building so they wouldn't burn too. Clara was so dumbfounded that she dawdled like a stone statue, too terrified to rush over and help.

Joanna joined her, and as the flames grew bigger, the temperature soared. They had to step farther into the trees to escape the heat. They huddled together, gaping as the inferno swallowed their world.

The forest was eerily quiet, as if the animals had scurried away from the danger. The only sound was glass breaking and the cracking of timber. Other than that, it was as if they'd been struck deaf.

"Where is Mutt?" Joanna asked after a bit. "You didn't let him in the house, did you?"

"No, and I thought I heard him bark. It woke me up, but then, when I listened more closely, it was silent."

"I'll walk around to check on him."

"No, Joanna! Don't walk around!"

"I won't go in. I have to be certain he's not stuck under a board or trapped in a corner. Don't move."

Joanna flitted off and vanished in the shadows, calling to Mutt as she searched. An eternity passed before she reappeared. She was cradling a huge bundle that was almost too large for her to hold, and Clara couldn't imagine what it might be until she neared and Clara saw it was Mutt.

"Oh, no!" she wailed. "Is he ... is he ...?"

"He's just hurt. Take off my cloak. Lay it on the ground so I can put him down."

Clara unhooked the cloak and spread it at their feet, then Joanna gently placed him on it. He had a fierce gash opened on his neck and down the front of his leg, as if he'd been slashed with an ax or a knife.

"Someone cut him!" Clara fumed. "He's such a good dog! Who would act that way?"

"I don't know," Joanna said, but she was glaring in a manner that told Clara she had her suspicions.

"Would Mr. Boswell have come early?" Clara asked.

"It was deliberately started, Clara. The window in my workroom was smashed in, and it looks as if a torch was hurled into it."

"But we were sleeping upstairs!"

"I realize that."

"Was it Mr. Boswell?"

"I can't guess right now. I'm too distressed, and I have to tend to Mutt. I must focus on that and naught else."

Joanna bent down and whispered to him in the soothing language she utilized when she was healing. He whined and licked her fingers.

His gash needed stitching, and they had medical supplies in their satchels, but it would be difficult to dig them out. Plus, it was so dark. Joanna probably wouldn't be able to see well enough to sew the wound.

They knelt with Mutt, petting him, comforting him, and glancing occasionally at their destroyed home. A wall collapsed, the roof fell in. They couldn't slow it down, couldn't stop it. They could only watch through the long night and wait for dawn to arrive.

MARGARET SAT AT A dining table in the coaching inn in Gretna Green where she, Sandy, Tim, and Tom had traveled so she could wed quickly. They'd finished breakfast, and Sandy was out in the barn, arranging a carriage for the journey back.

The boys were...somewhere. She wasn't sure where, but they'd show up.

The four of them had cantered to Scotland on horseback, but they were returning at a leisurely pace. With the marriage accomplished, there was no reason to hurry.

They'd argued over whether to have Tim and Tom accompany them. They could have left them with Sandy's in-laws, his deceased wife's parents and the boys' grandparents. Sandy had a cordial relationship with them, but it would have caused a delay where they'd have had to explain themselves.

They'd been afraid his in-laws would be upset to learn he was marrying again—and so abruptly too. He couldn't bear to shock them, so he'd inform them later, when he could calmly clarify what had happened and that there was a stepmother in the picture.

As to Margaret, she felt they were carrying an enormous negative burden by having to elope, and she wouldn't increase the load by angering Sandy's in-laws.

So they'd brought Tim and Tom along, and she was glad they had. They'd been raised around horses, so they were excellent equestrians, and they'd galloped with Sandy and Margaret as if they'd been made for hard riding, which of course they had been.

They'd delivered a sense of fun to the escapade, so their frantic trip seemed like a family decision. Margaret wasn't merely attaching herself to Sandy. She was joining herself to all three of them. She had a husband and a pair of sons she adored.

She hadn't written a note to Jacob, so she had no idea if he'd even notice she was gone. She was that inconsequential to him and the estate, but Sandy would definitely be missed. His presence was too vital, and they'd debated whether Jacob might chase after them if he ever deduced their intent.

She truly didn't think he would, but then, what did she know about her brother?

He'd incensed Sandy to such a high degree that Sandy wouldn't continue working for him. They would leave Ralston Place immediately. Sandy had a bit of money saved, so he could rent them a house, then begin applying for jobs. He was renowned for his expertise with animals, and he was positive he'd be offered a better position elsewhere.

She was positive too, and she refused to believe otherwise.

She heard the boys before she saw them. They tromped in the front of the building, the door slamming after them. They were like a force of nature: serious, tough, loyal, smart. In other words, they were possessed of their father's best traits.

They were such physical beings. They pushed, shouted, and punched. Their boots were always scuffed, their elbows always scraped, and their trousers usually had a hole in the knee by the end of the day.

Life with them was exciting, loud, and exasperatingly splendid, and she couldn't figure out how she'd endured so many quiet years with Mr. Howell. How had she survived all that festering silence?

They blustered in and marched over to where she was alone in the corner and finishing her tea.

"We have a surprise for you," Tom said.

"I love surprises. What is it?"

Tim had his hand behind his back, and Tom nudged him. With a flourish, he whipped out a bouquet of wild flowers. "We didn't pick any for you for the wedding. Pa was regretting that you had to marry without flowers."

"Oh, you two . . ."

Tom added, "Pa says we've been bachelors for too long, that we have to get accustomed to having a lady in the house again. We can't forget things like flowers."

She pulled them close, one in each arm, and gave them a tight hug.

It only lasted a second before they squirmed away. They didn't like to be cuddled or have their hair ruffled, but she did it anyway.

"We decided on an important issue too," Tom said, "and we're hoping you'll like it. You see, we've been wondering what we should call you."

"It doesn't seem appropriate for it to be *mother*," Tim explained. "We had a mother, and we miss her very much."

"I understand perfectly," she said, "and I wouldn't expect to take her place."

"You're not Mrs. Howell anymore, and it would sound odd for it to be Mrs. Sanders. Or even Mrs. Sandy, so we've agreed on Mother Margaret. Would that be all right with you?"

Tears flooded her eyes. She couldn't help it. "Yes, Mother Margaret would be marvelous."

At witnessing her wave of emotion, they were horrified, and Tim asked, "Have we upset you?"

"No, I'm happy."

They cocked their heads as if she was a very strange creature, and Tom asked, "You cry when you're happy?"

"Yes. It's another thing you bachelors will have to learn."

She hugged them again, and the instant they grew restless, she released them and said, "Find Sandy and check if the carriage is harnessed. Fetch me when it's time to depart."

They stamped out, and she listened to them go, chuckling at the ruckus they made. They were handsome and polite, so no one minded the commotion they generated. When they went by, people smiled.

The front door opened again, and she glanced up, assuming it would be Sandy, but when she realized who'd arrived, she scowled so ferociously she was amazed her face didn't crack.

"What are you doing here?" she said to her brother. "And if you imagine you can stop me, you're too late. I'm married."

She held up her hand to show him the gold band on her finger. He smirked, then staggered over and plopped down on a chair. He appeared weary and spent, as if he hadn't slept in days.

There was a basket of scones on the table, and he grabbed one and gobbled it down. "Where is Sandy? Has he abandoned you already?"

"Very funny. If you must know, he's out in the barn, renting a carriage. His sons are with us too, so if you're about to cause a scene, I wish you wouldn't. I can't have them watch their new uncle being an ass."

He didn't respond to her taunt, but seized her teacup, gulped the contents, then put down the cup with a hard smack. "You asked what I'm doing here, and I have absolutely no idea."

"You . . . what?"

He looked to be at a loss for what had to be the first time ever. "After I discovered you'd eloped, I was so angry. The hideous traits I've inherited from Mother surged to the fore, and I left home, hell-bent on catching you, but it's a long way to Scotland. I had many dull hours to ponder my intentions."

"What have you determined?"

"I'd just like you to be happy, and I've always liked Sandy. He's steady, reliable, and accursedly loyal. Who wouldn't choose that type of man as a husband for his sister? If he loves you as much as he claims, why shouldn't I let him have you? I'm too . . . too British, I guess."

She sputtered out a laugh. "I guess you are too. We both are."

"When he asked to wed you, I was focused on problems that don't matter. I was contemplating bloodlines and class distinctions, and he was offering to cherish you forever. You had a rough experience with Mr. Howell, and I probably could have prevented the betrothal, but I didn't. I've always regretted that I didn't protect you."

"I don't blame you for it. You remember what Mother was like. It was so difficult to stand up to her when we were younger. It was easier to capitulate than to fight."

"Yes, and you paid the price for that. If you can have a kind husband now, why shouldn't I want that for you?"

"All of that occurred to you while you were riding to Scotland?"

"Yes, and I can't fathom my purpose. I'm sorry I was so horrid to you. Have I missed the ceremony?" He pointed to her ring. "It seems as if I have. I would have liked to attend."

"My goodness," she murmured. "You're being so gallant. I suppose I have to retract every insult I hurled over the past week."

"I suppose you have to too, and if I inquire nicely, would you wed again once we're back at Ralston Place? Could we have a second ceremony? I'd like to walk you down the aisle. Father would be glad about it, and I'd like everyone at the estate to be there—for you *and* for Sandy."

She did burst into tears then. The boys had pushed her to the brink, but Jacob had shoved her over.

"Don't weep," he muttered. "Please! I didn't think I could possibly feel any worse, but if I've made you cry, I might have to throw myself off a cliff."

"I can't help it. This whole exploit has been so draining. I'm thoroughly exhausted. I don't have an ounce of sense or energy remaining."

He dug a kerchief out of his coat so she could dab at her eyes.

"Are you happy though?" he asked. "You look happy. Well . . . except for the tears. You're definitely sending me conflicting messages."

"I'm very, very happy."

Noise erupted out by the front door, and Tom stomped in, calling, "Mother Margaret, are you still here?"

"Yes, Tom, I'm here," she called back. She explained to Jacob, "That's the name my boys have picked for me: Mother Margaret."

"Pa says to tell you ten minutes." Tom strutted over, but when he saw Jacob, he halted and dubiously studied him. Then, his tone a tad cool, he said, "Hello, Captain Ralston."

Margaret said to Jacob, "This is Sandy's older son, Tom." She smiled and added, "He's *my* son too."

"Hello, Tom," Jacob said.

"He's planning to join the navy in a few years," Margaret said. "I told him he could talk to you about it, but we've been so busy running away that there hasn't been any time."

"I would love to talk to you about the navy," Jacob said. He could be very charming when the occasion required it. "It's a fabulous career to have, and it would be perfect for you."

On the trip north, Sandy hadn't spared the boys from the truth, so they were aware that Jacob had been vehemently opposed to the marriage. Margaret had piled on plenty of snide comments she shouldn't have voiced, so Tim and Tom had no illusions about what had transpired.

Tom scowled at Jacob and dared to ask, "You won't cause trouble, will you? For if that's why you've arrived, my Pa and I won't let you. My brother either. Margaret belongs to us now, sir, so we have to always protect her."

"I'm not about to cause trouble," Jacob insisted. "I was furious initially, but I've calmed down, and I'm delighted that you're fond of Margaret. She deserves protecting, and I'm sure you and your father will take good care of her."

"We will. Pa says she's not too good at taking care of herself, but we'll get her squared away."

Jacob raised a brow and grinned at her. "It sounds as if the new men in your life know you quite well. From this moment on, I suspect you'll be in excellent hands."

"Dammit."

Sandy mumbled the curse, then glanced around to be certain no one had heard. He never liked to use foul language, but he was standing outside the coaching inn's barn, and who should strut toward him, but the exalted, pompous Captain Jacob Ralston.

Where had he come from? And why would he slither in when everything was over? It was too late to stop them.

Sandy and Margaret had endlessly debated whether her brother would bestir himself to chase after her. Sandy had assumed he would simply because he was such a conceited ass, and he'd be eager to put Sandy in his place.

In the past, Sandy wouldn't have risked absconding with Margaret, but he'd had about all of the Ralston family he could abide. For thirty years, he'd been denigrated and snubbed by them.

He'd tolerated their awful mother, Esther—because he'd had to tolerate her. He tolerated their ward, Kit Boswell—because . . . because . . .

Why had he? In his dealings with Kit, he'd had to ceaselessly degrade himself merely to keep his job so his boys would be safe, but he was widely respected in the community, and—when he attended auctions and horse races—he was repeatedly offered better positions at higher salaries.

He tolerated Jacob Ralston because he was never present to throw his weight around. With his exhibiting some of his mother's worst traits, Sandy had had enough.

He'd stayed at Ralston Place because he'd always worked there. It was habit. It was loyalty. It was . . . stupid. A few days earlier, when he'd stood in the manor as the Captain had complained that he was too lowly for Margaret, he'd suffered a flare of temper that hadn't burned out.

Normally, he viewed himself as a very placid fellow, but the Captain had lit a spark under decades of umbrage, and Sandy couldn't tamp it down. Margaret was his now, and that fact couldn't be changed. Not even by a pompous, angry brother.

He braced his feet, fists gripped behind his back so—if the arrogant oaf insulted him—he wouldn't pound the man into the ground. He supposed the Captain was a brawler, but so was Sandy. If it came to blows, they were the same size, and it would be a fair fight.

"Hello, Sandy," the Captain said as he sauntered up. "Fancy meeting you here."

"Captain."

"I just talked to Margaret."

"We're wed, so if you were intending to berate me, you should think again. I should first explain that I quit."

The Captain scowled. "What do you mean?"

"I *mean* that I resign from my post. Since you don't believe I'm suitable to be your sister's husband, I've decided *you* are not a person I want to work for anymore. I'm no longer your employee, so if you offend me or disparage her, I will beat you to a pulp."

"I wasn't planning to protest your marriage."

"Oh." The comment dumped cold water on Sandy's ire. "What were you about to say then?"

"I'll start with this: I don't accept your resignation."

"I don't care. I quit anyway. It's a thankless proposition to toil away for you."

"I'm sorry you feel that way."

"This journey to Scotland clarified numerous issues for me," Sandy said. "I exhaust myself, keeping the estate in fine shape. For you! But why must I strive so valiantly? *I* supervise the employees. *I* ensure the crops are planted and the orchards trimmed. *I* learn when a tenant's widow needs her roof repaired, yet I have to grovel to Boswell every second. My patience for that type of nonsense has vanished."

"I don't pay you enough money."

"I know you don't," Sandy raged, "and this will be a great surprise to you, but I constantly receive job offers."

"I'm *not* surprised by it. Who wouldn't like to hire you?"

"I've refused them because I told myself I should be faithful to you, but I'm tired of it. I will latch onto the next proposal that's tossed at me. I'll load up my wife and my sons and go to a spot where my contributions are valued."

The Captain actually laughed in his face. "Are you finished? You won't let me get a word in edgewise."

"Well, I predict you won't tell me anything worth hearing, so why listen?"

"How about this? I'm glad you're my brother-in-law."

"What?" The man might have spoken in a language Sandy didn't comprehend.

"I fumed all the way here, and after many miles had passed, I couldn't figure out why I was so incensed."

"It's probably because you're a Ralston and you people simply strut and preen."

"It's pretty much the truth. I've always felt guilty that I didn't stop my mother from marrying Margaret to Mr. Howell. I didn't help her when I should have, and she suffered because of it."

"I won't argue the point."

The Captain extended his hand, as if they should shake and become friends. "Congratulations. I'm delighted for you, but remember this: If you ever hurt her, I'll kill you."

Sandy scoffed. "I'd cut off my right arm before I'd hurt her. I've loved her my whole life, and I always will."

An awkward silence festered, with the Captain's hand still extended, and Sandy never liked to be an ass. He clasped hold, gave it a firm shake, then pulled away.

"Would you do something for me?" the Captain asked.

"That depends on what it is."

"Take Margaret on a honeymoon. She deserves one."

"I don't have time to waste. I have to hurry home and find a new job."

The Captain tsked with exasperation. "Wasn't I clear? You're not quitting. I won't permit it. Margaret said you're heading to England, but why don't you head to Edinburgh instead? You can be lazy; you can sightsee and enjoy yourselves. The boys can ride south with me, so you and Margaret can be alone for a week or two. You'd trust me with them, I hope."

How was Sandy to answer that question? "I guess I'd trust them with you."

"It can't be overly romantic to have them watching your every move with your bride."

"Our escapade has been a family affair. My sons like her but, because she's a Ralston from the manor, they study her as if she was hatched from an egg. They have to get used to having her around."

"They can get used to her when you're back." The Captain patted him on the shoulder. "I hate that I forced you and Margaret to run away, and I'd like you to start off on a better footing with her. I want her to have a *real* honeymoon."

Sandy blew out an irked breath. "I suppose she and I can travel to Edinburgh."

"I made her promise too that we'll have a second ceremony when you're home. We'll have it in the church and invite the neighbors."

Sandy frowned, as if he hadn't heard correctly. "You'd do that for her?"

"I'd do it for both of you." The Captain's cheeks reddened, as if with chagrin. "Don't bite my head off, but I have to ask this: Have you the funds to spend two weeks in Edinburgh? Might I slip you some? It could be a wedding gift."

Sandy smirked. "Yes, I have money for a trip. I'm not a pauper. My employer is a miser with the wages he pays, but I'm adept at saving my meager pennies."

The sly insult drew another laugh. "You're my sister's husband, so I imagine I'll have to give you a raise. If I don't, she'll nag me to death. You're welcome to reside in the manor too, if you'd like. You can have a suite of rooms in the west wing."

"I'd rather we stay in our own house. We'll settle in quicker."

"I understand, and you have to call me Jacob."

"I'll think about it."

"And we'll be implementing some changes."

"What kind of changes?"

"Kit has received all the favors I owe him. He has to search for a different job somewhere else—so you can have his. You're doing his anyway. You should have the income and the title."

Sandy snorted with disgust. "I won't offer an opinion about it. It would stir a pot of controversy, and you'd have Boswell as your enemy. He's a vindictive oaf, so that could never be a wise idea."

"Don't worry about him. I know how to handle Kit. We'll worry about you and me and how we go forward from this point on."

"I'm willing to let you worm your way into my good graces."

"Maybe we both have to behave better," the Captain said.

"If we quarrel, it will distress Margaret, and I don't intend to ever distress her."

"Exactly so, Geoffrey Sanders. Exactly so."

HOWARD PERIWINKLE WAS ROLLING down the road in a posh carriage. He was on a mission to speak with Joanna James and was still a few miles from her cottage outside Ralston village. He glanced out the window, and he observed the strangest sight.

They'd just passed a young lady and a girl who'd stepped into the grass so his vehicle could race on by. They had satchels strapped to their backs as if they were vagabonds, and the young lady was dragging some sort of bedding contraption. It looked as if there was a . . . a . . . dog lying on it? Was she pulling an injured dog?

He was positive it was Miss James. Who could forget that gorgeous red hair? It couldn't be anybody else.

"Stop the carriage!" he shouted, and he pounded on the roof. "Stop please!"

The driver called to the horses, and the conveyance rattled to a halt. The team hadn't expected to be reined in, the driver either, so it took a minute to completely cease its movement.

He'd been loafing at Barrett Manor with Libby Carstairs and Caroline Grey, the other *Lost Girls* who'd survived the shipwreck with Miss James. Miss Carstairs was marrying very soon, and they wanted Miss James to attend the wedding, to sit in the front pew as an honored guest with Miss Grey. Miss Carstairs's fiancé, Lord Barrett, had sent Howard to fetch Miss James to his estate.

He was in Lord Barrett's coach, accompanied by several of his servants, which made him seem grander and more important than he actually was.

He was a newspaper reporter for the London Times, and he'd written the stories about Miss Carstairs being Little Henrietta Pendleton. He'd also found Caroline Grey—Little Caro from the shipwreck—and after he'd delivered her to Barrett, Miss Carstairs had decided he was a handy fellow to have around. He was working valiantly to ingratiate himself so he'd have a good seat during the wedding ceremony.

The entire nation adored Miss Carstairs and wished they could attend, but there was limited space in the church, so only a few dozen people would view it in person. Howard would pen articles, and describe it so perfectly, that everyone in the kingdom would feel as if they'd been there too.

At his having summoned the driver, the servants were disconcerted. They knew they were traveling to transport Miss James to Barrett, and they were excited to have a role in bringing the third *Lost Girl* to Miss Carstairs.

An outrider peered in the window. "Is there a problem, Mr. Periwinkle?"

"Did you see that woman we passed?" he asked. "I think it's Miss James."

"We're still a distance from Ralston," the man said. "Why would she be walking on the road? I hope she hasn't encountered some difficulties."

"Open the door so I can talk to her. We flew by her so fast; I'm not totally certain it's her."

Howard jumped down and went toward the pair, and he waved to her. "Miss James? Joanna James? Is it you?"

The woman studied Howard as if she couldn't place him. Finally, she nodded. "Yes, I'm Miss James."

He kept on, trying to appear harmless. "It's me, Howard Periwinkle. We met recently. I write for the London Times, and we chatted about it being the anniversary of the shipwreck."

"Oh, yes, hello, Mr. Periwinkle. Our conversation might have happened a century ago. Why are you in the area again?"

He was close enough to discern she was in a dire condition. The girl too. Their faces were smudged black, their clothes dirty, and he could smell smoke emanating from their possessions. Miss James's hands were wrapped with bandages, as if she'd injured them.

When he'd bumped into her earlier in the summer, she'd been pretty, vibrant, and full of vigor. Now she looked beaten down, abused, and without a friend in the world.

"What's wrong, Miss James? You're a tad undone. Why are you so far from home?"

"We've had a spot of trouble."

The girl piped up with, "Our landlord evicted us, and we were supposed to depart at dawn, but before we could, our cottage caught fire. We barely escaped with our lives."

He peeked down at the makeshift bed Miss James was pulling with straps attached to her shoulders, and he said, "Is that a . . . dog? Is he hurt?"

"Yes," the girl said. "Whoever started it—"

"Someone started it? Deliberately?" He was aghast. What type of fiend would commit such a crime?

"Yes, someone started it"—the girl's fury was evident—"and he attacked our dog, probably with a hatchet." The girl pointed to Miss James's bandages. "Joanna burned herself, trying to grab our bags out of the inferno."

"I'm most distressed by this news," he told them, "and I'm so glad I've arrived!"

Miss James seemed to find her manners. "Mr. Periwinkle, this is my niece, Clara. And our dog, Mutt. I apologize for our being in such a sorry state."

"Don't fash yourself, Miss James. I'm relieved to have stumbled on you when you could obviously use some assistance. Will you allow me to provide it?"

"Normally, I'd be too proud, and I'd insist I don't need any help, but in light of our predicament, I shouldn't act so stubbornly."

He gestured to the carriage, to the driver and outriders who were watching the scene unfold.

"I was on my way to Ralston to speak with you," he said.

"Is it time for the reunion?" Tears welled into her eyes. "I fear I'm not in much of a position to meet my old companions."

"It's better than a reunion. Miss Carstairs is getting married shortly."

"That is splendid to hear," Miss James said. "With it being such a terrible day in my own life, I'm happy to know there's a celebration occurring. Who is her husband to be?"

"She's marrying very high. To Lucas Watson, Lord Barrett? They've sent me to fetch you to the wedding. Will you come?"

"We're in such bad shape. We can't show up at Lord Barrett's door, looking like homeless waifs—which is exactly what we are."

Clara said, "Beggars can't be choosers, Joanna. I believe we should go with Mr. Periwinkle. Maybe your friends at Barrett can explain what we should do next."

"Just so, Miss Clara," Howard agreed. "There is a kind and considerate group of people waiting for you at Barrett. Let me take you to them."

Miss James began to cry, tears dripping down her cheeks, and she was too worn down to swipe them away. "May I bring my dog? He'll be fine; he merely requires a quiet period to heal. I can't leave him behind."

Howard's heart wrenched with dismay. She was even prettier when she cried. Almost as pretty as Miss Carstairs, whom he would love forever. He'd like to hug her, to promise her everything would be all right, but it would have been completely inappropriate.

But Miss Carstairs and Miss Grey would have her fixed in a trice.

"Of course you may bring your dog," he murmured. "What's his name? Mutt?"

"Yes, Mutt," Clara said.

"A grand name it is too."

Mutt woofed softly, and Howard patted him on the head, then he motioned to the outriders, bidding them to aid the two females.

He stood to the side, observing as the servants fussed over them. They and their wounded animal were settled in the vehicle, their meager possessions too, and he grinned with satisfaction.

Howard Periwinkle was saving the day for the *Lost Girls* yet again! What a story he would have to tell!

He went over and climbed in too.

Chapter
20

Jacob was nearly home, but he turned his horse down the lane toward Joanna's cottage. Tim and Tom were with him, so he should have ridden on by, but he felt as if magnets had grabbed hold of him and forced him to stop.

The prior week, he'd left Ralston Place in an enraged hurry to chase after Margaret and Sandy. As a result, he hadn't sent a message to her. When he didn't visit again, what must she have thought of his behavior?

She probably suspected he'd climbed into her bed, and then—having lifted her skirt like the worst cad—had gotten what he'd craved and was finished with her. He hoped she didn't presume that to be the case, but how else would she have viewed it?

"Do you know Miss James very well?" Tom asked, bringing his horse up alongside.

"Yes, I know her very well. How about you?"

"Only in passing. We were wondering: Can she cast magic spells? Pa says it's superstitious nonsense, that there's no such thing as magic and she's just a normal person who's learned some doctoring, but the stable boys claim she's really powerful. They've watched her change her dog into a bird."

Jacob laughed. "First, I agree with Sandy, and I don't believe in magic. Second, I know her dog quite well too. His name is Mutt, and he can't fly—no matter what the stable boys tell you."

Tom scowled. "Are you sure?"

"I'm very sure."

Tom called to his brother. "The Captain says her dog can't fly."

"She can't fly either," Jacob said, "but she has some interesting talents. She's a very powerful healer, and she might be a clairvoyant too."

"She can see the future?"

"I think she can."

"Could she see mine?"

"We'll ask her. She won't always consent. She has to feel you're not the sort who would judge her badly for it."

"I wouldn't judge her. I promise."

On the trip from Scotland, he'd let the boys' chatter alter into a drone, while he pondered his life and what direction he'd like it to take. During the long miles, he'd arrived at some decisions.

He was eager to marry, but not Roxanne. Bizarre as it sounded, he yearned to marry Joanna. It was such an outlandish prospect that it might push the Earth off its axis. Family members would faint. Acquaintances would snicker behind his back. Strangers would ridicule him to his face.

But *he* would be delighted forever. From the moment he'd met her, his father's ghost had been hovering, ordering him to pay attention, to note what had been placed right in front of him. That was Joanna James, the most beautiful, exotic, intriguing woman he'd ever encountered.

Most men would pick her to be a mistress rather than a wife. She'd be kept hidden to supply illicit entertainment, but he wouldn't live like that.

His father had navigated those depressing waters, and it had delivered him to a spot where he'd loathed his wife so completely that he was constantly gone. It meant Jacob had grown up thinking he'd hate to be a father, but suddenly, he *wanted* children! Fancy that!

Previously, the notion had appealed to him in a vague way. A man was supposed to sire sons after all, but Tim and Tom had made him realize how grand it would be to have a few sturdy, rambunctious boys of his own.

His children would know him well, and he'd be a steadying presence who would guide and mentor them on their road to adulthood. Jacob would bring that dream to fruition—with Joanna. She was the oddest choice he could settle on for a bride, but she would give him a happy home, happy children, and a happy life.

She'd marry him, wouldn't she? If he asked, wouldn't she accept?

As the possibility arose that she might decline, his pulse raced with alarm. She was such a peculiar woman. She didn't believe he was much of a catch, and she had that idiotic aversion to matrimony, so he'd have to wear her down. On contemplating how amusing it would be to persuade her, he grinned, ready for a battle he was determined to win.

He burst out of the foliage to her gate, prepared to jump from the saddle and rush to her door, but the sight that greeted him was so disturbing that he wondered if he wasn't in the wrong meadow.

Her cottage had burned to the ground. The roof had caved in, and three of the walls had collapsed. He could see charred furniture in the wreckage, the detritus of her world reduced to ashes. The smell of smoke was still heavy in the air, and the forest was very quiet, as if the animals were hunkered down, mourning what had occurred.

Had she and Clara survived? Surely Fate wouldn't be so cruel as to take her from him!

"Oh, no," he mumbled, and he leapt down. The flames had been so hot that even the fence was charred.

"What happened?" Tom asked as he trotted up and climbed down too. Tim did the same.

"You boys stay here," he said. "I should check the rubble."

"Should you? It might be dangerous."

"I'll be careful," Jacob replied.

He didn't explain that he would be hunting for charred remains, although it wasn't likely he could learn much from a visual survey. He'd have to send some men with axes and shovels to pull down the structure and dig through it.

There were no buckets lying around, so there was no indication that anyone had fought the fire. Then again, she lived so far from any neighbors. Who would have noticed the situation and pitched in to help?

He never should have left her in the isolated house! He should have insisted she move to a safer location.

The ruins were cold, so the fire had raged days earlier. He snooped as much as he dared, but there was no evidence they'd perished. He'd have to investigate more thoroughly to be certain though.

He walked over to where Tim and Tom were observing his every step.

"Was there any sign of Miss James or her niece?" Tom asked. "They weren't ... well ... they weren't trapped in it, were they?"

"No. It appears they escaped."

"That's a blessing, isn't it?" Tim said. "We should think so."

Tom added, "Perhaps they're in the village, staying with friends."

Did Joanna have friends in the village? Jacob had no idea, but he nodded. "Perhaps so."

He studied the mess, feeling bereft and disoriented. He'd pinned so many hopes on her. He'd been anxious to implement shocking, marvelous changes, and they all included her. She had to be all right. She and Clara both. He refused to consider any other conclusion.

"Let's head off," he said. "I have to get home."

"What about Miss James and her niece?"

"There might be news at the manor, and we'll find them. I have no doubt."

⌀

LIBBY KEPT MEANDERING OVER to glance out the front window. Then Caro would join her. Mr. Periwinkle was almost to Barrett, and he'd sent a quick rider with the thrilling report that Joanna was with him. They would arrive any minute.

Apparently, Joanna had suffered some difficulties, and she had an orphaned niece and an injured dog with her. She would need some advice, some strong defenders, and some tender, loving care, which Libby would provide in spades.

"Would you sit down?" her fiancé, Luke, asked. "You're nervous as a cat in a thunderstorm."

"You always say that to me," she responded.

"Well, it's always true. You won't make their carriage wheels turn any faster by staring down the road."

Caro's fiancé, Caleb, added, "In fact—if you constantly peek outside—it will make the wheels turn slower. It's that old adage about how a watched cake never bakes."

"You two are too obnoxious to abide," Libby told them. "Why don't you slither away and engage in some manly pursuits—like drinking or cards? Leave the women to focus on what's important."

Caro came up to stand next to her, and she slipped her hand into Libby's. They held tight, gazing down the lane. Then . . . ?

The coach lumbered out of the trees.

"It's them," Caro murmured, and Libby practically shouted, "They're here!"

The news raced through the manor with lightning speed. The entire house had been waiting for Joanna, and the sense of excitement was too potent to describe.

Libby and Caro ran off together, hands still linked, and they dashed to the driveway. Behind them, a crowd filtered out: Luke and Caleb, her half-sister, Penny, who was planning the wedding, her cousin and Penny's handsome husband, Simon Falcon, the butler, Mr. Hobbs, and the other servants.

The vehicle approached in a dreamy sort of snail's pace, and as it rattled to a halt, there was a moment of breathless anticipation, where Time itself seemed to cease its ticking.

In a normal world, they'd have politely tarried while a footman set the step and greeted the occupants, but Libby had never been a patient person.

She hurried over, dragging Caro with her, and before an outrider could jump down, she opened the door herself and peered inside. "Joanna James! Where have you been? I've been looking everywhere for you. For twenty years, I've been looking!"

Joanna—small of stature and pretty as ever—leaned out and tumbled into Libby's arms. Libby caught her, Caro too, and the three Lost Girls of the Caribbean began to cry.

⁓

"I've had a great life."

At hearing Joanna declare it, Caro and Libby smiled and teared up again. They'd been crying off and on for hours and couldn't stop.

They were in Libby's bedroom. Joanna was stretched out on the bed, having been bathed, coddled, and dressed in clean clothes. Lord Barrett had locked them in, so they could talk without pause or interruption.

Libby's story was known by everyone in the kingdom. When she'd been returned to England, Harry Carstairs had blustered forward and claimed to be her uncle. The navy had handed her over without investigating. She'd been a talented, flamboyant child, and he'd trained her for the stage.

She was England's darling, and people adored her. In recent months, due to Mr. Periwinkle's newspaper articles, it had been revealed that she was Henrietta Pendleton too, so she was Lord Roland's daughter. In a few days, she would wed Luke and become his countess.

Her life had played out as if she were a cursed princess trapped in a tower, and the romantic ending—with her marrying Lord Barrett—had pushed her fame to stunning heights.

Caro had been given to her cruel grandfather who'd tormented her. Once he'd passed away, her uncle had assumed control of the family, and though he'd acted kindly on the surface, he'd been just as cruel—and very corrupt too.

Before Caro's father had perished in the shipwreck, he'd explored in Africa with Sir Sidney Sinclair and had wound up owner of a diamond mine. The money had been dumped into a trust fund that Caro's male relatives had hidden from her so they could spend her fortune on themselves.

She'd been treated like Cinderella, but that horrid era was over. Their shenanigans had been exposed, and their many crimes were being prosecuted. She was free of them, and she was about to marry Jacob's half-brother, Caleb Ralston.

Joanna had been astonished to find him in residence at Barrett, astonished to learn that he was about to wed Caro, and she was frantically trying to figure out what it indicated.

She'd been biting her tongue, wondering if she should mention her connection to Jacob. She knew Jacob viewed Caleb in a cordial way, but she wasn't sure of Caleb's opinion in the other direction. With her only just walking in the door, she hadn't been keen to raise a difficult topic, and at the moment, she wouldn't ponder Jacob.

He'd been recalled to the navy, and she couldn't imagine when he'd return to Ralston Place. When he did, would he still be fond of her? Would he ride to her cottage to see her? When he found it burned to the ground, the meadow cleared by Kit Boswell, what would he think? Would he even recollect their fleeting amour?

"Tell us more about your Aunt Pru," Libby said. "What was she like? I remember your mother quite vividly."

"That is so lovely to hear. It warms my heart."

Joanna's mother had lived for several weeks after they'd staggered onto their island. In the beginning, there had been six adults with them, but they'd gradually died from illness or injury. Joanna's mother had been the last one to go. She'd cut her foot, and it had become infected. Their health had been so depleted that she hadn't been able to survive it.

"Did your aunt look like your mother?" Caro asked.

"Yes, she looked like her, and they were a year apart in age. They were completely similar in temperament, so it was like being with my mother all over again."

Caro and Libby sighed with pleasure.

"I missed both of you so much," she said, "and we tried to contact you. Caro, we wrote to your grandfather and suggested a visit, but we received such a nasty reply that we didn't attempt it again."

Caro's jaw dropped. "I never knew!"

"I wish now that we'd continued to pester him. I can't guess if it might have improved your circumstances, but Aunt Pru was like a force of nature. She wouldn't have stood by and let you be abused."

"I can't blame her for avoiding my grandfather. He was such a bitter, unhappy man. I can just envision the terrible remarks he'd have penned about me in a letter."

"And Libby," Joanna said, "we tried to see you too. We read a newspaper advertisement that you'd be performing in a nearby village, so we bought tickets, but you weren't in the show. We inquired of the manager afterward, and he advised us that you'd accepted another engagement and weren't there." She chuckled. "He wouldn't refund our money, and Aunt Pru was so mad."

Libby clucked her tongue. "I used to nag at my Uncle Harry that I wanted to find you. For years, he claimed it was impossible to discover where you were, then, once I was older and grew more adamant, he lied and insisted he'd written to the navy, and they'd lost the records."

"No!" Joanna protested. "That is so malicious. Why would he act that way?"

"He was a wily character, and I could never divine his motives. I was such a gullible dunce that I believed whatever he told me."

Caro said, "I never understood their keeping us apart. Why couldn't we have been allowed to remain friends? It never made any sense to me."

"Tell us more about *your* life," Libby said to Joanna, "and I swear I'll stop interrupting. I'm constantly blabbing about my own past, so you never finish with yours. It sounds as if you were the only one of us who was content."

"I was very content."

"Mr. Periwinkle informed us that you were living at Ralston Place, which belongs to Caleb's half-brother, Jacob. You're aware of how they're connected to us, aren't you?"

"Oh, yes, I'm aware of it," Joanna said.

"How did you end up there? And have you met Jacob? If you have, does *he* realize who you are?"

"And what happened to you?" Caro asked. "When you arrived, you were positively bedraggled. You and your dog were injured. What was the cause?"

Joanna launched into a lengthy story, admitting the truth about her parents, about her father's vicious wife who'd chased her mother out of England. She told them about her female ancestors, the special gifts they had that scared so many others. She explained how they'd learned over the centuries to be vigilant and careful.

She told them about Clara being born and discarded by her mother. She told them about moving to Ralston Place in order to conceal Clara's whereabouts from her despicable kin.

Previously, Joanna had assumed that was the impetus, but with Kit Boswell and Roxanne Ralston winding up in the same spot as Clara, she was wondering if Pru hadn't transported her and Clara to the estate for a reason.

Pru had firmly believed in pre-destiny. Perhaps she'd read Clara's and Joanna's cards and had decided their fate lay at Ralston. Who could be certain?

Joanna told them about Kit Boswell and Roxanne Ralston being Clara's parents, how they'd resolved to be rid of Clara. Then, she confessed why Roxanne had wanted Joanna gone too.

"You had an affair with Jacob Ralston?" Libby appeared stunned.

"I wouldn't call it an affair," Joanna said. "That would indicate a protracted relationship. This was more of an illicit flirtation."

Libby and Caro exchanged an odd glance, and Joanna's spirits sank. Had she revealed too many details? They'd blithely accepted her description of her powers and ancient knowledge, but maybe a carnal amour was too much.

"Do you hate me for it?" she asked, her mood plummeting.

"Gad, no," Caro said. "We've been talking about how Miles Ralston's ghost seems to be hovering. I'm convinced that he brought Caleb into my life. Now *you* have been seduced by Jacob. It can't be a coincidence."

"The last time I spoke to Miles Ralston," Joanna said, "he and I were alone on his ship, and we were about to dock in Jamaica."

"We never saw him again," Libby said with quite a bit of dismay.

"He was holding me on his hip, and we had a very solemn conversation—well, as much of a solemn conversation as you can have with a four-year-old. I asked him to always watch over us, and I think he is. I think it took him awhile to locate us from the other side, and once he managed it, he went to work to ensure we wound up safe and happy."

"You gave him this task?" Libby said.

"Yes, and for two decades, I've been waiting for him to get on with it. I'm back with you and Caro again, and I feel as if he's finally behaving as he promised he would."

"I wouldn't necessarily agree that everything is fixed," Caro said. "Caleb is marrying me, but what about you and Jacob? Has matrimony crossed his mind? From my own experience with the Ralston men, they have to be hog-tied and dragged to the altar."

"Jacob would never wed me," Joanna said. "He's very conscious of his elevated status as Miles's son, and he's too far above me. He actually told me that."

Her reply had Libby and Caro hooting with laughter. After they calmed down, Joanna asked, "What's so funny?"

Libby answered the question. "Jacob Ralston might assume he's too top-lofty to marry you, but my fiancé will have a very different opinion about it. In situations like this, he's a stickler for the proprieties. He will never sit by and let a cad slink away after a maiden has been ruined."

"Would you like to wed him, Joanna?" Caro asked. "Luke and Caleb could persuade him for you. They both know him, and they could pressure him into it."

Joanna shut her eyes and pondered the notion. Would she like it?

She tried to imagine herself as his wife, residing at Ralston Manor, having Margaret Howell as her sister-in-law. His relatives would share Margaret's view of her, and they'd be vehemently opposed to a match. Joanna refused to wedge herself into such an awful morass. And what would she do with a husband anyway?

It didn't matter how deeply she cherished Jacob. He was a *man*. By his very nature, he felt it was his God-given right to lord himself over any female. But Joanna deemed that type of arrangement to be ridiculous. How could two such disparate people ever come together in a sane way?

"No," she said, "I don't want to wed him. I love him dearly, but I can't fathom how it would ever work."

"If you love him," Libby said, "how could you walk away? I'd never be that noble. Why won't you fight for him?"

"It's not that. It's just that I'm too independent. The first time he bossed me, I'd pack up and leave."

"It's what I kept telling myself about Luke," Libby said. "When he proposed, I thought I'd wind up killing him before we were through, but he's growing on me."

"He dotes on you like a besotted idiot," Caro said.

"You mention it like it's a bad thing," Libby responded.

Joanna studied Libby's body, noticing the gentle aura surrounding her. She focused on Libby's stomach and said, "Could I put my hand on you for a moment?"

"I suppose."

Joanna climbed off the bed and knelt in front of her. She placed a palm over her womb and held it there as she concentrated intently. Finally, she *saw* what she was searching for.

She smiled and whispered, "You're going to have a baby."

"I'm . . . what?" Libby looked pole-axed.

"A baby." Joanna added, "A boy."

Caro smirked at Libby. "You'd best hurry and get Luke's ring on your finger."

"Are you sure?" Libby asked Joanna.

"Yes, and now that I'm with you again, I can deliver it too."

"A boy . . ." Libby murmured. "Luke will be so glad."

Joanna glanced at Caro and pointed to her stomach. "May I?"

"I'm almost afraid to let you," Caro said.

Libby chuckled. "It doesn't hurt, Caro. Don't be a ninny."

Joanna laid a palm on Caro, and she searched for an eternity, then said, "Not yet. But soon."

Caro pulled her close and hugged her so tightly she couldn't breathe. Libby scooted off her chair and joined in the embrace. They cried and chatted and cried some more.

When their knees and backs grew tired, and they drew away, Libby—always a nuisance—asked, "How do you know such eerie magic? How can you predict such mysterious events? Are you a witch?"

Joanna shrugged. "I might be, but I'll only ever admit it to the two of you. If anyone else inquires, we'll simply say I have some peculiar quirks."

"A witch in the family..." Caro mused. "My world becomes stranger by the day."

⌒

"ARE YOU FEELING BETTER?"

"I'm feeling perfect."

Caro sighed and snuggled herself to Caleb's chest. They were nestled on a sofa in a cozy parlor, sitting by a dying fire. She was talked out, and she could barely keep her eyes open.

"What has Joanna's life been like?" Caleb asked. "I would have inquired myself, but in case it was horrid, I figured I shouldn't pry."

"Of the three of us, she had the only sensible upbringing. She was claimed by her mother's sister who was a midwife and healer, so it was her nature to be kind. The women in their family have that calling."

"Joanna too?"

"Yes. She delivers babies and nurses the sick. She brews potions to treat various illnesses."

"Like an apothecary?"

"Yes, sort of. She's a clairvoyant too."

"My goodness. I'll have to ask her what she sees in my future."

Caro scoffed. "You don't need a clairvoyant to inform you. You'll live happily ever after—with *me* as your bride." She sat up so she could look at him. "Guess what she told me."

"Besides her confessing to qualities that make her incredibly odd? With that red hair of hers, I can't imagine what it might be."

"You're aware that she's at Ralston Place."

"I could hardly forget. Has she met my half-brother?"

"Oh, she's *met* him all right."

Caleb scowled. "What is that supposed to mean?"

"You won't like it."

"Tell me."

He had a difficult relationship with Jacob Ralston, but recently, Jacob had reached out to Caleb, hoping to be friends. He'd even invited Caleb to a September party where, according to Joanna, he would announce his engagement, but Caro doubted Jacob would be marrying Roxanne Ralston.

He might wed in September, but it wouldn't be to his cousin.

"I need you to visit Ralston Place for me," she said.

"You can request any favor, but probably not that."

"I have some disturbing news about Jacob, and I can't confide in Luke. I'm scared about how he'd handle it."

"Uh-oh. I don't believe I'll like where this is headed."

"No, I don't believe you will."

Caleb blew out a heavy breath. "He seduced Joanna?"

"Yes, and then out of the blue, his relatives claimed he was recalled to duty without any warning. After he *left* and was no longer around to protect her, they burned down her house and chased her off the property. What I'm worried about is this: Is there a chance he's a cad and he didn't really return to the navy? His kin insisted it was true, and Joanna didn't question their story, but might he have used it as an easy excuse to be shed of her after she was ruined?"

"You think he might be loafing in his front parlor at Ralston Place?"

"I'm not acquainted with him, so I'm trying to persuade myself it's not that. I'm telling myself he's your brother, and he wouldn't act that way."

"I hate familial quagmires," Caleb said. "I assume I'm riding to Ralston Place to find out if he's there."

"Would you?"

"And if he is? I'm guessing I have to drag him here and force him to wed her."

"Well, you Ralston men do need a bit of a shove toward matrimony."

"When must I go?"

"How about first thing in the morning?"

Chapter
21

"WHAT HAPPENED TO YOU?"

"I cut my leg."

Jacob was in Kit's office, watching as he limped in and eased onto a chair. He'd taken Kit's spot behind the desk, so Kit was forced to sit across from him. Kit was very conscious of his status, so it was a petty act on Jacob's part, yet he was enjoying the paltry snub.

He'd been struggling to figure out what would become of Kit once Sandy and Margaret returned. Kit didn't have an income except for what Jacob paid him. If Jacob sent him packing, he didn't have any friends to offer shelter. From the time he'd been a little boy, everything he possessed had come to him from the Ralston family.

He'd never appreciated it though.

"How did you cut it?" Jacob asked.

"Oh...ah...I tripped and sliced it on a fence post. The slash is very deep, and it's not healing." Kit snorted with a grim amusement. "It's too bad Miss James vanished. I could have used her to clean it out."

"Where do you suppose she is?"

"I can't imagine. With a girl like that, any destination is possible. Maybe she hopped on her broom and flew away."

"Very funny."

There had been no word about Joanna and Clara. Jacob had servants questioning the neighbors, and he'd posted inquiries in shops and taverns over quite a wide area, but there had only been one reply. A teamster had been driving by in his wagon, and he'd smelled smoke in the woods, so he'd stopped to check for a fire.

The cottage had already burned to the ground, with a few hot spots remaining, and there had been no sign of Joanna or Clara. No one had seen them in the village, on the road, or anywhere else. It was as if they'd disappeared into thin air.

Jacob was such a conceited ass that they'd rarely talked about *her*. Their conversations had always focused on him, so he had no idea who she might call upon if she was in trouble. It was definitely difficult to search when he had no information.

"You seemed fond of her," Kit said. "Were you ever able to lift her skirt?"

"Shut up, Kit. Even if she and I had dallied, I'd never tell you about it." Kit pulled out a kerchief and dabbed at his brow, and Jacob said, "You're a bit feverish."

"I'm injured! The wound is infected, and I'm not feeling well."

"I apologize; I should have left you in your bed. Have you summoned the doctor?"

"He's in London for the week." Kit waved a hand, as if his health was of no consequence. "The housekeeper gave me one of Miss James's ointments, so I'll be fine. What did you need?"

Jacob pointed to a document on the desk. "I had an audit commenced, remember? Of the estate accounts?"

"Yes, I remember, and from how you're glaring, I'm betting it wasn't good news. If we've suffered losses, I hope you don't intend to blame me. I can't control the weather or make your tenants work harder."

It was typical that Kit would deflect any culpability, and Jacob was weary over the entire situation. He never liked to quarrel, but honestly! If he hadn't commissioned the audit, how long would Kit have continued to steal?

Instead of delving to the heart of the matter, he said, "Sandy and Margaret will be back soon."

"That will be so bloody awkward. Sandy's ego is as big as a barn, and after she raised him up like this, he'll be unbearable."

"He can be cocky," Jacob blandly agreed.

"Have you any advice as to how I should deal with him? He was our stable manager, and now, he's your brother-in-law. How, precisely, am I to boss him? Margaret has created an incredible fiasco."

Jacob was about to say, *You'll be gone, so you don't need to worry about the problem.*

Suddenly, a footman knocked and poked his nose in. "I realize you asked not to be disturbed, Captain, but you have a visitor, and the butler thought you should be apprised immediately."

"Who is it?"

"Apparently, it's your half-brother. Mr. Caleb Ralston?"

Jacob's jaw dropped in surprise. "Caleb is here? Really?"

"Yes. Will you meet with him? The butler brought him into your library."

"Well...ah...yes, I'll meet with him. Give me a minute to wrap up with Mr. Boswell, and I'll be right there."

The boy hurried off, and as his footsteps faded, Kit said, "Caleb Ralston has waltzed in our door? He has some nerve. What could he want?"

"I can't imagine. He must have dire news to impart, so I better hear what it is." Jacob stood and said, "We'll finish this discussion after I've chatted with him."

"Should I accompany you? You don't suppose he's come to borrow money, do you? Or to request a favor? We could present a united front to dissuade him."

Jacob scoffed. "Caleb owns a gambling club in London, so he's rich and very powerful. I doubt he's seeking a loan or a favor." Jacob extended the audit report. "Would you like to review this while I'm talking to him?"

"I'm not hale enough. I'll have to study it later."

Kit was looking more sickly by the second, and Jacob said, "You should head for your bed. Can you make it on your own? Or should I summon a servant to assist you?"

"I can make it on my own."

Kit's injury had rendered him more churlish than usual. He pushed himself to his feet and limped out. Jacob trailed after him, watching until he lurched around a corner.

He wondered if Kit was telling the truth about how he'd hurt himself. He was in genuine pain, but it might have been caused by any ominous mishap. For all Jacob knew, he'd been shot by a jealous husband.

He put Kit out of his mind and went in the other direction. Evidently, his brother had strolled in bold as brass. Jacob had seen him earlier in the summer. Initially, their conversation had been stilted, but they'd gradually gotten the hang of it. Still though, they weren't chums, so why had he arrived?

He wound through the house until he approached the library. The butler was hovering in the hall, appearing anxious, as if he might be scolded for allowing the rogue to enter.

The man straightened and said, "It's your half-brother, Mr. Caleb Ralston, Captain."

"I hope you poured him a whiskey."

"I have."

"Then that will be all."

Jacob marched on, but Roxanne blustered toward him.

"I just learned about our visitor," she said. "Shall I serve as your hostess?"

"No, thank you. I don't need a hostess."

His response was more abrupt than he'd intended, but since he'd returned from Scotland, he couldn't deduce how to handle her. She was constantly underfoot, eager to have him recollect the reason she was in the manor.

She hadn't departed for London as she'd threatened, and she'd grown overly sweet and solicitous, as if she was trying to hold onto him by pretending to be someone she wasn't. Unfortunately for her, he couldn't forget what she was really like: icy, disdainful, posh, extravagant.

As with Kit, he had to devise a solution for her. Once he declared the engagement to be over, what would become of her? Was her fate his problem?

He couldn't decide, and with Caleb inside the ostentatious room, he wouldn't fret about her. He closed the door in her curious face.

Caleb was over by the sideboard, refilling his glass, and Jacob said, "Caleb Ralston! When you were announced, I couldn't believe my ears."

"Hello, big brother."

It was a jest of sorts. They were the same age, and Jacob was a few months older than Caleb, proving their father had been an immoral dog.

Caleb tipped his glass in welcome, and Jacob walked over and poured his own drink. He motioned to the desk. "Let's sit. Shall I bring the decanter? Will we have to keep ourselves fortified?"

"That depends on how you answer my questions."

"Has a calamitous situation arisen?"

"We'll see, I guess."

Jacob sat behind the desk, and Caleb pulled up the chair across. Jacob wanted to wait silently for Caleb to begin, but he was too bewildered.

"What could have dragged you here?" he asked.

"I should probably start by saying I'm surprised to find you in England."

"Why would you be? I'm home on furlough until the end of September."

"It's what you told me that evening in London, but I was praying you'd left."

It was an odd remark. "Why would you pray for that?"

"Because—since you're at Ralston Place—this will be a tad difficult."

"You're speaking in riddles."

"First off, I have a message from Luke Watson."

"I didn't realize you were acquainted with him. How's he been?"

"He's good. In fact, he's better than good."

"I've haven't talked to him recently. What's occupying his time?"

"I'm predicting this will astonish you—it certainly astonished me—but he's marrying in a few days."

"You're joking! Who is his bride?"

"I don't mean to shock you, but it's Libby Carstairs."

As far as Jacob was aware, there was only one woman in the world with that name. "Are you referring to Libby Carstairs, as in, *The Mystery Girl of the Caribbean*?"

"The very one."

"How did that happen?"

"I'll let them tell you about it." Caleb reached in his coat and drew out an envelope that had a gold border. He laid it on the desk. "You're invited to the wedding, and I should apprise you that the entire kingdom is begging for an invitation, so you're incredibly fortunate."

"I'm flattered and stunned."

"I'm marrying too, as soon as I can haul my sorry behind back to Barrett."

"What? I just saw you in London. You didn't mention it."

"It occurred rather fast."

Caleb's cheeks heated, providing evidence that he'd misbehaved with his fiancée.

"Who is the lucky girl?" Jacob asked.

"It's Caroline Grey."

The name was familiar, and Jacob scowled. "I should know her, shouldn't I?"

"She is one of the three *Lost Girls* who was rescued by Father with Miss Carstairs."

Jacob gasped. "*You* are marrying one of them?"

"Yes, and Caroline will be delighted to clarify how it transpired. I'd be too embarrassed to explain it myself."

"I'm ... floored. Will I sound deranged if I state that I've felt Father's ghost hovering all summer? Might he be bringing us together? Is he making sure we bond with those girls for some reason?"

"You won't sound deranged for thinking that. I've suffered the same impression this summer too."

"I've met the third girl. Joanna James?"

Caleb grinned. "Now we get to the real purpose of my visit."

"You're here about Joanna? Where is she? She was living in my woods, but her cottage burned down, and she vanished. We've been searching for her, and I've been frantic with worry."

"Have you been?"

Caleb looked dubious, and Jacob said, "Ah ... yes? I've been very worried."

Caleb grabbed the decanter and filled both their glasses. He sipped his whiskey and studied Jacob over the rim.

"I started this discussion," Caleb said, "by declaring myself surprised to find you in England."

"Why is that?"

"It seems that your alleged friend and estate agent, Kit Boswell, told Joanna you had been recalled to duty. Apparently, you fled in a hurry, and he had no idea when you'd be back in the country."

"Oh, for pity's sake. Why would Kit even have been talking to her?"

"Not only did he *talk* to her, but he claimed that he'd decided to level her cottage and clear the meadow where it was located."

"He...what?"

Caleb motioned to Jacob's glass and said, "Drink up, Brother. This story goes downhill from here."

⁓

"Were you able to listen in?"

"No. Jacob shut the door in my face."

Roxanne was in the bedchamber in the manor that Kit had commandeered for his own use. He was limping and too wretched to walk over to his own home, which was a huge indicator of his deteriorated condition.

Jacob was down in the library, having a private chat with his half-brother, and Roxanne was aggravated. She didn't like a single incident to occur in the mansion without her gleaning every detail.

"What could he want?" she asked Kit.

"How would I bloody know?"

"I don't like him showing up like this."

"As if I care."

Kit was seated on a chair, the leg of his trouser rolled up to reveal his calf. A bandage was wrapped around the wound, and he was slowly unwinding it.

Once it was free, he said, "What is your opinion? It's looks hideous to me."

"I agree. It's disgusting."

"It's definitely infected, and it would be nice if you could exhibit some sympathy. I received it because of you."

"Me! Why would it be my fault? You're mad to blame me."

He'd warned Miss James that men would arrive to level her cottage, but he'd been lying. He hadn't intended to bring any men, for he and Roxanne couldn't have had any witnesses to her eviction.

She'd simply had to go without delay, so he'd snuck over in the middle of the night, the plan being to light a small blaze that would get her moving. She was precisely the sort of obnoxious snot who would have tarried forever, and they'd needed her to vanish while Jacob was in Scotland.

But as Kit had tiptoed toward the rear of the house, merely to set the grass on fire, Miss James's dog had rushed up and delivered a furious bite that had torn his trousers and left a deep gash. In a panic, Kit had hurled his torch—through a window! He swore it was an accident, but as a result, the entire building had burned to the ground.

After a teamster had reported the inferno, Kit had acted concerned and had had some men search the rubble. Miss James and her niece's remains weren't there, so they'd escaped, but if they'd perished, Roxanne wouldn't necessarily have mourned.

Kit's injury was swollen and inflamed, the dog's teeth marks clear, and Roxanne wondered if it might kill him in the end. She wrenched her gaze away. She wasn't a nurse, and she wouldn't pretend to be.

"Where do you suppose the little trollop is?" she asked.

"I have no idea, but Jacob is hunting for her everywhere."

"I'm betting she took your threat to heart. I'm picturing her on the other side of England."

"You better hope so. If he finds her, there's no predicting how angry he'll be."

"I know, Kit. I know. Don't lecture me."

Their conversation might have erupted into a full-blown quarrel, but a housemaid stopped out in the hall.

"There you are, Miss Ralston," she said. "The Captain needs you in the library."

"I'll be right there." She couldn't imagine what the servants would think of her being in Kit's bedchamber, and she waved at his leg for her excuse. "Mr. Boswell has cut himself, and he had me check it for him. It's very bad, so would you have the housekeeper send up an ointment?"

"I will, Miss."

The girl glanced furtively at Kit, then she flitted off, no doubt to hurry down to the kitchen and gossip about what she'd observed.

"What could Jacob want?" Kit asked.

"Maybe he's decided to introduce me to the high-and-mighty, Caleb Ralston."

"He owns a gambling business in London, so he's much richer than Jacob, and you're such a mercenary. You might like him more than your fiancé."

Roxanne didn't reply to the taunt. "Good luck with your leg. It would be terrible if you had to have it amputated."

As she strutted out, he muttered, "Castrating bitch."

She grinned and marched down the stairs. She hadn't been joking about his condition growing dire. When she thought of that dog's teeth puncturing his skin, she shivered with distaste. Who could guess what disease the animal might have planted?

"Serves you right, you vain ass," she mumbled under her breath, then she forced a smile and walked faster.

Jacob had followed Margaret to Scotland, and in the interim, Roxanne's plan had been to travel to town, but once Kit had chased Miss James away, there hadn't been any reason to leave.

Miss James had been the impediment to Roxanne's happiness, but with the vixen gone, Jacob would forget her quickly enough. Roxanne was ready to proceed to the wedding, and she simply had to get him accustomed to the notion again.

She'd confronted him about Miss James, and he'd been incredibly embarrassed, and she would use his humiliation to her own advantage.

He could likely be coerced into handing over numerous boons to wipe away some of his misdeeds.

She headed straight to the library, and the butler was lurking. He saw her and said, "Miss Ralston is here, Captain."

"Send her in please," Jacob responded.

Roxanne hadn't known what to expect as she entered the room. She'd figured Jacob would introduce her to his bastard half-brother. Or perhaps his brother was staying for supper or for the night, and she'd have to arrange it.

Well, she would do whatever Jacob required. In that, she would be grace personified.

"You needed me, Jacob?" she said as she swept in.

She looked beautiful and glamorous, and she wanted his brother to be envious, but as she assessed the two men, a bit of anxiety flared.

Jacob was seated at the massive desk, and his half-brother was standing behind him, like a sentinel guarding his back.

"Sit down, Roxanne," was Jacob's answer to her greeting.

There was a chair positioned directly opposite him, and it was obviously for her. There was a perception in the air that an inquisition was about to start—and she would be the tortured party.

She nearly refused his command, nearly stomped out, but from how Caleb Ralston was glaring, she suspected he might run her down and drag her back.

She strolled over and eased down, taking an inordinate amount of time to adjust her skirt.

"From how you're glowering," she said to Jacob, "it appears you're angry. Have I upset you? If so, let me apologize."

Caleb Ralston snorted at that, and Jacob said, "This is my brother, Caleb."

"Hello, sir."

He didn't acknowledge her by so much as a dip of his head, and a niggle of panic ignited. Those blasted rumors from Florence! Had they caught up with her?

"Is this about the duel in Italy?"

The question burst out; she couldn't swallow it down, and Jacob blanched. "No, but that's probably a subject we'll have to address before we're finished."

"Her foibles in Italy are irrelevant," Caleb Ralston said. "You have plenty of proof without it."

Roxanne scowled ferociously. "Mr. Ralston, as you and I are not acquainted, there's no need for us to converse. I should like to speak to my fiancé in private. Would you leave us?"

"No."

The arrogant oaf looked so much like Jacob—same eyes, same mouth, same broad shoulders—that it was uncanny. Their bigamist father, Miles, had definitely passed on some strong traits.

"What's happened?" Roxanne demanded of Jacob, seizing the initiative. "Why are you staring at me with such . . . such malice?"

"Caleb brought me some interesting news."

"On what topic?"

"On *you* and some of your history."

"Your half-brother and I only met this very moment, so I can't imagine what details he could possibly possess."

"Tell me about you and Kit."

"Me and . . . Kit?" She frowned, pretending confusion. "What about us? I loathe him and it's a mystery to me why you continue to employ him. He's rude, lazy, and incompetent, and his very presence at the estate is a disservice to you."

"I'm not talking about your current relationship. I'm talking about a decade ago when you and your mother lived in Telford."

Her heart fell to her feet. Somehow, she managed to keep her gaze steady. She would deny and deny until she drew her last breath.

"I didn't know Kit a decade ago."

"He had kin there for a few years, and he visited them in the summers."

"I really don't recall."

"Don't you?" The query hung in the air between them, then his expression grew a tad cruel. "I don't necessarily judge you for your affair. He always viewed himself as quite a rake, and you had to be...what? Fifteen? I'm sure the liaison spun out of control before you completely understood what was occurring."

"I'm a virtuous woman, and I'm astonished that you'd raise such a hideous accusation."

Jacob chuckled nastily. "Give over, Roxanne. Your sins have been exposed. What's truly aggravating me is how you've practiced your subterfuge. The family previously intended a match for us, yet secretly, you were an unwed mother. You birthed Clara, then you fled the country without a hint to any of us."

"You're spewing nonsense."

He ignored her. "Then, when my mother suggested we finally follow through with the engagement, you raced home to marry me. It must have come as a shock to find Clara here too."

"I'm totally bewildered as to who you mean."

Jacob had a method of staring a person down, one he'd perfected on the sailors under his command. Who could stand up to him when he glared like that?

She glanced down at her hands, unable to persist with their visual battle, but her mind was awhirl as she struggled to devise the best path. A fraught silence festered, and Caleb Ralston filled it.

"Joanna James is safe and staying with my fiancée. She told me how you nearly murdered her and Clara. You stabbed her dog, then set their house on fire—with them in it—so they'd die in the blaze."

"Shame on you, Roxanne!" Jacob scolded. "What were you thinking?"

Before she could stop herself, she said, "I didn't do anything to the pathetic trollop. It was Kit's idea."

Caleb Ralston tsked with offense. "When I meet a woman like you, I wonder how the Good Lord lets some of you bear children."

"It was Kit's doing, was it?" Jacob's tone was even, his deportment calm. They might have been discussing the weather. "I figured you'd blame him for any mischief, but this isn't about Kit. This is about you and how you've deceived me for so long."

"I didn't deceive you! How would I have?"

Caleb Ralston butted in again. "Are you deaf, Miss Ralston? Or are you stupid? You had a child out of wedlock, then you snuck to Italy so Jacob wouldn't learn of it. You paid the midwife to make your daughter disappear. Then, years later, when you discovered she was living in Jacob's woods, you attempted to murder her all over again."

"Murder her!" Roxanne huffed. "That's insane."

"What precisely," Jacob asked, "were you assuming Joanna's aunt did with Clara? Did you suppose she drowned her in a stream? Did you hope she left her in the forest for the fairies?"

"You have no right to criticize me," she fumed, abandoning any pretense. "You can't imagine what that period was like."

"Exactly. I can't imagine it, and I'm not criticizing you. Not over Kit seducing you or you having a baby as the result. If there's condemnation occurring, it's because you were going to wed me, despite this debacle. If you'd told me about your mistakes as a girl, I'd have tried to forgive you. But you didn't. You'd have been my wife, and you'd have strutted around in my home, while you and Kit snickered behind my back over how you'd tricked me."

"It wasn't like that."

"What was it *like* then?"

Jacob's fury was bubbling to the surface and about to boil over. If it washed over her, how could she keep from being scalded?

"You agreed to marry me," she said, "and I won't allow you to cry off."

"After what's been revealed, you think I'd proceed? You're the kind of woman who would kill her own daughter. You're a monster, and I declare our nuptial contract to be null and void."

Roxanne bristled. "I didn't start that fire!"

"I don't believe you. I'm certain you were at Kit's side, directing his aim." Jacob peered over at his brother. "Get her out of my sight. I can't look at her another second."

Caleb Ralston pushed away from the wall. He walked over, grabbed her arm, and lifted her to her feet.

"Let's go, Miss Ralston."

"To where?"

"You're being arrested, and there are men waiting in the driveway who will convey you to the jail."

She laughed, as if it was the most ridiculous comment she'd ever heard. "Arrested on what charge?"

"Attempted murder—for now." Her knees gave out, but he didn't permit her to fall. He simply tightened his grip and continued. "I suspect it will be arson too, as well as destruction of property, false dealing, breach of promise. I'm very rich, and I can hire the best lawyers in the land to help Jacob skewer you. The prosecutor will likely pile on so many felonies that we'll have to have a book printed to list them all."

She tried to wrench away, but couldn't, so she turned her beseeching gaze to Jacob. "Jacob, please. Don't do this! You can't want to."

"I do want to actually. I want to very, very much. And just so you know, I've decided to wed Joanna James."

"What? No! I refuse to step aside."

"After I'm her husband, I will adopt Clara, so she'll be mine forever. You don't care about her, but I shall be delighted to be her father."

He nodded to his brother, and Caleb Ralston said, "Come, Miss Ralston. We're escorting you to the magistrate, then you'll be locked away until your trial. In light of the seriousness of your crimes, you shouldn't plan on ever being released."

"This isn't right! I'm guilty of nothing!"

Neither of them would listen, and she was so disoriented, she could barely keep her balance. She'd thought she'd been invited down to the library to play hostess for Jacob, to pour tea, to charm his half-brother. But she was being arrested? She was on her way to jail?

She was a modest, ordinary female. How was she to grapple with such an outrage?

Caleb Ralston dragged her out so fast that she didn't manage a final glimpse of Jacob. She was marched to a carriage, her wrists and ankles bound with a rope, then Mr. Ralston tossed her in and shut the door.

Despite how she wrestled and begged, he didn't heed her, and he didn't let her go.

***

"What did you need?" Kit glared at Jacob and said, "I'm in no condition to navigate the stairs, and it was cruel of you to demand I attend you down here."

Jacob was seated behind his grand library desk, and he waved Kit to the chair across. Kit limped over and eased down, wincing in pain as he knocked his wound against the chair leg.

"You're looking worse by the second," Jacob said.

"I'm feeling worse."

"It's too bad Miss James ran away. She might have been able to help you."

Kit shivered, desperate to forget the curse she'd leveled, then he scoffed. "I'm not sure I'd have let that witch lay her hands on me, and I use the term *witch* literally. The woman was unnatural, and we're lucky she's gone."

"Are we?" Jacob studied him in an unnerving way. "We'll be making some changes at the estate."

"You brought me down to talk about the estate? It couldn't have waited until I was better?"

"No. My news is a tad urgent."

"May I hope it involves that pompous bastard Sandy? He can't be rewarded for his mischief with Margaret."

Jacob didn't offer an opinion on the comment, but said, "A bit earlier, I tried to discuss the audit with you, but you weren't interested in the results."

"I was interested! I'm simply miserable. Can't we dicker over it later?"

"It doesn't appear to me that you'll improve any time soon."

Jacob was drinking a glass of whiskey, and Kit wanted to ask if Jacob would pour him one too. A shot of fortification would be beneficial, but from Jacob's glum demeanor, Kit received the distinct impression that he oughtn't to request any liquor.

"Could we get on with it?" Kit was too grouchy to be sociable. "I'd like to head back to bed."

"Yes, we can get on with it. How about this? You're fired."

Kit couldn't have heard correctly. "What?"

"You're fired. For embezzlement."

"Now just a damned minute!"

"I will be hiring investigators to search your bank accounts. Any money that's left? I'll find it."

"I've never stolen a farthing from you," Kit furiously fumed. "If some idiotic London accountant claims otherwise, let him raise the allegation to my face!"

"It's hard numbers, Kit, and you never were very good at math. You didn't hide your larceny very well either. It was a simple matter to unravel it." Jacob sighed, as if Kit was a great burden, then he added, "Unfortunately, I'll never recoup the income that was squandered due to your mismanagement of my affairs. It's a loss I'll have to swallow as unrecoverable."

"I've been terrific at my job! It's not my fault if crops fail or the weather won't cooperate. You can't blame me for the stupid decisions and laziness of your tenants."

"I can absolutely blame you." Jacob grinned evilly. "And I *am* blaming you, so I'm rectifying the situation immediately. You're fired, and I'll be giving your post to my brother-in-law."

Kit's fever was muddling his thought processes, so it took him a moment to deduce to whom Jacob referred. When he realized the truth, he bristled with offense. "You're giving my job to Sandy? Tell me you're not."

"He's always run the property anyway, so we're merely making it official. He's been the stable influence behind the scenes who plastered over your mistakes."

"I can't believe you'd treat me this way," Kit muttered. "After everything I've done for you! After everything we've meant to each other! As my reward, you'll toss my position to that insolent braggart?"

"I'm giving him your house too. Margaret is supposedly barren, but I'm an optimist. I pray they have a dozen children, so they'll be needing more space."

"But ... but ... where am I to live? Am I moving into the manor? I guess I could be happy with a suite in the east wing."

"You won't be moving into the manor."

Jacob's tone was so icy that a shiver slid down Kit's spine. "What are you intending for me then?"

The door opened, and Kit glanced around to see a tall blond man enter the room. He looked rich and important, and Kit figured he'd finally met the notorious Caleb Ralston.

"Is she settled?" Jacob asked him.

"Yes," his half-brother said. "She spat and complained and cursed all my unborn sons, but she's ready to go."

"Who is ready?" Kit asked, but they ignored him.

Instead, Jacob said, "Kit, this is my brother, Caleb."

Kit nodded his head. "A pleasure, Caleb."

The bastard snidely retorted, "You and I will never be on a first-name basis. You can call me Mr. Ralston."

Prick!

The Ralston men could be the most arrogant asses in the world, so there was no point in hurling a scathing response. Especially when he was feeling so poorly. He'd never start a fight he couldn't win.

To soothe over the awkward introduction, he said, "I apologize that I didn't rise to greet you, but I've injured myself."

Jacob smirked. "You told me you cut yourself on a fence post. I'd like to see your wound."

"It's quite ghastly," Kit replied, "and I'd rather not display my bodily parts in front of your half-brother."

"Show me," Jacob commanded. "I'm afraid I must insist."

The brothers stared him down, demanding he obey—as if he were the lowest pot boy in the kitchen. If he'd been more hale, he'd have jumped up and stomped out, but he simply didn't have the energy to make a scene.

He blew out a heavy breath, then lifted his trouser leg and unwrapped the bandage.

"Stand up and turn around," Jacob said.

Kit tried to push himself to his feet, but he was faint and off-balance. Caleb Ralston marched over, grabbed his arm, and hefted him up. He was taller and broader than Kit, and with Kit's health so reduced, he seemed impossibly large and imposing.

He bent down for a closer view, then he scoffed. "It doesn't look like any cut from a fence post I've ever seen. It looks to me like a dog bite."

Kit blanched before he could conceal his reaction. "Don't be absurd. Where would I have gotten a dog bite?"

"Where indeed?" Caleb Ralston mused.

He shoved Kit onto the chair, and Kit reapplied his bandage. The brothers continued to glower, and Kit's pulse raced with alarm. Why had Caleb Ralston arrived? Clearly, he'd spread rumors that had upset Jacob, but he was a stranger to Kit. Why would he possess any information that might be detrimental?

Jacob switched topics without warning. "Tell me about you and Roxanne."

"Me and . . . Roxanne?" Kit's sense of being off-balance increased. "Why would you ask about her? I can't abide her, and if you wed her, you'll be sorry forever."

"After she gave birth to Clara—"

Kit gasped; he couldn't help it. "What was that?"

"After she birthed your daughter, what did you think happened to Clara? Obviously, Roxanne didn't retain custody. Did you imagine she was sent to an orphanage? Were you told she was put out for adoption? What?"

"I have no idea who or what you mean."

"It's too late to lie," Jacob said. "Your secrets have been exposed. I realize you assume you chased Miss James away in a panic, and I have to admit, you were adept at terrorizing her, but she's safe and fine, so *you* must explain yourself to me."

"As with your London accountants," Kit blustered, "if Miss James has spewed falsehoods about me, you should produce her at once. Let me question her. We'll find out how brave she is when she's staring me in the eye."

"I wouldn't force her to endure your awful company ever again."

Jacob's expression was incredibly condemning, and it was gradually dawning on Kit that he was in a great deal of trouble. He'd merely planned to scare Joanna James, to be sure she'd leave, but apparently, he should have been a little more violent with her. If she was dead, she wouldn't be sitting in a hidden location and tattling.

"Jacob"—Kit's tone was soothing and conspiratorial—"you can't believe her over me, can you? I don't carry the surname of Ralston, but I'm a member of the family. Your mother adored me."

Caleb Ralston snickered. "Don't drag that shrew into this mess. Not if you hope to make any headway with your groveling."

Kit kept his gaze locked on Jacob. "We were raised together, Jacob. We grew up like brothers! You always said so."

"No, *you* always said so." Jacob gestured to Mr. Ralston. "I have two brothers: Caleb and Blake Ralston. You were never included in that group."

"What a perfectly horrid remark." Kit started to tremble and sweat copiously. He pulled out a kerchief and mopped his fevered brow. "You've yanked away my job and my home, and now, you're glaring as if I'm some sort of . . . of . . . felon."

Caleb Ralston said, "It's a good label for you."

Kit turned his furious attention to Mr. Ralston. "Sir, I am having a private discussion with Jacob. Would you depart the room so he and I can talk without you constantly interrupting?"

"I won't depart. I'm having too much fun, listening to your absurd alibis."

Jacob piped in with, "I'm having you arrested."

Kit's innards clenched. "Arrested! For what?"

"You'll be charged with arson, destruction of property, embezzlement, and . . . attempted murder."

"Who have I tried to murder?"

"Focus Kit. It was Miss James and Clara—who is your daughter."

"Her niece is not my daughter, and I didn't try to murder anyone."

"There's no use denying it," Jacob said. "You lit their house on fire while they were asleep. We're lucky it was only an *attempt* at murder. If you'd been more cunning, it would have been a full-on homicide."

Kit quailed with dismay. "You're joking, aren't you? Is this some kind of game? Some kind of trick? What are you thinking?"

"I'm *thinking* that my family has given you every single thing you've ever had, and you were never grateful for any of it."

"I've worked hard for you!"

"I suppose I could line up the servants and ask their opinions."

"The servants love and respect me."

Both brothers laughed at that, and Jacob said, "What about you and Roxanne? Stop pretending you never had intimate relations with her."

"I can't win this argument. It's a lie, disseminated by Miss James to ruin me. If I refute it, you'll ignore my protestations of innocence."

"Roxanne has already confessed, so there's no reason to keep up the ruse."

Jacob's comment fell between them like a death knell, and Kit seethed, "The bitch confessed? I warned her to shut her mouth."

"I figured that was your plan, but I'd like you to be honest with me. Once in your sorry life, admit your folly."

"Why should I?"

"Because I expect this will be the last time you and I ever speak to one another, and since this will be our final conversation, I'd like to hear the truth."

It suddenly occurred to Kit that he'd always taken their friendship for granted. Now, with Jacob claiming it revoked, he was sick with regret and wondering how he'd carry on without Jacob.

Jacob couldn't intend to sever ties, and Kit needed to get them back on firmer ground. Perhaps he should beg for mercy. Jacob was demanding candor. It Kit supplied it, would it help?

"We were children," he said. "She was fifteen, and I was but a few years older, so you shouldn't judge us. It was just one of those unfortunate scandals that engulfs young people."

"As I told Roxanne, I don't judge you for the affair. I judge you for your conduct afterward. I judge you for keeping the situation a secret. I judge you—and I condemn you—for letting me proceed to an engagement with Roxanne, while you snickered and bit your tongue."

"We didn't mean any harm."

"You had a daughter with my fiancée! You hid the information for over a decade, and you didn't mean any harm?"

"Your mother arranged the betrothal without apprising me. What was I supposed to do? When Roxanne waltzed in the door, should I have tossed her out?" Kit leaned toward Jacob, hoping he appeared sincere. "We were protecting you! We recognized how the facts would wound you, so we agreed to bury them. We did it for you!"

Caleb Ralston snorted with disgust. "That is the most self-serving, ridiculous excuse ever uttered."

"You were protecting me?" Jacob's skepticism was alarming. "And when you threw that torch through Miss James's window, when you could have killed her and your daughter, how would you describe your actions then? After Clara was born, you still haven't clarified what you presumed happened to her. Did you think Clara was smothered after the delivery? Did you assume she was given to the fairies to raise?"

Kit's cheeks heated. "Roxanne told me she was adopted."

"When you realized she was at Ralston, what then? You didn't kill her when she was a baby, so you decided to kill her now?"

"I simply wanted to scare them," he vehemently insisted. "Roxanne and I thought they should leave the area, but Miss James is such an imperious shrew that we didn't feel she'd go unless she was pushed."

"That sounds like an admission to me," Caleb Ralston said, "and I'm a witness."

"I . . . I . . . am not admitting to anything," Kit hurried to claim, "but whatever occurred at Miss James's cottage, it was Roxanne's idea. She was determined you never discover her past. I yearned to confide in you, but she constantly threatened me. You ought to know too that she was chased out of Italy because two lovers dueled over her, and there's been gossip that she entertained a hundred different men in Florence. You shouldn't marry her! It would be a huge mistake."

Kit sensed he was babbling, but his fever was making him lose track of the issues. He'd expected that the news about Roxanne and Italy would be a welcome revelation, but Jacob and his half-brother glared as if he'd posed a complex riddle.

"I'm delighted that Joanna's dog attacked you," Caleb Ralston said. "I wish he'd ripped off your entire leg."

"Please tell me that vicious animal is dead," Kit said, when he probably should have remained silent.

Whenever he closed his eyes, he could see that malicious beast leap out of the dark as Kit approached the cottage. The only bright spot of that whole wretched night was how he'd whacked the dog with his ax. He'd been praying ever since that he'd slain the loathsome creature.

"That vicious *animal*," Caleb Ralston said, "is alive and healing just fine. But I'm predicting the bite he inflicted will kill you painfully and slowly. It will save the courts from having to waste energy punishing you."

Jacob rose to his feet, looking like a judge about to pass sentence. He studied Kit's deteriorated condition, and he laughed in a cruel way.

"I have been kind to you," Jacob said. "I have given you a good life, a good job, a good home, and every minute that you were wallowing in my largesse, you were betraying me."

"I never betrayed you!"

"You embezzled from me. You let my property fall into a state of disrepair that will require years to mend. You nearly allowed me to engage myself to a trollop who wasn't worthy of being my wife."

"Will you listen to me? I didn't know about the engagement in advance! Your mother didn't inform me."

"But when you *did* learn about it, you conspired with Roxanne to hide your sins from me."

"I can explain."

"Well, there's the problem for you, Kit. I don't care what your explanation might be." He nodded to his half-brother. "Get him out of my house."

"Gladly."

Caleb Ralston marched over and yanked Kit to his feet with such force that it wrenched his injury. He wailed in agony and asked, "What's happening? Where are you taking me?"

"You must concentrate, Kit," Jacob said. "You keep becoming confused. You're under arrest, and there will be a lengthy list of charges. The worst ones will be the arson and the attempted murder."

Caleb Ralston sneered, "Those are hanging offenses."

At hearing the word *hanging*, Kit fainted. When he roused again, he was in a carriage and rumbling down a rough road. He didn't recollect how he'd arrived there or who had carried him. He was lying on the floor, each bump of the vehicle causing him to bounce and jostle his wound.

He tried to sit up, but he was stunned to find that his wrists and ankles were bound with a rope. He groaned in anguish, and Roxanne appeared in his line of sight, leaned over from the seat above. She was the only other occupant, and she was fettered as well.

"You only had to do one thing, Kit," she spat. "You had to shut your mouth."

"Where are we going?" he asked.

"To jail—you bloody fool."

"I told Jacob this was your fault," Kit said.

"I told him the same, but apparently, he didn't believe either of us. He seems to assume we're accomplices."

"His half-brother, that Caleb fellow? He said I might be hanged for starting that fire."

"It's no more than what you deserve for ruining my life."

"I ruined *your* life? I'm quite sure that's an exaggeration. You were completely capable of ruining it without any help from me."

Roxanne crushed her foot onto his leg, right on his wound. He howled with outrage, but she simply stared out the window. Despite how he begged, she didn't raise her foot, didn't ease the pressure, and he wasn't strong enough to kick her away.

"THOSE ARE THE TWO most despicable people I've ever encountered."

Jacob smirked in agreement. "I'm amazed that I put up with Kit for so many years. I'm even more amazed that I almost wed Roxanne."

"You definitely dodged a bullet there."

"You are a master of understatement."

"Have we handled all your crises?" Caleb asked. "May we head to Barrett now? I'm anxious to marry Caro, but she'll be thinking I've changed my mind and fled."

"I need to pack a bag, write a quick letter, and speak with two boys so I can have them pack too. Then I'll be ready."

"Who are the boys?"

"Their names are Tim and Tom Sanders. Their father is my stable manager, and he's out of town. I'm watching them while he's away, so they have to accompany us. Their father would skin me alive if I left without them."

"I can't have them slowing us down. Can they ride?"

"Like the wind."

"Who must you write to?"

"My sister, Margaret. She eloped last week—with their father. It's why he's away from the property."

Caleb laughed. "It sounds as if your side of the family is just as deranged as mine. Did you try to stop them?"

"I thought about it. I even chased them to Scotland, but then, it occurred to me that she's twenty-eight, and she can decide who she wants as her husband. They stayed on to enjoy a honeymoon, but I'd like them to come to my wedding."

"You're awfully certain Joanna will have you."

"I'm not certain at all. She feels I'm a pompous snob."

"She's right, but I suppose you'll wear her down."

"I hope I can, or Luke will wring my neck."

"He won't have time to notice your misbehavior. He's too busy, doting on his bride. It's embarrassing to observe how he fawns over her."

They were in the driveway, waiting as the dust settled behind the carriage whisking Kit and Roxanne to jail. Caleb gestured to the house and said, "Could we cease our dithering?"

"I'll hurry."

"Don't forget to bring a fancy suit. You have your own wedding to attend—plus two more besides."

Jacob peered up at the sky and asked, "Do you believe there's really a Heaven? If so, do you imagine Father is looking down on us?"

"There might be a Heaven, and if there is, he must be up there. I can't fathom how these three Lost Girls found each other on their own. Someone seems to be guiding their steps."

"And ours." Jacob grinned. "Let's head to Barrett and get married."

Chapter

22

JOANNA WAS IN HER bedchamber at Barrett. Caro was sitting on a chair over by the window, and Mutt was loafing on a rug by the fire. Joanna was kneeling next to him, checking his stitches.

He was healing nicely, with no sign of infection, and he was able to walk with a slight limp. It would be awhile before he'd run after a rabbit, and he'd probably never be as fast as he once was, but he was much better.

"How is he?" Caro asked, and when he heard them talking about him, he thumped his tail.

"He's much improved," Joanna said. "In another day or two, I'll remove the stitches."

"I wish I had your nursing skill. It must be satisfying to possess such a useful talent."

"It's satisfying, but it can be dangerous too. I can't ever forget how my mother and I were chased out of England because of her abilities."

"I don't think it was her healing ability. I'm quite sure it was her illicit amour with your father."

"In my Aunt Pru's version of the story, the romance was all my father's fault. My mother constantly tried to break it off, but he was like a bad penny. He kept turning up."

"Do you ever wish you could meet him? What if you have a few half-siblings out there in the world? Wouldn't it be interesting to speak to them? You've always been so alone. What if you approached them and they welcomed you into the family?"

Joanna scoffed. "Or what if they were horrid? I couldn't bear to get my hopes up only to have them dashed. And what kind of man could my father possibly be? He supposedly loved my mother, yet he wouldn't intercede to protect her. I realize it will sound silly, but I blame him for the shipwreck and for her dying on our island."

"That *is* silly. I blame the weather."

They chuckled, then Joanna gave Mutt a final pat and went over to the chair beside Caro.

They'd just been to the village church, to check Libby's wedding preparations. Flowers were being delivered by the wagonload, and a team of housemaids was polishing every inch of wood so the building gleamed. It would be a festive, glorious occasion, and everyone was determined that each tiny detail be perfect.

Libby had asked Caro and Caleb to make it a double ceremony, to wed with her and Luke, but Caro had declined. Libby was a national celebrity, and Luke was an earl. Caro wouldn't dare butt into the middle of their grandeur, and Libby couldn't change her mind.

The wedding rehearsal would be held the following afternoon, and—since the vicar would be there—Caro and Caleb would have a quiet ceremony after it ended. It meant they'd have two weddings in two days, one very posh and splendid and one very small and private.

Joanna would sit in the front pew at both, and at the pretty notion, she could have burst into tears. Fate was a strange creature. She'd waited twenty years to find Caro and Libby, and they'd crossed paths at exactly the right moment.

"Will Caleb return today?" Joanna inquired. He'd had a problem arise at his gambling club in London, and he'd rushed to town.

"He promised he'd be here," Caro responded, "and I'm telling myself he will be."

"He won't have gotten cold feet, will he?" Joanna teased. "He wouldn't have boarded a ship and sailed for America?"

"Oh, his feet will be so cold that they'll be blocks of ice. Those Ralston men are such confirmed bachelors. A woman needs a chain to drag them to the altar, but I have Luke on my side now. He'd wrestle Caleb down the aisle for me."

They smirked together, then Joanna sighed wistfully. There was so much nuptial cheer in the air, and she was nostalgic for the what-might-have-been she could have pursued with Jacob.

She'd been raised to believe she shouldn't wed, but she would have loved to be his bride. She wondered where he was and when he'd be back in England. Did he ever think about her? Did he ever regret how they'd parted without a goodbye?

With her being reunited with Libby and Caro, she would be entwined in their lives, and Jacob would be too. He was Caleb's half-brother, so he would be Caro's brother-in-law and a member of Caro's extended family. He was also friends with Luke from their service in the navy, so Joanna would socialize with him in the future.

She was trying to deduce how she felt about that. She was fairly certain he wouldn't be marrying Roxanne, but he'd eventually marry someone. If he strolled into Barrett Manor while Joanna was there too, if he had a wife with him, how awkward would the encounter be?

Her choices with regard to him had all been wrong ones. She hadn't warned him about Roxanne or Kit Boswell, hadn't told him they were Clara's parents. She'd like to contact him through the navy to inform him of how they'd burned down her cottage, but she'd moved away from the estate and wouldn't ever return, so how could any of it matter?

It might be years before he was home again, so why would he care about her or her cottage?

Caro glanced over at her and asked, "Why are you smiling?"

"I was just pondering how ridiculous I am. I make awful decisions."

"I disagree. You showed up at Barrett when we needed you most."

"My arrival was an accident brought on by catastrophe. It didn't occur because I was being shrewd and pragmatic."

Clara ran in and announced, "Miss Caro! A footman sent me to fetch you. Mr. Caleb has been sighted. He's about to ride up the lane."

"He didn't abandon me after all," Caro said. "Is he alone?"

"No. There appears to be a whole group with him."

"A whole group? Who could it be?"

Joanna said, "Maybe it's some wedding guests."

"That would be lovely."

"Will you come down?" Clara asked Caro.

"Definitely." Caro stood and looked at Joanna. "Will you come too?"

"I'll be there in a minute. I should pack my medical bag. I left my supplies scattered on the floor."

Caro rested her palm on Joanna's head, and she grinned oddly. "I'm betting everything will be fine now. In fact, I'm sure of it."

"In my view," Joanna said, "everything is already fine. How could my life get any better?"

Caro and Clara hurried away, and Joanna dawdled, listening as their strides faded. It dawned on her that she was very despondent, which was idiotic. What was there to lament?

Yes, she'd lost her cottage, and yes, Jacob had departed without a goodbye, but it was futile to bemoan that sad conclusion. He'd been very clear that he'd never wed her, and *she* had insisted she wasn't interested anyway.

Their split was so recent though, the loss of him so raw. She felt wounded and bereft, as if she'd never recover, but she would. She was with Caro and Libby. Clara and Mutt were safe, and Luke had invited her to stay at Barrett forever if she wanted. He was trying to locate a house for her.

With those blessings raining down, what reason had she to complain?

Suddenly, Mutt rose to his feet, and his tail was wagging like mad. He gave a woof of welcome, and he was practically quivering with joy.

"Who is it?" she asked him.

He seemed to say, *Just wait until you see!*

Footsteps sounded, two pairs approaching, and one of them belonged to Clara. She was giggling, whispering, then she peeked in the door and said, "Guess who's here?"

She was being so sly that Joanna was a tad alarmed. "I can't imagine."

"Surprise!"

Clara eased away to admit her companion, and when Joanna peered over, if an angel from Heaven had been standing there, she couldn't have been more astonished.

"Hello, Joanna," Jacob said. "I hear you weren't expecting me, and you'll be so stunned by my arrival that you might faint."

Mutt woofed again, demanding to be noticed, then he hobbled over. Jacob leaned down and petted him. "Let me look at you, you poor boy! How are you?"

Man and dog engaged in some extensive male bonding, then Jacob straightened and said to Clara, "Would you take Mutt out in the hall? I have to talk to Joanna."

Joanna's pulse raced. She was nervous about being sequestered with him. She was still overly besotted, so he might coerce her into any insane conduct.

"You and Mutt don't need to leave," she told Clara.

"Yes, you do," Jacob countered.

Clara motioned to Mutt, but he wasn't keen to miss the excitement, so Jacob motioned too, and he limped over to Clara.

"When can we come back in?" Clara asked.

"When I have good news," was Jacob's answer. "It might be awhile though. I have to explain some things. I'll fetch you the instant it's arranged. Don't go far."

Joanna had no idea what he meant, and before she could seek clarification, Clara shut the door. Jacob turned to her, and his expression was very cunning.

He was more handsome than ever, his color high, his hair tousled by the wind on the trip to Barrett. She was so glad to see him, and she yearned to fall into his arms, but that would be humiliating.

From the moment they'd met, he'd pursued an amour. She'd allowed herself to be seduced, but he didn't really want her. No, he wanted from her what her father had wanted from her mother. He craved a physical affair with a paramour who was exotic and out of the ordinary.

For a brief interval she'd toyed with the notion of permitting him to treat her that shabbily. It's how her ancestors had typically dealt with men, but she couldn't continue down that shameful road. Not when she'd been reunited with Libby and Caro.

Though it was disgusting to accept, she was jealous of the wonderful men they'd found, men who loved them, men who would move the world to have them. What had Joanna found? Naught but a coward who'd been scolded by his sister for kissing her under a rose arbor. Once his sister had complained, Jacob had severed all ties.

What woman would tolerate such a feckless swain? Not Joanna James. That was for certain.

He sauntered over and plopped down on the chair Caro had vacated. He repositioned it first, so they were facing each other, their feet and legs tangled.

"Aren't you curious as to why I'm in England? It's obvious you're dying to be apprised."

"I might be curious," she blandly responded.

"You were informed that I was recalled to duty and that I left immediately."

She nodded. "I may have been told a story like that."

She wasn't about to stagger into a discussion of Kit Boswell and how dangerous she viewed him to be. She was no longer a resident of Ralston Place. Any issue he had with his family was none of her business.

"I wasn't recalled to duty. Would you like to know *where* I was instead?"

"I suppose."

"I've been in Scotland."

She scowled. She truly couldn't bear to be dragged back into his life, but she couldn't keep herself from asking, "Why were you there?"

"Do you remember the last time we spoke? My sister, Margaret, was anxious to wed Sandy."

"Yes, and you were a complete ass about it."

"They agreed with you and eloped."

Joanna laughed. She couldn't help it. He was so pompously convinced that he was better than Sandy, but Sandy was the nicest person ever. Margaret was lucky she'd glommed onto him when she had the chance.

"It serves you right for being such a beast about it," she said.

"I figured you'd feel that way, but when I initially learned of their plan, I was livid. I chased after them, and I would have stopped them, but on the lengthy journey, guess what occurred to me?"

"I don't know. Your mental wrangling has always been a total mystery to me."

"I realized I didn't care who Margaret married. When my mother sold her to Mr. Howell, I should have intervened, but I didn't, and I've always regretted it. Sandy is a terrific fellow, and I decided she should have the opportunity to be happy with him."

"That's big of you." Her tone was very snide.

She wasn't concerned about Margaret or who she wed, and she was still smarting from how Margaret had pressured Jacob to end their flirtation.

Had either of the snooty siblings noted the obvious? Margaret had been intent on preventing Jacob's liaison with a female she deemed inferior, but then, she'd run off with a man just as unsuitable. They were such conceited idiots, and Joanna was sure the hypocrisy would have escaped them.

"Thank you for telling me about them," she said. "Will there be anything else?"

"Oh, I have a ton of items to address. First off, I apologize for racing to Scotland without sending you a message that I was leaving."

"There's no reason you would have notified me. It's not as if I had a connection to you that would have warranted any courtesy."

"I was simply so furious that you never crossed my mind."

"Well, that certainly makes me feel special."

She wished he'd finish and go away, but he was very obtuse. He wouldn't recognize her pique or her annoyance.

He continued, undeterred. "I wasn't pondering you when I departed, but as the miles sped by, you gradually became front and center in my musings."

"Meaning what? You could be speaking in riddles."

"I was reflecting on Margaret and how she'd forged ahead with Sandy after I'd warned her she shouldn't. I actually had the audacity to claim he wasn't worthy of her."

"You've always been a bit blind."

"After thinking about them constantly, I began thinking about you and me."

"There is no you and *me*," she churlishly retorted. "You're being ridiculous."

"When I returned from Scotland, I went by your cottage—before I proceeded to the manor. You can't imagine how shocked I was to stumble on the rubble."

"You can't imagine how shocked I was to have lived through the inferno."

He grinned slyly. "I know who started the fire."

"So do I." Or at least she had her suspicions.

"It was Kit," he said, confirming them. "He's admitted it too. Were you aware that Mutt attacked him in an altercation? He nearly wrenched Kit's leg off."

"Good." She wasn't usually vengeful, but she was delighted that Kit had suffered. "He almost killed Mutt. He almost killed me and Clara. I'm not sorry if he was injured."

"He was more than injured. His wound is infected. He may die from it."

"I hope he can find a skilled doctor to tend him."

Jacob chuckled. "I told him he was stupid to have chased you away. You're the one person who could have nursed him back to health. He was quite feverish though, so I doubt he grasped the irony."

She recollected how she'd hexed him, and it was gratifying to discover that her power had been so effective—and that it had worked so fast too.

"What will happen to him?"

"He's been arrested, and once I'm home, he'll be tried for attempted murder."

She frowned. "Who did he try to murder?"

"You, you silly girl! He insisted he simply planned to terrorize you, but I'm not sure that's true. I'm betting his motive was more felonious than that."

"I hadn't really considered his actions being that dire, but he could have easily murdered us. I woke up and smelled smoke, so we escaped before the flames grew too intense."

"He's committed other crimes I should point out. He's been embezzling from me for years."

"He's a fiend, so I'm not surprised. Who will run the estate for you now?"

"Sandy has agreed to it, but I've been debating whether I shouldn't retire from the navy and manage the property myself. I've never been interested in it, but that was because my mother's presence kept me away. With her not being there during my recent visit, I enjoyed myself very much."

"You should take an interest in it. You're lucky to own it. I've never thought you were grateful—about anything."

He snorted at that. "My cousin, Roxanne, has been arrested with Kit, and she'll be prosecuted with him."

"On what charge?"

"I believe she was out in the woods that night when he threw his torch through your window. If she wasn't, I figure she sent him over there, so it will be arson and attempted murder."

"Could I tell you something about them? Something awful?"

"I don't suppose it would be the fact that they're Clara's parents?"

She blanched. "How did you find out?"

"You don't seem to realize that your chum, Caroline Grey, had Caleb fetch me here. Actually, he rode to Ralston Place to see if I'd been recalled to duty. They were worried I seduced you, then rid myself of you by having Kit lie and claim I'd fled England. While Caleb was with me, he blabbed your secrets."

"I thought Caleb had an emergency in town."

"He had an emergency all right, but it was with me. He had to discover my opinion on several issues."

"What issues?"

"I'll get to those in a minute. First, how long have you known about Kit and Roxanne? Why keep the information to yourself?"

"I found out a few weeks ago when Roxanne stopped by my cottage. Clara was there too, and they look exactly alike. I was suspicious."

"You didn't know before then?"

Joanna shook her head. "My Aunt Pru, the woman who delivered Clara? She wrote me a note about it, but she begged me not to peek at it unless there was an important reason. Once the truth was revealed, I was conflicted about my role. I was afraid you wouldn't believe me or that you might kill the messenger. I was also afraid of *them* and how they might retaliate."

"Fair enough." He nodded. "I've been wondering about this: Would you have let me walk down the aisle with Roxanne? With what you'd unearthed, could you have?"

"Well, Captain Ralston, I'm certain you'll deem me mad, but I was positive you wouldn't be marrying her."

"How could you be so sure?"

"I read your cards and learned that you would wed someone else— and wind up very happy."

"You're so convinced that your talents provide correct answers. Have you ever been wrong?"

"Not very often. Humans have free will, but they end up where they're destined to be. Occasionally, they take a circuitous route to where they belong."

"Did the cards tell you who I'm meant to marry? If it's not Roxanne, who will it be?"

"I have no idea."

The notion left her very sad. Now that she was with him again, she was being bombarded with affection. They'd had such a brief amour, but they'd grown so close. Her potent feelings hadn't had a chance to wane. Where was she to put the fond sentiment rolling around inside her?

"I broke off my engagement to Roxanne," he said.

"I should hope so. You couldn't wed a woman who's been charged with attempted murder."

"You don't seem to be aware of what this indicates."

"You're a bachelor again."

His sly grin popped out once more. "Yes, and I can start searching for another bride. I'm very excited about it too. When I decided to proceed previously, I had my mother deal with it for me."

"Since she picked Roxanne, I can't laud her for her choice."

"I heartily concur, so now, I can select a candidate who *I* view as being perfect for me."

He was staring at her like the cat that ate the canary. Or maybe it was more like a wolf toying with a mouse. She couldn't bear it. She was so in love with him that she felt sick with regret.

She pushed back her chair and stood. "I can't discuss this with you."

"Why not?"

"Because it hurts me, you dunce."

"Why does it hurt?"

He reached out and tried to hold her hand, but she yanked away and staggered off. If he touched her, she couldn't focus, and she might utter any humiliating comment.

"I'm a very proud woman, Jacob Ralston, and you chased me until you caught me. You used me badly, then tossed me aside. You bluntly and brutally apprised me I could never be worthy of you, and I can't dawdle as you wax on about your next fiancée. All the while, I'd have to remember that you would never have considered me!"

His grin became even more sly. "Why, Joanna James, I could have sworn that you told me—over and over again—that you would never marry."

She was aggravated to have him hurl her own words back in her face. "I might have mentioned that once or twice."

"But what if you met a kind and loyal man, one who loved you madly? What would your opinion be then?"

"I . . . I . . . can't answer a hypothetical question."

"Why not? Are you afraid your attitude about matrimony just might be ridiculous?"

He stood then too, and he stepped toward her. She lurched back, and they moved across the floor in a sort of awkward dance. Finally, she bumped into the wall and could go no farther. He swooped in and slapped his palms on the plaster, trapping her between them.

"You, Miss James, are the most infuriating female."

"You believe that because I've never been in awe of you."

"No, you haven't ever been, but why is that exactly? I'm handsome, rich, and renowned. I'm landed and important, and I have a famous name and ancestry. The only thing I lack is a fancy title, yet none of my qualities appeal to you."

"I don't care if you're landed and important. Those traits don't interest me in the slightest."

"What would interest you then? I'm so curious to hear."

"If I ever broke down and wed, it would be to a man who adored me, a man who couldn't live without me. He'd have to be my friend, my partner, my confidante. He'd have to be secure enough in his own ego to let *me* be me, but as I've discovered, there are very few men like that out in the world."

"So you'll remain a spinster."

"Yes."

"You'll be content with that conclusion."

"The women in my family always have been. I'm sure I will be too."

"There's one little problem with that scenario."

"What is it?"

To her great consternation, he dropped to a knee and clasped hold of her hand, their palms connecting in a sweet way rather than a raucous one. There was only one reason a man put himself in that position, and she blanched with dismay.

"What are you doing?"

"You know what I'm doing, so be silent and listen to me."

"No. You're teasing me, and it's cruel of you to behave like this."

He scowled. "Why would you imagine I'm teasing?"

"You're about to propose, but you don't mean it. You were very blunt that day at my cottage. You are the grand and glorious Jacob Ralston, and I am lowly, inconsequential Joanna James. You're the biggest snob I've ever encountered—except perhaps for your sister. You could never stoop down far enough to wed me."

His scowl deepened. "Are you finished?"

"I guess."

"Then be *silent* and listen for once." She opened her mouth to offer another remark, and he laid a finger on her lips. "Hush! It's my turn to talk. You claim you'd wed if you could find a man who adores you. Well, Joanna James, *I* adore you."

"Yes, you probably do, but so what?"

"So what?" He grumbled with frustration. "You are so obstinate! I can't figure out why I'm bothering with you."

"Neither can I. Your sister revealed how she views me. Your other relatives would feel the same, and they'd never agree to a match between us. Your friends would laugh behind your back, and your acquaintances would insult you to your face. There's an odd impulse driving you, so you're not thinking clearly."

"*I* am not thinking clearly?"

"No."

"Would you like to hear another secret Caleb shared with me?"

"Not really."

"He advises me that—when you last spoke with my father on his ship—you asked him to watch over you."

Her cheeks heated. "I might have."

"This is *him* watching over you. This is *him* leading me to your side. I will confess that it took me awhile to heed his message."

"What message is it you assume he's delivered?"

"He's telling me that I will never be able to walk away from you.

I tried! I told myself it was for the best, but every time I avoid you, it feels as if fetters are strapped to my ankles to draw me back. *You* are the one who believes in Fate and destiny. Not me. You can't stand here and declare you don't belong with me. My father, God rest his soul, will never give me any peace until you accept what he's arranged for us."

She started to tremble. All summer, his father's ghost had been hovering. Libby and Caro had noticed him too. He'd been such a central character in their lives, and it made perfect sense that he'd intervene.

"You imagine your father brought me to you?"

"I'm certain he did."

Joanna stared down at him, and she was riveted by the blue of his eyes, by the tenderness of his gaze. He was so handsome, so mesmerizing. He kissed her hand, then said, "Joanna James, will you marry me?"

It was on the tip of her tongue to refuse him, but she swallowed down the words. She would love to have him for her very own, but she was so conflicted. It seemed very, very right for them to end up together, but it seemed a complete blunder too. Weren't they too different?

"I can see your mind whirring," he said, "as you devise a thousand reasons why you shouldn't."

"It's much more than a thousand."

"You presume it would be horrid, but what if you're wrong? What if we wound up blissfully content?"

"You don't want to wed me!" She practically wailed the comment. "When your sister pointed out how ridiculous a notion it was, you instantly split with me. It kills me to admit she was correct, but she was!"

"My *sister* married my stable manager so she can be happy, so she can have the life she chooses for a change. Why can't I have the life I choose?"

"You think that life should be with me?"

"Yes. I absolutely think that."

Her trembling increased. "Well, it's a deranged decision. I simply can't fathom what is spurring you on."

"I haven't been clear, but then, I'm not very eloquent. I want you to be my wife—so I can take care of you. I want you to fill my home with your quiet joy and your soothing presence. I want you to fill my days with wonder, excitement, and delight. I want you to constantly surprise me and teach me how to be a better man."

She was quaking so hard that she could barely remain on her feet. "Would you get up? Please?"

"No. Not until you stop being so stubborn."

She tried to lift him, but he wouldn't budge.

"Marry me, Joanna. Say *yes*. Tell me you will."

"If I ever considered marrying," she tentatively ventured, "I would only do it for love. It's the only way I could convince myself to proceed."

He raised a brow. "Aren't you in love with me? Don't you dare deny it."

She debated her reply because—once she voiced it aloud—they would be careening down a new road. "Yes, I love you. I love you more than life itself."

He nodded quite smugly, as if it was the precise response he'd been expecting. "Guess what? I love *you* even more than that—if it's possible."

Finally, he stood, and he dipped in and kissed her. She'd never been able to resist him, and she couldn't now. She wrapped her arms around his waist and held him tight, feeling as if—should she release him—she might simply float off into the sky.

As their lips parted, he said, "You still haven't answered my question."

"*If* I agree, you'd have to let me continue with my healing." Gad, was she contemplating it? "You'd have to let me birth babies, brew potions, and tend people who are ill. You couldn't prevent me or wish I was a different type of person. You will never change me, so you'd have to swear you're prepared for that type of wife—and you'd have to mean it."

"Why would I seek to change you? You are fascinating, annoying, and remarkable. I'd like you to always be exactly who you are."

"Clara and Mutt would have to stay with us."

"That's not even an issue. In fact, I'd like to adopt Clara. Would *you* like that?"

"You would? Really?" Who could reject such a dear man? "And . . . you have to reflect on whether you should retire from the navy. I couldn't wed you, then have you vanish for years at a time. I couldn't live like that."

"I've come to the same conclusion. I won't be like my father. I won't sire children who never see me, who never know me. I should be at home."

"At Ralston Place? Are you sure? You never liked it in the past."

"No, not in the past. But I can be content there in the future—because you'll be there with me."

"Oh, Jacob . . ."

It was the sweetest thing he could have said. The comment seemed to yank down the walls she'd erected to keep him at bay.

"I never thought I'd marry," she said.

"I understand that about you."

"I never thought I'd find someone to wed. I never thought there would be a man who was perfect for me, but it's you, Jacob. Will you have me?"

"Are you certain? Don't promise unless you are."

She gazed at him, her affection wafting out. He would be faithful, loyal, and kind, and he would be *hers*. He would protect her from the slings and arrows the world would inflict, but—with him by her side—those arrows would bounce off.

"I'm certain," she vowed. "I can't bear to be Joanna James another second. I'm ready to be Joanna Ralston."

"Mrs. Jacob Ralston . . ." he mused. "I like the sound of that."

He drew her into his arms again, then he was kissing her like a fiend, the two of them laughing, twirling in circles, growing so wild that they knocked over a table.

The door was flung open, and Clara and Mutt rushed in.

"Are you all right?" Clara asked. "We heard a crash."

"It was just us being happy," Joanna said.

"Why are you happy? Is it good news?"

"It's very good news."

Jacob told her, "Joanna and I have decided to marry."

"She said *yes*?" Clara asked.

"She said *yes,*" Jacob replied.

Joanna extended her hand, and Clara hurried over. They pulled her close, the three of them huddled together in a hug that went on and on. Mutt trotted over, his tail wagging, and he barked his approval. They pulled him close too, and Joanna smiled, thinking that it was a splendid start to her very own family.

She shut her eyes and glanced toward the heavens, and she sent a message to Jacob's father.

Thank you for giving him to me.

A clear response popped into her mind: *You're welcome.*

She sighed with gladness and hugged everyone a bit tighter.

Epilogue

"Is everyone ready?"

Lady Penny, Libby's half-sister, asked the question to no one in particular. The church's vestibule was packed, and Joanna glanced around, trying to count how many were squeezed into the small area, but it was impossible to tabulate them all.

Libby and Luke probably should have wed at the cathedral in London, but they'd decided on the local church at Barrett instead. It held a few dozen people, so invitations had been as valuable as gold nuggets. The individuals who'd received them felt as if they'd won a grand lottery.

The organist was playing a quiet hymn, and they were waiting for Luke to step out to the altar with the vicar. His best man would be Lady Penny's new husband, Simon Falcon. He was Libby's cousin, and after the vows were exchanged, he would be Luke's brother-in-law.

Libby's sole bridesmaid would be her old friend and costumer, Edwina Fishburn, who'd stood by her side through a life of tribulations.

"Do we remember the order?" Lady Penny inquired.

She was as organized as an army sergeant, and the crowd straightened, and there was a general murmuring of *yes*. They'd attended the rehearsal the previous day, so they'd practiced their parts and were eager to proceed.

Sandy's sons, Tim and Tom, were the ushers, with Lady Penny having dug up clothes for them to wear. They dawdled behind her, prepared to leap into action and carry out any command she leveled.

"Clara," Lady Penny said, "you'll go down first and toss your flower petals." Clara beamed with pride and lifted her basket to show it off. "You'll scoot into the front pew on the left. Be sure there's room for Joanna and Jacob."

"Caro and Caleb," Lady Penny continued, "or should I say, Mr. and Mrs. Ralston? You're next. Front pew on the right. Joanna and Jacob, you'll be after them. Front pew on the left." Lady Penny checked her notes. "I will follow and sit by Caro, so don't forget to leave some space for me."

"I won't," Caro said.

"Then Fish will go down, and Libby will be the only one remaining." Lady Penny frowned at her father, Lord Roland. "My lord Father, can you get Libby down to Luke? You won't faint, will you?"

"I won't faint," Lord Roland replied. "I didn't have the chance to walk *you* down the aisle, Penny." Lady Penny had eloped with Simon Falcon, so it was still a sore spot between them. "I'm glad *one* of my daughters was kind enough to let me have this wonderful honor."

Libby had met her father at a house party earlier that summer. After it had been revealed that she was his long-lost child, Little Henrietta, they'd had a rocky start to their relationship. But now, they were fully reconciled and as close as a father and daughter could ever be.

Libby rose on tiptoe and kissed him on the cheek. "Father won't faint. He's too stalwart to quail with anxiety. Not when I desperately need him to be steady."

Everyone smiled, and some people dabbed at their eyes.

It had been such a traumatic and dramatic few months for all of them. With it being the twentieth anniversary of the shipwreck, Joanna,

Libby, and Caro had been unusually distressed, bombarded by painful memories and recurring nightmares. Then they'd crossed paths with the men of their dreams, but none of their amours had been easily pursued.

Libby had ended up in jail. Caro had run away from her male kin, then she'd been robbed and left penniless on the streets of London. Joanna had had her cottage burned down around her.

Caro and Caleb had wed the prior afternoon, after the rehearsal had concluded. It had been a private ceremony with just Libby, Joanna, Luke, and Jacob as witnesses. In a thrilling turn of events, Jacob had served as Caleb's best man.

The two brothers had bonded during Caleb's trip to Ralston Place, and Joanna was certain, in the future, they would be the siblings that family circumstance had prevented them from being in the past.

As to her own wedding, she'd let Jacob pick the time and venue, and he'd chosen to have the banns called at their local church in Ralston village. It meant they'd marry a month hence, with the neighbors and servants joining in the merriment. His chief concern had been the fact that Margaret and Sandy were still in Scotland on their honeymoon, and he didn't want to proceed without them being able to participate.

Joanna was praying that Margaret wouldn't be too shocked about what had occurred when she'd been away from home and not present to stop him. Hopefully, now that Margaret had made her own ill-conceived marriage, some of her snobbery would have waned. Joanna was an optimist, and she would embrace the positive expectation that Margaret would become a fond sister.

Mr. Periwinkle bustled up. He appeared jaunty in a new suit he'd purchased for the occasion. Libby had offered to have him sit toward the front of the church during the ceremony, but he'd been aghast at the idea, viewing himself as too lowly a person to be seated with the more important guests.

He was hovering in the background, scribbling copious notes, and jotting down quotes from the spectators. Libby had given him permission to pen whatever articles he liked about the wedding, as well as the days of celebration afterward—if he promised she would always be described as beautiful and extraordinary.

Since the poor man worshiped her, there was no chance he'd write his stories any other way.

"How are you, Miss Joanna?" he inquired. "Are you happy?"

"Must you ask that question, Mr. Periwinkle? Can't you judge my delightful mood just by looking at me?"

"And how about you, sir?" he said to Jacob. "How does it feel to be marrying one of the *Lost Girls*?"

"It feels amazing. How would you suppose? I don't know how I'll be patient enough to wait an entire month for my own festivities."

"If your famous father could be here today," Mr. Periwinkle asked, "what do you imagine he'd say to you?"

Jacob smirked. "I imagine he'd chastise me for taking so long to propose to Joanna. Were you aware that when I met her, I didn't realize how she was connected to me?"

"Miss Joanna!" Periwinkle exclaimed. "How could you keep the news from him?"

Joanna chuckled. "I didn't want to tell him all my secrets at once. A woman needs to be a bit mysterious, don't you think?"

Jacob linked their fingers, and he leaned over and kissed her—right on the mouth. Mr. Periwinkle wandered away, writing furiously in his notebook, no doubt recording that they were so much in love that they'd dare to brazenly kiss. But then, romance was definitely in the air.

The organ volume swelled, and Lady Penny said, "It's eleven o'clock. Let's get in line."

As she shifted people around, Joanna pulled away to grab Caro. They went over to Libby who was at the rear of the group. Her father stepped away so they could have a private conversation.

"When we were on our island," Joanna said, "you were my family. You were my sisters."

"You were mine too," Libby said.

"And mine," Caro added.

"We were the *Lost Girls* of the Caribbean," Libby said, "but look at us now! Who could have predicted we would arrive at this wonderful spot together?"

"I always knew we'd find each other again," Joanna told her. "Fate wouldn't have been so cruel to kept us separated forever."

They peered toward the heavens and Libby murmured, "Thank you, Captain Ralston."

They were convinced Jacob and Caleb's father had been protecting and guiding them through the arduous summer they'd endured. He'd led them to this perfect moment, where they were united—sisters again—and about to watch Libby march down the aisle.

"You're the most gorgeous bride who ever lived," Caro said to Libby.

"Of course she is," Joanna agreed. "Would we have expected anything else?"

"No," Caro said.

"My sisters, my best friends," Libby said, "you're here to celebrate with me. What better wish could have been granted?"

Libby opened her arms, and Joanna and Caro fell into them. They began to cry; they couldn't help it, and Lady Penny rushed over and yanked them apart.

"Libby," she scolded, "I refuse to have you grow so emotional that you're bawling like a baby. Stop it or your face will be mottled, and the guests will notice."

They were dabbing at their tears, laughing, weeping. Caleb came and eased Caro away. Jacob came and took Joanna. They moved into the line Lady Penny had arranged. Down by the altar, the vicar appeared, prayer book in hand. Luke followed him out, accompanied by his new brother-in-law, Simon Falcon.

In their wedding finery, the two men were handsome and dashing, and Luke was clearly impatient to get on with the ceremony. He stared to the back of the church, visually willing Libby to hurry so he could become her husband.

Clara started down, tossing her rose petals side to side, then Caro and Caleb went after her.

Joanna was still crying, and Jacob pulled a kerchief from his coat and dried her eyes.

"Next month, it will be our turn," he whispered. "All these people will be there to see you and me. What do you think of that?"

"I think I am the luckiest girl in the world."

THE END

About the Author

CHERYL HOLT IS A *New York Times, USA Today,* and Amazon "Top 100" bestselling author who has published over fifty novels.

She's also a lawyer and mom, and at age forty, with two babies at home, she started a new career as a commercial fiction writer. She'd hoped to be a suspense novelist, but couldn't sell any of her manuscripts, so she ended up taking a detour into romance where she was stunned to discover that she has a knack for writing some of the world's greatest love stories.

Her books have been released to wide acclaim, and she has won or been nominated for many national awards. She is considered to be one of the masters of the romance genre. For many years, she was hailed as "The Queen of Erotic Romance," and she's also revered as "The International Queen of Villains." She is particularly proud to have been named "Best Storyteller of the Year" by the trade magazine Romantic Times BOOK Reviews.

She lives and writes in Hollywood, California, and she loves to hear from fans. Visit her website at www.cherylholt.com.